While You're There

ABBY MILLSAPS

ebook ISBN: 978-1-7370947-2-2
Paperback ISBN: 978-1-7370947-3-9

Edited by Joanne Machin
Cover Design by Cover Couture www.bookcovercouture.com

Also By Abby Millsaps

When You're Home

Book One in the Hampton Hearts Series

Content Warning

While You're There is a steamy new adult romance that includes mature themes, substance abuse, fertility issues, references to infidelity, and language that some may find offensive.

Please read the Note From the Author on the next page for additional details. The note includes spoilers.

Note From the Author

I wanted to take a moment to expand on the content warning for While You're There. I wrote this story with an abundance of empathy and concern for both my characters and my readers. This book includes conversations and portrayals of fertility treatments, and there are on-page descriptions of miscarriage and the grief that follows.

Although these are hard topics to write and read about, I approached them with as much care as possible. The miscarriage storyline in particular was reviewed by sensitivity readers. That said, I understand these are deeply personal and complex issues for many people. Please prioritize your mental health and read at your own risk.

To anyone who's ever crumbled—

It's okay to fall apart. It's okay to break.
Sometimes we don't see what's right in front of us when it's whole.
There's beauty in the broken.

Chapter One

Tori

"Honestly? I think I liked it better when you two were pretending you weren't together," Jake confessed from behind the bar of Clinton's Family Restaurant.

Tori felt Rhett smile against her face, his two-day stubble tickling her chin. Jake's words didn't stop him from moving his mouth down her jawline and placing another kiss in the crook of her neck. "I love you, Victoria Thompson," he murmured low enough so only she could hear. "You look gorgeous tonight. I'm so goddamn lucky you're mine." His fingers swept under the hem of her skirt and brushed against her inner thigh.

His hand was only resting an inch above her knee, but a thrill of desire zinged straight to her core. She peered down at her legs parted on the barstool and watched his strong, tan forearm flex ever-so-slightly as his hidden hand made delicate circles against her skin.

She let out a breathy sigh. She couldn't wait to get home—or hell, even just to his old Prelude parked behind the restaurant—and continue this game.

This was the Rhett she remembered from high school. This was Rhett not holding back, not toeing the line. This was Rhett playing full out.

The shift had been sudden but certain. As soon as she agreed to marry him, it was clear he was done holding back. There was a reignited confidence in the way he touched her, spoke to her, approached her. It was like journeying somewhere new and coming home at the same time.

"Seriously? Can you at least take it to the walk-in cooler? You two could obviously use some privacy."

Tori was too preoccupied to verbally respond to Jake's ribbing, but she managed to fling a tater tot in his general direction.

"Hey! Don't mess up my immaculately kept bar, baby," he scolded as he retrieved the tot from the floor and glared at the pair of them. "I have to close by myself tonight since Mister Big Shot MBA needs his beauty rest for graduation."

Rhett slowly removed his hand from under her skirt, swiveling his bar stool to right himself.

"Don't try to put that on me, bro. I barely work here anymore. You would have closed by yourself tonight regardless," Rhett shot back at his best friend. "I wouldn't even be in Hampton tonight if it wasn't for this one," he reasoned, cocking his head toward Tori.

She couldn't help but smile and roll her eyes as she looked between them. Hanging out at Clinton's. Joking around and ragging on each other. Everything about this night felt right.

Well, most everything. As hard as she tried to push down the anxiety that was always threatening to crest to the surface these days, Tori couldn't help but think about her follow-up ovarian cancer screening from earlier in the week.

Inconclusive.

Those were the results of her pelvic exam and ultrasound. She had been so sure she would be diagnosed with cancer, but that wasn't the case. Dr. Ritter had explained that without a visible tumor, she couldn't make an official diagnosis. But between the elevated bloodwork and her genetic history, Tori was sure she knew what was lurking inside her. The dreaded 'someday' had finally caught up with her, but she was done running from the fate that had haunted her for so long.

What happened next was up to her. Dr. Ritter suggested a PET scan to try and identify any rapidly changing cells that weren't visible on the ultrasound. She also suggested an exploratory biopsy, but that felt ridiculous and redundant. If Tori was having surgery, she was having *the* surgery: a prophylactic hysterectomy with bilateral salpingo—oophorectomy, just like she had always planned.

She already knew in the back of her mind what she wanted to do. Now it was just a matter of logistics and timing between her school schedule and Rhett's work schedule.

"I guess I'm just salty you're taking Tori and Maddie down to Easton tomorrow and leaving me behind," Jake lamented.

Tori beamed at the reminder. She was excited to head to Easton the next morning, to help Rhett pack up his apartment and move back to Hampton for a few weeks before he had to start his job in Norfolk, Virginia. She was so proud of her boyfriend—no, not boyfriend—her *fiancé*, and she couldn't wait to celebrate with him this weekend.

Rhett reached over and wrapped his arm around her shoulders, leaning in to whisper in her ear. "We have to get up early tomorrow, but if we leave right now, we'll have time..."

She didn't even let him finish his suggestion before she found his lips, answering his question with an eager kiss.

"What's this? Is the walk-in cooler occupied?" Mike joked as he approached the bar. Jake snickered at the jab. As the owner of Clinton's Family Restaurant and Tori's current employer, Mike Hobbs had had a front row seat to the Tori and Rhett Show over the last several years. Still, his scolding made the blood rush to her cheeks. That, or Rhett's relentless ministrations under her skirt were really starting to take effect.

"No sir. We're regular paying customers tonight," Rhett defended. "I just wanted to take my fiancée on a proper date before we head out of town for the weekend, but that seems to be causing some problems around here." He cocked one eyebrow, playfully challenging his former boss and mentor.

There was that word again: fiancée. He had found a way to use it as often as possible over the last week since he had proposed to her at his family's cabin on the lake in Michigan. She instinctively looked down at her ring: a two-carat diamond shone brightly in the center of a gold twisted pave halo band. The ring had been his grandmother's. Rhett admitted that he knew the ring was intended for her the moment he received it, even though they weren't even dating at the time. It had been a perfect fit when he slipped it onto her finger Monday night.

"Oh, come on," Mike replied. "You know I'm just teasing you, Wheeler. I'm happy for you two. I wish I could say I'm surprised, but ya know..."

"Alright, I think we've had enough Clinton's hospitality for one night," Rhett declared as he shifted off the barstool and reached for his wallet. He pulled out several bills, passed them across the bar to Jake, then nodded in Mike's direction. "I've gotta get my girl home. We're out of here."

His girl.

Home.

Rhett's hand rested on her low back, right along the waistband of her skirt. She let him guide her through the dining room toward the back door of Clinton's.

Tori pushed through the door and gasped when she saw the pink and purple cotton candy sky. The sun had set, but dusk hadn't given way to the stars just yet. She would love to try to recreate the colors the next time she had the chance to paint. As soon as they got to the car, she reached for her phone so she could take a picture for reference.

"Second most beautiful thing I've seen tonight," Rhett murmured into her ear, pressing up against her from behind and winding his arms around her waist. Goosebumps flared up and down her legs in response to the short stubble on his jaw tickling her neck. His fingers stroked under her shirt along her ribs.

Tori leaned back into his arms and craned her head, letting him support more of her weight. He placed a feather-light kiss on the side of her neck, but it wasn't enough. It would never be enough. He knew what she wanted without her having to ask. He tightened his hold and bent forward, meeting her lips in a demanding kiss.

He removed one hand from her shirt and moved it up her torso, between her breasts, over her throat. He took hold of her jaw and gripped her chin, holding her face possessively as he deepened the kiss.

"I can't get enough of you, V." He moved his mouth to the pulse point below her ear. She blew out a heady sigh of satisfaction. The feeling was mutual. She wanted his hands everywhere. She wanted his mouth to consume her.

"Good thing you don't have to try and get your fill anymore. You're stuck with me now," she reminded him. He nipped at her earlobe and moved a hand back down to rest against her stomach, creating a barrier between her and the car.

"I've waited six years for you to want me to stick around, beautiful. I plan to spend the next sixty making sure you know you made the right choice." His roaming hand travelled south, sliding down her body until he was cupping her between her legs on the outside of her skirt. He pulled her closer still, sending a jolt of wanting to her core as he pressed his rock-solid erection into her from behind. The tip of his middle finger was aligned perfectly with her clit, but he didn't apply any pressure or give her the friction she craved.

She needed more. She slinked away from him slightly, turned around, and slammed her mouth into his. He pressed her harder into the car now that her back was to it. His mouth moved against hers, his tongue alternating between sweet caresses and demanding assaults. She moaned into his kiss, wanting him to possess her completely. They were both panting in short, rapid breaths, their desire for each other surpassing their need for air.

Tori worked a hand in between their bodies, running her nails down the center of his chest, letting her fingers graze along the dips of his well-defined abs. Her teasing didn't last long before her hand landed on what she really wanted. She stroked him lightly once, testing just how far he was willing to let this game go. They were standing outside, up against his car, in a downtown Hampton parking lot, after all.

Once she realized he wasn't going to pull away, she gripped him harder. His length filled her entire hand and then some, his heat warming her palm through the strained fabric across his zipper.

She wasn't satisfied with just holding him through his pants though. No, she wanted to make him feel just as needy as she'd been feeling all night. She continued to kiss him as she worked her free hand into the short hair at the nape of his neck. Then, with her other hand still firmly holding his cock, she stroked his length in the middle of the parking lot.

Rhett grunted but froze, his lower lip caught between her teeth. She nipped him once before opening her eyes and tilting her head in question.

"What do you want, V?" he breathed into the inch of space between them.

"You."

"You want to do this here?" He raised an eyebrow and held her gaze as he tried to call her bluff.

She gave him a coy smile, biting down on her bottom lip as her eyes trailed up and down his body. He looked so damn good tonight. Crisp white polo with the collar turned down to show off his taut neck muscles and sharp jawline. Tight dark jeans that hung low on his hips and emphasized the taper of his waist. Of course she wanted to do this here. She wanted him, always.

She squeezed his dick again, this time gripping him tighter and holding on for longer as she imagined exactly where she wanted to feel him right now. She released her hold on him for a moment, just long enough to find the tab of his zipper.

"Tori," he groaned, resting his forehead against hers as she slowly pulled the zipper down. "Tell me right now if we're really doing this, beautiful. I'm three seconds away from lifting your skirt and pushing into you against this car."

Her pussy clenched in response to his words. If she'd had any doubts before, her answer was now crystal clear. She looked around, scanning the parking lot for movement. There were a few other cars around, but that was it. They were tucked away on one end of the lot, their bodies positioned so that no one could see their lower halves unless they were standing right behind Rhett. As long as he kept his pants mostly pulled up...

"What's it going to be, beautiful? Yes or no?" he demanded as he tilted his hips forward.

She smirked, meeting the rhythm of his body as she pushed back against him. She finally released his zipper, now completely undone, before starting in on his belt buckle. "It's not no."

"Fuck," Rhett muttered as he realized just how serious she was about this. He pushed her hands out of the way and undid the belt himself. "How quickly do you think I can get you off?" he asked, a devilish smile playing across his face.

"Well, you haven't made me come for almost twelve hours," she teased as she laced her arms around his neck. "So... three minutes?"

He gripped her chin and brushed his thumb across her bottom lip. "Is that an invitation or a challenge?"

"Both," she sighed, reaching into his open fly to grasp his smooth, solid shaft. He hissed in a breath on contact before lowering his head to speak directly into her ear.

"You watch the back door of the restaurant. Don't take your eyes off the alley. I'll watch the other side of the parking lot to make sure no one comes from that direction." He ran his tongue up and down the column of her neck as both his hands found their way under her skirt. He lifted the front of it, bunching the fabric and suspending it between their bodies.

"We've gotta be quick, so let me get you..." His words stopped as soon as his fingers made contact with the only barrier between them. "Oh. I see. So by 'it's not no,' you actually meant your panties were soaking wet?" He stroked her clit through the dampened fabric once, twice, then a third time with just enough pressure to send a full-body shudder from the crown of her head to the tips of her toes.

Tori looked up at him through her long lashes. "I didn't cause that," she purred. "You did."

Rhett smirked as he continued stroking, pushing aside her underwear and dipping two fingers into her folds.

"And you also really like the idea of being out in public, partially exposed, right here where anyone could possibly walk by."

"That too," she confessed with a shaky breath. She tried to rise up on her tip toes, lowering herself quickly to gain more leverage against his hand. She wanted so much more, and she wanted it now. But Rhett stayed steady, giving her just an inch, circling her entrance with the same two fingers. He knew exactly what he was doing.

"My fiancée, the exhibitionist," he whispered as he slowly scissored his fingers inside her.

"Rhett, please." She was so wound up, so ready for him to tip her over the edge and send her spiraling. They had been finding their pleasure in each other for years, and yet every interaction was still an unexpected and delicious ride. She'd never tire of being loved by this man.

"What do you want, V?" he asked again.

"I want you," she begged.

"Then take me. Line me up and put me inside you, beautiful."

His words alone were almost her undoing. She frantically worked to turn down the zippered edge of his pants and free his dick from his boxer briefs. Rhett bent his knees slightly, granting her better access and giving them a deeper angle.

She pushed up onto her tip toes, grasped him at the base, and ran his length through her arousal. She lined up the head of his cock with her entrance, just like he instructed. She rolled her hips forward and closed her eyes, savoring the deep, satisfying sensation of his length pushing into her. Then she opened her eyes and locked him in her gaze.

"You feel so good," she panted as she worked him in, inch by delicious inch.

"And you feel like home." Once he was fully seated inside her, he stilled, letting them both adjust to the sensation. The fullness was overwhelming, her longing to feel him everywhere finally sated. He bowed low to kiss her, pushing his tongue in and out of her mouth before he started thrusting in and out of her with the same rhythm.

He moaned her name between kisses. He sucked on her neck and gripped her hip possessively with one hand as he held her panties off to the side. Her taut underwear brushed against her clit every few strokes, shooting a wave of friction through her that was more pleasurable than painful.

She would gladly spend the entire night in this parking lot with her fiancé chasing their pleasure, but she knew they were on borrowed time. As if he could read her thoughts, Rhett spoke up in a husky voice.

"You said three minutes," he reminded her. "Time's up." He reached a hand between them and rubbed her clit in quick, tight circles as he continued to thrust. "Come for me, beautiful."

Her brain couldn't make sense of the buildup. They'd only been at it for a few minutes—how was she already right there? She didn't know where to focus, what to do. Instead of trying to figure it out or fight it, she chose to surrender. She relaxed back and let her head rest on the roof of the Prelude as Rhett continued to drive into her, to rub all over her, to do all the things she wanted and needed that he instinctively knew to do.

She hit her peak and screamed, both the suddenness and the intensity of her climax catching her by surprise. Within two seconds of the first wave of pleasure crashing through her, she felt Rhett's hand cover her mouth. Her eyes shot open on contact.

"Shhhh," he soothed as he continued to ram into her. His frantic, feral expression revealed just how close he was to his own release. She could feel her own slickness coating his hand. Without conscious thought, she licked the length of one of his fingers.

Rhett's eyes widened as she continued to suck and bite at the hand that gripped her mouth. They locked eyes, and he groaned as she felt him tense inside her. She was still clenching around his dick from her own orgasm as he filled her with his release.

They stared at each other, breathless, for what felt like eternity: their eyes locked in wonder, their bodies still joined. If anything positive had come out of all the pain and drama they had endured over the last few months, it was this. This connection. This love. This version of them was better than it had ever been before.

Rhett moved first, stepping back slightly and finally removing his hand from her mouth. "Fuck, Tori... you are *so* loud."

"You like that I'm loud," she retorted, reaching up to kiss him before readjusting her underwear and skirt. Rhett fixed himself quickly, but cupped her face in his hands as soon as he was done.

"I love everything about you." He lowered his forehead against hers before kissing her on the nose. "Every-fucking-thing."

CHAPTER TWO

Tori

"Explain to me how I ended up in the back of my own car for this little adventure?" Maddie huffed from the backseat of her Lexus RX. Tori watched Rhett's grip tighten on the steering wheel as he drove along Willow Drive. It was early, and the sun was just starting to rise. Tori wondered not for the first time that morning if Maddie was hungover or if she was actually still drunk from the night before.

"Well, Maddie Girl, we needed to take your car to fit all the stuff I still need to bring home from Easton, and even though you *knew* that was the plan, you don't seem fit to drive this morning." Tori watched, amused, as Rhett shot Maddie a look through the rearview mirror. "Plus, V gets carsick and can't ride in the back."

Maddie grumbled something ineligible as she reached up between them to adjust the input on the sound system. "My car, my music," she muttered as she cranked up the volume and the quick cadence of a YUNGBLUD song filled the car. She was purposely pushing her brother's buttons. It was going to be a long four hours if they were going to bicker the entire drive.

"What is this shit?" Rhett demanded after a few beats. Tori recognized the song, but there was no way she was interjecting.

"*This shit* is my current favorite song, bro. I can put it on repeat if you aren't familiar with it?" she taunted. "Since when do you listen to punk-rap? I thought your favorite band was One Direction?" Maddie settled back into her seat and adjusted her seatbelt. "I contain multitudes, Everhett."

"Did you just quote Whitman? Don't ever let anyone tell you the Hampton High curriculum isn't as good as Archway Prep."

To Tori's surprise, Rhett didn't say anything else about the music. She took the opportunity to turn around from the front seat and assess Maddie's getup. She was wearing big aviators that took over half of her face, her platinum blonde hair piled high on top of her head in the messiest of buns. She had rolled up her hoodie behind her head as a pillow so her toned arms were bare and on display in a fitted camisole. She finished the look with an oversized pair of grey sweatpants that probably didn't belong to her.

"Do you want me to stop and get you coffee, Maddie Girl?" Rhett offered.

"Oh God, yes please. Coffee is a must." Maddie yawned as she stretched out longways across the bench seat of her SUV.

"Then turn this shit off and check the attitude."

Tori swallowed her smirk, not daring to insert herself between their sibling standoff. Maddie made another indiscernible noise before she relented. A few seconds later, the first chords of an old John Mayer song came through the speakers.

"There we go," Rhett coaxed, eyeing his little sister through the rearview mirror again. "One extra-large double dirty chai coming right up."

Rhett parked the car in one of the many available spots in front of historic downtown Hampton. Clinton's was just a few buildings down the way. Tori instinctively looked around to see who was working the opening shift. She spotted Jake's and Lia's cars parked side by side. She felt bad they were working so early this morning since they had both closed the restaurant last night, but attending Rhett's graduation was her priority this weekend, and she knew they wouldn't give her a hard time about having to pick up the extra shifts.

"Coffee with cream?" Rhett asked Tori, reaching over to squeeze her knee before he opened the driver side door. She nodded.

She watched him cross the street, his lean frame moving with confidence across the familiar sidewalks of downtown Hampton. He was dressed down for the car ride, sporting worn jeans and an old Archway sweatshirt. That didn't stop her from gazing appreciatively at his long legs and admiring the way he moved with authority, then held the coffee shop door open for two women walking out.

"When's the last time you were in Easton?"

Maddie's question was innocent enough, but Tori felt a hint of embarrassment creep into her consciousness at her future sister-in-law's inquiry.

"It's been a while, honestly. I haven't visited Rhett at college since his junior year. Jake and I came down together for his twenty-first birthday."

Maddie sat up straighter at her confession. "What? So you've never even been to this apartment we're about to pack up?"

Tori shook her head.

"That seems crazy."

She smirked. Maddie didn't know the half of it.

Rhett always seemed to find a reason to come home to Hampton during his first few years at college. His visits only increased in frequency when he and Tori reignited their relationship with a friends-with-benefits arrangement designed to let them indulge in their mutual attraction but keep things casual.

Tori had suggested he date other people during that time as a means of self-preservation: she needed him to not get too wrapped up in what they were doing, in the soul-deep magnetism that always seemed to pull them back together.

They had spent the last three years in a tumultuous battle of push-and-pull. Rhett wanted more. She refused to let him get in too deep.

Everything had come to a head a few months ago when she finally gave in and admitted she wanted to be with him as much as he wanted her. Unfortunately, things didn't fall together as easily as they had hoped. Tori had always insisted he see other people as part of

their arrangement, so he had been casually dating a girl named
Chandler for a few years.

Things between Rhett and Chandler were more involved than she
had realized, even though he claimed he didn't have real feelings for
the other woman. Tori believed him, but that didn't make the
situation any less messy when Chandler showed up in Hampton
unexpectedly a few months ago. It had taken a health scare and a
panic attack to make things crystal clear for both of them.

They were together now, finally and completely. It had been a
long, unconventional road to get to this place. Tori knew Maddie's
questions wouldn't be the last they'd have to answer about their
relationship, or about how they got to this place so quickly.

"Rhett came home to Hampton a lot," Tori finally offered in reply.
"And I usually work at least two shifts at Clinton's on the weekends.
Since we weren't technically dating over the last few years, there
wasn't any reason for me to go visit him."

That was close enough to the truth. She knew she didn't need to
mention anything about Rhett's ex-girlfriend for Maddie to
understand the subtext of her defense. She hadn't visited Rhett at
Easton over the last three years because Chandler was at Easton.

Rhett opened the driver's seat door then, cutting their conversation
short. He carefully balanced two cups in one hand as he handed her
the third.

"There ya go, beautiful." He placed his own cup in the cup holder
before turning back to his sister and handing over her drink. "Are we
ready?"

"Ready," Maddie confirmed.

Rhett settled in and buckled his seat belt. He glanced over at Tori
then.

"You okay, V?" he asked softly as he put the car in reverse, then
turned toward the highway.

"Mhmm," she hummed, taking a long sip of her coffee to prevent
herself from having to fully answer his question.

Thankfully Maddie piped up again. "What are Mom and Dad's plans for tomorrow?"

"Dad's flight gets in late this afternoon. They're going to head to Easton early in the morning so they don't have to worry about getting a hotel room tonight. The MBA ceremony isn't until noon, so they'll have plenty of time. Mom made reservations for brunch afterward, then we'll finish loading up the cars and head home."

Tori took another sip of her coffee, letting her mind wander as Rhett went over the plans. An uneasiness made its way into her consciousness as she thought more about the weekend ahead. She had been so wrapped up in everything that had transpired over the last two weeks—from getting the phone call about her abnormal test results to Rhett coming home for her, to their engagement and her follow-up scans. When he told her the plans for the weekend, she had just gone along with it, knowing he would take care of the details and all she had to do was show up. She hadn't had time to dwell on what it would feel like to visit his college apartment for the first time.

As if he could sense her spiraling thoughts, Rhett reached across the central console and brushed his fingers across her hand. "Are you sure you're feeling okay?" She couldn't get away with a change in posture, a slump of the shoulders, or even a sullen expression without him noticing.

"I'm good," she insisted. She let him take her hand, interlacing their fingers and squeezing. She lifted her eyes from their hands to his face. The sharp angle of his jawline moved slightly as he chewed on the inside of his cheek. He had a dark shadow of scruff from not shaving over the last few days. The memory of that stubble sandpapering against her neck last night was enough to make her cheeks flush.

"Simmer down," he whispered as he side-eyed her. He didn't need to take his eyes off the road to read the thoughts that had started to creep into her mind. Tori bit down on her bottom lip, then lifted their joined hands to her mouth. She started by placing a gentle kiss on Rhett's knuckles, but then subtly licked the space between his middle and ring fingers, just like she'd done when he'd held his hand over her mouth to keep her quiet last night. His whole arm tensed before he pulled away from her grasp.

He didn't need to say a word for Tori to know he was as annoyed with her teasing as he was turned on. She loved to rile him up in the car, to see him lose a bit of that stoic control he asserted most of the time.

"So what are your plans for the next few weeks?" Maddie interrupted their flirtation from the back seat. She was sitting up now, looking a little more awake and a lot more sober, thanks to the boost of caffeine.

"What do you mean?" Rhett asked as he subtly adjusted himself before he placed both hands back on the steering wheel.

"I mean, are you moving back home to our house? Is Tori moving in, too? I think I deserve to know if I'm getting one or two new roommates..."

Maddie's questions weren't outlandish, but they were things they hadn't talked about yet. Tori assumed Rhett had already thought through these things, but between her follow-up doctor's appointment earlier this week and just trying to find a new semblance of a routine for this new version of their relationship, they hadn't had a chance to talk about what was next.

"Well," he started, glancing over at Tori cautiously. She smiled at him, confirming that she didn't mind discussing this with Maddie, even if they hadn't figured out all the details yet. She trusted him to know how to proceed and navigate the next few months. Hell, she was counting on him to have a plan and to handle things the way he always did.

"A lot of what I have at Easton can just go with me to my new apartment in Virginia. I'm going to store all the boxes in Mom and Dad's garage and in my room until I move at the end of the month." Rhett reached for Tori's hand again. This time, she knew better than to tease him as he sought her comfort.

"Tori and I will be at the house some, but we'll stay at her house, too. Paul doesn't mind me sleeping over now that we're engaged."

That was true. Her dad had told her a few days ago that Rhett was welcome to stay with them until he moved to Virginia in May.

It helped that her dad was a little distracted these days, too. He had finally admitted to Tori that he was seeing someone. She knew he had gone on a few dates earlier in the spring, but he hadn't offered any additional information, and she hadn't pushed him for details. It wasn't until she caught him trying to sneak back into the house at seven a.m. a few days ago that he admitted he was dating a woman named Tricia. She was genuinely happy for him, in addition to feeling like a significant weight had been lifted off her shoulders. The emotional burden of caring for her father had taken its toll after all these years.

"It's going to be a busy couple weeks with a lot of back and forth," Rhett continued. "I've got to be in Norfolk on Wednesday and Thursday this week."

"But you'll be back on Saturday before I go to prom, right?" Maddie asked, hopefulness apparent in her tone.

"Absolutely. I wouldn't miss it. You know that. We have a few appointments on Friday, so I'll be home early Friday morning." Tori didn't miss the way he referred to her surgery consultations as *their* appointments.

"Okay." Maddie nodded. "So are you also moving to Virginia in a few weeks, Tor?"

She winced at that particular question. Moving was another thing they hadn't discussed yet, but Tori was firm in her position. She didn't want to give up her job at Clinton's, and she was still two years away from earning her graphic design degree from Holt State. She couldn't imagine leaving Hampton and abandoning her dad, even if he had someone else in his life now. Getting both preventative surgeries was her top priority, so she wouldn't be moving to Virginia anytime soon. She was pretty sure Rhett already knew her stance on the issue, but she responded cautiously, just in case.

"Eventually." She glanced over at Rhett, curious as to how her answer would land. He turned his head to meet her gaze and offered her a confident, easy smile. "I'm not ready to move just yet. I want to finish up my degree, and I plan to have both surgeries I need this year if possible. It'll be easier to do that in Hampton."

"Gotcha. So you'll probably move to Virginia once you guys get married?"

Tori raised her eyebrows, but she stayed quiet, letting Rhett respond to his sister.

"We're getting married soon, Maddie. Like, really soon. I want Tori to be on my insurance before she gets her first surgery this summer. I plan to commute back and forth between Norfolk and Hampton for the foreseeable future. I already talked to Grandad about telecommuting and splitting my time between home and the office so I can be with Tori through everything."

Maddie let out an exaggerated squeal. "Wait, so there'll be a wedding this summer?"

"There'll probably be a wedding within the next month." He glanced over at Tori again, and she knew he was seeking reassurance. She nodded in earnest, smiling at the eagerness she could feel coiling off his body. His posture straightened at her confirmation. He winked at her before returning an easy smile.

"Holy shit. My head is spinning, and it's definitely not just from this hangover. Okay, okay. So you're obviously not getting married this weekend. And next Saturday is my prom. So should I save the date for Memorial Day weekend?"

Tori hadn't realized how limited their options were when it came to setting a date. But Maddie was right: the next two weekends were booked, then Rhett would be moving to Virginia the first week of June. "I hadn't even thought about that..." Now her head was spinning, too.

"I did," Rhett replied to them both. Of course he had already thought about it. Had she really expected anything less from her calendar-loving Golden Boy?

"Memorial Day weekend at the cabin could be really special." His eyes didn't leave the road, and she knew he was trying to play it cool.

He had been forced to tread lightly over the last few years, always deferring to her to call the shots in their friends-with-benefits relationship. But she heard the hopefulness in his voice, and she was more than willing to let him take the lead when it came to wedding planning.

"Yeah," Tori confirmed. "Yeah, it would be."

Rhett's face erupted into a grin. Tori felt the blush rise in her cheeks at his eagerness. The timing of their engagement and the rush to the altar didn't take away from the fact that she was irrevocably in love with the man sitting beside her. There was so much they had to figure out and discuss, but Tori had no doubt in her mind that marrying Rhett was all kinds of right.

CHAPTER THREE

Tori

"Alright, I think we should divide and conquer to get this done as quickly as possible," Rhett announced as he unlocked the apartment door and held it open for them. Maddie walked in first, turning her head to roll her eyes at Tori.

"Put me to work," Maddie offered as she stretched her arms over her head and yawned.

Rhett set down the stack of flat boxes he'd carried up from the car. "I'll work on packing up my bedroom. Maddie, if you don't mind unplugging the TV and my gaming system and packing up everything in the living room, that would be great. And V, can you clean out the fridge and kitchen cabinets? I want to keep the beer glasses and the cookware, but you can pitch almost everything else. If you're not sure if you should pack it, just pitch it. I want to take as little back with us as possible."

"What about the furniture?" Maddie asked.

"My buddy Tanner's coming by tomorrow morning. He's taking the couch, the bed, and the kitchen table. I'll just buy new stuff in Virginia."

Maddie nodded before grabbing a few boxes off the stack and walking further into the room. She moved through the apartment easily, like she already knew her way around. That made sense, but it reminded Tori of how foreign this place was to her.She glanced around the apartment. It was a newer unit, painted in light greys and whites. It wasn't homey, per se, but it was certainly nicer and cleaner than should be expected for a single college guy's apartment. *He wasn't exactly single when he lived here,* she reminded herself.

"Is this weird?" Rhett asked. He took a few hesitant steps toward her, outstretching his arms as he approached. Tori walked to meet him without hesitation and let him wrap her in a hug.

"It's okay," she muttered into his sweatshirt, her head buried into the crevice between his arm and his solid chest. She couldn't lie. It wasn't *not* weird to be in the apartment that he had shared with his ex-girlfriend, the woman she had required him to date so he could be with her.

"I want us to pick out everything for the Virginia apartment together." He spoke softly into her hair, not breaking their embrace. "That's why I'm not bringing much home. I know you can't move to Norfolk with me right away, but it's going to be my place just as much as it's going to be yours."

"I'd like that. Let's just get this done so we can focus on celebrating you tomorrow." She squeezed him for extra emphasis, then rose up on her tiptoes to kiss him. He responded to her kiss by weaving his hand into the hair at the nape of her neck. He teased his tongue against her lips, willing her to open to him, to let him deepen their connection.

She smirked against his mouth and shook her head. "Look alive, Wheeler. We've got work to do."

They spent the next several hours packing boxes and filling garbage bags. Tori felt her mood deplete with her energy as the afternoon dragged on. She assumed she'd come face-to-face with parts of Rhett's past this weekend, but she hadn't been prepared for the near-constant reminders of Chandler.

First it was the start of a grocery list on the dry erase board on the fridge, each item scrolled in a loopy handwriting that definitely didn't belong to Rhett. Then it was the half-empty bottle of spiced vanilla sugar hand soap at the kitchen sink. By the time she had pulled out the third container of expired light Greek yogurt, she'd had enough.

Knowing that Rhett had a longtime but not exclusive girlfriend back in Easton hadn't bothered her before. Hell, she had been the one to insist on it. But seeing the physical evidence of the other woman's presence in his life grated on her nerves in the most jarring and unexpected ways.

"How's it going out here?" Rhett asked as he emerged from the bedroom.

"Just great," she clipped out, slamming the door of the fridge closed so hard it rebounded and popped back open.

"V...?" he dragged out the question as he approached her. He offered out an arm, inviting her into a hug, but she refused to lean into him. The rational part of her brain knew that Chandler was out of the picture for good, that he was committed to her, and that they were engaged. But all the subtle reminders of the other woman had completely soured her mood.

She had been the one to insist that Rhett date other people if he wanted to do the friends-with-benefits thing with her. But how, and more importantly why, had that caveat evolved into what appeared to be a full-blown relationship with one single person? He said he was never serious about Chandler. He told her he'd never committed to being exclusive with Chandler. Yet the evidence of just how deeply she had been intertwined in his life was undeniable. Undeniable and upsetting.

"What's wrong?" he demanded in frustration as she folded her arms across her chest and leaned against the fridge.

"Nothing's wrong," she snapped. "I just wasn't aware how much you loved key lime pie light and fit yogurt."

"Oh shit," Maddie muttered from the living room.

She had no real reason to be defensive. But she couldn't stop herself from lashing out. She wasn't even upset with Rhett. The only person she was actually mad at was herself.

"Tori," he finally whispered as he figured out the root cause of her outburst. She watched as the realization clicked in his mind. He reached out for her again. "Come here... please?"

She huffed out another breath but closed the space between them and let him pull her into his arms. He held her gently against his chest, one arm wrapped around her waist while the other hand cupped the back of her head. She felt part of her anger melt away on contact. His embrace served as a physical reminder of where things stood now.

"Please don't let being here get under your skin, beautiful. I can't even tell you the number of times I wished you were here with me over the last three years."

That was the heart of the issue. She didn't want to let any reminders of Chandler take away from what they had now or where they were heading. She had the utmost confidence in her relationship with Rhett. But that didn't mean she'd be able to just forgive herself for requiring the arrangement that had brought the other woman into their lives to begin with, or that she could easily forgive him for actually following through.

———

Rhett groaned as he flopped down onto the bed. "That was a lot more work than I thought it was going to be."

Tori pulled on the T-shirt she planned to sleep in before turning around to join him. She slid under the sheets, her body instinctively making its way to the middle of the mattress. "Come here, you," he instructed as he pulled her body into his. "Thank you for all your help today." He kissed the tip of her nose. "How are you feeling now?"

"I'm fine," she replied automatically. That was partially true. She had cooled down from her earlier outburst, a lot of her frustrations dissipating once the apartment was completely packed up and cleared out. She still felt some lingering irritation about all the artifacts from Rhett's other relationship she had stumbled on, but she wasn't interested in rehashing the same fight again tonight.

"Are you tired?" he asked. She knew the subtext of his question. Never mind that his sister was sleeping on the couch just one room over.

"I am," she admitted, running her nails against the short hair along Rhett's neckline. "And I've got cramps because my period started this afternoon."

He shifted next to her, moving one of his hands down her back so he could knead into the spot that always bothered her whenever she had her period. She sank into his touch, savoring the way his strong fingers worked the muscles at the bottom of her spine.

"That feels so good," she moaned in satisfaction. He continued to soothe her tight muscles as he trailed kisses along her neck and collarbone.

"Can I get you anything? Water or painkillers? I think I packed up a bottle of ibuprofen earlier, but I can go find it."

"No, I took some after dinner. I'm okay," she insisted. She almost hadn't said anything about her cramps. She knew he would spring into action and go overboard in his efforts to comfort her. But that was Rhett. He prided himself in taking care of his people and doing whatever was in his power to take everyone else's pain away.

He had stopped kissing her at that point, but he continued to massage her low back, his face nestled in the crook of her neck. "Will you be sad to leave here tomorrow? This apartment has been your home for the last few years."

Rhett's hand stilled as he raised his head to look at her. "This place was never home, V. Home has always been wherever you are."

Chapter Four

Rhett

Rhett rolled over on the familiar mattress in his now bare apartment bedroom. He knew Tori was there—all the reasonable parts of his brain told him he had nothing to worry about—but he still wanted visual confirmation. She lay next to him, her oversized T-shirt crumpled up around her stomach, her legs splayed out in the center of the bed. It was surreal having her here, seeing her next to him in a bed she'd never been in before. But lying next to her now scratched all the happy places in his brain. He felt more settled and more inside his own body just lying next to her and feeling her presence.

He quietly lifted his arm and let it rest across her back. He didn't want to wake her. They didn't need to be up for at least another hour. He just wanted to feel her solidness next to him.

He had to do things like this a lot lately to remind himself that everything that was happening was real. Less than two weeks ago, they hadn't even been on speaking terms. Now, they were together, truly and completely. They were engaged, and based on the conversation they had yesterday in the car, they were going to get married in a few weeks. It was just going to take a bit of time for his adrenals to get the message that he could relax and trust in their relationship now.

It wasn't lost on him that the catalyst for their current relationship was everything Tori had feared for so long. But she was a fighter, and he was going to be by her side through it all. He would make sure she had the best care possible, regardless of cost. He would be the one to take care of her after her surgeries. They would get through this, and once they cleared this hurdle, they would have the rest of their lives to look forward to together.

He watched his own hand rise and fall with the deep inhales of her breathing. She was always beautiful in his eyes, but he especially loved to watch her sleep. She had put so much effort into preventing him from getting too close over the last few years. He had gotten in the habit of trying to wake up before her when they were together so he could savor the moments when she wasn't pushing him away.

His eyes scanned her body from the soft curve of her hips up the small of her back to the hand she had resting across her pillow. His gaze lingered on her ring, and he felt his heart swell with pride. He could distinctly remember his grandmother wearing that ring. He was so grateful she left it to him.

Now that Tori was on board with Memorial Day weekend at the cabin, they could start making wedding plans in earnest. They would share their plans with his parents at brunch. He knew they would support whatever they wanted to do, and he was counting on his mom to step up and help him and Tori over the next two weeks.

Rhett reached for his phone on the nightstand, curious about the marriage license procedures in the state of Michigan. He swiped to unlock the device, but his hand froze when he saw the message notification on the screen.

Chandler: Hey, I know you're in Easton this weekend. I really need to talk to you. Can we meet up?

Fuck.

Rhett didn't click on the message. He didn't want his ex to know he'd read her text. He set the phone back on the nightstand as gently as possible, slowly releasing the device like it was a motion-activated bomb.

Rhett raked his hand through his hair. Should he wake Tori up? He couldn't stand to just lie here when he had something big to tell her. He wasn't willing to let anything come between them now. She looked so peaceful sleeping, though, and she didn't need to be up for a little longer.

He shoved off the bed and headed for the bathroom instead. He could shower and get coffee going for the girls. He grabbed his phone and brought it into the bathroom with him, just in case Chandler attempted to call or text him again.

Tori was awake by the time he was done showering, still sprawled out on her stomach in the middle of the bed with her head turned to face him. "Good morning," she offered in a sultry tone, cocking one eyebrow as she assessed his towel-clad body.

"Good, you're up." Rhett sighed, hurrying over to the bed to sit down.

"What's wrong?" She sat up quickly and scooted to the edge of the bed to meet him. He didn't want to panic her, but he couldn't reign in the frantic energy he felt from seeing Chandler's text.

"I have to tell you something."

"Okay."

"I woke up to a text from Chandler." He paused. He wanted to give her a moment to process what he just said.

"And?" she prompted. She moved to sit next to him, swinging her legs over the side of the bed to mirror his posture.

"And? She texted me! I haven't heard from her for two weeks, and now it's the morning of graduation, and she decides to reach out? I haven't even opened the message yet. I didn't text her back, V, I swear." He heard himself rambling, but he couldn't seem to slow his thoughts or control his tone.

"Hey. Hey, look at me," she demanded as she took his hand and interlaced their fingers. "This isn't a big deal. I don't understand why you're so upset about this... Wait. Are you freaking out because you think *I'm* going to freak out?"

He didn't say anything in response to her question, but he felt the tension in his chest loosen a bit as she named his exact concern.

"Rhett, you didn't do anything wrong. Will you please look at me?"

He slowly turned to face her, steeling himself for whatever was about to happen next.

"I'm not upset that your ex texted you. That's literally not within your control. I know I freaked out on you yesterday about Chandler... but that was just my own insecurities coming out. This isn't like before. We aren't sneaking around. We're together. We're *more* than together," Tori reminded him as she held up her left hand to flash her engagement ring. "I appreciate you wanting to tell me right away, but you don't need to worry. There's nothing Chandler could say or do to come between us now. Right?"

"Right," he answered in a rush. Her words only went so far to ease the anxiety he'd let build up since he first saw the text.

Tori must have sensed he still didn't feel settled. She ran her hand up his bare arm before letting it rest at the nape of his neck. "You're okay, Ev. We're okay. Chandler trying to text you isn't a big deal. I trust you to handle it. You can text her back and tell me about it if you want, but I know where we stand." She finished her declaration by placing a soft kiss on his lips. Rhett greedily accepted her affection, pulling her into his chest and exhaling.

"I didn't mean to freak out," he muttered into her hair. He hugged her even tighter, letting the connection between their bodies soothe his frayed nerves. "It was like a bad case of déjà vu to be lying in bed next to you and see her name on the screen."

"Rhett. Seriously. Let it go. We're good. Today is supposed to be about *you*. I can't wait to see you walk across that stage. I'm so proud of you, and I'm so glad I get to be here with you today."

She was right: There was a very different version of how today could have gone, one where she wasn't here with him at all. He didn't want to live in the past or worry about the mistakes they had both made to get to this place. They were here together now, and there was nothing anyone could say or do to change the fact that he would be marrying Tori in just a few weeks.

"Okay, so if you take that path, it'll cut through the quad, and you'll see the stage," he instructed as he pointed out the directions.

"Got it," Tori chirped, grabbing her bag before she exited the car. "Ready, Maddie?" She turned around to confirm his sister was coming with her.

"Hey," Rhett called out once she exited the car but hadn't closed the door. She turned back to him, smiling. "I'm so glad you're here, beautiful." He winked at her, relishing the fact that this was the first of many celebrations for them this month.

She held up a finger to indicate he should wait. He didn't care that he was stopping traffic in the middle of campus on the morning of graduation: He would do any damn thing she asked him to do. His eyes followed her as she walked around the front of the vehicle. The way her body moved in that yellow dress... He rolled down his window when she reached his door, almost certain he knew what she wanted. She leaned in quickly, half her torso entering his space on the driver's side of the car. Instead of kissing him, she hovered two inches away from his face, her eyes gleaming with a sultry gaze. "I love you, Everhett Wheeler."

She tasted like coffee and sweet cream. She smelled like rosemary and mint. She kissed like they were about to be separated for an indefinite amount of time, her mouth confirming the words she had just whispered. It wasn't until a horn blared that he remembered he still had to park the car. He reluctantly ended their kiss as Tori hurried across the street where Maddie was waiting for her.

He drove to the small parking lot behind the business building that almost always had a few open spots. Miraculously there were only three other cars in the tucked-away lot. He parked the SUV before digging out his phone.

He finally felt calm enough to return Chandler's text. Now that he had Tori's blessing, he just wanted to check her off his list and be done with it. He hadn't found anything that belonged to her when they cleaned out the apartment yesterday, so he didn't know what the hell she wanted to talk about. Still. He felt like he owed her the opportunity to gain the closure she needed before he left Easton for good.

Rhett: Hey. Congrats on your graduation today. I just got to campus and have to head to the stage soon. Want me to call you later?

He hoped the offer to talk on the phone would be enough for her, or that maybe she wouldn't see his text right away. His hope was short-lived when he felt his phone vibrate in his hand less than a minute later.

Chandler: Where are you?

He shook his head and contemplated his next move. He had plenty of time to get to the ceremony since he had found a parking spot so quickly. But did he really want to sully the day by talking face-to-face with his ex-girlfriend? Guilt crept in and beat out the selfishness he was feeling.

Rhett: I'm in the lot behind the business building. I can wait 10 minutes if you're close?

Chandler: I'll be right there.

He fiddled on his phone while he waited, opening and closing apps without really paying attention to anything on the screen.

Chandler: I'm here. Where are you?

He had forgotten he was in Maddie's car. He hopped out of the front seat and scanned the parking lot. She must have spotted him first, because she was already striding toward him.

"Hey," he offered timidly once she was within earshot.

"Hi," she replied curtly. She was dressed up for graduation in a pale pink strapless dress and matching open-toed heels. It was supposed to be a joyful, happy day for them both, but Rhett could tell just by her tone that she was seething. Her eyes scanned the parking lot around them, almost as if she was checking to see if anyone else could hear their conversation. She seemed to be looking everywhere but at him.

"How was graduation?" She was the one who'd insisted on meeting up, but he didn't want to make this any more uncomfortable than it needed to be. He could be cordial.

"It was fine. Long, as expected. We took pictures by the fountain and are about to head out to eat. My parents keep asking about you. I haven't told them that we're not together anymore, so..."

Shit. Was this why she wanted to meet up with him? If Chandler hadn't admitted to her parents that they were over, was she still hanging onto the illusion that there was a chance they would get back together?

"Chandler, listen. I'm sorry for how things ended. I know it probably seemed abrupt, but it really is over between us."

"I know that," she hissed as she wiped a stray tear from her cheek. "After almost two weeks of total silence from you, don't you think I fucking know that?"

Rhett recoiled at her tone but still felt a subtle pull to take a step toward her. Part of him wanted to wrap her into a hug and comfort her. But he couldn't do that. She might read too much into it, and he couldn't give her any false hope about where things stood between them.

"So why did you text me? What did you want to talk about?"

She continued to avoid meeting his gaze as she smoothed her hands down the front of her dress. "Do you remember the weekend after you went to Virginia?"

The memory of that weekend was painful. He had gone to Virginia for a few days, then came back to school and stayed in town instead of going home even though it was Easter weekend. Tori and her dad had spent the day with his family while he went to Chandler's parents' house for dinner. He knew now that Tori's scans had been the next day. He always made a point to be in town for her appointments, but they'd had a blow-up fight the month prior, and they weren't even on speaking terms at the time. It would be a long time before he would forgive himself for not being in Hampton for Tori's appointment.

"Rhett?" Chandler snapped.

"Yeah. Yeah, I remember. I didn't go home to Hampton that weekend, and we went to your parents' house for dinner."

Chandler let out a gaff and moved her hands to her hips. "Right. You didn't go home to Hampton to *her*." The last word came out of her mouth like something vile. "Of course that's what you remember about that weekend."

"Hey," he warned. His voice came out lower and harsher than he expected. "I don't know what you thought you were going to accomplish today Chandler, but I'm not interested in rehashing the past with you in a parking lot. I didn't agree to meet up with you just so you could disrespect my fiancée."

Her entire body went rigid. He swore he heard her gasp.

Fuck. She obviously didn't know he was engaged, and that was a really shitty way for her to find out. He hadn't meant to rub his relationship with Tori in her face. But he also was done pretending that he wasn't devoted to the love of his life.

"You're engaged?" she deadpanned.

"Yeah, I am. Tori and I are engaged. Listen, Chandler... Fuck..." Rhett raked his hand through his hair, desperate to rewind the last ten seconds and take back the pain he had just caused. "I didn't want you to find out like this. I know it probably seems rushed, but..."

"You're engaged to the girl who you always swore was just a friend? You're going to get married sometime in the next few years to your side piece back home after ending *our* three-year relationship less than two weeks ago?"

Hell. No.

She didn't get to talk about Tori like that. She didn't get to have an opinion about his relationship at all. This ended now.

"Nope," he declared defiantly. "I'm not going to marry my 'side piece' in a few years. I'm going to marry the love of my life at the end of this month." He threw her words back at her like he was batting away a grenade.

Chandler teetered on her heels as his words landed exactly as he had intended. *Good*. Now she was getting it. This wasn't a game. Not anymore. He was done playing with her. Hopefully this would be the last time he had to shut down Chandler Cunningham.

"Fuck you, Everhett. You almost had me fooled. I wanted so badly to believe that you would eventually grow up, that you could eventually move on. I should have known it would always end like this. Congratulations on your graduation. And your engagement. I left my key fob to the apartment on my hook in the entryway."

Chandler turned on her heel and stalked off, her shoulders shaking in the undeniable tell that she was crying. Rhett felt a deep-seated guilt for the pain he had inflicted. He had no intention of hurting her when he agreed to meet up with her, but now the damage was done.

There was residual regret nudging at his conscious. He still wasn't sure why she wanted to meet up with him in the first place. The only positive outcome from their encounter was that Chandler probably wouldn't want to talk to him anytime soon. Or ever again.

He knew there was very little he could do to undo the pain he had caused. He had to accept that he had made a lot of wrong calls and stupid mistakes where Chandler was concerned, but that they had all lead him back to Tori. That was what mattered.

He grabbed his gown and cords from the trunk of the car, then strode with purpose to the front of campus. He was graduating with his Master's degree today, and when he drove back to Hampton tonight, he was leaving with a degree, a fiancée, and the promise of the life he had always dreamed of.

CHAPTER FIVE

Rhett

Rhett scrolled through his calendar app for the third time that morning. It was early. He hadn't slept well again last night. He wasn't used to sleeping at Tori's house, but his room at his parents' house was littered with boxes and all the random things he wanted to take to Virginia so they didn't have a choice. Plus, he didn't want to have to face off again with his dad.

He sat up a little straighter against her headboard and rubbed the sleep out of his eyes. He needed a run. Or a drink. He doubted he had time for either.

Graduation had been a shitshow between the Chandler incident and the unexpected push back from his father during their post-graduation brunch. He never dreamed that when he pitched the idea of having their wedding up at the cabin in a few weeks, his parents wouldn't be completely onboard.

It wasn't the wedding itself or the rushed timeline that caused the discord. It was the flurry of questions his father had spat out over his plate of steak and eggs. Questions that were uncomfortable at best, insulting at worst, and that left such an uneasiness in the air that none of them were able to finish their meals.

Why were they getting married so soon?
Why wasn't Tori willing to move to Virginia with him?
What contingencies had he included in the prenup?

What did her preventative surgery plans mean for his future, for their family legacy?

His mom at least had the decency to shake her head and scold Peter Wheeler when he brought up Tori's health and how it might affect the Wheeler "legacy" as he had not-so-subtly worded it. That wasn't the worst of it, though. His dad shoved out of his seat and upended a saltshaker when Rhett revealed that they didn't have a prenup.

He couldn't believe his own father had assailed them like that at brunch, on the day of his graduation no less. His dad had known Tori since she was five years old. She shouldn't have to provide a character assessment or credit check to officially join the family after being part of their lives for nearly twenty years.

Nothing was resolved or accomplished from their face-off besides the lingering tension that followed them home to Hampton. Rhett was pretty sure the issue wouldn't come up again. His dad would be at the wedding, and then he would resume his fifty weeks of travel per year. As long as he was confident his mom was on his side, he didn't give a shit what his dad thought about his marriage, his money, or his future.

Thankfully, his mom had agreed to help him with the wedding planning and seemed genuinely happy for them to get married. Now that the date was set, he had even more to do. He had to leave for Virginia tomorrow morning for a quick two-day trip. He was in the final stages of hiring his executive assistant for NorfolkStar Transport, and he wanted to conduct the final round of interviews in person. He needed to be there in person to hire the person who he would trust to manage his schedule.

Then Tori had three back-to-back consultations on Friday. He knew she was set on having a risk-reducing hysterectomy as soon as possible. Her follow-up scans had come back inconclusive, but because of the elevated CA-125 levels in her bloodwork and her genetic history, there was a chance that she already had a very early stage of ovarian cancer. Unfortunately, without evidence of tumors or an official diagnosis, she had been warned that she may get some

pushback about being so proactive about prophylactic surgery. Rhett
wanted to be there for her on Friday to help navigate those
conversations and to feel out the surgeon they were going to trust
with her life.

He sighed again, accepting that the only way to tackle the next few
days was to put his head down and push through. He would have to
head back to his house at some point today to pack a bag for Virginia.
He wondered idly where he had put his garment bag when they
unloaded the cars on Sunday night.

Rhett was pulled out of his own head by Tori rolling over next to
him. He turned to gaze down at her, noticing the slightest pinch
between her eyebrows. "Good morning, beautiful."

"Hey, hot stuff," she replied, her voice still heavy with sleep. "What
are you stressing about over there?"

He offered her a tight smile. She could always tell when his mind
was working overtime.

"Just thinking about everything we have going on this week." He
shifted onto his side and wrapped an arm around her. She shimmied
closer to him, lining up her back against his bare chest. He could feel
the warmth of her body through the thin T-shirt she had slept in last
night.

"Are you worried Memorial Day weekend is too soon?" she asked as
she traced small circles on his forearm.

"Nope, not at all," he replied without hesitation. "The wedding is
what's going to get me through these next two weeks. It's all the other
stuff I have to do between now and then that feels daunting.
Memorial Day weekend will be perfect. I can't wait to marry you." He
nuzzled his face into the crook of her neck, letting his lips savor the
delicate skin stretched along her collarbone. He felt her shiver in
response to his words and his mouth. They both stayed silent for a
minute, relishing in the stillness of the morning.

Being in bed together was a sacred shelter. He could call up all the
resilience and strength he needed when he was holding her in his
arms. He had waited so long to be able to just hold her.

The calm didn't keep against his reeling thoughts, though. He was the first to break the silence. "So what's your work schedule this week?"

"I have to work dinner shifts tonight and Thursday, then I open on Saturday morning."

"Wait, you have to work tonight?" He had to catch a flight to Virginia before sunrise tomorrow. He'd been counting on spending the day with Tori before he had to leave her for a few days.

"I do. I feel like I need to get back on somewhat of a normal schedule after all the random time off I've had lately. I've barely worked this month. I can't work on Friday because of my appointments, then I marked off Saturday night and all of Sunday to be with you..." Tori trailed off as she ran her nails up and down the inside of his arm.

"You know it's okay to work less with everything we've got going on, right? I hate the idea of you running yourself ragged when we don't need the money." He had already called his bank guy earlier in the week and had Tori added on to all his accounts. He was going to take care of his wife in every way possible, including financially.

Tori stilled in his arms, her body rigid in response to his words. She moved her hand off his arm and moved ever-so-slightly away from his hold. "Do you think we need a prenup?" she whispered.

Goddamnit. His father's tirade had obviously gotten to her. "Of course not."

"You know everyone's going to think I'm marrying you for health insurance or your money."

"Bullshit. Don't let my dad's ridiculous power play get to your head, beautiful. Anyone who knows us—hell, anyone who's ever seen us together—knows that we've been in love for years. What's mine is yours now that you're mine."

Tori craned her neck back to smile at him. "Okay," she relented. "I'm sorry that happened yesterday. I've never seen your dad fly off the handle like that."

Rhett blew out a long breath. He was so disappointed by how everything had gone down. "I know. It sucks. I'm still in shock, honestly. I could tell my mom and Maddie were caught off guard, too. But I guess, in his defense, he hasn't been around much over the last several years. His only context for our relationship is that we dated in high school, then still hung out together whenever I was home."

"That's true. I don't think either of us expected things to end up like this, so we can't expect other people to understand it either." She rolled over and buried her face in the crook of his arm. Her hair was a frazzled mess, and she still had crease marks from her pillow on one cheek. She had never looked more beautiful.

"I love you. I'm marrying you. That's what matters now, and that's what I'm going to focus on for the next few weeks as we get through all the craziness ahead. Are we good?" he asked, brushing a loose strand of hair out of her face and tucking it behind her ear.

Tori nodded and closed her eyes in response to his touch. The sweetest smile played across her face. "We're good."

"I'm going to run some errands this morning, then try to go on a long run. I've still got to pack for Virginia, and I have to call into a few meetings this afternoon. But I'll drive you to work this afternoon, okay? Just let me know what time you want to leave."

Tori nodded again but, this time, opened her eyes to meet his gaze. "You know I've been driving myself to work for the last six years, Ev."

He ran his thumb back and forth over her bottom lip before moving in to kiss her. "Yeah, I know. But it used to be our thing. Driving through downtown and just being in the car with you? That's one of my favorite places to be. Sometimes I think you don't totally get it."

"Get what?"

"That the entire time we were apart—from the minute you broke up with me that summer, then when we were sort-of-together, and especially over the last few months—I just wanted to be wherever you were that entire time."

Tori's gaze softened and she pouted out her lower lip. "Thank you for never giving up on us."

He couldn't get enough of this new version of their relationship: of her softness toward him, of her easy acceptance of his love.

"Never," he vowed as he kissed her forehead and rose out of bed to take on the day.

CHAPTER SIX

Tori

Work was incredibly slow, even for a Tuesday. Tori had only waited on three tables during the first half of her shift. The last two hours were going to drag.

"You want me to put some food in for you, baby?" Jake asked from behind the bar. Their boss Mike was next door, working on renovations for The Oak Barrel Tavern, which meant Jake was in charge tonight.

"I'll put in an order in the back and take my break in twenty if that's okay?"

"Sounds good." He turned back around to refill the water glasses of the two people sitting at the counter. A hockey game had just started on the big screen hanging behind his head. Maybe the game would draw in a few more patrons tonight.

Tori did a final check on her table, but they said they were fine and they had already paid. When she made her way to the back, she found Lia leaning against the point-of-sale system, working the straw of a large Styrofoam cup between her teeth.

"This sucks," her best friend declared. Tori nodded in agreement. They'd be lucky to each leave with twenty dollars in tips tonight.

Not that I need the money anymore. She was still coming to terms with the idea that she would just suddenly have access to Rhett's money. She knew she shouldn't have expected anything less, but it had been jarring when she had logged into the bank app on her phone earlier that week and saw the insane amounts of money associated with the multiple accounts in both their names.

"Yeah, it does," she commiserated. "This weekend will make up for it, though. The weather should be nice enough for people to sit on the patio."

Lia side-eyed her, obviously skeptical of her optimistic overview. She narrowed her eyes slightly while working the straw back and forth in her mouth, but she didn't have a chance to add to the conversation.

"Order up!" one of the cooks called from the back. Tori watched with relief as her best friend grabbed the plates and headed back into the main dining room. She wasn't trying to hide her new tax bracket necessarily, but she knew Lia would have plenty to say about her newfound fortune. Tori would have to deal with her twenty questions eventually. Just not tonight.

Tori put in the order for her usual salad, adding a side of fries in case Jake was hungry, too. She planned to sit at the bar and keep him company during her break.

"You've got a new table, Tor," Lia announced as she pushed back through the kitchen doors. Tori flinched at the sharpness of her tone.

"Uh, do you want to take it?" she offered, worried that Lia was upset with her for getting another table on such a slow night.

"Nope," she popped the P as her eyebrows shot up. "He's asking for you."

"He?"

"Fielding. He's out there, and he insisted on being seated in your section instead of just parking his stupid-hot body at the bar like he normally does."

Tori scrunched her eyes closed and pinched the bridge of her nose between her thumb and forefinger. A pit of guilt festered in her stomach as she thought about how she had been intentionally ignoring Fielding over the last few weeks. They had texted a few times, and he knew her follow-up appointment hadn't been good, but she hadn't actually seen him in person since the day after she had a panic attack at his house.

"You better tell him tonight, Tori."

She glanced down at her left hand. She had purposely left her ring at home just like she had for every shift she had worked since getting engaged. She told herself she didn't want anything to happen to the ring while she was bustling around Clinton's. Not having to answer any prying questions about her engagement was just an added bonus.

"Tor."

"I know, I know. I wasn't trying to keep it from him, I just..."

"Yeah, I know. Just get it over with. It'll be okay. Jake told me I could take off early, but I'll stay for the rest of your shift, even if he wants me to clock out."

Tori squeezed her best friend's arm appreciatively, steeling herself for the difficult conversation she'd been avoiding for weeks.

She spotted him the second she stepped out of the kitchen. Fielding was seated in the booth closest to the windows. It was big enough for at least eight adults. Even his six-two frame looked small in such a large space.

"Hey, you," she offered as she approached the table.

"Long time no see, Victoria."

He hadn't even looked at her yet, but she knew he was pissed. *He has every right to be*, she reminded herself. She had basically ghosted him. She felt guilty that she hadn't made more of an effort to reach over the last few weeks. There was also a residual embarrassment swirling around inside her because of the panic attack she'd had in front of him.

"I know. I've just had a lot going on..."

Fielding glanced up at her then, his eyes searching her face. "Yeah. I figured that much out on my own. I've called you multiple times. I've texted you. I've been worried about you. And now I feel like a loser coming here and demanding to be seated in your section, like this was the only way I could see you." He gripped the edge of the table as he started to slide out of the booth. "This was stupid. I'm gonna go. I shouldn't have expected..."

"No! Don't go. I'm sorry, Field. I know I've been a shitty friend. But I want you to stay."

He continued to rise out of the booth, taking his time to straighten to his full height. Tori was increasingly aware of the intensity of his gaze as he continued to stare down at her. What was he searching for? Eventually he shook his head and cleared his throat.

"Fine," he relented. "That was way too easy, though. You must have some sort of magical spell cast over me, Victoria Thompson. Are you a witch? I don't know that much about witches. I'm going to have to look that up. I feel like I should have at least made you work..."

"Oh, stop," she interjected, giving him a solid shove that did nothing to dislodge his footing.

"I missed you," he murmured, finally meeting her eyes and offering her a head tilt and a half smile.

"I missed you, too." It was the truth. She had spent more time with Fielding over the last few months than she had with anyone else in her life. Rhett's absence had left an impossibly bleak hole in her heart, but she discovered that she felt less lonely when she was with him.

"Will you hang out with me if I move to the bar?"

"I'll do you one better. I just put in my dinner order, so I'll sit and eat with you."

Fielding reached out and wrapped her into a side hug as they approached the bar together. Tori stiffened slightly in response to his touch before catching herself. She wouldn't be worried about Jake or Cory hugging her, so why was she so on edge about Fielding's gesture? He was her friend, and a good one at that.

Jake gave Fielding a one-nod chin lift when he slid onto a stool on his usual side of the bar. "Long time no see, Haas."

Fielding rolled his eyes. "Pretty sure I woke up on your couch still drunk this morning, man."

Tori grinned at the boys' easy exchange. She had missed this: hanging out at Clinton's, listening to their banter. She walked past the bar and headed back to the kitchen to check on her food.

If she thought she was going to have a moment to herself, she was wrong. Lia was waiting for her at the point-of-sale computer, and Jake was shoving through the door behind her, hot on her heels.

"Tori, you've gotta tell him you and Rhett are engaged." Her chest tightened in response to Jake's demand. His mouth was set in a hard line, his eyes as dark as his tone.

"That's exactly what I told her," Lia added as she placed one hand on her hip.

"Way to pile on, guys," Tori muttered as she crossed her arms and leaned back against the drink station.

Jake widened his stance and matched her posture, crossing his large arms across his chest as he assessed her up and down. "Baby, you don't get it. That, or you're doing a hell of a job pretending not to get it. Fielding has been asking me about you every day for the last two weeks. I keep assuring him that you're fine, just busy. I haven't said a damn thing about Rhett or the wedding. But at this point, I'm just straight up lying to him for you, and I'm sick of it. I'm done. If you don't want to be friends with him anymore, that's fine. But I do. So you..."

"Of course I want to be friends with him!" she shot back.

"Then act like a friend. He deserves to know what's going on."

"He's right, Tor. He deserves to know what's going on," Lia echoed. "At this point, not telling him is the same as lying about it. Do it here so he can't freak out on you."

Tori raised her eyebrows in defiance. "Why would he freak out on me?"

Jake and Lia said nothing, but they both gave her knowing looks. There was no way Fielding wasn't going to react to the news, and she sincerely doubted his first response would be one of congratulations. Tori had been clear from the beginning that she only wanted to be friends with Fielding, and he had taken that in stride. But that didn't stop him from flirting and jokingly declaring his love for her on a regular basis.

"You guys were hanging out multiple days a week for the last two months, baby. And you and Rhett weren't together during any of that time. He doesn't know anything about your relationship over the last ten years. I agree with Lia: do it here. That way, I can make sure he keeps his cool and gets home safe tonight."

Tori felt a wave of nausea rise from her stomach to her throat. Did Jake really think Fielding was going to react *that* poorly? Not for the first time in the last two weeks, she wondered what the hell she was supposed to even say to Fielding about her fiancé.

"Order up!"

She spun on her heel and grabbed her food before making her way to the bar. She didn't glance up when Lia and Jake both brushed past her, Lia heading to check the tables in the dining room and Jake taking his position back behind the bar.

Fielding's eyes lit up as she approached. "You ordered me fries?" He didn't wait for Tori to reply before grabbing a handful and shoving them in his mouth.

"I actually ordered fries for Jake, but I'm sure he doesn't mind sharing," she teased. She didn't dare glance over at her fiancé's best friend, but she could feel his eyes boring into her. "So…" she started, scraping her fork against a piece of spinach, hoping the right words would just come to her if she stared at her salad long enough.

Fielding glanced between Tori and Jake as he reached over to snag more fries. "When will you guys know your schedules for Memorial Day weekend? We're going to open up the pool at my mom's house that weekend. Dem and I want to have everybody over."

Tori eyebrows shot up. He had just given her the perfect opening. Technically, they already knew their work schedules that weekend: Rhett had called Mike as soon as they picked a wedding date to make sure Jake, Lia, and Cory could all be off at the same time. Once Mike knew why half his staff needed time off, he made the decision to close Clinton's for the entire weekend. Rhett said it was Mike's idea, and she hadn't asked if Rhett offered to buy out the restaurant for those three days. She just let him handle it, grateful that all their friends plus their boss would get to celebrate with them.

"We have plans that whole weekend," Jake answered from behind the bar.

Shit. She was up.

"Fielding, I have to tell you something." He turned to her and reached across her plate for a few more fries. "Rhett and I are engaged, and we're getting married Memorial Day weekend."

Fielding froze in place, two fries dangling a few inches from his mouth. A small blob of ketchup dripped onto the bar as he held the food suspended in the air.

"I know it probably seems unexpected," Tori gushed, not wanting to sit in the awkwardness of his reaction, "but after Rhett came home a few weeks ago, everything clicked. We've dated for years, we just weren't open about our relationship some of the time, so even though it didn't seem like anything was going on..."

Fielding interrupted her rambling. "You got engaged after you got that call at my house?"

"No, not right after. We got engaged that weekend..."

"When?"

"What? What do you mean when?"

"What day did you get engaged, Tori?"

She had to think for a minute. Everything had been happening so fast, it felt like the days blended into each other. "Friday," she finally concluded.

"So two days after you had a panic attack at my house"—Fielding nodded in a show of understanding—"one day after I spent all morning and afternoon with you so you wouldn't have to be alone," he confirmed. His face was expressionless, but she didn't need to see the emotions on his face to hear the hurt in his words.

Fielding lifted a hand to the back of his neck, scowled at her, then nodded toward Jake. "And you knew all this?"

Jake had remained unmoving during their exchange, his big arms crossed in front of his chest as he leaned against the ice machine. He didn't respond to Fielding's question, but his lack of denial was confirmation enough.

"Fan-fucking-tastic," Fielding muttered under his breath. He swiveled his barstool to face her again. "You told me you didn't date, and I believed you. I respected what you said, Tori. Now you're *engaged*? How do you go from not dating to being freakin' engaged? *That's* why I haven't heard from you these last two weeks, isn't it? So what was I then? A placeholder? A distraction? A plaything while Wheeler was away? I'm the last to know, aren't I?"

The intensity of his outburst shocked her. Anger radiated off him in waves. The tension only increased as he sat there fuming, waiting for her to respond. She didn't even know where to begin.

"Field, please, I would have told you sooner, but I just haven't had a chance..."

"No shit, Tori. You haven't had a chance to tell me, because you won't even talk to me! You've been avoiding me for weeks!" His rebuttal was loud enough to draw attention from the two other patrons sitting at the bar. They were both staring, although one at least had the decency to pretend to glance down at his phone when Tori looked in his direction.

Jake pushed off the ice machine and made his way over to them. "Hey," Jake called Fielding's attention off of Tori, his voice low and steady. "She's on the clock right now, and I'm the manager tonight. Don't doubt for one goddamn second that I won't ask you to leave if you can't keep your cool."

Fielding stared back at Jake. His expression shifted from outraged to detached as he absorbed his friend's warning.

Fielding smirked before speaking again. "I'll take a double whiskey sour, bartender," he ordered, his coolness obviously in place just to challenge Jake's authority.

Tori exhaled and pushed her plate away. She wasn't hungry anymore.

Jake wordlessly poured and delivered Fielding's drink before turning to her. "I'll ask Lia to stay and close out your section tonight, baby." She nodded her thanks, silently communicating to Jake that she had it under control.

Fielding took a long drink, draining half the glass in one gulp. He winced before he spoke again. "Are you marrying him for health insurance?"

Tori squirmed at the directness of his query. Fielding was too perceptive. She knew people were going to talk—to gossip about their seemingly rushed race to the altar. She expected half the town to wonder if she was pregnant. Only someone who knew about her medical situation would think about the insurance aspect, and only someone as bold as Fielding would dare to ask.

"No. I'm marrying him because I love him and he asked me," she stated as confidently as she could muster.

Fielding stared down at his drink, rimming the top of the glass with one finger. The silence between them grew more awkward with each passing second. He picked at the corner of his drink napkin for a few more moments before he finally looked up to meet her eyes. She didn't see pain or anger in his gaze like she expected. Instead, there was determination.

"Because you know he's not the only person who cares about you that has money," Fielding stated nonchalantly. He threw back the rest of his drink. "Another double," he said to Jake from across the bar.

Tori's body tensed in defense. What the hell? Had he not just heard her? She loved Rhett. She wanted to be with Rhett. She was marrying Rhett because she loved him, not because she needed health insurance or wanted his money. She knew Fielding was upset, but she didn't have to sit here and subject herself to an emotional thrashing.

"Are you done?"

"I'm just barely getting started, baby."

She winced at his use of Jake's nickname for her.

"I'm serious, though. If this is about insurance or money, I can help. I want to help. I know Wheeler's family is well off, but I don't think you understand how much I'm worth. I don't have to work another day in my life if I don't want to. I have more money than I know what to do with. Tori, if you need help…"

She blanched at his words. "You're unbelievable," she muttered. "I just told you, it's *not* about money. I love Rhett. Rhett loves me. Maybe the timing of everything is faster than it would be if I wasn't sick, but Rhett and I being together has always been inevitable."

"Inevitable," he repeated slowly, as if he was testing out the word on his tongue. "So you're settling?"

Tori gritted her teeth at his dismissiveness. She didn't know if Fielding was still trying to justify the situation in his mind or if he was just being cruel. "Shove off, Field. I'm not going to sit here and listen to you insult me like this. Enjoy your drink." Tori hopped off the bar stool, determined to walk away from his insults and judgement.

"Fuck…" he muttered under his breath before reaching out for her. His hand landed on her upper arm before it brushed up to settle on her shoulder. "That was a dick move. I don't know what's wrong with me tonight. Tori, please, don't go."

She paused as she felt his hand cup the curve of her shoulder, his fingers applying the slightest edge of pressure. She couldn't help the blush that crept up her cheeks when she saw Jake approach.

He set down Fielding's new drink, then retreated to give them privacy. Or at least the illusion of privacy. She knew Jake wouldn't go too far or take his eyes off them now.

"Look, I'm sorry. I know I'm being an asshole…"

"Yeah, you really are," she quipped as she shrugged off his hand.

"Think about this from my perspective, Tori! We've been hanging out multiple times a week, every week. Over the last few months, I never wondered if I was going to see you or Jake. The three of us together wasn't an if, it was a when. *We* were inevitable. The last two weeks have sucked without you."

Tori settled back in her seat and sighed. Everything he said was true. So much of her life over the last few months included Fielding, and she'd be lying if she didn't admit she missed him, too.

"That morning after the party was the first and only time you ever mentioned Wheeler's name to me. Imagine my surprise when, all of a sudden, you're on the floor at my house, begging me to call him for you. Then the next day he shows up at your house and takes you away. I had no idea what was going on, Tori. I didn't know where you went or when you'd be back."

Fielding deflated with his confession. He looked so earnest sitting next to her now.

"Do you know how worried I've been over these last two weeks? I knew something had to be wrong. You've barely responded to any of my texts, and I haven't seen you since he came back to town. I had considered so many explanations for what was going on, and I thought I was prepared to see you tonight. But fuck. I didn't expect you to tell me you're engaged."

Tori absorbed everything Fielding said. His defenses were finally down, and it was clear she had hurt him. It was her turn to apologize now.

"I'm sorry for not being a better friend or keeping in touch over the last few weeks, Field. Everything happened so fast. I was sort of avoiding you, and that was stupid. I should have told you about the engagement sooner."

He nodded as he took another sip of his drink. He set his gaze across the bar before he spoke again. "So were you just using me to distract yourself while you waited for him?"

"No, Field, I swear. I wouldn't do that. I love spending time with you, and I value our friendship. I'm not just saying that, either. I never expected to even like you. You're cocky and goofy and pretty full of yourself for my taste," she teased in an attempt to lighten the mood. "But hanging out at the Valet House and having lunch together became the best part of my day over the last few months. You were never just a distraction."

"So it was real?"

The question gutted her. The sincerity of his voice, the weight of what he was asking. Tori had insisted that she only wanted a platonic friendship with Fielding, and he had respected that boundary. But she would be lying to herself if she tried to deny that she felt a deeper connection to Fielding than she did to any of her other friends. They had both felt that spark the moment they met.

"It was real. Our friendship is still real," she clarified, not wanting to let any false hope linger between them.

Fielding was silent for a few beats, absorbing her words as he finished off his drink. "Okay. I can accept that. So we can still be friends?"

"Yes, of course. Nothing has to change between us, as long as you understand that I'm with Rhett."

"I get it. I'm fine with it," he said a little too quickly. "I think I've already proven that all I'm after is your friendship, Victoria. I love spending time with you, and I haven't eaten a decent sandwich in nearly two weeks since you've been gone. I'll forgive you for ghosting me if you promise we can pick up right where we left off."

Tori nodded and exhaled a long breath. She wasn't about to give up their friendship just because she was getting married.

Fielding's smile transformed into a smirk. "So do you have to ask Daddy Wheeler's permission before we can make plans?"

Tori glared at him. "Nope. That's not going to fly. Rhett is going to be my husband in a few weeks. If you and I are going to stay friends, you have to respect him."

"Fine," Fielding rebuffed, waving his hand through the air for extra emphasis. "I just want to be able to hang out with you on a regular basis like before. That's okay, right?"

"Absolutely," she promised. "My schedule is sort of crazy this week, but I'm free tomorrow if you want to hang out then?"

"Deal." Fielding smiled sincerely at her before he raised his empty glass in Jake's direction. "I'll have another."

Jake rejoined them and gave Fielding a pointed look as he reached for his glass. "I'll serve you, but you're not driving tonight."

"No shit, man." His tone was playful, his consent a peace offering. Fielding knew better than to push it when it came to Jake's tolerance for impaired driving.

Fielding leaned into Tori's personal space for the briefest of moments. She could smell the whiskey on his breath mixed with the scent of his expensive cologne. It was a familiar scent, a smell that reminded her of lazy afternoons and easy conversations. "You gonna offer to drive me home tonight, Thompson? That's what friends do for each other, right?"

She smiled back and shook her head. "I can't. I mean, I would, but I didn't drive tonight. I bet your buddy Jake would love to cart your drunk ass home in the Jeep," she quipped before picking up her plate to carry it into the kitchen.

"Wait!" Fielding called after her before she pushed through the kitchen doors. Tori stopped in her tracks, turning around quickly when she heard the urgency in his voice.

"I've got one more condition before we're back to being besties." Fielding paused for dramatic effect. "Can you bring me more fries?"

Tori rolled her eyes. They were going to be okay.

CHAPTER SEVEN

Rhett

It had taken Rhett most of the day to prepare for just two nights in Virginia. He was glad that Tori had to work after all. He didn't need much—toiletries, a suit, a few shirts, his dress shoes, and his laptop— but his things were packed up in multiple boxes strewn between his bedroom and his parents' garage, so it was impossible to just quickly grab what he needed. It didn't help that he kept getting distracted by his ever-growing to-do list and the onslaught of emails pinging his inbox.

His body relaxed slightly as he eased the Prelude out of their neighborhood and onto one of the two main roads in town. The air was filled with the pungent, earthy tang of fresh mulch. New buds graced the tall trees that lined both sides of the road, creating a canopy that connected right above the parallel yellow lines.

He had lived in Hampton his whole life. Even when he went away to college, this town had always been home. It was unsettling to think about moving more than an afternoon's drive away from everything he knew and everyone he loved. Relocating to Virginia was always going to be hard, but now that he and Tori were together and soon to be married, it felt even more complicated.

They should be house hunting together. Instead, he was moving hundreds of miles away, and she claimed she didn't want to even think about moving or finding a place of their own yet. He understood she had other priorities. He wasn't worried about long distance as much as he was just frustrated that after all this time of wanting to be together, they technically were, but they weren't going to physically live together anytime soon.

Rhett parked as close to the side door of Clinton's as possible. He'd just be in and out tonight. He knew Jake was working, and as much as he'd love to hang out and catch up, he was anxious to get Tori home and get some sleep. He needed to be up in five hours to head to the airport for his flight to Virginia.

He tugged at the side door of the restaurant and felt the familiar give when it opened. What he didn't expect was the peel of laughter that greeted him as he stepped inside. His mouth involuntarily turned up into a smile just from the sound of her laugh. He had missed her all day, and now he was especially glad he insisted on driving her to work. The few extra minutes in the car together would help him get through the time apart over the next few days.

But it wasn't just Tori and Jake still inside the restaurant when he walked in. Fielding Haas was also sitting at the bar, right next to his girl. Rhett pocketed his phone and stood up a little straighter as he approached. He wrapped his arms around Tori from behind, affectionately brushing his hand along her shoulder as he gently squeezed.

"Hi, beautiful," he murmured into her ear.

"Rhett!" She sounded surprised, even though he had texted her ten minutes ago to say he was on his way to pick her up. "I didn't even hear you come in. You didn't have to come get me. I would have just come out to the car."

He brushed his lips against the side of Tori's neck, lingering longer than he normally would for such an intimate gesture in public. He felt her pulse pick up in response to his affection. "I don't mind coming in for you. You know that."

Rhett lifted his eyes to find Jake behind the bar. "Hey, bro," he said before looking over and adding, "Haas," in greeting to the other man. It was civil. And it was also all he was willing to give.

"Wheeler." Fielding matched his tone as he twirled his keys on one of his fingers. A few tense seconds passed. No one said anything for one breath, then two.

Finally, Rhett broke the silence. "Is Mike in the back?" He still had one arm wrapped around the front of Tori's chest, his chin resting in the dip between her shoulder and her collarbone as he held her. He had missed her all day. Just her physical proximity to her now was soothing to his wound-up nerves.

"Nope," Jake answered. "He's been putting in a ton of hours next door trying to get everything up to code for the final planning commission meeting in a few weeks. He's either still over there, or he already went home."

"So you're the boss tonight?"

"I'm the boss tonight," Jake boasted with a sly smile.

"And it looks like you're staying open late?" Rhett challenged, cocking his head toward Haas.

"Nah, front door's locked and we're closed. Fielding's just waiting on me. We're going back to my place to chill."

Rhett didn't let the surprise register on his face as he took in the information. Jake had told him that he and Tori had both gotten closer with Fielding over the last few months. He obviously hadn't realized how close.

"Alright, let's go," Tori interjected. "*You* have an early flight tomorrow," she reminded him, kissing his arm before uncoiling it from around her body. She slid off the barstool and grabbed her bag. "Will I see you Thursday, Jake?"

"I'll be here, baby."

"And I'll text you when I get up tomorrow, Field," she added as she smiled at the other man. Rhett tensed at her promise, his molars immediately finding the fleshy part of the inside of his cheek and biting down to thwart an outward reaction.

Fielding nodded. "I'm going to run out to the store before you come over. I'm pretty sure no one has bought groceries at the house since the last time you and I went shopping. Text me your list, 'kay?"

Rhett watched Tori's profile as he processed everything Haas said. None of the information was landing right or sitting well. He tasted a distinct rust flavor just as he realized how hard he was biting on the inside of his cheek.

"Goodnight, Fielding," she replied before taking Rhett's hand and walking toward the door.

"Goodnight, Victoria," Haas responded with more flirtation in his voice than necessary. Why the hell did he always have to call her by her full name?

Rhett held the side door open, then quickly strode past her to open the passenger door of the Prelude. Once she was securely inside, he slammed it shut and let out a frustrated sigh. He had been so inside his own head—worried about graduation and his schedule and Tori's appointments on Friday—that he hadn't given Haas another thought since he and Tori left for Michigan a few weeks ago.

Seeing him sitting next to his fiancée tonight was like being doused with a bucket of ice water. Fielding Haas was trouble. He knew it in his bones. He felt it in his gut. He hated that he had such a visceral reaction to the guy, but he just couldn't shake it. He knew there was almost no way to bring up his feelings without starting a fight. He also knew there was no chance he wasn't going to bring it up.

"How was your shift?" he asked, trying to sound casual as he put the car in reverse and backed out of the parking spot.

"It was super slow tonight."

Rhett nodded, feeling a small sense of relief that she didn't have to worry about slow shifts and low tip nights anymore.

"So you had plenty of time to hang out with Haas?" he inquired, the words coming out sharper than intended.

He felt Tori's guard go up. Instead of replying right away, she rolled her window down and rested her elbow on the opening while her fingers drummed on the doorframe. He could smell the promise of rain in the air, the scent of ozone mixing with the tanginess of the fresh mulch spread along the flower beds around the downtown area. It was the distinct perfume of springtime in Ohio.

"Fielding showed up around eight tonight. We did spend some time hanging out and catching up since I've barely talked to him over the last few weeks."

Was she being nonchalant just to heckle him? He was pissed. She knew he was pissed. And they both knew he didn't have a right to be pissed. Tori had developed a friendship with Fielding Haas in Rhett's absence over the last few months. His instincts told him that Fielding wanted to be a lot more than friends with his girl. That sense of knowing, compounded with the fact that Fielding had placed a bet with his roommates that he could get Tori to sleep with him, formed Rhett's unsavory opinion.

Tori broke him away from his own thoughts. "Hey. Don't sit there and stew, Ev. Fielding always comes into Clinton's when Jake and I are both working. It's our thing."

"I didn't realize you two had a *thing*."

"Don't," she warned, snapping her head around to glare at him.

Rhett kept his eyes fixed on the pavement, his hands in perfect position at ten and two. He side-eyed her through his peripherals. "I don't trust him, Tori," he confessed as he coasted down the main road toward their neighborhood.

"Well, I do," she shot back. "And Jake does too. Fielding and I are friends. We're good friends, actually. We got close over the last few months. He was there for me when..." She trailed off, realizing six words too late that she had tiptoed into a landmine they had both been trying to avoid.

"When what, V?"

She didn't respond, instead turning to look out the window again.

"When what? Just say it. He was there for you when I wasn't?" he pushed, anger coiling through him as he gripped the steering wheel harder.

"That's not how I view it, but yes. He was there for me when you and I weren't together. He was there for me when I first got the call. He was there for me when I needed a friend. I like spending time with Fielding. We made plans to hang out tomorrow, actually."

Rhett didn't think his grip could get any tighter as all the rage he was feeling pooled in his knuckles.

"I'll be in Virginia tomorrow," he reminded her.

"So?" she shot back, looking back at him with a scowl on her face. "What does that have to do with what I do tomorrow?"

"Tori, please," he tried again. "You know I don't like Haas. I don't trust him. I'm not going to tell you who you can and can't hang out with, but..."

"You've got that right," she interrupted. "I'll hang out with whoever I want, whenever I want."

Rhett let out a long exhale, running his free hand through his hair as he turned onto Sunset Drive. He mentally catalogued all the facts he knew about Fielding: his reputation as a partier when they were in high school together at Archway Prep. The notoriety of his lifestyle now that he was back in Hampton living off his trust fund and working valet for some of the local restaurants. The bet he had made about getting Tori to sleep with him. The challenge he had issued to Rhett when they faced off the day after she got the call about her bloodwork. There was just too much against him for Rhett to trust the guy.

"I didn't mean it to sound like I was trying to tell you what you could and couldn't do, beautiful. I would never do that. But I've known Haas a lot longer than you have."

Tori narrowed her gaze before rising to his challenge. "Yeah? Well, I know him a lot better than you do."

Rhett sighed, defeated. "That's fair. I guess I don't know him that well. I just worry based on what I *do* know about him. The Fielding Haas I know isn't a good guy. You and Jake keep telling me otherwise, and I trust you, but I don't trust him."

"You have nothing to worry about, Rhett. I'm with you. I love you. Please don't make my friendship with Fielding into something bigger than it is." She reached across the center console and interlaced their fingers.

He knew he shouldn't push it. But he couldn't stop himself from trying. "Will you invite Jake to hang out with you guys tomorrow just so I don't worry?"

"No."

He knew he had gone too far. But he didn't care. And he wasn't done.

"Tori, the last time you hung out at Fielding's house, shit hit the fan. If something happens to you while you're alone with him..."

"Rhett, *stop*. This isn't two weeks ago. This isn't two months ago. Nothing is going to happen while I'm with him. And if it did, I can take care of myself. I trust Fielding. He is my friend. He also knows that you and I are engaged, and I told him he has to respect that part of my life if he wants to keep being friends. I made that inexplicably clear to him tonight."

Her words lightened the dark clouds that had been swirling up in his mind. He put the Prelude in park in her driveway before turning to face her. He let out a long sigh, resigned to the fact that he didn't have a leg to stand on in this fight. He didn't like it, but he recognized that didn't matter in this situation. He would have to work through his worries about Haas on his own. And he would maybe have a little chat with Jake about him soon, too, just in case.

Acceptance settled in his mind as he glanced down at their joined hands, but that sense of resolve evaporated when he saw what was missing. "Where's your ring, V?" he questioned, staring down at her bare hand as all the anger that had just started to settle swirled back up in his chest.

She tried to pull her hand out of his before replying. "I always take it off for work."

"I didn't realize it was something you would take on and off so easily," he bit out.

Tori yanked her hand away from him, her green eyes set in a glare.

"You need sleep. You're tired and pissy. I'm not going to let you pick a fight tonight, especially before you have to get on a plane and leave tomorrow."

Rhett knew she was right. But he didn't like her tone or the fact that she was right.

"Fine," he clipped as he unbuckled his seatbelt. He was more than ready for bed, already dreading the alarm that would start to chime in four and a half hours. Tori's arm reached across his chest before he could open his door.

"I think you should just go home," she suggested. Her words came out soft, but they jolted his insides, poking at all the anxiety that had bubbled up over the last twenty minutes.

He froze on contact as a fresh wave of panic coursed through his veins. They had been apart all day, and he was struggling to reconcile where things stood between them now. "What do you mean?" he choked out.

"Hey, we're okay," she insisted as she raised a hand and brushed her fingers along the side of his face. "I just don't want to fight anymore. I know you need sleep. And I know you slept like shit in my bed last night." She gave him a knowing look that told him arguing was futile. "Just go to your parents' house, Rhett. We're okay. I just don't want to get into anything before you go to Virginia. I don't want either of us to worry about anything while you're there."

Everything she said made sense. But still.

"You're sure?" he asked. It was more of a plea than a question, but she didn't know that.

"Yes. I'm sure. I love you. Goodnight." She kissed him gently before exiting the vehicle and walking up her driveway.

Rhett silently cursed himself for letting things escalate like that. He should be following her into the house right now. But he couldn't leave it alone. He couldn't *not* safeguard what was his and stand his ground where Haas was concerned. He didn't want to have to worry about her while he was away. But he also wasn't able to explain that to Tori in a way that made sense.

Defeated, he backed out of her driveway and made the turn onto Sunset Drive. He didn't have time to figure out anything tonight. He barely had time to sleep before he had to get back in the car and head to the airport.

CHAPTER EIGHT

Tori stretched her arms over her head before she opened her eyes. Her room was illuminated by the soft morning light that crept in around the window blinds. Little specks of dust danced in the sun streams next to her bed.

She instinctively reached for her phone to check the time. 9:42 a.m. She had slept in later than she had in a while. Even though she had insisted Rhett was the one who needed sleep last night, she knew she needed a good night's rest as well.

She couldn't help but wonder if she was extra tired because there could very well be cancer cells multiplying rapidly in her body. Her "inconclusive" test results had been the most frustrating report possible for someone who had been worrying about when cancer would rear its ugly head for the last ten years. She was growing increasingly anxious for the three surgery consultations on Friday.

She took in a long, steady breath, and reminded herself that she was doing everything in her power to stave off the disease that had killed her mom. She didn't need to worry about cancer today. She had a plan, and things were happening as quickly as they could, given the circumstances. A deep, elongated exhale helped her put her worry away for now.

She opened up her messages app to read the three texts Rhett had sent her so far that morning.

Ev: Good morning, beautiful. I'm heading to the airport now.

Ev: Landed in Norfolk. I'm already excited to come home to you on Friday.

Ev: I'm sorry again about last night. I hope you have a good day. Tell Fielding I said hi. Call or text me if you need anything.

Tori sighed contentedly. She was grateful their fight wasn't going to trickle into today. Sending Rhett home last night had been the right call because it felt like they were starting fresh this morning.

V: Hey you. I hope you slept well last night. I'm just now waking up. How's your day so far?

Rhett's response came through less than a minute later.

Ev: Hey lazy bones. My day is better now that I've heard from you. I slept well enough. I don't think I'll be taking too many of those 6 am flights in the future. So far the interviews are going well— there's one candidate who really stands out.

V: Ahh I'm sorry you're tired, Ev. It's been a crazy couple weeks. We'll catch up on sleep this weekend.

Ev: You know that's not the only thing I want to catch up on. I miss you so damn much.

V: Oh yeah?

Ev: Oh yeah. We have the house (and the pool... and the hot tub...) all to ourselves this weekend, remember?

She smiled and let out a little sigh as she thought about all the catching up they could do that weekend. A second text came through before she had a chance to respond.

Ev: I've gotta get ready for the next candidate. I love you. I hope you have a great day. Promise me you'll call or text if you need anything?

She sensed the subtext to his question, but he obviously wasn't going to bring it up or fight her on it now. She decided not to call him out on it. She had made her case last night, and bringing up Fielding right before he had to focus at work wasn't fair. She didn't want or need to make him worry unnecessarily.

V: I love you too. I'll be fine, but if I'm not, I promise I'll call.

Fielding glared at her and shook his head as she carried over their empty glasses from the table. "Do you know how mad I am at you right now, Victoria Thompson?"

She tried to keep her face stoic as she challenged his sarcasm. "Me? What did I do this time?"

"You've been keeping your secret waffle recipe to yourself for months. I can't believe you've never made these for me before. I love waffles. I am a waffle aficionado. And yours are some of the best I've ever had. You've been holding out on me, and I honestly might not ever forgive you." He delivered his entire monologue without breaking character. He only stopped glaring at her long enough to take the glasses from her hands and load them into the dishwasher.

"Joke's on you then, Field. If you don't forgive me, how am I ever going to make them for you again?" She watched as he closed the dishwasher door and bit down on his lip to hold back a laugh. The entire morning had been like this: playful and light, just like things had been before. Their banter was interrupted by the slam of the side door.

"Hey hey, boys and girls!" Anwar announced as he stepped into the kitchen, followed closely by Fielding's twin brother, Dempsey. "What smells so good in here?"

Tori glanced up in time to see Anwar play-punch Fielding in the arm before moving further into the kitchen. Dempsey followed behind, offering his brother a subtle head nod as he passed. It was still disorienting to see the Haas brothers side-by-side. They were almost painfully good looking with their curly blonde hair, lagoon blue eyes, and deep summer tans. The looked more like surfers from California than fuckboys from Northeast Ohio.

She made her way over to the kitchen table to wipe it down before she replied. "Hi guys. We just made waffles. I already put away the leftovers, but there's plenty in the fridge."

"Dude," Anwar gawked. "You made waffles? I guess that makes up for you ditching our boy here for the last few weeks, huh?"

Tori shot a questioning glance at Fielding. She knew based on their conversation last night at the restaurant that he had been upset by her absence over the last few weeks. She didn't realize he'd been jolted enough that his roommates had noticed.

Fielding didn't meet her gaze, instead shoving Anwar in response to the jab. "Dem, you're going to love them," he added, turning to his twin. "They taste as good as, if not better than, Mom's. They just might be best waffles ever."

Dempsey stilled at his brother's words, his eyebrows drawing together in a scowl. Dempsey was the more serious twin, and he was definitely quieter than Fielding, but she hadn't ever seen him look that intense before. Was he pissed that she was here? Maybe Fielding had confided in Dempsey about what had gone down over the last few weeks.

Anwar, seemingly unaware of any of the tension coiling between the twins, opened the fridge and took a whole waffle out of the Ziplock bag then bit into it like a cookie. "Shit," he moaned in approval. "These are really good." He moved through the kitchen to grab a plate from the cupboard. "I'm gonna do this properly, though. These babies deserve it. You want me to heat you up some, too, Dem?"

"Nah. I think I've lost my appetite. You're a dumbass," Dempsey muttered to Fielding before he replaced Anwar in front of the fridge and started to rifle though the contents. Fielding didn't react to his brother's remark, instead standing frozen in place in front of the sink. His gaze was set ahead of him, but he didn't seem to be looking at anything in particular. Tori had no idea what to make of that. She had never seen the Haas brothers do anything but joke around with each other.

"So," Tori tried again, desperate to break up the tension, "what's everyone up to today?"

"We've got to work tonight," Anwar replied, cocking his head in Fielding's direction.

"Oh, shoot. I didn't realize you had to work later, Field." She was disappointed that her plans for the evening weren't going to work out after all.

"Why? Did we have plans I didn't know about?" he asked with a sly smile.

This guy. He never missed an opportunity to flirt with her. She really had missed him over the last few weeks.

"Sort of. I was going to ask you to help me with a project tonight."

"I'll help you. What do you need? I'm sure one of the guys will switch with me."

Dempsey smirked as he finally raised up from the fridge, a carton of eggs in his hand.

"Nice to see things are back to normal around here. Playing house like a married couple again," he teased as he found a pan and turned on the front burner. Fielding flipped him off as the other Haas twin turned to the stove. Tori scrunched up her nose at the marriage comment. Did Dempsey know she was engaged? She glanced down at her ring finger out of habit, just now realizing she forgot to put her ring back on that morning.

Fielding scowled. His frustration with his brother couldn't hide the apparent pain behind his eyes. "Ignore him. He's just pissed about the waffles."

Tori's heart softened when she saw the look on his face. Whatever had set Dempsey off was a bigger deal than either brother had let on or was willing to admit out loud. She nodded, offering Fielding a reassuring smile. He didn't have to tell her anything if he didn't want to, but she would be happy to listen if he wanted to confide in her.

Fielding shook his head slightly, tousling his messy curls in the process. "Okay, back up. What did you need help with tonight?"

"Ah, it's not a big deal." Tori tried to brush it off. "I just have a ton of canvases to prep for Camp New Hope, and there's a lot going on over the next few weeks. I thought maybe I could talk you into coming over and helping me if you weren't busy?"

"I would love to help. Camp New Hope... that's the camp you went to after your mom died, right?"

Tori beamed up at him. She was certain she had only mentioned the camp and her volunteer position once or twice before. The fact that he remembered meant the world to her.

"It is. Our biggest program of the year is the summer sleepaway camp. It's not until July, but I'm in charge of all the arts and crafts for both weeks, and it's just easier to prep things in advance. I would say we could do it another night, but between my crazy schedule this week, and the fact that I promised our volunteer coordinator she could pick up the first set of canvases tomorrow, I need to at least get started tonight."

"I got you, bro," Anwar interjected from the table. Tori had almost forgotten he was there.

"Are you sure?" Fielding asked, glancing over at his friend.

"Yeah, I just texted Teddy and Cole." Anwar held up his phone for emphasis. "I'm sure one of them will step up and switch shifts with you if they know it's for Tori."

Fielding grinned. "Looks like we're getting crafty tonight, Thompson. What time should I be over?"

Tori pulled up into the Wheelers' driveway around four p.m. that afternoon, curious to see what her mother-in-law was up to. Anne had texted her while she was hanging out with Fielding and asked her to stop by. She made her way around the side of the house and pulled open the sunroom door out of habit. When she stepped into the Wheelers' well-appointed kitchen, she was instantly overwhelmed by the chaos in front of her.

Anne was talking through a Bluetooth headset, pacing between the fridge to the sink. She had a file folder in her hand, and a stern look on her face. Maddie and Lia were sitting at opposite ends of the kitchen table with stacks of paper and envelopes between them. They both had their heads down and hadn't seen her walk in yet.

"Tori!" Anne exclaimed once she spotted her future daughter-in-law in the doorway. "Oh, sweetie, I'm so glad you're here!"

Everyone's attention turned to her as she slipped off her shoes. "What's all this?" she asked, realization dawning on her as she asked the question.

"This is wedding planning central! Do you think Rhett would leave town without giving me a detailed task list and timeline?" Anne asked.

"Nice of you to finally join us, Tor." Lia shot her a questioning look from behind a stack of envelopes. Tori smiled sheepishly as she made her way over to an empty seat at the kitchen table.

"I had plans with Fielding today. Anne didn't even text me until a few hours ago."

"I'm sorry for the late notice, sweetheart. Rhett made me promise not to text you until after lunch time. He said you needed rest and insisted we start without you," Anne explained. Another call must have come through her headset because she wordlessly turned on her heel and resumed her pacing.

"Is Fielding that tan, blond-haired, blue-eyed hockey player that Rhett hates?" Maddie interjected. "He's hot. We would make really cute kids."

Tori rolled her eyes but held her tongue as she reached across the table to pick up one of the stuffed envelopes. The thick paper felt lush in her hands. She traced the outline of an embossed W in the upper left corner as she realized what exactly she was holding. Her eyes grew wide as she took in all the piles in front of her.

Lia lowered her voice before replying to Maddie. "That's him. Or at least that's one of him. Fielding's a twin. He's just fifty percent of the Haas Fuckboy Team." Maddie's eyes grew twice their normal size, a salacious smile blooming on her gorgeous face. Of course Lia's description of the Haas brothers would pique her interest even more.

Tori pinched the bridge of her nose, thankful Rhett wasn't here to overhear this exchange. But Lia wasn't done. "So yeah, we've been sitting here all afternoon working on wedding invites while Tori's been hanging out with the trust fund fuckboy who wants to get in her pants."

"Lia!!" Tori scolded, whipping her head around to make sure her future mother-in-law hadn't just heard that. "What is wrong with you?" she hissed. Her voice came out just above a whisper so as not to draw Anne's attention. Maddie appeared to be fighting back a smile as she bit down on her lower lip.

"What?" Lia retorted. "It's obvious he wants you, Tori. Anyone with eyes can see he's into you."

"Fielding and I are friends. *Just* friends. I don't think of him like that at all."

"Gee, I would hope not, considering I've given myself three paper cuts so far while stuffing invitation envelopes for your wedding to Rhett."

Tori crossed her arms across her chest and glared at her best friend from across the table. Before she could come up with a clever retort, Anne strode over and commanded their attention.

"Alright, ladies, let's wrap these up so we can start on the favors," she instructed before turning to Tori. "I'm so glad you're here, Tori. We need to talk about dresses, and I want you to look over the guest list Everhett and I put together. I think we got everyone on your dad's side of the family, but I wasn't sure if there were any relatives on your mom's side that you'd like to invite? Or if your dad wanted to bring a date?"

Tori shook her head to both questions. Her mom had been an only child, and both sets of her grandparents had passed away. She had very little family left in the world besides her aunt from Philadelphia and a great uncle who lived in an assisted living facility. And although her dad was dating someone, she was certain it was still too new to invite her to the wedding.

"Not to worry. It's a small guest list as it is. We're inviting around eighty people, but since it's so short notice and over a holiday weekend, I think we can expect forty to fifty guests tops. Here"—she thrust a spreadsheet into Tori's hands—"look this over, and once you sign off, we can talk about dresses."

Tori's eyes glazed over as she took in the detailed, color-coded spreadsheet. If anyone had ever wondered what traits Rhett got from his mom...

She gazed up at Anne in wonder. "I can't believe you did all this."

"Oh, sweetie, it's nothing. I'm happy to help. Rhett gave me strict instructions not to stress you out with any of the wedding plans, so you need to tell me if I'm overstepping or if you want to be more involved. We've got to get most of the major to-dos checked off our list today and tomorrow since I'll be in prom mode all weekend with Maddie." Anne grinned down at her daughter and affectionately stroked her silky blonde hair. She was so in her element right now. "But I've already got a room block reserved for guests at the inn near the cabin, the caterers and rentals are all booked, and these invitations will go out tomorrow overnight express," she exclaimed as she clasped her hands together.

"I can't believe this is all really happening!" Maddie squealed in excitement.

Tori shook her head slightly, reveling in her own disbelief. "I know," she admitted. "I'm glad Rhett was so on top of everything we'd have to do to pull this off."

Speaking of Rhett... It was almost five p.m. now, so she assumed he was done with interviews for the day. Tori slipped her phone out of her pocket and shot off a quick text.

V: I'm currently holding one of our wedding invitations!!

Ev: Hey, beautiful. It's so good to hear from you. What do you think? Do you like them? I've only seen the PDF proofs.

V: They're gorgeous. You should see your house right now. Your mom has Maddie and Lia stuffing envelopes.

Ev: Yeah, I got the impression she was going full speed ahead. I hope that's okay?

V: It's more than okay. I'm grateful you two have it covered.

Ev: I can't wait to marry you, V. And I really can't wait for the honeymoon.

Tori stared down at her phone, puzzled. Honeymoon? They hadn't talked about any sort of honeymoon. Between rushing to pull together the wedding and Rhett moving to Virginia the first weekend in June, there wasn't time for anything else.

V: What honeymoon?

Ev: The honeymoon I've been secretly planning since the moment you agreed to marry me.

Tori's eyes went wide as she read his message.

"Who are you texting, Tor?" Lia asked.

Tori glanced up at her friend from across the table and shot her a pointed look. "Who do you think I'm texting?"

"Tell my brother I said hi," Maddie chimed in as Lia muttered something about "just checking" under her breath.

V: I didn't think we would be able to go on a honeymoon. I thought you have to be in Virginia the first weekend of June?

Ev: You thought I was going to miss out on the opportunity to take you on a real vacation? I'd be more inclined to skip the actual wedding than our honeymoon.

V: You're crazy!!

Ev: Yeah, crazy about you.

A second text came through before she could reply.

Ev: I can't wait to marry you, but I feel bad we've had to rush everything. I want to take my wife on a real honeymoon. We have time. We have almost a full week between the wedding and when I need to be in Norfolk, and our health insurance won't kick in until June 1 anyways. You in?

V: I'm in. Where are we going?

Ev: Let me worry about that. It's someplace you've never been. I want to surprise you.

V: Can I have a hint?

Ev: There will be sand.

Tori grinned from ear to ear at the thought of a sandy beach vacation with Rhett. Just the two of them. Together. Married.

V: I love you.

Ev: I love you too. Call me tonight before you go to bed, okay?

"Tori, what can I order you for dinner?" Anne asked from across the island in the kitchen. "I'm just going to call in so we can get as much done as possible." Tori set her phone down before turning to reply.

"I can't stay for dinner. I'm so sorry. I promised my dad we'd eat together, then I have plans tonight."

Lia chimed in once again. "What kind of plans would those be, Tor?"

Tori glared back at her best friend for the dozenth time that hour. "I have to prep eighty canvases for Camp New Hope tonight. I already thinned out the gesso, so I can't put it off without wasting it," she explained coolly.

"And who's helping you with that?" Lia asked without looking up from the envelope she was stuffing. It was a valid question. Her best friend had helped her with this task several times in the past, and Lia knew it was easier as a two-person job.

"You're welcome to come over and help," Tori replied, circumventing the question with an offer she knew Lia wouldn't go for.

Whether she sensed the tension rising between the two women or she was solely focused on checking off her task list, Anne chose that moment to interrupt them.

"No worries, sweetheart. I shouldn't have sprung all this on you. I'll send you an itinerary for the next two weeks so we don't mix up our schedules again. The next big to-do will be dress shopping. I have an appointment scheduled for all of us on Monday afternoon, if that works for you girls?" She was looking at Lia and Maddie now, who both nodded without looking up from their tasks. "Perfect. I have a seamstress coming with us so we can make alterations at the same time."

Tori felt a slight tenseness in her chest, right over her heart. As much as she loved Rhett's mom, the idea of picking out her wedding dress next week without her own mom there felt bittersweet. She inhaled deeply, steadying herself as the reminder of why her mother wasn't around reared its ugly head in the corners of her mind.

"It sounds like you've thought of everything," Tori marveled.

"Oh no," Anne countered, her hands both raised up for emphasis. "I'm just the task master. This is all Everhett."

CHAPTER NINE

Fielding looked up from his canvas and gave her a megawatt smile. "I feel like I'm exceptionally good at this. If being a rich prick doesn't work out for me in the long run, I just might have a future in canvas prepping."

She watched as he carefully smoothed gesso over the wrapped edges of one of the last canvases, his forearm a chiseled display of lean muscle and tanned skin as he gripped the sponge and focused on making long, even strokes like she taught him a few hours ago.

Tori shook her head and laughed. "You're such an ass. That, or you've been inhaling too many paint fumes. Want to get some fresh air?"

She didn't wait for his reply before she made her way to the opposite end of the garage and pulled two camping chairs down from a shelf.

"Good thinking."

"Let's sit outside," she suggested, already walking over to hit the garage button and fully open the door. She watched as Fielding ducked under the still-rising garage door, opening his camp chair and unfolding it with ease. Instead of sitting down, he turned and took the chair she was carrying out of her arms so he could open it for her. He set her chair down next to his own, close enough that the armrests almost overlapped.

"Was Dempsey in a better mood after I left the Valet House?" she asked, trying to sound as casual as possible. She didn't want to pry, but she'd been thinking about the waffle incident on and off all day.

"Yeah, he's good now. It's been a stressful week with our mom. I ended up crashing at Jake's last night, so he stayed with her overnight and probably didn't sleep much." Fielding didn't glance over or meet her gaze, instead resting his head against the low backrest of the camp chair and gazing up at the night sky. Tori focused on his profile as he stared up at the stars. The sky was clear tonight, and the air was cool with a slight breeze—the ideal temperature for sleeping with the windows open. It was a perfect late spring night in Ohio.

"Is your mom sick?"

Fielding blew out a long sigh. "If I tell you something, do you promise not to bring it up to Dem? Or to anyone, really?" She felt like she knew where this conversation was headed, but she resisted jumping to conclusions. This was a big enough deal that Fielding actually looked nervous, an entirely new look for him, and one she'd never seen before.

"I promise." She reached the short distance between their chairs to squeeze his hand. He glanced down at their hands for a moment and smiled before lifting his eyes to meet hers. The intensity in his gaze registered as a pinprick of warning. *Too far,* she thought to herself as soon as she realized she was toeing the fine line of friendship. She feigned a yawn, pulling her hand away from Fielding's so she could cover her mouth. She smiled back at him before settling both her hands in her lap.

"Second request," he continued. "Please don't think differently of me because of what I'm about to tell you. You can't worry about me or act weird when we're at Clinton's. I swear, Tori, I'm always in control and aware of how much I'm drinking, and Dem and I do a good job of keeping each other in line. There's not a day that goes by that I don't think about it. Sometimes I'll go a month or two without having a single drink just to prove to myself that I could do it if I wanted to. Or needed to."

"I would never judge you," she assured him. A single beat of silence lulled between them before Fielding spoke again.

"My mom is an alcoholic." He said the words slowly and evenly, not letting any emotion inflict his tone. "And not like, a 'sloppy drunk' type of alcoholic. More like a 'black out from alcohol poisoning and pill mixing a few times a month and have to be hospitalized' alcoholic."

Tori nodded her understanding but remained quiet, waiting for him to continue.

"It's bad. It's really bad. I don't even know how it got so bad. She rarely drank when we were little. She might have had a glass of wine at dinner, but other than that, I don't ever remember her with a drink in her hand. Fuck," he muttered, scrubbing a hand through the mass of blonde curls on top of his head. He left his arm lifted, resting his hand on the back of his neck. "It's crazy to think about that now that I say it out loud. Anyways, things got bad when my dad left, then things got worse when Dem and I went away for school. That's why we both came back to Hampton after college. Well, that's why I came back, and that's why Dem followed."

"What do you mean?" Tori cut in, her curiously getting the better of her.

"After winter break of our senior year of college, I decided I would move back here after I graduated. She's a mess, but I know how to handle her, and at least then we would both know she was safe. I was prepared to do it alone. I could fucking handle it myself if he would just trust me... but Dempsey refused to let me move home by myself. He gave up a huge job opportunity to move back here with me. Then as soon as we got back into town, his fiancée called things off between them."

"Dempsey was engaged?" Tori hush-whispered as she sat up straighter in her chair. She knew she shouldn't interrupt him again, but she couldn't help it.

"Yeah. Her name was Brooke. She was great. Dem really liked her, and I'm pretty sure she liked him for more than just his money. But once we came back to Hampton, I think they both realized it wasn't going to work. There's just not a clear path forward. Dem and I... we're sort of just on hold, waiting for something horrible to happen before we can finally move on with our lives."

"Hey," Tori breathed out, reaching between the chairs again to place her hand on his arm. "Don't talk like that, Field. She's your mom." Her voice nearly cracked on the last word. Tori didn't know who she felt worse for—Fielding, Dempsey, or their mother. "It's not hopeless. There's got to be something she can do. Has she ever tried getting help?"

Fielding let out a loud gaff, shaking his head at the suggestion.

"It's hard to explain how bad it really is without seeing it for yourself, Tori. It *is* hopeless. She's been in and out of rehab for the last ten years. I think she's been three times this year already, and it's only May. It's just a waiting game at this point."

"What do you mean?"

"We're just waiting for her to black out and not wake up one day. Or overdose. We're waiting for it to kill her."

Tori gulped, trying hard not to judge the crassness in Fielding's words. She took a deep inhale, letting the cool and slightly damp night air steady her before she spoke again. "I'm so sorry, Field. It's not the same circumstances, but I know what it's like to watch a parent struggle. To watch them suffer and to feel helpless as they slip away. I'm really sorry you have to deal with that."

He shrugged and met her gaze straight on. His eyes revealed more sadness than his words had allowed. "It is what it is. It just sucks not knowing if we'll be playing this game for a few more months, a few more years, or a few more decades."

"If things are that bad, why don't you guys live with her?"

"We did when we first moved home. But it's not healthy for us to be there all the time. She's going to drink regardless. It affects Dempsey more than me, really, but then I get pissed at her for how it affects him, and then he gets defensive that I'm mad at her, and then we're all stuck in this horrible feedback loop. We have a housekeeper and a driver and a few other people on payroll, plus a ton of security cameras throughout the house, so it's not like she's there all by herself. We've lived at the Valet House with the other guys for a little over a year now, and it's just better that way. Dem and I take turns checking on her. One of us goes over there to put eyes on her every day."

"What would you be doing if you hadn't moved home to Hampton?" Tori asked, hoping the subject change would cut through some of the sadness radiating off her friend.

"Hell if I know." Fielding sighed as he ran his hand through his hair again. "I might have kept going with school. I was in the top three percent for my program. Or maybe I would have traveled or decided to just start working. Our dad is in real estate development, so I could have worked for him. He's got offices all over the country, plus locations in London and Tokyo. I could have taken my pick and moved anywhere I wanted," he admitted wistfully to the stars.

"Wait, what did you major in?" She had never even thought to ask him about his degree.

"Pre-med," Fielding responded with a healthy dose of cockiness.

"No freakin' way!" she exclaimed, hitting him on the forearm for emphasis.

"What? You don't believe me? Do you think I'm some sort of slacker? I was in the top ten of my graduating class at Arch. You and Wheeler were together when he went there, so you know how academically challenging it is."

"Oh, I know it's a lot of work, but I always thought you just had to be really smart *or* really rich to go to Archway Preparatory Academy."

He smirked and cocked one eyebrow at her. "How about really smart, really rich, *and* really good looking? You're looking at the full package right here, Victoria Thompson."

"You're such an ass," she scoffed for the second time that night. She couldn't resist ribbing on him again, but she also couldn't help but return his smile. "Hey." She nodded once, softening her tone and holding his gaze. "I appreciate you telling me all this. And I swear I don't think differently about you because of any of it."

"I knew you wouldn't."

Chapter Ten

Rhett

Tori let out a long, heavy sigh. He knew she had to be exhausted by now. They had spent the last five hours in waiting rooms and doctor's offices, making their case for the preventative surgery his fiancée was hell-bent on having as soon as possible.

The first doctor of the day let her lay out her case, and she even looked through her bloodwork and the huge file of scans they brought with them. But she told Tori there was no rush to do anything anytime soon in her opinion. She said she would only feel comfortable proceeding with an exploratory laparoscopy, with the goals of biopsying any questionable cells and preserving as much of her anatomy as possible.

Tori ended that meeting as soon as she realized it was a waste of time. She literally stood up, thanked the doctor for her time, and walked out. It took Rhett a few seconds to process what had even happened. He was glad he had the wherewithal to collect all of her files off the desk before following her out the door.

The second appointment had gone even worse. That doctor insisted she was too young to be making a decision like this. He had the audacity to ask Tori what her future husband would think of her taking away his ability to have a family.

It took no time at all for Tori to snap back at him. "He's fine with it. In fact, I brought him with me today," as she pointed to Rhett.

The whole thing would have been a disaster had it just ended there. But it didn't. The douchebag kept going.

"What do you think of all this nonsense?" he had asked smugly, cocking an eyebrow that told Rhett he would judge him based on the answer he provided.

It was the wording. It was the dismissiveness. It was the fact that the doctor thought Rhett should have any say whatsoever in what Tori chose to do to advocate for her own health.

"Not my body, not my call," he had responded as he pushed to his feet, turning to Tori to gauge what she wanted to do. One look at the crushing disappointment in her eyes told him all he needed to know. They walked out of that office hand in hand without another word.

Now they were sitting in the office of the third and final doctor of the day. Rhett pinched the bridge of his nose as he rested his elbows on his thighs. His shoulders and neck were tight from the early-morning flight he had taken that morning.

If this meeting was anything like the others, he didn't know where they were going to go from here. These doctors were supposed to be the best of the best. Maybe there were better options in Norfolk? Or hell, maybe they should research beyond Ohio and Virginia. He'd take her anywhere if it meant she could get the kind of surgery she wanted and the care and respect she deserved.

"You okay, Ev?" Tori whispered, pulling him away from his own racing thoughts.

He sat up straighter, turned to face her, and smiled. "I'm good. I'm frustrated for you right now, but otherwise I'm fine. Honestly I should be asking *you* that question." He reached out to take her hand, squeezing once before raising it to his mouth and placing a feather-light kiss on her knuckles.

"I didn't think it was going to be like this," she confessed as she cast her eyes down at their joined hands.

"Yeah, me neither. But don't get discouraged yet. I've got a good feeling about this one." He didn't, but he needed to give her something to hold onto. He needed to give himself something to hope for.

As soon as he spoke the words out loud, the door opened behind them and in walked a petite woman in a long white coat. She settled into the leather chair behind the desk before crossing one leg over the other, unzipping a portfolio, and reaching for a pen.

"Hi there." Her eyes focused intently on Tori. "I'm Dr. Silko. What brings you in today?"

Rhett watched as Tori sat up straighter in her chair. He squeezed her hand once before dropping it, trying to encourage her as she started her pitch for the third time that day.

"Hi. I'm Tori, and this is my fiancé, Rhett. We're here today because I recently received abnormal results during a semi-annual breast and ovarian cancer scan. I have the BRCA1 mutation, and my mom had breast cancer and ovarian cancer. She died of ovarian cancer when she was thirty-nine."

The doctor nodded to acknowledge everything Tori said and maintained her intense gaze. "I'm sorry to hear about your mom. I spent some time looking through the records you sent earlier today. You're enrolled in Dr. Ritter's genetic study, correct?"

Rhett sat up a little straighter. This doctor had obviously done her homework.

"Correct. I started in the program when I was fifteen. My latest scans were on April 22. The mammogram was clear, but there were abnormalities in my CA-125 bloodwork, which hadn't actually been tested since the previous year. I went back a few weeks ago for a follow-up pelvic exam and ultrasound."

"And let me guess," Dr. Silko interjected. "The results were inconclusive."

"Yes!"

Rhett exhaled, trying to hold his emotions steady as he felt Tori's excitement start to grow. He was liking this doctor so far, but he didn't want either of them get their hopes too high. At least not yet.

"That's typical for a follow-up appointment like that, unfortunately. There's just not a good diagnostic test for ovarian cancer. At least not yet. If you don't have an actual tumor or rapidly changing cells that light up a PET, you're not getting a diagnosis."

Tori was propped on the edge of her seat, hanging on the doctor's every word. "So the reason we're here today is because I want to schedule a prophylactic hysterectomy. I know I'm young, and I understand the long-term consequences of what I'm choosing to do. But I've made my decision, and I'm confident this is what I want."

"Completely understandable. No woman grows up knowing what you know about your genetic history and doesn't understand the risks and benefits of a decision like this."

"You—you're the first doctor to believe that, I think," Tori stammered.

Dr. Silko glanced over at Rhett for just a beat before refocusing her gaze on Tori. "When did you first start thinking about preventative surgery?"

"The day I got the results back from my genetic panel when I was fifteen."

"And you're twenty-four now," she confirmed as she glanced down at Tori's medical records. "So, nine years ago?"

Tori nodded. Rhett wondered where the doctor was going with this line of questioning.

"So what I'm hearing is that you're looking to schedule a preventative, risk-reducing procedure. You aren't making this decision because of the bloodwork and inconclusive results you just received. You've known for a long time that this would be the course of action you would take one day."

"Yes. Exactly!"

Rhett reached over toward Tori's chair and rested his forearm on her arm rest. He didn't go as far as to reach for her hand. He just wanted to remind her he was there in case she needed him.

"Do you perform prophylactic hysterectomies with BSO? Would you do it for me?"

He held his breath.

"That is my area of expertise, and yes, I would be happy to take you on as a patient. There's standard paperwork and hoops we need to jump through to make it happen, but most insurance companies now cover preventative surgery when it comes to BRCA1 and other mutations. Tell me about your ideal timeline. Is this something you're hoping to do soon? Or in the next few years?"

He risked glancing over at Tori when he felt her gaze on him. He locked eyes with her, immediately recognizing the utter relief welling up behind unshed tears. This was it. They were finally here. A mix of excitement and relief coursed through his own body. A small pang of fear was present, too, but he knew these procedures were inevitable. More than inevitable, they were necessary. They were what she needed to feel whole.

"Well, we're getting married next weekend," Tori explained. "And then we're going on a honeymoon." She glanced over at him with a sly smile. Rhett winked in response, too elated to hide the excitement they were both feeling because of this appointment.

"Ideally I would like to have surgery at the end of July. I have a commitment during the first two weeks of that month, then I'd like to be able to return to school in August."

Dr. Silko winced. It was the first less-than-enthusiastic indicator she'd given them up until that point. Rhett shifted forward in his seat, anxious to know what wasn't going to work with Tori's proposed timeline.

"The end of July isn't unrealistic for surgery. But thinking you'll be able to drive and return to life as normal within a month might be overly optimistic. Everyone heals differently, so it's not impossible. If you have a lot of help and support throughout your recovery, that helps, too."

"I'll make sure she has all the help and support she could ever possibly need," he asserted, nodding solemnly at the doctor.

"Good. I don't see any reason why we can't move forward with scheduling a July date then. Although I will put this idea out there for consideration: Usually, women opt for the risk-reducing mastectomy first if that's part of their plan. I'm sure you know that from your research, so I won't try to convince you to go that route. Knowing that the greater risk is currently ovarian cancer, I think you're smart to do it this way. But if you're going to consider a mastectomy sooner rather than later, it may be wise to have the first surgery in July, give your body a chance to recover and heal and get used to the replacement hormone therapy, and then have the mastectomy at the end of the year."

Tori glanced over at him with an uncertain look on her face. He wasn't sure what to make of the suggestion either. He knew she would be tempted by the prospect of having both preventative surgeries by the end of this year. But was it tempting enough to fall behind in school? Would her determination trump her pride and independence?

She finally turned back to Dr. Silko with the same look of uncertainty. "Can I think about it for a few days? I want to check in with my advisor at school and talk it over with Rhett and our families."

"You can take some time to think about it if you promise not to think about it too long. My colleague Dr. Brennan is a dual-trained plastic and breast cancer surgeon. She's based out of Cleveland, and she's the best. The work she's doing with sensation and nerve preservation is phenomenal. She's who you want, and I know she's almost fully booked for the rest of the year."

Everyone fell silent for a few beats. It was all good information, but it was a lot to take in. Rhett suddenly felt like maybe he should have been taking notes. He bit down on the inside of his cheek to stop from smirking. Tori would have teased him mercilessly if he had showed up to these appointments with a notepad.

"What are you thinking, beautiful?" he prompted.

"I'm thinking this is everything I was hoping to hear today." She smiled at him before turning back to the doctor. "This is what I want to do. And I want you to be my surgeon. What do we have to do next?"

Dr. Silko offered them a tight smile and a confident nod. "You'll need to come into my practice for a new patient intake appointment before we schedule the surgery. I can have my office call you on Monday to set that up. I'll also get in touch with Dr. Brennan if you'd like, to put you on her radar now. She and I work together on a lot of cases like yours."

"Yes, please contact her," Tori replied almost instantly.

"Let's talk logistics. What considerations have you given to fertility preservation?"

Tori sat up straighter. "I know the options. That's not in the cards for me," she stated with finality.

"What are you doing now to prevent pregnancy?"

"I've had a copper IUD since I was sixteen."

"And when was the start date of your last period?"

"Last Saturday, May 11."

"Okay, so you'll need to schedule a time to come in and have the IUD removed before surgery. I can do it during your new patient intake appointment if you'd like, but then you would need to use alternative contraception until we do the full procedure."

Tori grimaced at that idea. "What's the latest it can possibly be removed?"

"I can take it out just a few days before your surgery if you'd like to keep it in place as long as possible. It can even stay in if you change your mind and decide to pursue fertility preservation."

There was another long stretch of silence. Enough time passed that Rhett shifted in his seat, assuming they were done and it was time to go. But then Tori spoke up again.

"Just—just to make sure we're all on the same page, what do you mean by fertility preservation?" Her question came out meeker than all her previous statements and responses. Rhett stilled as he picked up on the hesitancy in her voice.

He knew where she stood on having kids. He was certain she wasn't interested in exploring any fertility preservation options. More likely, she was asking this question for his sake. He hated that she thought that was necessary.

"Assuming we're moving forward with the prophylactic hysterectomy with BSO, I'll be removing your uterus, ovaries, and fallopian tubes. Fertility preservation means we would harvest and store your eggs in case you want to have biological children in the future."

"So that would mean doing an egg retrieval now, then having to use a surrogate for IVF later?"

"Correct. In your case, fertility preservation would involve stimulating ovulation so multiple eggs mature during one cycle. Then we would harvest them and freeze them, either as eggs or fertilized embryos. If and when you want to use them, you'd have to use a gestational carrier, and they would undergo IVF. It's worth mentioning that insurance doesn't cover all aspects of fertility preservation or surrogacy, the and there are yearly storage fees and other costs to consider."

"Money isn't a concern," Rhett said before turning to face Tori. His face softened as he tried to reassure her. "We don't have to talk about this if you don't want to. I know where things stand. I'm good," he whispered under his breath. If his suspicions were right, then this whole conversation was for his benefit, but she didn't need to do this. He didn't need to hear it. He'd always known her choice.

The conversation might have concluded there if the doctor didn't follow up again. "The expenses associated with IVF and surrogacy are usually the biggest obstacles individuals face when they're considering fertility preservation. Can I ask why you've ruled it out as an option if money isn't a concern? If it's because you don't want children, that's perfectly acceptable. I would never question that response. I'm not judging your choices, just seeking to understand."

Dr. Silko glanced in Rhett's direction in a clear effort to turn the conversation into a dialogue. He had no plans to interject again unless

Tori specifically asked him a question.

Tori didn't reply right away, but she did finally reach for his hand. He interlocked their fingers and gave her a gentle squeeze.

"There's no way I can do that to a child," she insisted, her voice barely above a whisper. He could hear the tremble in her tone without looking over at her. Grief had held her hostage for the last twelve years. It robbed her of her adolescence, and in a way, it orphaned her, too.

When Tori's mom died, she also lost her parental relationship with her father. Suddenly she was his caretaker, the support person he relied on just to put one foot in front of the other. Paul Thompson still lived in that grief most days. He relied on his daughter emotionally and financially. Tori never let the weight of caring for her father drag her down, but that didn't mean it wasn't a burden she consistently had to bear.

"I can't in good conscience make the choice to bring another life into this world and know that I may not be around for them. I won't do that to them. I won't do that to Rhett. Or worse, I can't bring a new life into this world knowing they might have to go through this exact same thing I'm going through now. I would rather never have a child than have a daughter who has to sit in this seat and make the choices I'm making today."

A daughter. He bit down on the inside of his cheek again, harder this time. He steadied his hold on Tori's hand as he tried to remain stoic. His feelings weren't her burden to bear.

Dr. Silko pursed her lips and tapped her pen against her portfolio a few times before she spoke. "One of the most surprising benefits of risk-reducing surgery is the dissipation of anxiety patients experience when it's done. By the time you've had both procedures, you will be even less likely than the general female population to have breast or ovarian cancer."

Tori nodded but said nothing else, so Dr. Silko continued.

"It's also worth noting that there's no chance of passing along the BRCA1 mutation to an embryo."

Tori continued to nod silently. She was going into shutdown mode. He had told himself he wasn't going to interject again, but he didn't want her to leave the office with unanswered questions.

"What does that mean?" he asked.

The doctor glanced over at him without turning her head before settling her gaze on Tori once again. "Preimplantation genetic diagnosis allows us to assess an embryo to detect whether it has certain mutations. It's a fairly standard procedure nowadays to check for birth defects, but in cases like yours, we can look for additional markers, such as tumor-suppressing genetic mutations."

This was all news to Rhett. He sensed it was news to Tori, too. Her fingers were rigid and unyielding in his hand. Her eyes were cast forward, unblinking. He had no idea what was going through her mind.

"You could guarantee my baby wouldn't have the BRCA1 gene?" Tori finally choked out. She sucked in a gasping breath before adding "I didn't even know that was possible."

He was on his feet the second he heard her voice crack. He gripped her elbow, encouraging her to stand up and let him hold her. He didn't care if they were in the middle of a doctor's office. He couldn't bear to watch her breakdown. He couldn't not hold her. Not after not being allowed to hold her like this for so long.

He wrapped his arms around her and engulfed her upper body, one palm settling against her back as he brushed the other hand over her hair. He could feel the rapid rise and fall of her chest against his as her breathing picked up. She made a muffled choking sound as a shudder worked through her.

"Hey, hey, shhh...." he comforted as he hugged her tighter. "You're okay. I've got you, V." She didn't respond, and he could feel the trembling in her body grow stronger, even as he held her. It took everything in him not to let his own body quake. He inhaled deeply, taking a steadying breath for her as much as himself.

He turned his head to meet the doctor's gaze as he continued to hold Tori in his arms. "I think we're going to need a little more time to process all this."

She nodded in understanding and gave him a sympathetic smile. "Tell you what. I'm going to give you my card with my cell phone number on it. Take the next few weeks to talk things over, and do your own research. We wouldn't be able to begin any sort of fertility preservation plan until the start of your next menstrual cycle anyways, so you've got a few weeks to figure things out."

Rhett unwound one arm and accepted the card from the doctor. He nodded appreciatively in her direction before picking up Tori's medical files. They may have more questions than answers after this appointment, but he was confident they could check one thing off their list. They had found the doctor Tori needed and deserved.

CHAPTER ELEVEN

"I just need a minute," she insisted as she shrugged Rhett's hand off her shoulder. She didn't even remember walking out to the parking lot, but they were somehow already at the car. She rested her elbows on the top of the Prelude and blew out a long, shaky breath before she glanced back at him. "I'm okay," she tried to assure him. The helpless look on his face told her he saw right through her words to the flurry of emotions threatening to spill over.

So much of what Dr. Silko said was exactly what she wanted to hear. But then there was the fertility preservation conversation. She thought she knew everything there was to know about egg retrieval and fertility treatments. She thought she knew it all. To find out that there was a way to ensure any biological children wouldn't have the same genetic markers that haunted her should have been joyful news. But it felt more like an unexpected earthquake to Tori.

The foundation of everything she thought she knew had just fractured. She was straddling a fault line, and she had almost no time at all to decide which direction to jump.

"V..." Rhett's voice was laced with concerned even as he stood on his side of the car to give her the space she requested. "What can I do for you?"

"I'm fine, reall..."

"Damnit, Tori!" He hit the roof of the car with such force she felt the vibration of the metal jolt up her forearms. He was back around the car and by her side in just a few strides. He spun her around and boxed her in against the passenger door, forcing her to meet his gaze. "Don't do this, V. Don't lie to me. You don't get to say you're fine and try to hold me at arm's length like before. I see you. I know what you're doing. But it's not going to work this time, beautiful. I'm in it. I'm right here with you. Your pain is my pain. There's no saving me anymore." He lowered his forehead and pressed it into hers, willing her to let him in and let him stay. "Let me be here for you."

She didn't have the energy to defend her bad habits. Now that he called her on it, she realized that was exactly what she had been doing. The tension in her muscles released and her entire body sagged. She wrapped her arms around his midsection and leaned in, knowing he would hold her up.

Rhett hugged her hard and worked one hand into her hair before kissing her forehead and pulling back to look in her eyes. "I love you," he vowed, "and I'm here for you. No matter what comes next. No matter what we decide."

"This is everything I was always afraid of," she admitted in a whisper.

"What is? The surgery?"

"No. This. Us. Every reason I resisted being with you is raging inside me right now," she choked out as a fresh wave of tears streamed down her face.

Rhett gripped her tighter. "Now is not forever. It won't always be this hard Tori, I swear. We are going to have a full and happy life together. You and me, V. It's you and me."

She wanted to believe him. But the reality of her own experience defied every reassurance he could offer. "What if it's not enough? What if even after the surgeries cancer still catches up with me sooner rather than later? You could be a widower in your 20s or 30s, Rhett. It's so fucking selfish for me to think—"

"Stop," he demanded as he dropped to his knees before her. He took both her hands in his, running his finger over her engagement ring before looking up to meet her eyes with an intense gaze.

"Listen to me right now, beautiful. I'm not going to promise you it'll all be okay, or that you won't get cancer someday. I know the reality of what we're facing. But even if this is it... even if all we get is a few years. It'll be worth it. This moment with you? In this parking lot? You and me, together? This is all I ever wanted. This is enough. You are enough. For my whole damn life, this one single moment is enough."

"Rhett..." she tried to interject. But he wasn't done. His blue-grey eyes were a storm of emotions as he bravely put words to her deepest fears.

"If you get cancer, and if you die way too young, I'll spend the rest of my life mourning you and what we had. But at least we had it, V. At least we had the chance to love each other full out."

She swallowed past the lump that had formed in her throat, letting his words galvanize her and banish all the fear and doubt in her mind.

"What do you need?" he prompted as he pushed to his feet and wrapped her up in another hug.

She sucked in a steadying breath, willing herself to rely on him and trust in his ability to take care of her. She didn't have to do this alone. Not anymore. Not ever again. "Take me home, Rhett."

They drove is silence as he navigated through the city and eventually merged onto the highway. "Do you want to talk about anything?" he finally asked once he set the car's cruise control.

Tori blew out a long sigh. She didn't want to talk, but she didn't want to shut him down again, either. "I don't even know where to start..."

"Just tell me what you're thinking. You can vent or we can talk shit about the first two doctors we met. You'll feel better if you don't keep everything bottled up. Just tell me the first thing that comes to mind."

She let out another long breath. "Fuck."

Rhett chuckled as he reached for her hand. "I can't remember the last time I heard that come out of your mouth, V." His tone shifted as he raised their joined hands and placed a kiss on the tips of her fingers.

"But it's definitely justified. That was a lot. You have so much to think about, and we have a lot to talk about."

"I know. I feel like everything I thought I knew and had figured out just changed."

He squeezed her hand a bit harder and glanced at her before shifting his gaze back to the road. "I think having both surgeries this year is a really good idea, and something you should consider."

"Yeah, I wasn't expecting that to be an option, but I think it's a good idea, too. Especially if Dr. Silko can get me in with Dr. Brennan. I'd be crazy not to do it. I know it means taking the semester or even the year off from school... and I'd probably have to take a lot of time off from work... but that would be okay now, because it's not like I'm racing the clock to get a job with benefits anymore, right?"

"Right. There's no deadline anymore. We have to get you well, then you can focus on finishing your degree."

Tori shifted in her seat to face him a bit more. "I'm good with that. Knowing I could just be done with both surgeries by the end of this year is a huge relief. It's just not how I expected things to go. The surgeries and the timeline aren't even what's throwing me off. I just feel like we have no time. She dropped that bomb about egg retrieval and fertility preservation, and we literally have the next three weeks to decide what to do."

"I'm sure we have a little more time than that..."

"Rhett. No. If I want to do this, we have to do it in June. Otherwise, I won't be able to have surgery in July. I researched everything there is to know about egg freezing years ago. Or, at least I thought I had. It takes two weeks, and it has to be all lined up with my menstrual cycle. I would need all these ultrasounds and shots, and then it would take a little while for my body to recover from the bloating and hormones. All that would have to happen *before* I could have surgery..."

She trailed off to give him an opportunity to share his thoughts, but he didn't say anything to fill in the silence. She was growing increasingly annoyed with his cool, stoic responses. She knew he was putting on an act for her—staying strong and steady to support her—but it felt like they weren't even having an actual conversation.

Rhett had to have opinions. This was his future, too. Why wasn't he being more candid? She didn't want him to just agree to everything she decided. They had played that game for far too long. She needed to know how he really felt about all this.

She was determined to get some sort of reaction out of him, one way or another. "I know you want kids."

"Not necessarily," he replied without hesitation.

"You can't honestly sit there and tell me your wheels aren't spinning after everything Dr. Silko said?" she pushed.

"You got me there," he admitted. He took his eyes off the road for a moment to glance over and offer her a smile that didn't reach his eyes. She *knew* he had been affected by the fertility conversation, even if he was acting unflappable. "What do you want to do? You know I'll do whatever you want."

"I don't feel right taking away this option from you."

"Tori. Please. I know what you're trying to do right now, and I won't allow it."

She whipped her head around at his declaration. "You won't *allow* it?"

"I said what I said," he shot back without taking his eyes off the road. "I love *you*. I want *you*. I never expected to be here with you... to have the privilege to be here with you. I've known for years that you didn't plan to have kids. That's always been okay with me. You're all I've ever wanted, beautiful. Nothing has changed for me, unless something has changed for you. So yeah, like I said, I won't allow you to pick a fight about this."

Tori swiped at the tears rolling down her cheeks before settling her hands in her lap. She glanced down at her engagement ring, momentarily distracted by the way it picked up the late afternoon light through the tinted windows of the car. A galaxy of sparkles reflected off the diamond and danced along the glove compartment and dashboard in front of her.

"Don't shut down on me, V. What are you thinking?" This time there was an ache in his voice, a familiar pang of longing behind his words. Freezing him out had been her go-to move for so long. She owed it to him to speak her truth.

"I don't want to make the wrong decision," she worried out loud. "I don't want to have any regrets. I never knew this could be an option, so I literally haven't thought about the idea of having kids in years. I accepted what I thought was the reality of the situation back when I was sixteen." She sighed, frustrated with herself for not keeping up with the latest fertility preservation research. She truly had no idea what was possible nowadays.

Yet today's revelation still didn't change her headspace. "If I have to make this decision in the next few weeks, I think my answer is the same. But I'm not confident enough to say that's what I'm going to want in the future, knowing what we know now. I just wish we had more time to process everything. I'm heartbroken that we don't have more time to decide."

"So what if we did it just in case?"

Tori stilled as his suggestion. There was no affliction in his voice; he still wasn't giving anything away. She believed him when he said he'd willingly and gladly go along with whatever she decided. She knew then that Mr. Logistics was simply analyzing the situation and presenting her with the options.

She let the idea marinate for a moment, but his suggestion didn't make sense. "Just in case of what?"

"In case you change your mind. Or, I guess in this case, just so you don't have to decide anything right now. If we move forward with egg freezing, you at least still have the option to have kids in the future. We would always have the option. But if you choose to not do it, you can't change your mind later. You're only twenty-four, V. And you heard what Dr. Silko said. After surgery, you'll be less likely to get breast cancer or ovarian cancer than the general population. What if in ten years you decide you want to be a mom?"

Everything he said made sense. Part of her wished it didn't.

"If in ten years from now, I decide I want to be a mom—-and that's a big if, and I would have to have totally clean scans between now and then with no scares or setbacks or anything—if that happened, we could adopt."

He agreed without missing a beat. "Absolutely. I'd be one hundred percent on board with that plan."

She huffed out a sigh. It was clear she wasn't going to penetrate his steadiness. She silently scolded herself for even trying. Her decision shouldn't be based on whether or not she could get a rise out of Rhett. It wasn't fair to use his reactions or lack of reactions to gauge her own response. She had to figure out what she wanted. And she needed time to figure it out.

"If—if we go through with it," she started, her voice trembling, "this whole summer is going to be even harder. On you. On me. On the start of our marriage. It won't be pretty, Ev. I remember reading about egg freezing years ago. It's a million appointments and hormone injections and just..."

Rhett didn't let her spiral. "We can handle it. I know it'll be hard, but I can hold us both up. I've got you, beautiful."

"If we do this, it isn't a guarantee I want kids. You understand that, right? I haven't had any time to think about this. We might go through all this and then never even..."

"If we do this, we're just buying more time. It's like getting an extension for a deadline. I swear to you, I get that."

Tori leaned forward, resting her elbows on her knees and burying her face in her hands. She was frustrated and defeated. "I don't want to have to decide this right now."

"Then don't. Let's not decide anything right now, let's just give ourselves the extension. Freezing eggs doesn't mean we're going to have kids. I can separate the two in my mind if you can."

"Okay," she relented. "You're right. I don't want to rule out anything unnecessarily if we don't have to, so let's do it, and decide later. Much later," she emphasized.

He reached over for her hand again, this time a genuine smile taking over his whole face as he took the exit for Hampton and glanced in her direction. "I love you. And I swear I would have been okay with whatever you decided, Tori. There's nothing I want more than you."

"I love you, too. So damn much."

"Hey. It's finally the weekend," he reminded her with a playful smile that lightened the mood.

"I know," she said as she returned his easy smile. What a week. Between working and wedding planning and Rhett going to Virginia and today's appointments, she was ready to just be with him. "I have to work open to two tomorrow, though, remember?"

His smile faded slightly, but he didn't protest. "I know. I remember. Can I please sleep over at your place tonight though? We can stay at my house tomorrow. Maddie will be at prom, and my parents are staying in the hotel where they're hosting the after-prom party. We'll have the whole house to ourselves."

Her breath caught at the earnestness of his request. She hadn't let him stay over on Tuesday night, then he'd been in Virginia on Wednesday and Thursday. "Of course you can. When you're home, you're mine."

"I'm always yours now, beautiful."

"Always."

———

"Hey, baby," Jake greeted her as she walked in through the side door of Clinton's. Tori stifled a yawn with the back of her hand even though she wasn't actually tired. Rhett had insisted they go to bed early last night after treating her to two full-body, toe-curling orgasms, so she had gotten plenty of sleep.

"Our Golden Boy actually let you drive yourself to work today?"

"Ha-ha. Good morning to you, too." She rolled her eyes as she approached the computer system behind the bar of Clinton's to clock in for her Saturday morning shift. "And yep, he sure did. He just got back from Virginia yesterday morning, then we had appointments all day. He's exhausted, so it wasn't hard to convince him I could drive myself six minutes into town."

"That's right. Your doctor appointments were yesterday. How'd that all go?" he asked as he leaned against the back bar and hooked one ankle over the other to assume the traditional Jake and Rhett bartender stance.

"We got off to a rough start. Just douchey doctors and some pushback I wasn't expecting," she clarified when Jake arched one eyebrow. "But then we met with an amazing doctor, and she was totally on board with my plan."

Jake nodded solemnly and shifted his weight. "So you're going ahead with surgery?"

Tori looked up from the computer and returned his gaze. She wanted him to see that this wasn't something she was taking lightly. "Yes. Ideally sometime this summer. Then I'll have the second one around the holidays. I know it means I'll miss a ton of work, and Mike will probably have to hire someone in my place. But it's really for the best..."

Jake's brow furrowed. "Hey, I know that, baby. I'm not questioning you. Or judging you. I want this for you. I want this for both of you, honestly. I'm your friend before I'm your manager. You know that, right?"

His sincerity struck a nerve. Tori quickly turned back around to the computer to finish clocking in before grabbing a collection of pens for her shift. She hadn't expected to have this type of conversation with Jake today, especially not this early in the morning. She avoided his gaze as she fiddled with the ties of her apron.

"This is stupid," he muttered. "Don't try to act all tough and hold me at arm's length in typical Tori fashion. I'm the one who picked you up off the damn floor at the Valet House when you got the call a few weeks ago, baby." He rolled his dark hazel eyes, then gave her a pointed look. She didn't react to his declaration.

"Can I at least give you a hug?" he huffed, clearly frustrated with her lack of response.

Tori didn't reply, but she shifted over two steps so he could wrap her up in his strong, bulging arms. Their contact cut through all the awkwardness of the last few minutes. He squeezed her almost too tightly as she rested her cheek against the worn fabric of his Clinton's T-shirt. The edges of his ink peeked out from the cuff of the sleeve on his left arm. She felt him kiss the top of her head as he continued to hold her, right there in the middle of the restaurant at six-thirty on a Saturday morning.

She inhaled his unmistakable Jake scent. He had been wearing the same cologne since high school: equal parts woodsy and floral. He smelled like an overpriced preppy clothing store. Even though she teased him about it, she secretly loved it. That scent always took her back: it transported her to memories of driving to football games with the top off the Jeep, of bonfires on weekends and carpooling to school, of stealing his hoodie in class.

Jake had attended Hampton High for his last two years of high school, and they had been as thick as thieves during that time. Although they both had Rhett, he had stable parents, beloved grandparents, a little sister, and a real home. Jake and Tori were each other's family their junior and senior years of high school.

Their bond seemed unshakeable until she broke up with Rhett the summer before college. She had broken his heart, and she had dented her friendship with Jake in the process. The breakup was bad enough. But then the real damage happened a few years later. Jake became even more distant when he realized his two friends were still hooking up but refused to confide in him.

He muttered something into her hair before he finally loosened his grip.

"Uh, come again?" she asked, smiling as he scowled down at her. She knew why he was scowling. This display of tenderness was out of character for her fiancé's tough-guy best friend. There was a distinct comfort to being held and loved by a friend who had been in her life for so long.

"I said, you know I'm here for you. I'll always be here for you, baby. Even if Rhett's not home. Especially when he can't be here. I've got you."

"I know that. You're the best, Jake." She squeezed him one more time for emphasis before starting to pull away from his hug. "Ya know, marrying Rhett is sort of like getting two husbands for the price of one. You're like my rowdier, bisexual backup husband," she joked.

Jake cringed at her jab. "Please do *not* say that in front of him. You know he's not good at sharing."

"Don't remind me." Tori rolled her eyes at the memory of one of their drunken escapades from years ago. Jake was right. Rhett was even-headed most of the time, but he was way too possessive when it came to her. He obviously hadn't enjoyed himself the night they let Jake watch them fool around in the hot tub, but that didn't stop the memories from making *her* top ten list.

"You don't think that's why he hasn't asked me to be his best man yet, do you?"

The question came out soft and vulnerable. Tori stilled, feeling slightly whiplashed from the quick change of tone. "Jake." She sighed, drawing out his name in an attempt to comfort him. "We've only been engaged for two weeks, and he's been so stressed trying to pack, move, graduate, take care of me, plan a wedding, and get things set up in Virginia. I feel like I've barely seen him myself. Cut him a little slack. I'm sure your very own best man proposal is coming soon." She poked him right below the ribs to elicit a laugh. Her finger rebounded off a tense coil of muscle on his stomach instead.

"Hey, maybe he won't forget *my* ring," Jake goaded, recalling how Rhett had proposed to Tori spur-of-the-moment, sans engagement ring.

"Or the condoms," she deadpanned. It would be a long time before anyone let Everhett Wheeler forget about the one and only time he wasn't actually prepared.

Jake smirked at the jab at his best friend's expense before going soft again. "This back-and-forth shit sucks, huh?"

"It really does. Why do you think I tried to hold him at arm's length for so long?"

Jake let out a grunt of resignation. "Hey, can I ask you something?"

"Anything."

"Did you end up hanging out with Field the other day?"

She sensed it was a leading question. The warning bells in her head told her she was walking into a trap. But she refused to feel like she was doing anything wrong by being friends with Fielding, so she replied truthfully without hesitation. "Yeah, why do you ask? You were here when we made those plans," she reminded him.

Jake held her gaze for a few beats, as if he was considering what to say next. She returned his stare with a cool, even scowl as she noted the judgement in his eyes.

"Be careful there, baby."

Tori bit down on her lower lip as she considered his words. Jake had had a front row seat to the way her friendship with Fielding had unfolded over the last few months. He also had the unique perspective of someone who had watched her and Rhett run circles around each other for the last ten years. There wasn't anyone else who understood the intricacies and complications of the tangled web of emotions between them.

Jake's warning wasn't unwarranted. Tuesday night's confrontation all but confirmed that Field had feelings for her. His reaction to her engagement was so intense—so painful to witness and experience firsthand—that there was no doubt in her mind that Fielding Haas had been hopeful that they could be more than friends one day.

But now that she was engaged to Rhett, it was a nonissue. She would make sure of it. Fielding knew where things stood, and she wouldn't let him forget it. It would have honestly been easier to cut him out of her life, but she had her reasons for wanting to maintain her friendship with Fielding. There was something nice about having a friend who wasn't connected to Rhett—having a friend who she knew was on her side one hundred percent of the time, no matter what. As much as she loved Jake, she never questioned where his ultimate loyalties laid.

She was confident she could maintain a friendship with Fielding without letting him get too close or think she wanted anything more.

"I will. I promise," she replied.

Jake blew out a long breath of acceptance before changing the subject. She knew if she didn't push back, he wouldn't force the subject. "Okay, good. Let's get this party started then, yeah? Locks are turning in twenty. Cory's working this morning, too, but he doesn't come in until eight. It's Market Day, so Mike will be on the Green most of your shift. Let me know if you need anything."

"Will do," Tori confirmed before heading back into the kitchen to start the coffee pots.

CHAPTER TWELVE

Rhett

"Finally," he exhaled, his arm extended up and over his head in a wave as his parents coasted up Willow Drive in his dad's Mercedes S-Class Coupe. Maddie's limo had just pulled away from the house ten minutes prior. After a full day of wedding planning and a few tenser-than-expected moments with his parents, Rhett was relieved to see them go. This was what he'd been looking forward to all week. They finally had the house to themselves. They were finally alone.

Tori sighed as she moved her body into his side and wrapped her arms around his waist. He lowered his raised arm and draped it on her shoulder, bowing down to kiss the top of her head in the process. "Hi," she greeted him as she nuzzled into his chest.

"Hey, you," he murmured, letting his fingers brush up and down her arm. "Why does it feel like we haven't been alone in weeks?" Rhett swept her hair off her shoulder and brought his mouth to the pulse point right below her ear. He savored the sensitive spot and relished that there was no longer any concern for who could see them.

A month ago, Tori would have recoiled from this kind of public affection. Now, he could kiss her in his driveway anytime he wanted. It felt so damn good to get to love her out loud.

"You slept over at my house last night," she reminded him before sighing softly and tilting her head to the side, exposing her neck and granting him more access. He felt her go soft and lean into him. He gladly accepted her weight, wrapping his arm tighter around her as he continued to trail kisses along the column of her neck.

"You've gotta know by now that I won't ever get my fill, beautiful. With you, I'll always want more." He spun her around so he could pull her into a hug.

"Well, we're finally alone, and I'm all yours tonight."

"You're all mine tonight," he confirmed, working his hand to the nape of her neck and squeezing gently for emphasis. "I've been dreaming about tonight all week. I plan to make the most of it."

"You and your plans," she teased. "I'm sure you've got the whole night already mapped out for us, so let's hear it."

"Dinner," he whispered as he ran his tongue from the edge of her collarbone up the side of her neck.

"Dessert," he breathed his intentions into the shell of her ear.

"And a show," he promised, hooking a single finger into the front belt loop of her jeans and pulling her body into his own.

Her breath hitched in response to his promises, the energy between them charging the air with an intensity that matched the incoming storm.

"You feel that, beautiful?" he murmured as he wrapped an arm around the small of her back and held her close. "That's because of you. That's what you do to me."

"Mhmm. I love you," she murmured in reply, running her hands up his arms before circling them around his neck.

"Promise to show me just how much tonight? I need you, V." His voice was husky now, his body and his mind equally excited for everything he had in mind.

"Ohh, I see how it is. *I'm* supposed to put on the show then?" She lifted her chin to brush her lips just an inch away from his.

"No, no, I'll do the work. But it's just you and me tonight. Phones stay in the house. No interruptions, okay?"

"It's gonna rain," she mused, keying up the tension between them as she withheld her kiss. He knew she was teasing him. Usually he loved the tension and relished the chase. But tonight, he needed to be in control. He needed to possess her in every way she'd allow.

"You don't think I've already checked the radar? No storms in the forecast. Just showers tonight. Your ass will be in the pool within the hour," he promised, finally letting his control snap as he pressed his lips into hers and slid both his hands into the back pockets of her jeans. She only let him kiss her for a few brief seconds before she pulled away. It wasn't enough. It would never be enough.

"Pool?" she questioned, cocking an eyebrow up at him.

"You heard me. We're having fun tonight, beautiful. I want to play."

"In that case..." She raised up on her toes to kiss him again, albeit briefly. "I'll race you in."

Tori took off toward the house before he even knew what was happening, laughing as she grinned back at him over her shoulder.

This girl. They needed this tonight, and they both knew it. They needed the lightness to counter all the hard and heavy that had been thrown their way over the past month. They needed the reminder of who they were together. Rhett was going to do everything in his power to give her all that and more tonight.

CHAPTER THIRTEEN

Tori

"Are you ever going to come in here and join me?" she called across the pool as she languidly swam through the water. Rhett was perched on the end of the diving board, Gatorade bottle in hand. He didn't answer her right away, instead lifting the green sports bottle filled with Jameson to his lips and taking another long swig. He winced slightly as he swallowed, his Adam's apple commanding her attention in the process.

He had established a rhythm to their game: stare, swig, smirk, repeat. He was working her up, propelling toward the inevitable. She knew it was all for her. Every stare. Every smirk. He was provoking her in all the right ways.

His strong, defined legs swung idly over the edge as his feet stirred the water below. She watched in rapture as his forearms flexed when he gripped the sides of the diving board. They'd been playing at this for almost an hour: Tori swimming in the pool by herself, taunting him, tempting him to join her; Rhett maintaining his position out of the pool, watching her, resisting her, perched above her on his throne.

The energy rippling between them had nothing to do with the humidity in the air. She was dizzy with want, and she knew he was right there with her. It was only a matter of who would yield first.

"I told you I wanted a show tonight," he countered. His sly smile was a tease and a promise and just—everything.

"A show, huh?" She peered over at him from the center of the pool where she floated. She didn't miss the way he was working his lower lip between his teeth. She quickly averted her eyes, trying to ignore the magnetic energy threatening to erupt between them. She could practically feel her body floating in his direction on its own volition. He was gravity. Who was she to try to resist gravity?

Rather than return his gaze, she looked back up at the threatening sky. Rain clouds shadowed the golden hour of twilight, casting everything around them into a deep pink and purple haze.

"Yeah. A show. Think you can do that for me, beautiful?"

He wants to play. If he wanted a show, she'd give him a show.

Tori righted herself in the water, treading in the center of the pool as she reached behind her back and found the clasp of her bathing suit top. She turned her body away from the diving board. She smiled to herself as she deftly unhooked the fabric that rested at the middle of her back. She glanced over her shoulder and bit down on her lip. She knew without looking that she had his full attention.

The straps of her top floated on either side of her as her soaking wet hair tickled her bare skin. She turned around as slowly as possible when she saw the heat in Rhett's gaze. If he wanted a show, she was going to give him a show. She could play this game, too.

She grasped the halter portion of her suit from around her neck and lifted, uncovering her upper body. She would have been fully exposed, if she wasn't already in the deepest part of the pool. She gathered her wet hair and collected it over one shoulder.

Rhett cleared his throat and made a noise that sounded like a combination of a growl and a moan. She whipped her head around and gave him a cheeky smile.

"Bring that to me," he ordered.

Her insides clenched at his command.

"But I'm not done. The show's not over."

"It better not be fucking over," he responded, his voice a full octave deeper than normal. "But you're not gonna need that again tonight. Bring it to me. Now."

Her body started moving through the water before she even made the decision to go to him. They had always been so attuned to one another, so keyed into the desires of the other. For as sweet and caring as he could be, Everhett Wheeler was an indomitable force when he set his mind to something.

She reached the diving board at the same second he extended his arm. He wrapped his hands around her forearms, steadying her in place so she didn't have to tread. They locked eyes, each one tempting the other to either come in or get out. This game was intoxicating in the best and worst ways. She desperately wanted it to be over as much as she never wanted it to end.

"That's mine," he ordered, jerking his chin toward the bathing suit top she still held in her hand.

"You're bossy tonight."

"You like it when I'm bossy. Now give me that top."

"A-And if I don't?" she stammered. Rhett smirked. They both knew she didn't have a leg to stand on, literally, as he held her suspended in the water.

"You're the most stubborn person I know, V. Stubborn. Determined. Strong-willed. So fucking strong. We both know you're not going to do anything you don't want to do. There's nothing I could say or do to convince you otherwise." He shrugged. "But we also both know you want to give that to me right now."

She released her grasp on the slick fabric as he snatched her top from the air before it fell into the water. He released both her arms, granting him the view she knew he was waiting for. His sharp intake of breath confirmed the moment his eyes landed on her bare chest.

"Good girl," he moaned as he threw her bathing suit top off to the side of the pool deck.

Tori smiled as she stretched out, floating on her back as her breasts crested above the surface. The humid night air barely registered against her skin, but her nipples pebbled under his gaze anyways.

"So goddamn beautiful." His words were muffled because her ears were half submerged. The filter of the water just added to the hazy, dreamy tension that continued to rise between them. "Hey, V?"

"Yeah?"

"Swim over to the shallow end and do a handstand for me."

She considered arguing with him but started to swim across the pool instead. Resisting Rhett was futile. She didn't know what he had in mind, but she was more than willing to let him call the shots tonight.

"I haven't done an underwater handstand in years." She reached the halfway point of the pool. She was still on her back, staring up at the swirling clouds, letting herself succumb to the humidity in the air and the heat from his gaze. Everything felt hot. Everything felt heavy. And yet she was floating. She felt so weightless she wondered if she could fly.

"Think you've lost your touch?"

"No way. Just thinking I might need a spotter. Any volunteers?" She held up the bathing suit bottoms she had just slipped off. In that moment, he was a bull, and she was the matador, waving her flag and testing his resolve with one extended hand.

Your move, Everhett Wheeler.

"You're trouble," he groaned, running a wet hand over his face and through his hair.

"Get in here and prove it," she taunted.

"We both know once I'm in, the show is over."

"Like I said—get in here and prove it."

Rhett just shook his head, narrowing his eyes on her from across the rippled surface of the water. "Go," he commanded. "You're going to miss it."

Curious, she turned away from him and made her way to the shallow end. She cut fluidly through the pool, each movement inspiring a ripple of water against her bare skin. When she reached the shallowest section, she turned back to him and cocked her head to the side in question.

Rhett didn't speak, but he nodded eagerly, urging her on as he cast his eyes up to the sky.

Tori dove forward, stretching out her arms until she felt the textured bottom of the pool scrape against her fingertips. She held her breath and starfished her fingers against the bumpy surface, extending her arms straight as she raised her lower body out of the water. She may have been in the shallowest end of the pool, but the water was still four feet deep on this end, meaning only her knees, calves, and feet reached out beyond the surface.

She held the handstand as she held her breath, feeling the cool, delicate raindrops tickling the soles of her feet. Each droplet was a kiss, each streak of moisture a caress. Memories flooded her mind before the sensation fully registered in her brain. Running barefoot through her backyard to meet him at the broken spot in the fence. Cannon ball competitions with Maddie and Jake. Stolen kisses and secret underwater touches when they thought no one was watching them. Handstand contests in the rain.

She let her arms give out, desperate to feel more than just the rain on her skin. She stood up and wiped the water from her eyes, keeping them closed for a few extra seconds. She knew he'd be right there when she finally came up for air. He'd always been right there.

She was right. He was in the water now, standing right in front of her, just out of arm's reach. He peered down through his wet, dark lashes, his grey-blue eyes a little hazy from the bottle he'd been nursing for the last hour. "How'd you know it was about to rain?" she marveled as she met his steady gaze.

"Do you remember?" he asked instead of answering her question.

"Of course I do. The summer that changed everything. Kissing you against the fence in the dark. Handstand contests in the rain. The summer we became Ev and V. How'd you time that so perfectly?"

Rhett took two steps forward, closing the space between them as he wrapped her in his arms. She felt his erection press into her stomach under water. The solidness of his desire reignited her own wanting. She hoped the show was almost over. She was ready for the grand finale.

"Lucky timing." He winked, giving up his secret as he bowed down to kiss her. His lips brushed against hers, his kiss filled with a reverence and tenderness she wasn't expecting after the last hour of teasing.

No sooner was Tori letting herself sink into the gentleness of his kiss than he switched gears. He wove his hand into the soaking wet hair at the nape of her neck, drawing her in and deepening their connection. Their bodies connected in the water, slick skin slipping and sliding into a heated rhythm.

There he is. Nobody kissed like Rhett. The tip of his tongue against hers inspired a jolt of wanting between her legs. She could taste the spicy notes of whiskey as he made love to her mouth. He applied just enough pressure to be possessive. She was consumed by him completely, but still she wanted more.

"Show's not over," he whispered as he kissed her once more before nipping at the shell of her ear. He clasped both her forearms in his hands, mirroring the position he held her in at the diving board, then started to guide her through the water toward the edge of the pool.

Tori planted her feet in objection. She glared at him through heavy lids, knowing damn well he knew what she wanted. Was he going to make her beg? Breaking away from this moment and getting out of the pool was not acceptable at this point. She was too far gone.

"I know you're close," he practically purred as he tried tugging on her arms again. "Come on," he encouraged with a slight cock of his head.

"Rhett," she whimpered as she tried to push her naked body against him. She couldn't help it. The last hour had been too much. She was done. She needed to finish. She needed him now.

"I've got you. Now come here."

"And if I don't?" she clipped out, testing him.

"Do you want to come or not?" he deadpanned.

She lifted her feet and obediently followed him to the edge of the pool without another word. She would follow him to the edge of the world if he asked right now.

The rain continued to fall. The tension continued to rise.

"I won't make you wait," he promised as he used his grip around her arms to lift her out of the water and set her on the edge. The bumpy texture of the pool's edge pressed into the backs of her thighs, but the contact was a welcome sensation to her wanting. He spread her legs, rising onto the first underwater step to expose himself from mid thigh up as he positioned himself as close to her as possible.

"Stay just like that," he instructed, peering up and down her naked, soaking wet body. He made quick work of his trunks, untying and stepping out of them without ever taking his eyes off her. He took one more step through the water to close all space between them. Tori let her head lull back in anticipation, her gaze returning up to the sky. She could see the clouds rapidly moving against the final brushstrokes of twilight. They were almost there.

"Is this okay?" he asked as he placed each one of her feet onto the edge of the pool, positioning her bent legs right up next to her ass. She was on display and exposed to him completely. She widened her legs a bit more and rested back on her forearms, inviting him in. She bit her lip and nodded, not trusting her voice to hold steady.

He bent down and claimed her mouth at the same exact moment she felt the head of his cock press into her entrance.

"Ev," she sighed in anticipatory satisfaction, loving the way he spread and stretched her. Loving the way she felt around him.

"Open your eyes, beautiful."

Her lids shot open on his command. He held her gaze as she felt him push in another inch. "I love you," he swore as he cupped her face in his hands. He was only a few inches inside her, but she was already about to explode around him. The angle was perfect. She could feel herself teetering on the edge, flutters of desire holding him inside her.

He lowered his hands then, resting each one on the inside of her thighs and gently spreading her legs even further apart. He stroked her skin and held her gaze, but he didn't push in any further. "Look at you," he murmured in reverence, his eyes cast down at where their bodies were joined. "Look at us." The tips of his fingers were brushing up and down her pussy.

Her breathing hitched in response to his words, to his touch, to his eyes fixated on the exact spot where he ended and she began. "Look at us, beautiful," he repeated, tipping his chin in encouragement as Tori cast her eyes between her legs. The sight of him sunk just a few inches inside of her was enough to ramp up the familiar tingle in her toes. Instead of pushing in, he continued to pet her soaking wet core.

"So fucking perfect," he praised as he used his fingers on both hands to gather her arousal and spread it up and down his shaft. "You want more, don't you, beautiful?"

Tori moaned in response to his question as she teetered on the edge. It was all she had left to give. She closed her eyes, ready to give in and fall apart.

"Hey," Rhett called her back to him, pausing his caresses and not pushing in any further, not allowing her to reach the peak she so desperately craved. She was panting. She was ready. He knew she was right there. Why wouldn't he just let her go?

"Look at us."

She glanced down again, transfixed as he used one single finger to trace the outline of her opening stretched around the girth of his dick. He ran his finger up and around, over and over, outlining the perfect arch of their connection. She had never seen anything so erotic in her life. Then he took that slick finger and moved it up an inch to rub tight circles around her clit.

"Now look at me."

She met his eyes and fell into the depths of their combined wanting. There was only this moment. There was only him. Everything she felt, everything she was: it was all for him.

"This," he breathed into the air between them as he finally pushed in further. She let her gaze follow his back down, locking in on the sight of their bodies becoming one. "This is mine. This is all I've ever wanted. You know it's always been you."

He pushed all the way into her then, giving her the solidness and the connection she had so desperately craved all night long. The pressure. The intensity. The claiming in his words. It was all for her.

He didn't even have time to pull out and thrust back in before she started coming hard. She knew it wouldn't take her long—but damn. She had never climaxed that quickly.

She watched in awe as her body pulsed and writhed around him. Wave after wave of pleasure had her moaning his name. He began to pound into her with fast, deep thrusts. Her orgasm seemed never-ending as the sight of their joined bodies inspired a second wave of pleasure to grip her from the inside. She had come so hard. He was still filling her so deep. She didn't think she could physically handle coming again right away. But Rhett obviously believed in her.

He bent lower and kissed her, momentarily distracting her with the warm, demanding thrusts of his tongue in her mouth. It wasn't until his thumb found her needy clit that she finally broke away and tried to claim she'd had enough.

"Rhett," she pleaded, thrusting her hips up to meet him thrust for thrust even as she questioned whether she could handle anything more. "It's too much."

"You've got another in you, V. I feel it," he growled as he continued to stroke demanding circles against her sweet spot. His thrusts were more frantic now, the erratic rhythm of his hips the most obvious tell that he was close. His mouth dropped open in a groan as she felt the first pulse of his climax shoot off inside her.

"Come with me, beautiful," he commanded, pressing down on her sensitive bundle of nerves with the pad of his thumb. She toppled over the edge with him, because of him. Damn him for always giving better than he got. Damn him for knowing her and loving her so well.

Chapter Fourteen

Rhett

"Come on, you," he directed, placing a hand on the small of Tori's back to guide her through the sunroom and into the house. They both moved slowly, as if they were still walking through water. Rhett was feeling the foggy pull of the Jameson combined with the post-release satisfaction he knew she had to be feeling, too.

"Mhmm, no more objections from me tonight. I like coming with you," she murmured, glancing back over her shoulder as they made their way through the kitchen. Her cheeks were flushed from the humidity and physical exertion. Her eyes took on a lush hunter-green hue that seemed almost too vibrant to be real. She looked so beautiful and satisfied.

"I love you," he replied.

The words he held back for so long still felt foreign on his tongue. But between all the whiskey he had consumed and the merciful reprieve from his break-neck schedule this week, he felt closer to Tori tonight than he had in ages. They were here. They were together. What else could he ask for?

"Do you want to eat and watch some TV?" she asked as they wandered through the living room.

Hell no. He finally had her alone. There wasn't time for anything but her.

"Up," he instructed instead of answering her question. He was feeling the alcohol even more now that they were out of the water.

"Ev," she cautioned, pausing at the base of the stairs and turning to face him. "You should probably eat something. I had a late lunch with Jake at the end of my shift, but I bet you haven't eaten since this morning, and you just drank a good amount."

She knew him well. But he wasn't interested in food right now.

"I fully plan to eat," he conceded, leaning in closer to nip at her bottom lip. He whispered directly into her ear even though they were the only people in the house. "But I want dessert first."

Tori shivered and gave him a knowing smile, shaking her head slightly at his diversion tactic. She knew what he meant. He knew she wanted it.

"Besides," he added seriously, "I know how much you hate the feeling of chlorine in your hair. Let's go upstairs."

This time she didn't argue. He followed behind as she took the stairs two at a time, skipping the second-to-last squeaky step at the top of the staircase. It didn't matter that they were the only ones in the house tonight. Or that they were getting married in a week. They had been avoiding that step as they snuck in and out of his room for more than a decade. Some things would never change.

Tori had the shower started and had already disappeared into his en suite by the time he walked into his bedroom. He discarded his swim trunks on the top of her pool robe before meandering over to his bedside table where his phone was charging.

What was meant to be a quick time check stopped him in his tracks and made his alcohol-fueled veins ignite. He had not one, but two missed calls from Chandler, about twenty minutes apart. No voicemail. No texts. Just two offensive red notifications in his call log. More misplaced attempts to manipulate him. Another way for her to punish him for what he'd done.

He was getting pretty fucking tired of seeing the name Chandler Cunningham on his phone.

He should just block her number. He had considered it at least a dozen times over the last week, ever since their pointless standoff in the parking lot of Easton before his graduation ceremony. But that seemed immature, and if he was honest with himself, he felt like he didn't have it in him to cut Chandler off completely. He wasn't sure they would ever be to a place where they could be cordial, but their friend groups were intertwined enough that seeing her again was unavoidable. There would be weddings. Reunions. All sorts of social gatherings and get-togethers in the coming years where he stood the risk of running into her. Blocking her number now would be a shitty move he might regret. But that still didn't mean he wanted to hear from her anytime soon.

Seeing Chandler's name jerked him out of the mental reprieve he'd been enjoying. All the stress, anger, and overwhelm that had dissipated over the last few hours returned in waves. It was like each reminder brought with it three more spiraling thoughts, all fighting for attention in his alcohol-soaked brain.

He released a drawn-out sigh, resigning to the fact that it might be another long night. If all that Jameson and some of the hottest sex of his life wasn't enough to sedate the anxiety coiled inside him, he didn't stand a chance of sleeping well. Again.

Frustrated, and really too drunk to be messing around with his phone, he pivoted and stalked into the bathroom. Steam rose up as he pulled open the glass shower door. Tori eyed him and worked her bottom lip between her teeth, giving him one of those signature looks that instantly made his dick hard. He returned her gaze, narrowing his eyes and licking his lips involuntarily at the sight of her dripping wet body in his shower.

Everything they had been through—all the heartache they had caused, both for themselves and for others around them—it was all worth it.

Rhett entered the shower and wordlessly dropped to his knees. She continued to watch him as rivulets of water cascaded down her body. He ran his palms up her legs, coaxing them open, requesting access, making silent promises.

He lovingly caressed the curve of her hip bones, the softness of her tummy, the little dips of her waist. She let out a gasp when he cupped her breasts in his hands, pinching both nipples before rubbing his thumbs back and forth to soothe the sting.

"Dessert?" She smirked, her eyes alight with excitement and desire.

"My favorite." He ran his hands back down her body and coaxed her to take a wider stance. He used one hand to pin her against the tiles of the shower while he worked his other arm in between her thighs. Once he was sure she was steady, he hoisted her leg up and hitched it over his shoulder.

"I won't let you fall, beautiful."

"I know."

"I've got you. Always."

She smiled down at him and dragged one hand through his wet hair. That was all the urging he needed to bring his mouth to her center. She was exposed to him, so open and primed after all the time they spent teasing each other in the pool.

He could feel her body quiver when he dipped his tongue inside her for a taste. He could hear her breathing hitch when he nudged up against her clit, taking the swollen bud between his teeth and sucking. She was so responsive to him, so willing to love him, to let him unravel her in every way possible. It may have been an unconventional path that landed them here, but it was worth it.

He licked and played and savored her until she was practically grinding on his face, finally sinking two fingers inside her to set off her third orgasm of the night. There really was nothing he loved more than making her come. Not even his own release matched the wholeness he felt when her body clenched around his hands, his mouth, his cock. Her satisfaction was everything. He couldn't believe he got to spend the rest of forever chasing her pleasure.

So fucking worth it.

"Okay, beautiful. Technically we worked backwards tonight. I got a show *and* my dessert, but we still need dinner. I'll go scrounge something up. What sounds good?"

Tori moved from the bathroom toward the bed, releasing an exaggerated yawn in the process. She had already slipped into one of his old Archway lacrosse T-shirts and was weaving her wet hair into a loose braid.

"Wait. You're going to bring food up here?" He didn't miss the skepticism in her voice.

"Aren't you tired?" he countered.

"Yes," she admitted, yawning again. "But I thought there was a 'no eating in Rhett's bed' rule? Who are you, and what have you done with my fiancé?"

He reached out for her and caught the hem of her shirt, reeling her in. He pulled her between his thighs and peered up at her with sleepy eyes. "Keyword there: fiancé. We're getting married. Actually, by this time next week, we *will* be married. That means this isn't just my bed anymore. You're tired and probably hungry. It's my job to feed you, even if it means an extra load of laundry."

Tori's eyes grew wider as a small smile played across her lips. What he wouldn't give to make her this happy all the time.

"What?" he asked defensively when she continued to stare at him.

"You just make me really happy," she replied without missing a beat.

He returned her affection with a grin of his own. Tonight had been exactly what they needed. Just the two of them. Just being together.

"Will you bring me some tortilla chips and salsa?" Of course she would ask for what was arguably the messiest food she could think of. She was testing him, and they both knew it.

"That might be pushing it, beautiful." He winked as he stood up and headed down to the kitchen to bring up exactly what she wanted.

Chapter Fifteen

Rhett

3:52 a.m.

Rhett stared at the numbers on his phone, so fucking frustrated that sleep still wouldn't come. Tori had fallen asleep in his arms around midnight. He spent the first hour watching her, hoping the rhythm of her inhales and exhales would lull him to sleep. But one hour turned into two, then three. Eventually he reached for his phone, trying to bore himself into slumber by reading the lost cargo reports from the last few months. He spent some time researching things to do on their honeymoon, as well as updating the shared task list for the wedding that he and his mom had been working from. But no matter how long he lay in bed, sleep just wouldn't come.

He had almost had it around three a.m. He felt the subtle tug try to take hold of his consciousness. Somehow the prospect of rest made his brain rebel even harder. The nastier highlights of the prenup fight with his dad came flooding back to him as his body experienced the same rush of emotions he had felt when they were actually at brunch that day.

Rhett sighed. This was the third night this week that he was going to see four a.m. on the clock. He knew he needed sleep. He didn't want to be sick for the wedding, and definitely not for the honeymoon. He made a mental note to up his supplements and to schedule in a few long runs this week to try to give his immune system a fighting chance against this fatigue.

He gave it a few more minutes before he brushed a loose strand of hair off Tori's face and gave in. He silently rolled to his side and got out of bed, grabbing his phone and pulling on a pair of joggers before hitting the stairs.

He meandered into the sunroom, not out of conscious thought exactly, but more out of habit. It sucked to feel this tired and out of it and still not be able to sleep. Maybe a change of scenery was all he needed for the grogginess to take hold.

The cool tiles of the sunroom floor sent a jolt of alertness through his body as he made his way around the built-in bar. He leaned against the edge of the polished wood, assuming the crossed-ankle position he usually stood in at Clinton's as he assessed the regiment of bottles all lined up at attention. His parents kept a very well-stocked bar, organized by spirit and color.

He let out a frustrated breath and pulled his phone out of his sweatpants. There was nothing new on social or in his inbox since he had last looked about ten minutes ago, just like he knew there wouldn't be. Who the hell did he expect to be up and posting at this hour?

He mindlessly opened the calendar app on his phone, glancing past the slew of conference calls and updates scheduled for the first half of the week. He felt a pang of guilt when he glanced at the end of the week. He was marked out of the office starting Thursday, all the way through the end of May. It was necessary time off for the wedding and the honeymoon. Then he needed the following weekend to move and get things set up in his new apartment in Virginia. He had to keep reminding himself that he didn't officially start working at NorfolkStar Transport until June 1, so he had no reason to feel guilty for taking time off for his own wedding. But still.

He closed the calendar app, hitting the call log right next to it out of habit.

Chandler's name appearing not once, but twice at the top of the list stirred up the same level of rage he had felt toward his father. He was done. He had no tolerance for anyone who thought they had a say in what happens next in his life. He wouldn't let anything or anyone get in the way of what he wanted—what he was so close to having, finally.

He swiped on each individual call, deleting the visual reminder of all the time he had shamefully wasted over the last three years. He wasn't trying to hide her calls. Tori had already made it clear that she trusted him, and that she knew he would handle any loose ends that needed to be handled. He just wasn't interested in letting Chandler's name linger on his device.

He repocketed his phone, feeling no sleepier than when he first came downstairs. If anything, he was more keyed up now. He was exhausted but wired and running out of ways to distract himself.

"Damnit," he muttered, leaning forward and reaching for the container he'd been itching to pull for the last ten minutes. The neck of the emerald-green bottle was a comfort in his hand. He turned on his heel and blindly felt around for a glass under the mahogany bar.

He poured himself what would be considered a triple in most establishments, forgoing any ice or mixers. He circled around the bar, hoisted himself onto a stool, and settled in.

Rhett glanced down at the dark amber liquid for a few moments before lifting the glass to his lips. He was already going to be hungover tomorrow. What was one more drink to cap it all off? One more drink, then he'd head back upstairs. One more drink, then hopefully, finally, sleep would come.

Chapter Sixteen

Tori

"Okay, for real though. Who gets to make the speech tomorrow?" Jake lowered his beer bottle and glared at Rhett from over the flames. Tori could barely hide her smirk as her fiancé stared ahead, giving nothing away.

Poor Jake. Rhett had been torturing him all week, skirting around asking him to be his best man, insisting they weren't even having a traditional wedding party. While that was technically true, there was a midnight-blue suit perfectly tailored to Jake's measurements hanging in a garment bag in the master bedroom of the cabin. But Jake still didn't know that, and Rhett seemed determined to keep it that way for as long as possible.

Maddie spoke up before Rhett had a chance to reply. "I don't care about the title all that much, but you should know something, Jakey. I talked to the DJ about my audio needs when he came to set up the stage earlier." She lifted her White Claw and took a long swig, hiding her telltale smirk behind the aluminum can. Tori assumed she was just joking, but she also wouldn't put it past the younger Wheeler to have planned ahead. Or to enjoy getting a rise out of Jake as much as her brother.

"I bet you did, Fourth Wheel," Jake shot back, resurrecting the childhood nickname she hated.

"Jacob Whitely," Tori warned. As Maddie's babysitter and the other female of their four-person group, it had always been her job to put the boys in their places when they were younger. Jake knew the scolding was in jest. That didn't stop him from turning his campaign on her.

"Tori. Baby. Please. I'm begging you. Just tell me what you know."

She had to bury her hands in her face to stop herself from laughing. She leaned into Rhett as he wrapped an arm around her shoulders, pulling her closer. She inhaled the the scents of sandalwood, salt, bonfire smoke and fresh lake air, a combination that left her feeling heady with desire and nostalgia.

"Ev," she pleaded in a whisper. "Put him out of his misery."

They had finally settled around the firepit after a full day of setup and last-minute wedding prep. The Wheelers hired a local food truck to cater the casual rehearsal dinner for their friends. Rhett's parents and his grandad had made a few speeches, welcoming Tori to the family and welcoming their friends to the cabin, then they all noshed on tacos and sliders. Tori had deliberately asked Rhett and Anne to try and keep the event small and intimate. This was exactly what she had had in mind.

Most of the guests had already made their way back to the inn. It was just their friends around the fire now. Everyone still here would be staying at the cabin with them tonight. Cory and Jake were set up to sleep downstairs, with Maddie and Aurelia bunking in the loft. Tomorrow Cory and Lia would stand with Tori during the ceremony, while Jake and Maddie would be at Rhett's side. They had decided on the pairings a few weeks ago, but it had been all too easy to goad Jake about his role.

"Fine," Rhett drawled out, weaving his hand through the hair at the base of her neck and pulling her in for a kiss. She expected a quick peck, but he took things further, running the tip of his tongue against the seam of her lips. She parted them and let him in, granting him access to deepen their connection as he worked his hand under the hem of her fitted white denim skirt. She barely had time to sink into his touch before someone spotted their PDA and started whooping. A cacophony of "get a room!" and "you're not married yet!" rose up as their friends banded together to taunt them.

Tori smiled against Rhett's mouth before pulling away. She blushed slightly as she took in the scene before her, as she looked from person to person and acknowledged how lucky she was that they were all here. They really did have the best friends. And the best boss for that matter, seeing as how Mike closed down the restaurant during a holiday weekend to allow half his staff to participate in their wedding. She sighed contentedly and leaned back into Rhett's side, resting her head in the crook of his arm.

It was crazy what could happen in just a few weeks. Less than two months ago, she and Rhett hadn't even been on speaking terms. Now they were here, hanging out with their friends on the eve of their nuptials, at her favorite place in the world, ready to face whatever came next, together.

She felt surprisingly calm for someone who was about to star in a seemingly shotgun wedding. A lot of that calm was thanks to Rhett. He and Anne had worked tirelessly to pull this all together in a short amount of time. She marveled at what they'd accomplished as she took in the ceremony floral arch by the lake and the stage and dance floor closer to the house. She knew they were both planners by nature, and that they threw a lot of money at this event to make it all happen on a holiday weekend. But it was still impressive.

She glanced over at her fiancé, waiting for him to finally admit to Jake that he was, in fact, his best man. He looked so handsome leaning forward on his knees: casual, steady, confident. He oozed happiness, and he seemed lighter today. She knew things were wearing on him lately, particularly after all her surgery consultations and the back and forth to Virginia.

Rhett hadn't been in bed beside her when she woke up that morning. As expected, he snuck out early to go on a run, dragging Jake and Maddie along with him, except both his running partners came back to the cabin a full hour before he did, claiming that six miles was more than enough for them.

She knew what he was doing, what he'd been doing for weeks. He was channeling all his stress and anxiety into any outlet he could find. He was running more. He was obsessing over his calendar more. He was working more. He was drinking more. He was pushing himself to the brink, wringing himself dry in the hopes he wouldn't feel it all quite as intensely by the end of the day.

Tori was grateful they were going on a honeymoon. He needed an actual vacation maybe even more than she did. She watched him for a few more moments, trying her best to really see him, to see past the in-control mask he wore so well. *He's okay*, she decided. And things were only going to get better from here.

She felt him sit up a bit straighter beside her as he ran one hand lazily up and down her bare arm. She wasn't cold—it was a warm summer night, even this close to the water—but his touch sent a shiver through her body nonetheless.

"You get to make the speech, bro," Rhett confirmed.

"For real?"

"Yeah, for real. What the hell kind of question is that?"

"Don't fuck with me right now, Rhett. I've had enough to drink tonight that I'm believin' every word you're saying. I don't care if there's a photographer showing up to take your wedding pictures tomorrow. I can't be held responsible for my actions if you're just playing and I have to beat you down in the morning."

Tori laughed and shook her head. Jake had really let loose tonight. She hadn't seen him drink much lately, not like he used to at least, so he was probably feeling it. She hadn't missed how Rhett had been nursing the same beer for most of the night. She wasn't sure if the guys had discussed it beforehand, or if her fiancé had just instinctively held back once he realized Jake was going to play full out. They had always had that kind of balance to their friendship: one ebbing when the other flowed, one filling in for the other when needed.

"You've been my best friend since we were five, bro. Of course you're my best man."

"Fuck. Why are you *just now* telling me this, the night before your wedding?"

Rhett gave him a pointed look across the fire. "Because I know you. And I know there would have been all sorts of shenanigans had I told you sooner. We didn't have time for any nonsense." That was the truth: this wasn't a typical wedding, and with the burden of planning already falling on Rhett's shoulders, Tori understood his reasoning for keeping Jake in the dark until now.

"Screw you, bro. We missed a major opportunity here. Could you even *imagine* the epicness of a Jake and Rhett *Bachelor* Party?"

"I could. And that's exactly why I didn't tell you sooner."

Jake scowled as he took another swig of his drink. She knew a lot of his reaction was for show—he was Jake, after all, so there was no way he'd stay mad—but she did worry they may have actually hurt his feelings. Rhett must have sensed it too, because he spoke up again before Jake could get another word in.

"Look, bro. I'll make it up to you when it's your turn, I swear. This just all had to happen a certain way, as quickly as possible. A bachelor party was never in the cards for me, but I promise I'll plan the most baller party ever for your bachelor weekend. We'll go anywhere you want," he vowed.

"One problem. Having a bachelor party would require me to get married."

Rhett cocked one eyebrow in challenge. "It would."

"That's so not fair. You know that shit's not happening anytime soon. Or ever."

"You never know. Maybe one day you'll meet Mr. or Mrs. Right. Or you'll decide you finally want to claim that inheritance." Tori winced. She knew the conversation was officially over now that he had taken it there.

Jake scowled before pushing to his feet. "Haha. You're *so* funny. I didn't know we were having dinner *and* a show tonight." Tori's face flushed in response to his word choice. Rhett didn't miss it either, based on the way he moved his hand further up her bare leg and playfully gripped her inner thigh. She had been thinking about his version of "a show" all week. She desperately hoped wherever they were going on their honeymoon had a pool. Or at the very least, a large tub.

"I'm turning in for the night," Jake declared. "I've got to work on a last-minute speech since no one had the courtesy to tell me I was the best man until the night before the wedding."

"Like you don't already have a speech written out and laminated," Lia chided before also standing up. It was only a little after ten, but Tori was glad to see it was going to be an early night.

Jake shot Lia a sly smile, dramatically looking from person to person around the firepit before he responded, "So what if I do?" Then he turned to Rhett and snickered. "Actually, I don't just have one speech written out. I have three different speeches ready. Three different speeches, all with varying levels of embarrassment. I was just waiting to see how long you were going to leave me in best man limbo before I decided which one I'm using tomorrow."

A collective groan rose up from the group as everyone started to rise to their feet and gather their things.

Tori couldn't help but smile at the promise of tomorrow. Tomorrow, she got to marry Rhett in front of all their friends and family. Tomorrow, they would declare their soul-deep love for each other, their commitment to forever, or to however long they got. Tomorrow couldn't come soon enough.

———

She squinted one eye open just a smidge as the biggest smile took over her face. She was lying flat on her back, reveling in the lingering blurriness of a really great night's sleep. She always slept well at the cabin, and she had slept even better than normal in Rhett's arms. They had forgone the traditional night before the wedding separation on purpose. They both wanted it this way: to fall asleep side by side and wake up together one last time before they became husband and wife.

There was already an excitement buzzing in her body. She opened both eyes and stared at the exposed beams of the cabin's ceiling. She loved the way the sunlight streamed in through the floor-to-ceiling windows, illuminating the master bedroom and filling the space with light. The cabin was beautifully decorated in white, cream, and linen, with little navy and gold accents throughout.

Today was her wedding day. She hadn't spent her youth dreaming of the perfect dress, a dream venue, the perfect partner. Yet here she was. She had it all. It almost didn't feel real. She almost didn't feel worthy. *Stop that*, she silently scolded herself. If she let herself think about it all too much, she would spiral.

She had no doubts about marrying Rhett. She wanted him more than she wanted anything. But she had spent so damn long convincing herself it wasn't fair to him or his future to stake her claim on what she wanted most in life. It was unnerving to constantly have to remind herself that it was okay to want what she wanted, that she deserved happiness, and that their love wasn't a sacrifice in his mind. She owed it to Rhett to believe that, today and always. She owed it to both of them to let him love her full out and to love him just as fiercely in return.

She slowly rolled to her side to take in her first look of the man who would become her husband later that day. He was sound asleep, lying flat on his back with one arm thrown over his face to block out the morning sunlight she loved so much.

She was glad he was still asleep. He'd been restless and not sleeping well lately. She'd caught him tossing and turning, getting out of bed at all hours of the night over the last few weeks. His insomnia was all stress-induced. It was hard to watch him struggle, knowing she was the root cause of some of his worry.

But she was confident that things were going to get better soon. The wedding was here. They were leaving at lunchtime tomorrow for their honeymoon. He'd be settled into his new apartment and officially full time at NorfolkStar Transport in less than two weeks. They'd be out of the in-between soon enough, and they could finally start to figure out some semblance of a routine. That's what a lot of this was about. Rhett would be better once things weren't so in flux.

She watched him sleep for a few more minutes, taking in the easy rise and fall of his chest and admiring the hard planes of his shoulders and arms. It was rare to catch him in bed like this, even when he wasn't struggling with insomnia. The man was almost always up first, making her coffee, getting ahead on emails, or going for an early morning run.

"Hi, beautiful," he murmured without opening his eyes. Her heart picked up in cadence on its own volition at the sound of his voice.

"Hello, almost-husband." She leaned into his space and draped herself over his chest. Rhett's arms circled her lower half on contact as he shifted her up his body. Once she was lying on top of him, he opened his eyes. A sly smile graced his lips as he began stroking her bare back underneath her T-shirt.

"Almost-husband, huh?"

"Yep. You've been promoted, Everhett Wheeler. You're more than just my fiancé today, but not quite my husband. Not yet at least."

"I'm more than ready for that final title," he admitted, raising his hips up just an inch so she could feel his morning wood. They had made love last night as quietly as possible since their friends were sleeping in the basement and the loft, but that didn't matter. His erection finding its home in the apex of her thighs inspired all sorts of ideas.

Tori realigned her body, then swiveled her own hips against the solidness beneath her. She ran her tongue along the outline of his collarbone, then bit down into the fleshy part of his shoulder.

"Hey, almost-wife?"

"Hmmm?" she hummed as she savored the skin stretched along the column of his stubbled neck.

"Don't start something we can't finish," he warned. Rhett reached over to the side table and flipped over his phone. "It's 8:40 already, beautiful. I don't think I'm even allowed to be here in another twenty minutes."

Damn. He was right. The girls had hair and makeup starting at nine, and she still needed to shower.

"But, but, but," she fake-protested, grinding her hips against him with each objection. She pressed her lips to his one more time, then raised her head to let her hair canopy around both their faces.

"Tonight."

One word. A million promises.

She smiled down at the man she loved, nodding her head so the ends of her hair tickled his bare chest.

"Tonight," she repeated, grinding her hips against him one more time for good measure.

Now it was Rhett's turn to let out a disgruntled moan. He rose up onto his elbows, forcing the muscles in his arms and upper chest to flex as he held the position. She couldn't help but scan up and down the body she was straddling. She admired the hollow V at the base of his throat, the defined ridges of his pecs and abdomen. She licked her lips without conscious thought.

"Victoria," he warned.

"Jusssst looking," she sing-songed. He loved it when she eye-fucked him, and they both knew it.

"Hey, I need to talk to you about something before I head out for the day."

She stilled at the shift in his tone. He wasn't teasing now.

"Is this an off-the-lap conversation?"

Rhett grinned and placed his hands on her hips, firmly holding her in place. "Nope, you're good. Please remain seated." He bit his lower lip and winked, which instantly forced her to clench her thighs together. She didn't know any other man in his mid-twenties who could get away with a legitimate wink.

"You love it here, right, beautiful?"

"Here? Like in this bed straddling you?"

"Here at the cabin," he clarified, his tone soft but serious.

"This cabin is one of my favorite places in the world. You know that."

"Good. Because it's yours now. Or ours, I should say."

Tori sat up straighter, bringing her hands to her hips. "Ours? What the hell does that mean?"

"It means you're home, V." He smiled again, one of the biggest, most genuine smiles she'd ever seen grace his gorgeous face. It was almost enough to distract her from what he was saying. Almost, but not quite.

"Seriously. What's that supposed to mean? My home is in Hampton," she countered. She wasn't mad, but she was confused.

"My parents are gifting us the cabin as a wedding present. We have so many happy memories here. They want us to have it. This place— this room—it's all yours now."

Tori mouth fell open, but no words came out. Anne and Peter were just giving them a house?

"They were going to surprise us during the reception," he continued, his teeth working the inside of his cheek as he tried to explain. "But I knew you would hate that. I didn't want to shock you or have you worry about what your dad would think about the gift." He knew her so well. "I insisted I had to tell you in advance or we couldn't accept. I'm sorry if that takes away from the whole surprise. My mom was disappointed, but..."

"This cabin? All this?" She waved one hand around them. "This is all *ours* now?"

"Welcome home, beautiful."

She let herself fall, felt her body fold over his as she smothered him with kisses.

Welcome home.

She'd been coming up to the cabin with the Wheelers since she was in middle school. Every inch of the gorgeous lake house was filled with memories. Each panel of wood already felt like home.

She gave him one last kiss and sighed against his lips. "Rhett... It's too much." That was the truth. The Wheelers had already done so much for them, especially over the last few weeks. They had paid for the entire wedding already—they didn't need to give them an additional gift.

"I thought you might say something like that," he murmured, blowing out a long breath as he gently shifted her off his lap and onto the bed. He turned to his side and propped himself up with one elbow. "Here's the deal, beautiful. My parents were planning to sell the cabin in the next few years anyways. With Maddie leaving for school on the West Coast, she'll probably only be home a few times a year, and after your surgeries are over, my mom wants to start traveling with my dad on his business trips like she did before we were born. They knew you and I were the only ones who would get any use out of this place in the future. And they know how much you love it. I knew you would have refused had we talked about it in advance, so I already accepted it for us. Please don't be mad," he begged, reaching out to stroke his thumb along the curve of her jaw. "I hated not running it past you, but I also didn't want you to stress about another big decision right now."

Everything he said made sense. Once she was done feeling unworthy of such an extravagant gift, she knew she was going to be unbelievably happy about owning this little slice of heaven.

"Who else knows about this?" she asked.

He winced. "Jake."

"So everyone?"

"No, no way. He swore he wouldn't bring it up to anyone or even to you if you didn't mention it first. He knows you, V. He knew how you'd react to all this. And the only reason I even told him was because I needed a gut check to make sure I was doing the right thing by not telling you in advance."

She had the momentary urge to make him sweat, just a little. But regardless of how she *thought* she should feel about being gifted an entire house, she couldn't help the genuine giddiness that dominated her thoughts.

"You did good, almost-husband," she confirmed, leaning forward to kiss him again.

"Yeah?"

"Yep. But wait. You don't expect me to live here, do you?"

"No, of course not. I know you want to be in Hampton. And this place is farther from Virginia. You can live at your dad's house or even at my parents' house, and I'll come home as many weekends as I can, just like we planned. Whenever we want or need to get away, the cabin is here for us. I don't expect us to ever live here full time. But I have the sneaking suspicion that these walls are going to feel more like home than anywhere else."

She sighed wistfully, looking around at the room she loved. "Honestly? They already do."

"This place is where we're happiest, V. It's where I feel closest to you, where I feel most like myself. Here, in this cabin, we're timeless. This place will always be a sanctuary for us."

A sanctuary.

A place where they were timeless.

A place to call home.

Tori closed her eyes and took a steadying breath as Rhett interlaced their fingers together. Today was already exceeding her every expectation, and she hadn't even gotten out of bed yet.

Her eyes shot open when a loud bang ricocheted throughout the room. The mattress was sinking in the middle before she could even sit up and get her bearings.

"Good morning, love birds!" Jake announced, shoving up further in between them before lifting both his ink-covered arms behind his head and making himself comfortable in the middle of their bed. "I actually expected to find you in a much more precarious position than this," he admitted, glancing up and down Tori's T-shirt clad body before turning to look at Rhett. "Sup, bro? You ready to go? I was told to get your ass up and out of here, and you know Mama Wheeler doesn't like to tell me anything twice."

Tori bit down on her lip to hold in her laugh as she shifted into a cross-legged position. She caught Rhett's eye and mouthed, "I love you," before setting her sights on the man in the middle of their bed.

"What the hell, Jake? Did you really just barge in here and dent the wall of *my* house on my wedding day?"

Everyone was silent for all of two seconds because of her phony outburst.

"You already know?!" Jake pressed off the pillows to join her in a seated position in the middle of the bed. He moved close enough that their knees touched. She could feel the eagerness radiating off her friend, his unbridled joy contagious. He was like a puppy ready to play, just full of energy and excitement and love. But she still felt compelled to give him a hard time.

"I know. And if you want to keep your best man title, you'll do well to not destroy my property. You have two minutes to get out of this bed and out of my cabin."

Jake smirked in response to her playful scolding then moved even closer to wrap her in a big hug. He brushed the hair away from her ear before lowering his mouth and speaking softly so that only she could hear him. "Happy wedding day, baby. I love you, and I'm so happy for you guys. Take care of my boy."

"Always," she promised, almost choking on the word after hearing the unexpected sincerity of his request. "Now get out of here for real. The sooner you guys leave, the sooner you can come back."

Jake rose from the bed and punched Rhett in the arm. He made quick work of collecting the garment bags from the closet and grabbing his friend's toiletries and overnight bag from the bathroom. He was obviously taking his newly minted best man title to heart. "Come on, bro. You heard the lady of the house. We're out."

Rhett stood up to leave, his gaze fixed on her as he slowly made his way around the bed. "You know you're making my dreams come true today, V."

Tori nodded, reveling in the solidity of his presence as he gently cupped her face in his hands. "Mine too," she admitted. She looked down at the white sheets before she spoke again. "I can't believe that we almost didn't make it. All the times I refused to admit how I felt, all the times I tried not to let you get too close..."

"Hey," he cut her off. "None of that. Not today. Hell, not ever again. We're done living in the past. It doesn't matter how we got here. You know I never gave up hope. I knew we'd get here one day."

"I love you."

"See you down there, beautiful." He kissed her forehead, lingering for longer than usual, offering a thousand promises about today and all their days to come. He straightened up and walked backwards toward the door, not taking his eyes off her the entire time.

CHAPTER SEVENTEEN

Rhett

There wasn't a nerve in his body that wasn't ablaze. That wasn't to say he was nervous. In fact, he felt the opposite. Rhett felt better—steadier—more like himself than he had in weeks as he stood by the lake, waiting for his bride. He was just all lit up inside. He felt so alive.

He caught the first glimpse of her emerging from the cabin long before he could really see her. Normally the walk from the porch to the lakeshore took no time at all. But right now, it seemed like miles stretched between them.

Even though he couldn't make out any of her features yet, he could feel her presence whispering to the deepest parts of his soul. It had always been like this between them—an instant spark, a constant hum. A soul-deep connection that bound them to one another years ago, when he was just a lanky preteen boy with a heart of gold, and she was just a strong-willed girl who would only go soft for him.

Tori's features came more into focus as she approached. She had one arm woven through her dad's arm while the other hand grasped a clean-cut bouquet of white calla lilies. The thin gold necklace she was wearing was new, or at least he hadn't seen it before. Her diamond chip earrings had been a birthday present he gave her when she turned eighteen. He had saved up for three months to afford them, proud he didn't have to ask his parents for money to buy his girlfriend a gift. He had offered to upgrade them before the wedding, but she wouldn't hear it. He wasn't surprised. She had loved him for so long, and the earrings were symbolic of that. The monetary value of the jewelry she wore was insignificant compared to what those earrings represented.

A light shove from behind pulled him out of his head. He turned to glare at Jake, only to find his best friend grinning at him from ear to ear.

"Bro," he exhaled. That was it. But Rhett knew exactly what he meant.

"I know," he responded as he matched Jake's grin, awestruck at the sight of his bride closing in on them.

Come on, V, he silently urged, ready to seal the connection between them that had been written in the stars above a broken fence in Hampton, Ohio all those years ago. Once she was standing by his side, he could exhale.

Tori's gaze lifted. She was less than ten feet away now, her spine long, her head held high. Her green eyes sparkled as they scanned their friends and family. She still hadn't looked directly at him.

That's it, beautiful. I'm here. I'm ready when you are. Let me be your last.

He was okay waiting. He'd waited for her for years. He would have waited even longer if that was what she needed. Hell, he would have waited forever if it meant they would be together in the end.

He knew what she was doing. It wasn't a taunt or a tease. She was honoring everyone else who had contributed to this day. She wanted others to feel seen. She needed them to know they were appreciated. She would make sure everyone else was taken care of before she'd finally turn to him.

Because once their eyes locked, it was over. This was it. Their beginning. His always end game. Once Tori finally met his gaze, he was never letting her go.

Paul Thompson took the final steps forward, wrapping Tori into a hug before slowly backing away. He looked up and met Rhett's eyes, his request playing across his features without any words passing between them.

Rhett nodded his acceptance, but that wasn't good enough for Paul. In two strides, they were toe-to-toe. One second later, his arms were around Rhett. He didn't say anything, but he didn't have to. A collective sigh came from the crowd when the two men embraced.

After a few more seconds, Paul pulled away, retreating quickly to find his seat.

Tori stepped up to fill in the space her dad had just vacated. Rhett instantly reached for her hand.

This was it. There was only this moment. There was only her.

She finally lifted her chin and locked eyes with him, the widest smile taking over her whole face as moisture welled in the corners of both eyes.

Everything they had ever been to each other and everything they were promising to be blended in that moment. Every kiss. Every heartbreak. Every secret. Every fear. It had been a long, hard road to get here. And he'd do it all again, a dozen times over, just to stand next to her today.

Rhett reached out his hands and wrapped them gently around her lace-covered arms, pulling her close. He bowed his head in reverence, not bothering to hold in the groan that escaped him.

He lowered his head even further to brush his nose against hers. "Damn, you're pretty."

"Everhett." She sighed, leaning into him and going soft in his arms.

"We made it, beautiful. We're finally here."

"We made it," she repeated, a single tear tracking down her cheek. He leaned in on instinct and brought his lips to the side of her face, kissing away the moisture and silently promising to be the one to kiss away all her tears from now on. He placed another kiss along her jaw, then tilted her head slightly so he could place another on her lips.

"I've got you," he vowed, tightening his grip and pulling her into a hug, careful not to catch the lace of the top of her dress or disrupt the perfectly pinned curls piled on top of her head.

A distinct throat-clearing caught his attention. It was then that Rhett remembered where they were and what they were supposed to be doing right now.

"Uh, you guys know you're not actually married yet, right?" Jake asked. "You've got to like, say the words and do the ring thing before you just stand there and force us all to watch you make out."

Rhett just shook his head, not bothering to turn around or tell him off. Nothing could get to him today. They were here. They were finally fucking here. And there was nowhere else he'd rather be.

Tori laughed softly, raising her hand to wipe away one more stray tear. "Really, Jake?"

"*There* she is," Jake stated proudly. "See? This is why I'm the best man. He's got you all teary-eyed and weepy before the ceremony even starts. You were gonna be pissed if you were crying in all your wedding pictures, baby. *I've* got you."

"I see those wheels spinning, Mr. Wheeler."

He smiled down at the woman in his arms: his girl, the love of his life, and now, his wife. *Fuck.* They were married. Tori was his wife.

"It's like you know me or something," he teased, bowing his head to place a soft kiss on her lips. They'd only been dancing together for two songs. One thing Rhett hadn't expected was how often he and Tori would be pulled away from each other during their own wedding reception. He wrapped her tighter into him, not willing to let her out of his arms anymore tonight.

"I'd like to think I can read my husband."

He groaned in appreciation. "Say it again," he urged.

"Say what?"

"You know what."

"Oh, you like it when I say husband?"

"Hell yes, beautiful. I waited years just for you to call me your goddamn boyfriend again. Hearing you call me your husband? It's an indescribable feeling. I know we just took our vows, but can you promise to never stop calling me that?"

She leaned in closer and whispered her reply. "Anything for you, husband."

Rhett lowered his head again to kiss her before trailing his mouth along her neck to find the sweet spot right below her ear. She sighed into him, gently scraping her nails against the short hairs above the collar of his suit. Every part of her leaned into him, like her body was subconsciously seeking as much contact as possible. He would never tire of feeling her go soft. After years of being held at arm's length, he would never tire of finally getting to hold her.

"I've got one more surprise for you tonight," he murmured into her ear.

Tori grinned up at him, shaking her head at the same time. "You're unbelievable, you know that? Don't you think planning our entire wedding and honeymoon and giving me a house is enough for one day, husband?"

He didn't miss the use of his new favorite word.

"Technically the cabin wasn't from me." He shrugged nonchalantly before turning Tori's body toward the lake and wrapping his arms around her waist from behind. He had seen the spotlight on the boat flash twice over her shoulder less than a minute ago. It wouldn't be long now.

"Oh, is this my surprise?" she teased, pushing her ass into his lower half.

"Behave," he scolded, bringing his hands to her hips to still her body against his. "Just watch."

The first firework illuminated the night sky two seconds later: a cascade of gold that looked double its actual size thanks to the reflection in the lake. A series of dazzling sizzlers followed the first explosion as everyone around them turned to watch the surprise show.

"Rhett!" she exclaimed, smacking his arm in disbelief as more bursts of light and color filled the sky. This was about to be more than just a few stray bottle rockets. Jake had $10,000 worth of pyrotechnics on the other side of the lake.

"Today's the first day of our forever, beautiful. I wanted it to start with a bang."

The line was cheesy, but she grinned up at him anyways before wrapping her hand around his neck. He rested his chin on her shoulder and held her tight, inhaling her familiar rosemary and mint scent as they stood together at the edge of the lake, husband and wife, at the cabin they could now call home.

CHAPTER EIGHTEEN

She ran her hands up and down the delicate lace of the white and blush body suit as she assessed herself in the bathroom mirror. How many times had she stood in this bathroom and peered into this exact mirror? She didn't know where all her nerves were coming from. Nothing was technically different. But everything was forever changed.

Tori finally understood why people said their wedding day was the happiest day of their lives. Happy wasn't a big enough word to describe how she was feeling. She couldn't even think of a single word that could encompass everything they had experienced that day. The memories would be with her, always.

The laughs and smiles and squeals of glee she shared with Lia, Maddie, and Anne as they all got ready together that morning.

The confidence and sexiness she felt when she took private photos in the bedroom that afternoon.

The magic of stepping into a beautiful wedding dress that fit like a glove.

The joy of seeing all their friends and family gathered to celebrate them.

Rhett's smile when they finally came together at the lakeshore. The way he pulled her in and held her tight like he was never going to let her go.

The love in her dad's eyes when he saw her in her wedding dress for the first time. The tenderness of his gaze when he handed her a small box and an envelope.

It was the sweetest surprise, the best wedding gift she could have ever possibly received. The box contained a delicate gold link necklace. No charms or jewels hung from the simple piece.

She smiled when she first accepted the gift. It was classic and simple and so perfectly him. "Daddy, it's beautiful. Thank you."

Her dad shook his head and averted his eyes to the envelop in her hand. "It's not from me. Well, technically, I picked it out and bought it, but I didn't originally buy it for you."

Tori's eyes grew wide as a sneaking suspicion crept into her consciousness. She ripped the unmarked card open more carelessly than she should have. Something told her she should take her time and savor the experience, but she couldn't let herself hope without confirmation.

A simple notecard rested inside the envelope. Her mother's handwriting filled the page.

My beautiful Victoria--

You have not heard my voice in years, but I hope you hear it now. I hope you feel me beside you as you read this note. I hope you feel me with you, always.

If you are reading this, it's because you are about to walk down the aisle and get married. I had a hell of a time convincing your father to do this for me. But I trust he waited, just like I trust that you two cared for each other over all these years. What I wouldn't give to blink away tears of joy as I watch the two of you walk arm-in-arm down the aisle at your wedding.

I don't know the person you're marrying, but I know my daughter. If someone has won your heart, it's because they have earned the honor of loving you. Do not let your own fears keep you from loving someone completely, sweet girl. To love and be loved is the greatest gift you can give your beloved and yourself.

Your father gave me this necklace the night before our wedding, and now we are both giving it to you. I hope the simple chain design reminds you that everything is connected. Even when a story seems to be ending, another has already begun.

I hope you are happy. I hope you are free. I hope you allow yourself to feel it all. I hope you get everything you want out of your one precious life. I hope you chose to spend that life with someone who adores you.

Please know that I hear you when you whisper to me at night, sweet girl. It may be years since you have heard my voice, but I always whisper back. I love you more than words. I am with you, always.

Until I see you again,

Mom

She hadn't had a chance to show Rhett the letter, but she told him all about the necklace when his fingers brushed against it during their first dance. The beautiful irony was that her mom did, in fact, know the man she was marrying. She had known him since he was six years old. Her mother knew him, and she had loved him. That Tori knew for sure thanks to the second envelope her father handed her after she opened the necklace. He called it the "only if" letter, which made sense once she read the second handwritten note from her mom.

Sweet girl,

If you are reading this letter, please remind your father that he owes me $50. I always knew you were going to end up with Everhett Wheeler.

Tori grinned at the opening line, tickled to see a bit of her mother's humor on the page. The letter continued:

Give Rhett all my love. Oh what I wouldn't give to see you two dancing together at your wedding! It seems silly to think about that now as I write this letter, considering you're only eleven years old, but a mother always knows. If that boy loves you with the same kind of ferocity he displayed as your friend growing up, then I know for a fact that you've made the right choice.

I want to tell you a secret. Although I'm sure it drove him crazy, I made your father swear to me that he would never mend the broken

spot in the fence. He didn't understand why I was so insistent, but I'm
sure I made a big enough fuss that he wouldn't dare fix it.
Sometimes we don't see what's right in front of us when it's whole.
Sometimes we don't realize the true value of something until it breaks.
And sometimes a broken fence is meant to stay broken. Otherwise,
nothing gets through. Not even the good things.
Take care of one another, and remember that there's beauty in the
broken. That's how the love gets in.
All my blessings and all my love,
Mom

She had always wondered if her mom had any inklings about her future relationship with Rhett. They hadn't officially started dating until they were fourteen years old. It had always been him, and her mom obviously knew it.

Tori held both letters to her chest, trying to absorb all the love and wisdom her mom bestowed upon her when she penned them years ago.

"Hey, V, you okay in there?"

Rhett's soft knock on the bathroom door brought her mind back to the present moment. She had no idea how long she'd been standing there, lost in thought, treading through memories. She let out a long breath to steady herself before responding.

"I'm good. I'll be right out."

She ran her hands down the see-through lace bodysuit she had picked out for tonight. She and Lia had made time earlier in the week to go shopping. Her best friend had encouraged her to break in the new rose gold Amex Rhett had ordered in her name. He didn't know it yet, but she had an entire suitcase of lingerie and new bathing suits packed for their honeymoon. The lingerie was for their trip, but she had also made good use of it earlier that day during her secret boudoir shoot. She wasn't the only one who could pull off a surprise.

Tori finished wiping the lipstick off her mouth and swapped it out for her favorite sweet mint lip balm. She left the rest of her professionally applied makeup in place, and she didn't dare touch the perfectly pinned curls of her hair. Rhett had leaned in close during the fireworks and mentioned something about messing up her hair just like he did on prom night. She was willing and eager to recreate that memory with him. She took in a deep breath, filling her lungs to capacity, before she finally turned and opened the bathroom door.

She stepped into the master bedroom—*their* master bedroom— and felt his gaze land on her immediately. He was perched on the end of the bed, stripped down to nothing but his suit pants.

Damn. He looked so good. Her husband was hot as hell.

"Fuck me," he groaned as she made her way across the room to join him.

"Oh, I fully intend to, husband."

"Seriously, V. You look *amazing*. You're a knockout. I don't even know what this thing is, but I want to rip it off your body right now."

"I'll let you rip it if you want."

He growled in response, hooking his fingers under the high-cut elastic above her hips and using his hold to steer her to him. She stepped in between his legs, wrapping her arms around his neck and bringing his head to rest against her chest.

"Not tonight," he relented, gazing up to look at her. "I feel like I'm gonna want to see this again."

She hummed as his hands ran up the sides of her body and over the lace. He lowered his head to settle in between her pushed-up breasts. His fingertips teased at the thin straps over each arm.

"Want to know a secret?" she purred, running her polished nails through his hair and pulling his head tighter against her chest, urging him on.

"You bought this in every color?" He found the edge of the lace cup with his teeth and pulled, exposing just a hint of nipple over the fabric. He lapped at the dark pink bud, teasing out more with each lick until her entire breast was exposed. He left the other side in place for now, instead grazing over the thin lace and pinching her through the fabric. Each lick, each pinch, each graze of teeth sent a jolt of wanting to her core.

Feeling emboldened by his response, Tori lifted one leg and moved it to the outside of his thigh. She straddled herself on his pants-covered leg, pulling on his hair again in encouragement as he continued to lick and nip her breasts. She lowered the strap of the second side for him and let herself spill out of the top of the bodysuit.

"Well, not this exact one," she finally responded as she started to grind up and down against his him. She would have gladly been riding something else already, but she wanted to draw out this night as long as possible. "But there's more where this came from. And there *are* lots of different colors."

Rhett's head snapped up as realization dawned on him. "Your shopping trip with Lia?" he inquired as he connected the dots.

"Mhmm," she confirmed as she grinded her hips back and forth again. The pressure on her clit was everything. Now if he would only resume what he was doing to her chest moments ago... "I figured if you could plan our entire honeymoon, I could at least have something new to wear each night. Plus, I needed options for the photoshoot I did earlier today."

His eyes grew wider as each confession spilled out of her. "What photoshoot?"

"The boudoir shoot I did right here on this bed," she confirmed. "The photographer will email me proofs in the next day or two." She couldn't help but smile when she thought about showing Rhett the pictures. There was nothing she could buy him that he couldn't buy himself. But this? This was the perfect wedding gift for the man who had it all.

"Fuck," he muttered under his breath, running his hand harshly through his hair, a fire blazing bright in his grey-blue eyes. "Up," he instructed, rising to his feet and displacing her from his lap.

"Rhett!" she protested, her body already missing the feeling of him below her. Was he upset about the photoshoot? He had explained a few weeks ago that all the vendors had been asked to sign NDAs because of his position at NorfolkStar. She double-checked the photographer's storage and backup processes, too. Everything had checked out.

He locked her in a searing gaze, his expression hard as he removed his belt. When she pouted, pushing out her lower lip, his eyes narrowed. "Do you really think I'm going to let your first orgasm as my wife come from you dry humping my leg?"

Oh. That was it. He wasn't mad about the pictures. Pride wouldn't allow her golden boy to give her anything but the best on their wedding night. She felt her cheeks heat as he simply smirked.

"Get on the bed, beautiful. Show me exactly how you posed for your little photoshoot today."

Tori bit down on her bottom lip again but didn't bother sassing back. She followed his instructions exactly, moving her body to the center of the white sheets, propping herself up on her knees, then spreading her legs as wide as they could go before lowering back down. She placed both her hands on her inner thighs, right along her bikini line, before finally lifting her head to meet his eyes.

Rhett had removed all his clothes by the time she looked up. He stood before her, gripping his own length, assessing her up and down as he stared at her exposed breasts and the way her fingertips teased at the fabric covering her core.

"*That* is how you posed?"

"Oh, Ev. Don't be such a stiff. This is just one of the ways I posed. And this is pretty PG compared to some of the other shots I took for you." She winked at him for good measure.

"You did this all for me?"

"Yes."

"These pictures are *only* for me?"

"Yes."

His gaze drifted down to where her hands were still resting on her inner thighs. "Did you touch yourself in any of the pictures?"

Heat crept up her neck as she thought about a few of the racier poses. Everything was tasteful, even the close up shots, like the ones where she pinched her nipples through the lingerie or let her own fingers find the sweet shot between her thighs. She wasn't sure she'd have the courage to take things that far when the shoot first started, but she felt so comfortable with the photographer. The two glasses of champagne she drank while she was getting her hair done may have also helped.

She did the photoshoot for him, but she did it for herself as well. She wanted to have something to give Rhett since they'd be apart so much over the next few years. She also wanted to have something to keep for herself, knowing that her body was going to change drastically over the next year because of the preventative surgeries.

"V?" he questioned when she didn't answer right away.

"Yes."

"Yes what?"

"Yes, I touched myself in some of the pictures I took today."

Rhett stroked himself faster in response to her words. He was still positioned at the foot of the bed, watching her. His voice was a full octave lower than normal. "And what were you thinking about when you touched yourself?"

She met his eyes with a heat she hoped matched his sultry gaze. She peered down at his long, hard dick and licked her lips. "My husband."

"Fuck me," he muttered for the second time that night as he finally gave in and joined her on the bed. "You never cease to amaze me, beautiful."

"Pretty good start to a marriage, huh?"

"I'll show you a good start to a marriage." He used his hands to ease her back, laying her down gently in the middle of the bed. He brought his mouth to her ear as his entire body hovered over hers. She could feel the heat radiating off him. She could feel the want pulsing between her thighs. The soul-deep attraction that had taken hold of them years ago was presenting as a physical ache tonight. She needed him now. She needed him more than ever.

"Here's the plan," he crooned in her ear. "First, I'm going to go down on you, because I want to know exactly what my wife tastes like on our wedding night." She gulped in response to his words.

"Then I'm going to take you from behind so I can fully appreciate this ass you were teasing me with on the dance floor." He groaned, digging into the fleshy part of her hip with one hand. "After that, I'm going to lay you back on this bed, on *our* bed in *our* house, and I'm going to worship every part of you. Because as much as I want to fuck you right now, it's still our wedding night, and tonight I will make love to my wife."

Leave it to Rhett to have a sex checklist for their first night as a married couple. He always had loved a good plan.

She didn't even have time to respond before he had made his way down the bed and settled in between her legs. "Lift," he instructed as he grasped both hips, encouraging her to lift up so he could pull her lingerie down. He peeled her out of the lacy one piece, folding it once before gently tossing it off to the side. Then he turned back to her, his gaze locked on her center as he lowered his head between her thighs.

"Rhett," she moaned in encouragement, running her nails against his scalp and mussing up his perfectly styled hair. He didn't tease her or delay giving her everything he had just promised. The lingering touches and his words alone had worked her up enough. He licked her from the opening of her pussy to the tip of her clit, adding pressure the closer he came to her tightly wound bundle of nerves. He repeated the motion, over and over again, lingering to lap at her most sensitive spot each time he landed on his target.

"I love your mouth," she cooed, finally giving in to the urge to raise her hips and thrust against his face. She didn't want to rush it—but she was desperate for more.

"Mhmm," he murmured between her legs, his growl sending a vibration through her core. "And how do you feel about my hands?" He teased her opening with just the tip of one finger, chuckling to himself when she shifted down the bed to force him deeper. He slid in effortlessly, her arousal coating his hand as he continued to eat her out like he was starving.

The combination of his mouth pressed against her and his hand working inside her had her whole body flushed with desire. She ran her fingers through his hair again before moving her hands up to squeeze her nipples. There was no better feeling than letting herself get lost in him. He kept her present. He held her steady. He prioritized her pleasure and had always found his own indulgences in getting her off.

She was lost to his rhythm, her mind solely focused on the pattern he had established now. Just when she felt her orgasm begin to build, he changed it up. He kept his hand in place, curling two fingers and instantly drawing out a moan with his ministrations. He worked his mouth up her body, kissing harshly against her hips, biting hungrily at the dip of her waist. When he took one entire nipple into his mouth, her hips jolted involuntarily.

He didn't move on like she expected, though. No. He took his time, savoring her, lapping at her nipple with the same rapt attention he had just showed her clit. He sucked the first pink bud to a taut peak, then ran his teeth against the sensitive tip. She pushed into his mouth, desperate for more of him. He bit down quickly before running his tongue over her breast to soothe the sting. He moved to the other side, repeating the sucking and the nipping and marking while driving her higher and higher. He matched each movement of his mouth with a stroke of the fingers inside her, bringing her body to the brink.

She lifted her hips up to grind against him, desperately seeking the friction she craved. "Rhett, please. I need you. Fuck me," she begged. She grasped at the back of his neck and dragged his face to hers, catching his lips in a demanding kiss.

"No," he spoke against her mouth before abandoning the kiss and working back down her body.

"No?"

"Not no—just not yet. I told you the plan. I want to make you come with my mouth first…"

"Everhett." She dragged out his full name in an exasperated plea.

"Victoria," he countered, holding her firmly by the hips, his chin resting just below her belly button. She glanced down to meet his eyes and got lost in the grey-blue irises she had been staring into for the better part of the last ten years. He smirked now that he had her attention, maintaining eye contact as he traced feather-light kisses down her stomach to her core. He flattened his tongue against her clit, applying pressure, giving her the friction she craved, and hitting the exact spot she needed to reach that perfect peak of pleasure.

He lifted his mouth away from her just an inch, just for a moment, just long enough to make his case. "Let me do this for you, beautiful. Let me take care of my wife. Then I promise I'll fuck you, and we can come together."

Tori closed her eyes again and surrendered to his desires. He was all business now—stroking her with his tongue, sucking her clit into his mouth, and nipping her with his teeth until she was a panting, writhing mess. Even after she fell apart he continued to savor her. He lapped at her folds and kissed her all over as she rode out the aftershocks of pleasure.

After her first orgasm, Rhett kept every promise he made that night: he took her from behind and sent her spiraling again as he pounded into her. Then he spent hours making love to her, making promises to her body, tethering their souls together in a flurry of passion and pleasure. They each came multiple times, only stopping once they were both completely sated. They started to drift asleep, tangled in each other's arms, Rhett still inside her. "I love you, beautiful," was the last thing she heard before they both gave in and closed their eyes on the happiest day of their lives.

CHAPTER NINETEEN

Rhett

"This is crazy!" Tori hadn't stopped smiling since they boarded the plane. NorfolkStar's private jet was on the smaller side, but it was the pinnacle of luxury: all modern technology and sleek edges, decorated in white and chrome. His granddad had let them borrow the private plane to fly to their honeymoon then back home again. He had kept the secret from Tori up until they arrived at the airport, feeling badass and a little smug when they bypassed the commercial terminal and drove straight to a tarmac where the jet was fueled and waiting.

"Buckle up, beautiful," he instructed, nodding toward the lap belt in her seat. They were positioned across from each other in plush executive chairs.

"So, husband"—he grinned at her casual use of what was quickly becoming his favorite word in the world—"now that we're sitting on a plane, are you finally going to tell me where we're going?" She shifted in her plush leather seat, stretching her legs across the space between them and resting them in his lap. She had already kicked off her sandals, so he instinctively wrapped his hands around her bare feet, kneading into her arches.

She looked impossibly beautiful sitting before him. She was wearing a flowy white sun dress with just a little braid across the front of her hair. She seemed perfectly relaxed, too, even though she'd only flown twice in her life. She was always so brave and unshakeable. He loved her fearlessness and willingness to try something new.

"Sure," he replied casually, like he hadn't been keeping this whole trip a secret for weeks. They only had six days together because he had to get back to Virginia for his first official week of work. He had researched and planned every second of this honeymoon, determined to give her the trip of a lifetime.

"We're going to Charleston, South Carolina. I booked us a private villa at a boutique hotel across the harbor from the city. We'll be ten minutes from downtown, twenty minutes from the beach. We're staying until Friday, and I have plans for each and every day."

The biggest smile graced her face, her joy radiating off her and warming every part of him. "What kind of plans?" she asked suggestively as she curled her toes in his hands.

"Oh, I've got plenty of those kinds of plans for you, beautiful, but I made other plans for us, too. Private garden tours. A gallery visit. Dinner at the chef's counter at one of the best restaurants in the city. A couple's massage. A day at the beach. Shopping at the market. A ghost walk."

"A ghost walk!?" she exclaimed.

He laughed at her outburst. He didn't know what the hell a ghost walk was either until the ads popped up on every vacation planning site he could find about Charleston. "I'm pretty sure it's just something tourists do, but I wanted to make sure we got the full experience. I'll hold your hand," he promised as he continued to massage her feet.

Just because they'd had a small wedding didn't mean the party didn't go on for hours last night. He knew they'd both be tired today after all the planning and buildup and then the actual wedding. He was glad he hadn't planned anything for their first day beyond checking in and ordering room service.

He watched with interest as Tori pulled out her phone and smiled as soon as her eyes focused on the screen. Their friends and family had been posting pictures and video on social since before they woke up that morning. They wouldn't get the official wedding pictures back for a few weeks, but it was fun to see so many candid shots of what had undoubtedly been the best day of his life.

"What are you looking at?" he prompted when her smile grew even wider.

"Just a few sneak peeks from the photographer."

"Oh, nice. I want to see." He held out his hand for her phone.

"These aren't wedding pictures," she admitted, biting down on her bottom lip as she gazed up at him through her lashes. If they were from the photographer, but they weren't actual wedding pictures...

Realization and excitement both hit at the same time. "Tori. Hand me that phone."

"I just texted them to you." She shook her head and continued to eye him from her seat. His hand was in his pocket so fast he was afraid he was going to fumble and drop the stupid device. He unlocked the home screen and navigated through all the notifications until he found her text.

He sucked in a breath and immediately zoomed in on the first picture. All he could do was stare. There she was, kneeling on the master bed in the cabin—on *their* bed in *their* cabin—wearing what looked like just a bunch of crisscrossed silky fabric that hugged the curves of her body and left almost nothing to the imagination. Not that it mattered—he had memorized every curve and contour of her body over the last several years. He didn't need a photo to visualize the woman he adored, but damn, it was still a pretty picture. He zoomed in a bit more, focusing on her expression. She wasn't looking at the camera, instead staring toward the window, the sun illuminating her face and giving her an angelic glow.

His angel. His love. His entire heart. His wife.

She pulled his attention back to her when she ran her bare foot up and down his thigh, teasing him before he caught her ankle in his grasp and forced her to still. "Behave," he muttered, glancing up from the phone to look into her eyes.

"I have that packed in my suitcase, you know."

Rhett held back a smirk as he just shook his head. *This girl.* He was so in love with her he could barely think straight. He let his hand wander a bit further up her leg, gently cupping her calf before his fingers brushed against the back of her knee. His phone vibrating in his lap doused the heat that was starting to build between them.

It was just a notification for the latest round of emails being sent to his work account. His colleagues knew he was on his honeymoon, and his out of office message was set, but that didn't mean business came to a halt. He expected his assistant Quinn to send him pertinent updates throughout the week, and he'd still receive all the standard reports each day so he could catch up at the end of their trip.

"I'm tempted to turn this thing off and just leave it off for the rest of the week," he mumbled, unable to resist the temptation to open the Mail app and clear out a few of the messages.

"So do it," Tori suggested. "What's the worst that could happen?"

What was the worst that could happen? He wasn't supposed to be working this week. He knew his assistant *and* his granddad would chew him out if he tried to respond to anything during his honeymoon. More importantly, he wanted to be fully present with and for Tori. This was their time. These were the memories they would cherish for a lifetime.

"If I forward you all our reservations and our itinerary, can we use your phone during the trip?"

She nodded, watching him intently as he made his decision.

"Okay then. I'm turning this off until Friday. But you have to promise me one thing, V."

"What's that?"

"You will tell me and, more importantly, you will *show me* the second anymore pictures like that come through."

"You've got yourself a deal, Wheeler," she promised, leaning forward to kiss him.

"So what do you think?" he asked tentatively, leaning against the rooftop balcony to gaze out across the harbor. The afternoon sun was still high in the sky, casting an ethereal light on the city of Charleston. The view was amazing, but it was nothing compared to the luxury of their accommodations for the week.

Their private villa was two stories and separate from the main hotel. It was called a villa, but it was really more like a small house, complete with a fully stocked bar and kitchen, a massive master bedroom and bathroom, plush robes, an electric fireplace, 24/7 room service, and every other amenity imaginable. The upper level opened up to an expansive balcony complete with a hammock, a plunge pool, and a little café table for two.

Tori sighed before reaching over to wrap her arms around his waist. "It's incredible. I can't believe this is my life right now."

"*Our* life," he amended as he wrapped an arm around her shoulders and kissed the top of her head.

"I can't believe we're really here. That we actually got to come on a honeymoon. These last few weeks... everything happened so quickly. I honestly don't know how you pulled it off. I didn't realize a honeymoon was even something I wanted until we got here. I can't wait to explore this city and just spend time with you." She shifted into the space between the balcony ledge and his body, her back pressed into his chest, then reached an arm up and cupped the back of his neck.

"Is that something you want to do more of, V? Do you want to travel?"

Her fingers stilled, but she didn't respond right away. When she finally replied, her voice quivered with uncertainty.

"I honestly never gave it much thought. The only thing I've really wanted for the last several years was to get a full-time job with benefits so I could have surgery. I accepted a long time ago that some things were just never going to be an option for me, so I never gave myself permission to dream. It sounds really sad and pathetic to say, but that was my reality."

Rhett hugged her tighter, trying to absorb the ache in her confession.

"It's not pathetic, but I don't want you to think like that anymore, beautiful. I want you to come up with the wildest, craziest ideas and give yourself permission to want them for your life. We can travel. You can paint. We can start a family. We can live on a remote island somewhere. Money isn't an issue, and it never will be. Now that we have a plan for your surgeries... I want you to dream. And I want you to let me help make those dreams come true."

She pulled her hand away to wipe an unshed tear before craning her neck back to look in his eyes. "I think I want to get my BFA." Rhett closed his eyes as her words sunk in. They had talked about this months ago, and Tori had dismissed the idea outright. A Fine Arts degree was more aligned with her passion for painting, but it didn't seem practical given the vision she had for her future.

"Since I'm going to take a year off school anyways for the surgeries, and since money isn't an issue, I might as well go for the degree I really want." She paused then, and he knew she was waiting for his reaction before she'd let herself continue.

"I think that's an amazing dream, V."

"And then when I finally graduate with my BFA, I want to go to Europe. I want to travel all over Italy and France. I want to go to every museum and see everything. And I want to do it all with you."

"We'll make it happen," he vowed, hugging her against his chest. There wasn't a dream she could come up with that he wouldn't spend the rest of his life working toward for her. She had been his dream for so damn long... and now he had everything. He wanted to spend the rest of his life helping her figure out and pursue dreams of her own.

"Rhett?"

"Yeah, beautiful?"

"I really don't know if having kids is one of my dreams. I spent so long playing caretaker to my dad. I don't even know if I'd be any good at it, considering my mom was only around for the first eleven years of my life..."

"That's okay," he responded without hesitation. "Really. I'm not opposed to the idea of having kids, but it's honestly not something I ever dreamed about for myself. I spent so long focused on just one dream," he squeezed his arms around her for emphasis. "My plan for my own future was always either just me, or you and me. The only thing I ever wanted for myself was you."

They were both quiet then, soaking in each other's words, basking in the blending of their dreams for the future. His biggest dream had already been achieved. It was her. It had always been her. Getting to love Tori out loud was all he wanted and all he would ever need.

"Do you want to call Dr. Silko and give her an update? Would it help not to have that hanging over your head while we're here?

She let out a soft sigh and turned around in his arms. "No. I still want to do the egg retrieval."

He tilted his head in question. "But you just said..."

"I know what I said. And I meant what I said. But if the last few months have taught me anything, it's how quickly the things we want and the things we think we know can change. A few months ago? I thought that right now we'd be broken up for good, and you'd already be gone to Virginia. Then I got that call... I can't even describe to you what it felt like to hear those words and feel them change me. Everything I thought I knew came unhinged in that moment. It was like my world tipped onto a new axis. I wasn't even scared. I just knew I needed you. After years of genuinely believing that you were better off without me in your life, suddenly, and with no concern for the consequences, I just wanted and needed you."

Rhett sucked in a deep breath, letting the inhalation steady him as he processed what she was saying. She was right. Life had a funny way of going sideways sometimes, which they had learned first-hand over the last few months.

"So I'm going to do the egg retrieval like we talked about," she concluded. "That way we don't have to make any final decisions now.

I have no desire or plans to have kids. But I also recognize that life doesn't always go how we think it's going to go. The call proved that to me."

"I love you," he said. It was all he could offer as his mind tried to make sense of everything she had just shared. He still wasn't used to Tori being so open and candid with him. It would take a long time before he got used to her not holding back.

"I love you too," she replied as she raised the back of her hand to her mouth to stifle a yawn. "I really am excited to head into the city and explore, but I think I'm going to need a nap. Or maybe a big coffee."

"Let's take a nap." He stretched out a hand as he headed back into the villa. She accepted his suggestion and slipped her hand into his, letting him lead her into the massive master bedroom. A cool blast of air conditioning hit them as they escaped the southern humidity. Tori made her way over to the bed, plopping down as another extended yawn escaped her.

Rhett chuckled to himself as he unzipped her suitcase and started to dig through her things. "Why didn't anyone warn us that weddings are crazy exhausting?" he mused as a huge yawn caught him by surprise. He shuffled around a few items in her suitcase—toiletries, sun hats, some lacy, sexy things that he'd never seen but couldn't wait for her to model—before he found his target. He pulled out an old Arch lacrosse T-shirt for her and a pair of basketball shorts from his own bag. His body forced out another yawn, as if he needed the reminder that they were both crashing fast.

"Here you go, beautiful." He handed her the T-shirt while he pulled off his shirt and quickly swapped out his shorts. Tori eyed him up and down as he changed, biting down on her lower lip as she assessed him. He didn't miss the mischievous glint in her gaze.

"V... We both need sleep," he chided.

"But I want you," she declared. Not a second later, another yawn caught her by surprise.

"If my memory serves me right, you've already had me several times in the last twenty-four hours." Rhett smirked. Their wedding night had exceeded every expectation in every way. It was almost unfathomable that they were still so hot for each other, so desperate to satiate the desire that ran between them like an electrical current. But somehow, after last night, he felt more connected and more deeply in love with his wife than ever. "And you can have me again, but not until we both rest," he insisted with a pointed look. He walked around to the other side of the California king and pulled back the covers. The crisp white sheets were a welcome invitation.

They met in the middle of the bed, their bodies instantly intertwining into a familiar, comfortable position. He wrapped his arms around her, cradling her body against his.

"I can't believe I really get to keep you," he whispered into her hair.

"Forever, Ev. Now and forever."

Her words wrapped him in a different kind of embrace: the confidence in her promise and the strength of her love serving as its own form of sustenance. Her love was all he needed, now and forever.

———

He didn't remember falling asleep, and he had no idea what time it was when he opened his eyes. He had been dreaming, which in and of itself was amazing. He couldn't remember the last time he had slept long enough or deeply enough to remember a dream.

He slowly came to, letting his body ease into awareness as he realized Tori was no longer in his arms. He ran a hand lazily down his face, the sensations from his dream still lingering.

It took a few more moments for him to realize that he wasn't just waking up from a hot dream: He was consciously living it. Tori wasn't in his arms anymore because she had retreated under the covers. Her entire body was resting between his legs, his rock-hard erection hovering just an inch away from her mouth.

He chuckled hoarsely, reaching down to pet her hair. "I legitimately thought I was dreaming. What time is it?"

"Shhh," she insisted. "It's the middle of the night, but I'm not tired anymore. Pretend you're still dreaming. Close your eyes and let me take care of you."

He groaned in response to her invitation, adjusting himself on the pillows and pushing down the duvet so he could watch.

She peered up at him through hooded lids. It was dark in the room —the sun had fully set, meaning they'd been sleeping for hours—but he could still make out her salacious smile, thanks to the ambient light coming in through the balcony windows. He gazed down at her again and realized they were both completely naked. She must have stripped them both before he woke up.

She's unbelievable.

Tori ran her hands up his inner thighs, letting her fingers linger on the taut muscles above his hips. She lifted her head and traced the same path with her tongue: first on the right hip, then on the left. She was kissing and licking and touching him everywhere but where he wanted to feel her most.

Rhett let out a long breath, willing himself to stay present. To not rush it. To enjoy this moment.

"Crazy to think I've never given my husband a blow job before," Tori murmured as she continued to kiss up and down his inner thigh. He felt her slide her hand up the opposite leg and wrap it around his balls. He couldn't help but let out a satisfied grunt.

He reached down and gently took hold of her chin. "No more teasing, wife. I want your mouth on me."

She moved her hand from his balls to his dick, circling his length with her fingers as she began to stroke him up and down. The motion was slow and drawn out, intimate and languid. She rested her cheek against the top of his thigh as she continued to jack him off. She gave no indication she was actually going to put him in her mouth like he requested.

"V…" It was a command as much as it was a plea.

He felt her shift again. She was still lying down between his legs, her head propped up just enough to be able to take him. He tensed as the tip of her tongue ran along the slit of his cock. She hummed appreciatively when the first drop of precum touched her lips. She ran her tongue back and forth along the underside of the crown of his penis. Every motion was drawn out as if she was savoring the most delicious meal.

"Tori," he hissed, his resolve to stay still and let her have her way with him quickly dissipating with each swipe of her tongue.

"I want you to take what you want, Ev." Her voice was shaky with need. Her desire to please him made him even harder. He wanted to fill her. He wanted to claim her, everywhere. He wanted to use his body to solidify every vow they had promised each other.

He growled in anticipation when she crawled off his lap and shifted onto her side. He rolled over to match her position, his erection perfectly aligned with her mouth. He moaned louder when she finally wrapped her lips around his cock, the wet heat sending shockwaves up his spine. She bobbed up and down his shaft, using one hand to keep his dick firmly held into her mouth while the other pulled on and massaged his balls.

Every lick, every suck, every bit of pressure had him buzzing. He loved everything about this woman: how she worked him up and worked him over. How she knew just what to do to make his abs clench in anticipation.

"Hey, Ev?" Her sticky-sweet tone pulled him out of his own thoughts. "You know getting you off gets me hot. I told you to take what you want. What I should have said was, will you please fuck my mouth?"

He didn't need to be told twice. He would do anything she wanted him to do, and she damn well knew it. If she wanted him to take his pleasure, he would take it.

He worked a hand into her hair, not forcing her head, but stabilizing her in place before he really let go. Tori whimpered around his dick in approval, granting him the permission he craved to abandon his restraint. He started slow, thrusting his hips forward as he fed her as much of his cock as she could handle. After a few more thrusts, she had taken him by the balls, literally, and was pulling him closer to urge him on. He picked up the pace and deepened the angle. This position allowed him to push all the way in and reach the back of her throat, eliciting a moan from both of them with every hit.

His legs began to shake when she loosened her hold on his sack and pressed up with one knuckle behind his balls. He lost the rhythm then, but she didn't let him falter. She used her free hand to rock his hips back and forth, relentless in the pursuit of his release.

He felt the first pull in his core as the tingling sensation danced along his spine. He muttered her name in warning, but knowing he was right there only seemed to spur her on. All he could see was the shadow of her head bobbing up and down. All he could hear was his wet cock slapping in and out of her mouth as he filled her. She continued to meet him thrust for thrust, moan for moan, driving him wild and sucking him hard until he shot into her mouth.

She didn't pull away, instead swallowing him down and continuing to lick and savor his dick through every tremor of pleasure. She gave his balls one last gentle tug before shimmying up the bed. Even through the darkness, he could see the satisfied smile gracing her swollen lips.

"You're incredible," he praised, peppering her with kisses as she caught her breath. She molded her naked body around his as he deepened the kiss. Their lips locked. Their limbs tangled. Rhett growled into her mouth when he tasted his own release lingering on her tongue.

"Your turn," he declared, pulling away from her mouth. He was already hard again. He was determined to be inside his wife as soon as possible. "Buckle up, beautiful. You had your fun. Now I want to show you how good I'm going to love you for the rest of forever."

He started soft, kissing and nipping from her jaw to her neck then back again. He moved down her body as slowly as possible, torturing them both as he tried to draw out her pleasure. They made love for hours, exchanging orgasms. Whispering their devotion in the dark. Feeling the other's one love through every touch, every kiss, every thrust, every tremor. It wasn't until the sun had fully risen over the harbor and the warm glow of morning filled the room that they were both satiated enough to go back to sleep.

Chapter Twenty

Tori

"I honestly couldn't imagine a better trip." She burrowed deeper into the crook of Rhett's shoulder. They were in their bathing suits and lounging on the hammock, her legs draped over his lower half while he had one arm behind her shoulders and the other possessively resting between the apex of her thighs.

They had been rotating between the bed, the plunge pool, and the hammock for the last few hours. It had become a daily routine: lazy afternoons spent basking in the sun, making love, and falling asleep in each other's arms on their private balcony.

Rhett chuckled into her hair before kissing her forehead. "You know we didn't actually do anything this entire trip, right?"

She let out a little sigh. There was a lot of truth to his statement. So many plans had been cancelled or changed over the last five days. They had done practically nothing, but the week had still been everything.

"I'm sorry we didn't do more. I still feel bad. I know you worked so hard to plan us the perfect honeymoon..."

"Shhh." He cut her off with a nip on her ear. "Stop apologizing. This week has been better than anything I could have ever planned."

"Do you really mean that?" She ran her fingertips along his collarbone, into the hollow of his neck, then back again. It wasn't like they hadn't done *anything*. Technically they had left the room twice to go to out to dinner, and they spent half the day at the beach on Wednesday.

But that was the extent of their honeymoon adventures, at least outside the walls of their villa. They had cancelled most their reservations and tours for the week, opting to explore each other's bodies and revel in their new union instead.

Tori had never had so much sex in her life. She had lost count of the number of times they had made love. She was sore in all the best ways, and yet it was like each encounter just amped up their mutual desire for each other. No matter how many times he made her come, or how spent her body felt, she could not get enough of him.

"Of course I mean it. I didn't realize it before we got here, but being hidden away from the world in this villa was exactly what we needed. I want this trip to be something we remember forever, beautiful. We deserve to be this blissfully happy after everything we went through to get here." He kissed her shoulder as he stroked her through her bikini bottoms.

She subconsciously pushed into his hand, her need to be touched by him insatiable. She opened her legs and tilted her hips slightly to grant him more access, although she doubted he'd be ready to go again just yet. They had both crashed into full-body orgasms in the plunge pool less than an hour ago.

"Do you think long distance will be harder or easier now that we're married?" she wondered out loud as she continued to grind her hips against his hand. He knew what she was doing, but he made no moves to pull away.

"Both. It'll be different for sure. We're not sneaking around anymore or trying to push down our feelings. It'll be easier in that way. But we have a lot of big things coming up this summer. We're in it together, though, and I'll be home as often as I can. You won't have to go through anything alone, V. You'll never be alone again." One finger crept under the hem of her bathing suit bottoms as he made his promise.

"I love you," she murmured as she tilted her chin to find his lips.

"I love you too." He didn't deepen their kiss, instead smiling against her mouth and gazing down to meet her eyes. "I did get you something to make long distance a little easier."

"Like a present?" she asked with a mischievous smile.

"Yes, like a present. Or presents, I guess. There's more than one." He stroked her again, this time inside the still damp fabric of her bathing suit, and applied a little more pressure. She couldn't resist pushing into his hand. She would never get enough of this man.

"Come on," he coaxed, circling two fingers against her clit for emphasis before removing his hand completely. "Let's go inside."

"What? No!" she protested at the loss of contact. "I don't even like presents all that much," she whimpered as she grasped his hand and tried to drag it back to her core. She was perfectly content to stay out here on the hammock and let him continue playing with her.

"I promise these presents will feel almost as good as my fingers do."

Tori cocked an eyebrow in question but stood up without further prompting.

"Go inside and take off this wet bathing suit," he instructed as he pulled at one of the strings on the side of her bikini. "Get on the bed naked, and I'll be right there."

She didn't need to be told twice. She rushed through the door, her hands already working at the strings to undo her suit. Her nipples pebbled as soon as the chilly indoor air hit her skin. A full-body shudder raked through her, but it had more to do with anticipation than with the air-conditioned room being too cold.

She climbed onto the enormous bed without hesitation, turning back in time to see Rhett pull a sleek purple box from his suitcase. He sauntered over and joined her on the bed, kneeling before her as he presented her with the gift.

She excitedly took it from him, anxious to see what he had waited to give her on the last day of their trip. It couldn't be something for the actual honeymoon, since tonight was the last night of their trip. He said it would feel almost as good as his fingers, though...

She raised her hand to her mouth and gasped when she flipped open the lid. Nestled inside the box was three silicone vibrators, each one a different length and shape, but all in the same matching pastel purple hue. She lifted her gaze to Rhett's face to find him watching her expectedly.

"They're supposed to be the best of the best— rechargeable and waterproof, with five cycles and ten intensity settings each." Of course he would be focused on the features. She rolled her eyes and cocked one eyebrow at him.

"You know I already have a vibrator at home," she reminded him, unable to contain the grin she'd been holding in for the last several seconds. She couldn't believe he would go to the trouble to research and buy her something like this. But maybe she shouldn't have been so surprised. Rhett had always been obsessed with pleasing her, on insisting she came at least once, but usually two or three times, before he'd focus on himself.

"I know that," he murmured as he crawled toward her on the bed. He kissed her bottom lip once, then he kissed her again, his tongue teasing against the seam of her lips as he lowered her back onto the mattress. "You can still use that if you want." He was hovering over her now with one hand caressing her forehead and hair while he used his other arm to hold his body suspended over her. "But I wanted you to have options when I can't be home with you. And I liked the idea of knowing exactly what you look like using these when we have phone sex."

Her pussy clenched at his words. She squeezed her legs around his hips, desperate for a bit of friction. She could already feel her arousal slick between her thighs. "Wait. So you want me to use these now and let you watch?"

"I do," he confirmed, giving her a sultry look that sent a spark right to her core.

"But... But I never orgasm as hard as I do when you get me off." That was the truth. Her own fingers and her tried and true vibrator worked well, but they didn't come anywhere close to giving her the deep, delicious satisfaction that Rhett was able to elicit from her body.

He bit down on her lower lip and pulled it between his teeth. "I've been making you come for years. I know there's no competition. But I bet you'll like these, especially if I watch you use them on yourself. Go ahead. Pick one."

Shit. He had her there. She was already wet just from the idea of his eyes on her as she touched herself. She was more than happy to play this game. She reached over and lifted the box to peek inside again. She selected the toy in the middle. It was shorter and wider than what she was used to, with a hole at the tip.

He kissed her once more before sitting back on his heels and spreading her thighs apart with his hands. His fingers started to caress right along the edges of her core. "I think you're going to like that one best. It's a suction toy, and it uses little air pulses against your clit. Get yourself warmed up," he whispered with a quick nod of his chin.

She moved her free hand between her own thighs, running two fingers up and down her folds before landing on her sweet spot. She looked down to see Rhett's eyes locked on her hand as he held her open with his fingers. She pinched her tight bundle of nerves once, moaning from the sharp sensation.

"Fuck..." he muttered to himself, biting down on his lip and letting out his own low moan. "Do that again," he ordered, his voice husky, a fire burning behind his grey-blue irises.

She did was she was told, petting herself once, twice, then letting her forefinger and thumb come together as she pulled on her clit. She opened her eyes to find Rhett staring right at her.

"You're so fucking beautiful. I love watching you touch yourself like that. Do you like when I tell you what to do, V?"

She pinched her clit again without any instruction, desperate for another hit of pleasure as his words sent flutters through her core.

Rhett smirked and shook his head slightly. "I'll take that as a yes. Show me what you're going to do to yourself when I'm not home."

She pressed the power button on the top of the device, her eyes widening in surprise when the vibrator came to life and emitted a low rumble. She replaced her fingers with the opening of the toy and gasped on contact. The little hole sealed around her clit perfectly, creating an instant pull that felt almost as good as when Rhett sucked her into his mouth.

Her hips started moving without conscious thought, her body craving more now that she'd had a taste. Once she established a rhythm, she looked up to see Rhett staring right at her. She moaned again when his eyes shifted to her pussy. Her pulse quickened as he gazed down between her thighs. She was so hot right now, so worked up because his eyes were on her. She wondered if she would combust just from his gaze.

"You like being watched like this, don't you, beautiful? You're so hot right now. I love watching you."

His words made her brain short-circuit. She couldn't think, let alone focus on what she was doing. She distractedly moved the vibrator away from her body, whimpering from the loss of suction. "Rhett," she begged. As much as she liked to be watched, it was torture knowing that the person who could meet all her needs was *right there* but not actually participating.

He smirked and shook his head slightly. He had to know what she wanted—but he had made his intentions to sit back and watch perfectly clear. She blew out a frustrated breath.

"Here." He took her free hand in his and raised her fingertips to his lips. He sucked two fingers into his mouth, running his tongue up and down the space between them and biting down on the tip. Once they were wet, he moved her hand between her own thighs. "Try this," he coaxed, guiding her hand to her center. He pressed her fingers into her opening, holding her leg with his other hand as he urged her to take over and resume what she had started.

"You come hardest for me when I give you both at the same time," he explained.

Fuck. She knew nothing would ever feel as good as Rhett's hands, mouth, and cock, but being instructed on how to get herself off by the man who knew how to make her body sing was still hot as hell.

She brought the toy back to her clit as she circled her own opening with her other hand. He was right. Of course he was right. The combination of sensations blended together and inspired the familiar tightness in her tummy, her core tensing with the promise of release.

"Keep going," he murmured as he crawled up her body and situated himself beside her. She saw him reach down and twist his own dick out of the corner of her eye. She loved that her pleasure was such a turn-on for him. It had always been like this between them. Their bodies were as attuned to each other as their souls.

Tori closed her eyes in concentration, reveling in the mounting tension. She let out a little yelp of surprise when she felt Rhett close his mouth around one nipple. Her hips bucked involuntarily, her breath coming in and out in ragged gasps now. She was so close.

"When we're on the phone, I want you to pretend I'm lying right there beside you. And when I tell you to come, I want you to come for me."

His words were her undoing. She rocked against the vibrator once more as her walls clenched around her own fingers. She was overwhelmed by the tightening sensations, by the ripple effect her orgasm had on her whole being. She came, and she came hard, her body seeming to float off the bed for a few seconds at the peak of her pleasure.

Rhett released her nipple from his mouth, licking between her breasts before laying his head on her chest. She ran her hands through his hair, holding him tight as she tried to slow her breathing.

"One down, two more to go," he murmured, lifting his head to raise his eyebrows suggestively. She smacked the side of his head and rolled her eyes.

"That was amazing, but I need a break. I have other needs, you know. Like food. And sleep." Her words were in jest, but he sat up quickly at her declaration.

"I'm assuming we're cancelling our dinner reservation tonight?" The knowing look he gave her told her he already knew the answer to that question. "You relax," he instructed as he rose from the bed and pulled the covers up to her chin. "I'll go call the restaurant and order room service."

She drifted off to sleep within seconds of him heading downstairs. When she woke up, the room was darker. Rhett's arm was wound around her waist, his grip tight even in sleep. She reached down and interlaced her fingers with his.

She felt him stir behind her and pulled her body closer as he readjusted his own position. It wasn't until he started stroking her ribs with their joined hands that she knew for sure that he was awake.

Tori felt a hint of melancholy as she lay in her husband's arms. Their trip was coming to an end. Tomorrow they'd reboard the NorfolkStar private plane and make two stops: Rhett would get off in Virginia while she continued home to Ohio.

She meant what she said earlier. She couldn't have imagined a more perfect trip or a more perfect start to their marriage.

She knew with certainty that resisting Rhett for so many years had been a mistake. His love was unshakeable, their fates inevitable. Agreeing to marry him was the best decision she had ever made.

"Can I ask you something?" she whispered, turning in his arms so they could talk face-to-face.

He didn't reply, but his easy smile encouraged her to continue.

"How did you stay so steady all those years when I was pushing you away?"

A slight grimace flashed in his expression. If she hadn't been watching him so intently, she would have missed it. "What do you mean?"

"I mean, I'm sure there were other girls... hell, I insisted you date other people. But it felt like you never gave up on the idea of us. I had to work so damn hard to keep you away and hold you at arm's length. How did you hold on for so long?"

Rhett let out a huff and ran his hand through his hair. She didn't mean to upset him by trudging up the rockier parts of their relationship. But she knew they wouldn't be here now if it wasn't for Rhett's commitment to the idea of what they could be. She was genuinely curious how he held on for so long.

He let out a long sigh and gazed up at the ceiling to avoid meeting her eyes. "Don't laugh," he finally replied. She nodded earnestly. She would never judge him for sharing his truth. "I'm sure it sounds sappy and juvenile, but our connection has always felt fated to me. There's just something in you that belongs to me. And so much of me, of who I am, belongs to you. You were meant to be mine, beautiful, and even if I tried, I could never belong to anyone but you."

She was stunned silent by his words. Not because the sentiment was new, or because she hadn't had similar thoughts herself. But hearing him explain it like that tugged at every piece of her heart and soul. His truth was her truth. They belonged to each other.

"I would have waited longer, you know," he confessed. "If things hadn't worked out like this... if you hadn't called me about your scans or if you ended our arrangement when I moved to Virginia... I would have held on anyways. I would have waited for as long as it took. I would have waited forever, just for the possibility of a life with you."

Tori felt a pang in her heart as tears formed in her eyes. This man. His devotion. How had she ever thought she could live without him?

"Our love—what we have? It's precious to me, V. *You* are precious to me. I'm going to spend the rest of forever showing you how grateful I am for this love."

She let out a muffled cry as he held her, stroking her hair and kissing her tear-stained cheek. As tempted as she was to just let him hold her, she couldn't let the moment pass without matching his confessions with promises of her own.

"I know I can't make up for all the years I held you at arm's length, but I want you to be so sure of us now, Ev. There's nothing and no one that can pull me away from you. Not now, not ever. I love you. I belong to you. And I plan to keep you forever, or for however long we get."

CHAPTER TWENTY-ONE

Tori

Lookin' good, married lady."

Tori's whole face lit up when she heard Jake call out to her from across the Green. She'd been back in Hampton since last weekend, but she'd been so busy she hadn't seen him yet. She had worked two shifts that week, but Jake hadn't been there either day. Her days off had been filled with organizing things between her and Rhett's bedrooms, writing thank you notes for the wedding gifts that continued to pour in, and helping Anne plan Maddie's graduation party. She also had a volunteer planning meeting for camp and had spent time with Fielding.

"Hey! I missed you! I'm glad we're both here today." She assessed their setup for the morning. It was Small Business Saturday at Market Day, and Mike had asked both her and Jake to staff the tents he had reserved on the Green. She was in charge of the Clinton's booth, responsible for running the coloring page station and passing out French toast samples. Jake was in charge of The Oak Barrel Tavern booth, passing out flyers for the grand opening next weekend, and handing out job applications.

It made her a little sad to think about Jake moving on from Clinton's to The Oak, even if it was literally next door. But it's not like she was going to be at Clinton's much longer either, at least not consistently. She was on the schedule for a few more weeks before she took off her annual two weeks to volunteer at Camp New Hope.

Then her hysterectomy was officially set for July 19. She'd have to be off work for at least six weeks afterwards, and Rhett was trying to convince her to come to Virginia for part of that time.

"Come here, you." Jake was around his table in three strides, pulling her into a huge bear hug. She returned his affection and squeezed.

"I feel like we have a million things to talk about and catch up on. Starting with the honeymoon?" He raised his eyebrows suggestively as they both started setting things up at their respective stations.

"Ha! You wish. You know I don't kiss and tell."

"True. You just hope someone walks in or hears you instead."

He wasn't wrong. She still blushed at his ribbing.

"I haven't done anything but laundry, errands, and cleaning since I got back to town. Bor-ing. I feel like *you* need to update *me* on what's going on."

"Same old same, mostly. Fielding and Dem invited us all over to their mom's place last weekend for a little Sunday Funday. You should see that house, baby. The pool is insane. I swear it's bigger than WaterWorks. They even have one of those freestyle automatic drink machines filled with a lot more than just Coke products."

"Rowdy valet boys drinking at the pool? Sounds like my scene for sure," she joked. "Did you happen to meet their mom while you were there?"

"Nah, she's on some spa retreat in Arizona or something."

Tori nodded, assuming the "spa retreat" was actually another rehab facility. She made a mental note to ask Fielding about that. He hadn't mentioned anything to her when they hung out on Thursday.

"Is our boy stuck in Virginia this weekend?"

She smirked at Jake's wording: "our boy," like they shared joint custody of Rhett.

"No, he's home. He got in late last night. He was sleeping when I snuck out this morning, thank goodness. He needed it."

Jake froze in place, his hands resting on the pile of menus he had just spread out along his table. "He's home now?"

"Well, he might have gone out for a run or something, but yeah, he's in town this weekend."

She watched Jake tighten his grip on the end of the table as the information sunk in. "What the hell? He sent me what I thought were a whole slew of drunk texts last night, including a picture of a bottle of Macallan 18 he was bragging about."

"I mean, maybe he had a drink at the airport?" she offered weakly. She hoped her nonchalance would defuse the tension marring Jake's features.

"So you're telling me Rhett flew in from Virginia last night. What time did he get in?"

"Honestly? I don't remember. I was asleep when he got home, so it was after eleven for sure."

Jake didn't say anything for a few minutes, instead standing in a wide stance and glaring at her while working his lip between his teeth. He was pissed. He was more than pissed. She didn't understand what the problem was or what they may have talked about in their texts to elicit this type of reaction.

"You were asleep. Meaning *you* didn't pick him up at the airport."

A spark of understanding tried to catch in Tori's mind, but she didn't let the embers take hold. She knew what he was implying. Rhett may have had a drink or two last night after the long work week, but he knew his limits. She buried the urge to defend him. She wasn't about to insert herself into a misunderstanding between her husband and his best friend. They could put on their big boy pants and figure it out later.

"Anyways..." She was desperate for a subject change. "What's going on with The Oak? Everything all set for Friday?"

Jake blew out a long breath before thankfully dropping the issue and responding to her question. "Technically, yes. We still need to hire another dishwasher and a few more bartenders. I don't feel like I have nearly enough staff yet."

"It's really cool that you get to be the manager, Jake. Mike trusts you completely. I'm proud of you."

"Thanks, baby. I've had my hand in this for almost a year now. I'm excited to finally see it come together. Are you coming to the grand opening next weekend?"

"Wouldn't miss it for the world," she promised.

The morning passed quickly. The Clinton's booth was always a crowd-pleaser on Market Day. Tori could barely keep up with the demand for stickers and crayons from all the kids working on their coloring pages. Mike or Cory ran across the street several times to refill the French toast samples. Jake was also busy, on his feet the whole time, chatting with their regular customers and making sure everyone knew about the newest bar in Hampton, Ohio.

It wasn't until the tornado test siren sounded at noon that Tori realized how much time had passed. She glanced over at her friend as he tidied up his pile of applications and menus. She mirrored his actions at her own booth, cleaning up so they would be ready to pack everything away when Market Day ended. There was no point in trying to talk when the siren was wailing.

It was the ear-piercing wail of the alarm that allowed Fielding to sneak up on them unannounced. Tori turned and saw him first, locking eyes with his light blue irises and returning his megawatt smile.

"I brought you food," he mouthed as he held up the familiar brown paper bag from Jersey Bagels. Her stomach rumbled as if on cue right as the siren finally stopped.

"Hey, man," Jake called once he spotted Fielding.

"Hey. You guys hungry?"

"Hell yeah," Jake replied. "I was about to text Cory to bring us something from Clinton's anyways. Perfect timing."

"I wasn't sure what you liked, so I ordered a few of everything," Fielding explained as he passed the bag to Tori. "Do you prefer butter or cream cheese?"

"Plain bagel, lightly toasted, butter," Jake chimed in before she could respond, rattling off her usual order. "What do you want from the restaurant, baby? I'll text Cory right now."

"Just my usual salad, no fries."

Fielding pulled out a chair from an empty booth across from them and positioned it between the two tables, forming a triangle so they could all chat as they ate. "So how's it going?" he asked as they dug into their bagels.

"Good. We've been swamped," Tori said. "Market Day only goes for another hour, though, and it looks like a lot of the usual vendors are already sold out and done for the day. It should slow down now that it's lunchtime."

Fielding nodded toward all the papers spread out in front of Jake. "What are you passing out? Menus?"

"Menus, grand opening flyers, and applications."

"Applications?"

"Yep, I need to hire a dishwasher and at least two more bartenders. Dude." Jake's eyes lit up. "You should totally apply."

Fielding reached across the table and picked up each one of the papers stacked on the table. He scanned the menu before looking over the application and shaking his head.

"Nah, think about it, man. If we both worked at The Oak, we'd only ever see each other at The Oak. Either one or both of us would always be working. Then who'd be in charge of keeping an eye on this one?" He slow-rolled his neck in Tori's direction and gave her a pointed look. Very few people had the gall to tease her the way Fielding did.

"But," he amended, turning back to the other man. "Dempsey might want to apply. He's been bitching all summer about needing to mix things up. I think he's itching for a change with our mom out of town for so long. I bet Cole and Teddy would apply, too. Cole was thinking about picking up another job, and Teddy and Anwar have been at each other's throats lately, so I could see him wanting to break away from the valet gig."

"Ohhh. Rich boy drama at the Valet House?" Tori asked in mock fascination.

"Don't try to get any gossip out of me, Victoria Thompson. You're the one who ditched us these last few weeks and missed out on my epic pool party."

She gave him a tight smile, not feeling quite confident enough to snark back about how she was a little busy on her honeymoon. The joke might have landed okay, but she didn't want it to come off as cruel.

"Order up, kids!" Cory called out to them as he approached with their food. He set everything down in front of Tori before turning back on his heel. "I wish I could stay and chat, but I've gotta get back. We're super busy in there."

"Cor, I'll text you later so we can make plans for next week," she called after her friend.

"Deal!" he hollered over his shoulder before crossing the road to get back to Clinton's.

"Speaking of next week," Fielding interjected, "when are we finishing those canvases?"

Tori dropped her eyes to her salad and spread a blob of dressing around to delay responding. Field had eagerly agreed to help her finish the prep work for Camp New Hope, but she felt a slight uneasiness about making plans in front of Jake.

"I have to work Tuesday, Thursday, and Saturday next week. And I have a doctor's appointment on Monday," she explained, avoiding the specifics of what exactly the appointment entailed. It was the first appointment to kick off the egg retrieval process. She knew the next two weeks were going to be busy and emotionally charged because of all the hormone injections, hence why she wanted to get everything done for camp sooner rather than later. "Want to plan for Wednesday or Friday?"

"I want both," Fielding declared.

Tori cocked an eyebrow at him, continuing to avoid looking at Jake over Fielding's shoulder.

"What?" Fielding asked defensively. "If we plan to hang out both days, the canvases will definitely get done, and we'll get to actually hang out, too, instead of just sweating to death in your dad's garage. Plus, you still haven't been to my mom's pool yet. We can work on the canvases on Wednesday, then go swimming on Friday. I'll make you breakfast."

He wagged his eyebrows for emphasis, which made Tori laugh. They both knew damn well that if they were together, she was cooking, although Fielding was great about setting the table and cleaning up. He was surprisingly domesticated for a privileged trust fund fuckboy.

"Fine," she relented. "But we have to hang out earlier in the day on Friday. I want to go to The Oak that night for the grand opening."

"Ahhh, that's where you're wrong, Victoria Thompson. I also plan to be at The Oak for the grand opening, so we will, in fact, being hanging out all day on Friday. I can DD in case you want to go wild and sip on half a beer."

She didn't bother arguing with him. Plans had officially been made.

CHAPTER TWENTY-TWO

Rhett

It wasn't hard to spot them on the opposite side of the Green. It also wasn't surprising to see Haas wedged between them, casually chatting with his wife and his best friend, his eyes seeming to linger on Tori whenever she spoke. He was too far away to hear what they were talking about, but whatever it was must have been riveting based on how Haas seemed to hang onto her every word.

Rhett blew out a long breath as he started to make his way across the Green. He kept his Ray Bans in place and bowed his head slightly. There were enough people out and about today that someone would eventually recognize him and stop to chat, but right now he just wanted to get to his girl.

She had been asleep when he finally got home last night. He found her starfished in the center of his bed at his parents' house. The tension of the day softened around the edges the moment he laid eyes on her. He had showered quickly, eager to wash away the stress of the week, before he climbed into bed. He had fallen asleep with relative ease, much to his surprise and relief. He wasn't sure if it was the familiar bed, the proximity to his wife, or the expensive whiskey he drank at the airport sky lounge. Business class travel had its perks. Whatever the reason, the cards were in his favor last night, the Universe on his side. He felt more rested today than he had since their honeymoon.

He slept in until almost eight am, which meant Tori had already left for work by the time he got up. He let himself enjoy a slow start to the morning, going on a long run out to the bike and hike trail and back before showering and getting ready for the day. He had only spent a few minutes glancing through emails, knowing that if anything needed his immediate attention, Quinn would let him know.

He had forgotten it was Market Day until he tried to find parking in the backlot of Clinton's and fell short. He assumed she and Jake had been stationed out here all morning. Maybe she would want to go out to lunch after her shift.

Jake spotted him first, offering a less-than-enthusiastic head nod in his direction before saying something to Tori he couldn't hear. He watched as Jake shoved to his feet and started tearing down the table and pop-up tent with the new Oak Barrel Tavern logo on it.

"Rhett!"

There she was. He grinned from ear to ear as his wife made her way around the booth to meet him.

"Hey, beautiful," he greeted her as he folded her into a hug. He pulled back and kissed her forehead before finding her lips. He didn't care if they were in the middle of downtown Hampton, surrounded by dozens of families. It had been seven long days since he had last kissed his wife.

"Missed you," she replied as she moved out of his hold. "We're just finishing up here." She cocked her head toward the booths. Jake and Fielding were making quick work of tearing down.

"Perfect. Can I take you out to lunch?"

"Oh, I just ate. Field brought bagels, then I had a salad, too. I'm stuffed. We can go out though, and I'll sit with you while you eat?"

Field brought bagels. Of course he did. Guess that's what he got for trying to enjoy a slow start to the day.

"I'm not that hungry either. I went on a long run this morning and made a huge breakfast when I got home. Why don't we go out to dinner tonight instead? I'll make reservations, and we can get dressed up. It is our two-week anniversary after all."

Tori laughed and shook her head, her wavy dark blonde hair waving with the motion. "It feels a little silly to celebrate a two-week anniversary when we've been together for more than ten years."

Rhett reached for her hand and gently pulled her back into his orbit. "I want to celebrate everything with you, V." He kissed her again, needing to feel her mouth pressed against him. Needing to remind himself that he was home, and they were together. Her presence soothed his frantic mind, her body comforted his frazzled nerves.

"I love you," she whispered before turning and walking away to help the guys clean up.

"Everhett!" a voice called out right as Tori stepped away. He inhaled, trying to savor what had just passed between them and commit the feeling of calm to memory. A hand brushed along his forearm before he had a chance to turn and see who had spoken.

He smiled at the middle-aged woman standing before him. He knew he wouldn't last long at Market Day without running into someone he knew. He was surprised it had taken this long. "Hi, Mrs. Riviera."

"I saw your wedding announcement in the paper last weekend and just wanted to tell you congratulations! Everyone always knew you two would end up together."

Rhett maintained his smile, laughing to himself about how easy it all looked from the outside.

"Thanks, Mrs. R. Tell Jasper and Becks I said hello, will you?"

"Sure! They'll be happy to hear I ran into you. Oh, is that Victoria over there? I must go tell her congratulations..."

"Ahh, I'm sure she'd love to chat, but she's on the clock right now. I'm not even supposed to be here distracting her." He held one finger to his mouth and winked, implying she was in on a secret. The woman's eyes lit up knowingly.

"Oh, of course. Mum's the word! Please pass along my congratulations."

"I will," he assured her, clasping his hand around hers before she walked away. He made his way over to where the gang was almost done cleaning up.

Tori met his gaze with raised eyebrows. "That looked like nosy Mrs. Riviera. Did you just run interference for me?"

He winked at her as he took a pile of papers and a bag of coloring supplies from her hands. "What are husbands for?"

"You're my hero. We would have been stuck here for another twenty minutes if she got to talking." Tori stretched up onto her toes to kiss him. A swell of pride rose up in his chest from her affection, especially in front of the other men.

"Wheeler. You here to help or just hold us up?" Jake clipped out as he finished cinching a pop-up tent closed into its carrying case.

"Hey, bro," Rhett greeted his friend tentatively, stepping forward to take the tent from Jake's hands. "What's going on?" His best friend was obviously on edge.

"Wasn't expecting you home this weekend after some of those texts last night."

What the hell was that supposed to mean? He didn't even remember texting Jake last night. He wasn't willing to tell him that, though. He ran his hands up and down his jeans a few times to stop his twitchy palms from reaching for his phone and checking his messages.

"What can I grab for you?" he asked instead, desperate to change the subject.

"Nothing. We're good here. Field, will you take all the Clinton's stuff so Tori can go?"

Rhett didn't miss the dismissiveness in his tone. Tori hadn't missed it either, based on the terse look she shot at Jake as she transferred everything she and Rhett had been holding to Fielding's arms.

"Thanks, Haas," Rhett acknowledged before taking a few steps back. What was going on with Jake? Rhett knew he'd been working a lot, helping Mike to get ready for the grand opening of The Oak. But his anger was obviously targeted at him since he seemed fully capable of speaking to Fielding and Tori with a sense of civility.

"I think he's just stressed about the grand opening," Tori assured him quietly as she stepped into his space. Rhett nodded once to acknowledge he heard her. But he knew Jake well enough to know there was more on his mind.

He was determined to try one more time, not willing to leave things so tense. "You working tomorrow, bro?"

Jake let out a disgruntled gaff. "I'm working tonight, I'm working tomorrow, I'm working every damn day next week." He ticked off each day on one hand.

"Cool. I'll come in early to help with brunch prep." Rhett turned on his heel before Jake could object, taking Tori's hand and guiding her down the little brick path that cut through the Green.

"Bye, boys!" she called over her shoulder as they made their escape. "Don't forget to clock me out, Jake!"

"I got you, baby."

"You know I don't have to work tomorrow, right?" Tori asked as she reached for his hand and interlaced their fingers. He didn't miss how she gently caressed his hand with her thumb as she held it. He needed the little extra reassurance after that encounter with Jake.

"I know. You don't mind if I go in though, right? I won't stay too long. And I'll bring food home so we can have breakfast together."

"Ohhh, are you going to let me eat in bed again?"

"Depends."

"Depends? Depends on what?"

"On if you're going to eat something that requires syrup."

"Ha!" she laughed out loud. "I knew the whole 'you can eat in bed' amendment wasn't going to last. Joke's on you, though, Mr. Wheeler. I've been eating in your bed all week."

He looked both ways for them before they started to cross the street to their cars. "You stayed at my house this week? Why didn't I know that?"

Tori shrugged. "I didn't really plan it. I went home every morning to take care of Penny and have breakfast with my dad. But I like being in your bed when you're not there. It smells like you."

"Our bed," he corrected.

"Our bed," she confirmed. "Okay, so we're going out to dinner tonight, and you're letting me eat breakfast in bed tomorrow, but what are we doing this afternoon?"

"I have a few ideas," he replied as they reached her car. "We've got the house to ourselves, and I'm going to make us a late reservation so we have the whole afternoon together. Let's go home, beautiful."

———

Rhett's "few ideas" were dead on arrival once he got home and checked his emails. A huge storm had torn through Norfolk unexpectedly around noon, washing out two bridges that connected to their main port. Dozens of staff couldn't get to work, and the entire weekend's docking schedule was going to be affected because of the storm.

He spent the afternoon stationed in the sunroom, on the phone and glued to his laptop as he worked with his logistics and ops teams to reroute or reschedule all that weekend's shipments. The storm was going to cause a ripple effect over the next several days, and it was going to cost them hundreds of thousands of dollars. The whole process was made more complicated by the fact that his team was gathered in a conference room at the office while he was sitting at home in Hampton. Because of Tori's first egg retrieval appointment on Monday, he wasn't due back in the office until Tuesday. The timing sucked.

He switched over to speakerphone as he made his way around the bar to refresh his drink. He peered out the sunroom windows and watched as Tori floated in the middle of the pool. She was wearing the navy-blue string bathing suit he loved, and she had the straps undone. Rhett smiled to himself as he poured his drink. He helped her slather on SPF 50 before she went out there. Those strings weren't hanging precariously in the water because she was worried about tan lines.

What he wouldn't give to hang up the damn phone, jump in the pool, and tug on those little strings dangling in the water. But he owed it to his team to stay on task as they worked through their emergency response plan. He had two cohorts on the ground in Virginia: his core staff at the office rescheduling shipments and freight carriers, then an auxiliary team trying to get in touch with all the dock staff scheduled to work that day, just to make sure everyone was okay. He'd been in touch with his granddad several times throughout the afternoon, too, but Jonathan trusted him to take care of the job he'd been hired to do.

He sat down at his makeshift workstation at the bar and glanced at the time. It was only four p.m. He had stupidly made their dinner reservation for seven, thinking they'd get to enjoy a swim and a nap and maybe an orgasm or two before going out that night. None of that was going to happen now.

Tori must have taken extra care to ease the sunroom door closed. If he hadn't felt her presence, he wouldn't have known she was there.

"Hey," she whispered, wrapping an oversized pool towel around her body as she stepped into his space. "You doing okay?" she asked, leaning in to run her hand through his hair. She had the height advantage for once as she stood next to where he was seated on a barstool. He savored the way her nails scraped his scalp, how her hand came to rest on his jaw. He turned slightly to plant a kiss in the center of her palm before nodding.

"Hang on," he mouthed back, reaching for his phone and hitting "mute" but leaving the call on speakerphone in case he needed to jump back in.

"Now we can talk. How's the pool?"

"Lonely."

"Sorry, beautiful." He sighed. "I had no idea this was all going to unfold today. Or that I'd have to be on the phone all damn day to work through it."

"Do you want a raincheck for our date tonight? I'm fine staying in and just hanging out if you need to be by your computer." She ran her hand up through his hair again, this time running her fingertips back and forth over the side of his skull. It was like she knew he had a tension headache forming right in that spot. He was so tempted to just slam his laptop shut and let her run her hands all over his body for the rest of the night.

"No way. I promised you a date, and we'd have to make dinner if we stayed in anyways. I'm taking my wife out tonight. All this should be wrapped up by then."

"Okay. I'm going to head back to my house to shower and get ready. I'll see if my dad's home from work and maybe take Penny on a walk. Want to pick me up just like old times?"

Rhett smirked, thinking about all the times he'd insisted on picking her up in his Prelude at her house rather than letting her walk between their backyards through the broken part of the fence that connected their backyards.

"I don't know, V... think your dad's going to come to the door and scowl at me as we drive off just like old times?"

"Nah. He knows I'm an old married lady now. He'll behave," she promised. She wrapped her hand around his head and pulled him into her slightly wet chest. She held him like that, with her hand on the side of his temple, pressing the side of his face into her body, while she rested her chin on the top of his head. He closed his eyes and savored the way she just knew he needed her touch. She rubbed her chin back and forth a few times, then kissed the top of his head. "Make sure to drink some water so you don't get a headache, 'kay?"

He nodded as she walked toward the sunroom door. "I'll pick you up at 6:45, beautiful."

"Love you," she replied as she slipped on her flipflops and let the door slam behind her.

CHAPTER TWENTY-THREE

Rhett

He eased his dad's S-Class Coupe into the turnaround in front of The Grille. It had been their go-to date spot for years, so it was fitting that they were celebrating their first date as husband and wife at the Hampton establishment.

If only Rhett could will his phone to stop going off in his pocket. He placed a closed fist around the vibrating device as he rose out of the car, key fob in his other hand. He made his way around the front of the bumper for Tori before a valet could reach her.

He opened her door and extended his hand to help her out of the car. "You look beautiful," he said once she was standing at full height. She really did. She had let her dark blonde hair dry naturally, so it looked all soft and wavy around her face. Her eyes were a bright emerald shade of green, set off by the strapless coral dress she was wearing. She had worn that same dress on their honeymoon a few weeks ago, and Rhett had vivid memories of how easily it fell to the floor as the zipper was undone.

"Tori!" a voice called from a few feet away, catching both their attention.

"Hey, Anwar," she replied breezily. *Shit.* Rhett had forgotten about the motley crew of fuckboys who worked valet at The Grille and some of the nicer restaurants in town when he made this reservation. He begrudgingly wondered who else was working tonight.

"Wow, you guys look good all dressed up. Nice wheels, Wheeler." Anwar smirked at his own lame joke before accepting the key fob for the car. "Fielding's working tonight, too. He's just out back," Anwar explained. Not that anyone asked him.

"Tell him I said hi," Tori replied as she took Rhett's hand. "I saw him this morning, but he didn't mention he was working tonight."

"He'll be right back if you want to..."

"Thanks, Anwar," Rhett interrupted. He'd already reached his Haas tolerance quota for the day.

"Oh, yeah, sure thing," the other man replied without missing a beat. "Enjoy your dinner!"

They were seated immediately in a quiet booth toward the back of the restaurant. They had sat in this same spot a few times before, but he couldn't remember the occasion. Maybe for a high school dance or for one of their graduations? Rhett blew out a long breath as his phone buzzed against his thigh.

He wanted to ignore it. He wanted to be here, to be fully present with his wife, instead of worrying about the latest updates from his team. He wanted to enjoy this weekend. And he wanted to take Tori's mind off the appointment coming up on Monday, the first in a series of appointments over the next two weeks.

There was so much he wanted. None of it was for the taking tonight.

"I'm gonna duck into the bathroom," he stated as casually as possible as he rose out of his side of the booth. "Order me whatever they've got on tap from Great Lakes if the server stops by before I get back." He knocked his knuckles twice on the table before bending down to kiss his wife.

Rhett had his phone out of his pants pocket before the bathroom door had even closed behind him. He leaned against the sink and let out a long breath. He started scrolling, first opening up the texts to see the most recent messages from his assistant.

There was nothing immediately pressing—just a continuous stream of updates as they juggled a million moving parts. He didn't mind all the notifications, and he was grateful for the play-by-play Quinn was sending him. This was the first big test of his leadership abilities. He was already ten steps behind by not being there in person. He needed to make sure his team knew he was available and that they could reach him for any reason.

He shot off a quick text to his assistant, letting him know he was at dinner so he might not respond as quickly over the next few hours. He checked email again, confirming it was just a lot of the same updates Quinn had summarized for him via text. The last notification came in the form of a missed call.

He clicked on his call log and almost threw the phone across the bathroom.

Chandler Cunningham.

Hell no. Not now. Not tonight. Out of all days for her to try to stir up trouble and be back on her bullshit... There was way too much going on to add Chandler's drama into the mix. He considered shooting off a nasty text to tell her off, but that would just be playing into her game. He refused to engage.

Rhett stalked back to their table, feeling no less settled than when he left to check his messages a few minutes ago. He lowered himself into the booth and gave Tori a tight smile.

She smiled across from him, looking so vibrant and carefree. She ran a sandaled foot up his calf through his dress pants as soon as he was seated across from her. "I ordered a couple appetizers since I wasn't sure what you were in the mood for."

"Thanks, beautiful," he replied as he reached for his beer. He took a long sip and exhaled. "Burning River?" he guessed, tipping his chin toward the glass in recognition of the familiar pale ale.

"Oh, you're good," she confirmed. "I asked the server to bring us a couple waters, too."

Rhett's phone vibrated in his pocket again, and he reached for it on instinct. He slipped it out halfway, then glanced down to read the text his assistant had just sent.

Quinn: Incoming. Jonathan just showed up and asked for a status update. I'm setting up the conference call now and will send you the link in the next two minutes.

Goddamnit. Things were under control. Or at least as in control as they could be, given the situation. He was handling it. And he had been keeping his granddad in the loop with hourly updates. But if his CEO wanted an in-person update on a Saturday night, Rhett needed to be in that meeting.

"Hey V? I'm so sorry, but..."

"It's fine," she assured him before he could even get out a full apology.

He still felt the need to explain. "Granddad just showed up at the office, and he's asking for an update. I can't leave my team hanging when I'm not even there..."

"Rhett. Really. Go make the call. I know this is a big deal, and you're not going to be able to think about anything else until it's handled and everyone is taken care of. You have to do what you have to do. Want me to order for you?"

"No, no, I won't be that long. I'll make it quick."

He rose out of his seat again and grabbed his beer before he headed for the outdoor patio, kissing Tori on the head as he exited.

Twenty minutes rolled into thirty. At the forty-five minute mark, Rhett found himself at the outdoor patio bar ordering another drink. Finally, just shy of an hour later, he was able to hang up and get back to his wife.

He approached slowly, noting how Tori's sun-kissed shoulders were slumped over as she sat alone in the booth, scrolling on her phone.

"Sorry, V. That was ridiculous," he offered as he ran his hand against the bare skin of her upper back. He let his fingers trail along her shoulder and her collarbone before grasping her chin. He leaned down to kiss her, trying to convey the sincerity of his apology as his lips glided against hers.

"Hmmm," she hummed against his mouth. "You upgraded."

"What?"

"I taste whiskey on that mouth I love."

"Ahh, yeah. The patio bar was open, and that call required it." He held up his half-full lowball glass for emphasis.

"Did something else happen?"

Rhett blew out a breath and ran his hand through his hair. He didn't want to spend their date night talking about work. But it seemed that was all his mind would allow tonight.

"Nothing new. But Jonathan showing up unannounced asking for updates sent everyone into a tailspin. Honestly, I think he was just stopping by to check in on them because he knew they'd been working all day, but my team got flustered and wanted to bring me in on the call."

"Rhett, if you need to get back ..."

He cut her off with a determined shake of his head. "No. No way. Our first egg retrieval appointment is on Monday, V. I can manage this from here. My team and I are still figuring out how to work together. And they're all going to have to get used to long distance, because this won't be the last time I'm not in town and things need handled. This is a learning experience for everyone, but it won't ever be this hard again." He shook his head in frustration. This wasn't how he wanted the night to go.

"Well, I ended up ordering for you after all. Steak frites, and a side of crab risotto to share."

"You're the best, beautiful."

"I know," she replied playfully. She reached across the table for his hand and interlaced their fingers. "Tell me about the rest of your week. I know today sucked, but how was your first official week at the office?"

Before he could even open his mouth to respond, he felt his pocket vibrate again. He let his head hit against the back of the high-backed booth and blew out another breath.

"Obviously not over yet." He grimaced as he fished out his phone to read the latest message from Quinn. "Hang on..." He opened up his email to glance over the new projection, typed out a quick reply of approval, then repocketed his phone.

"Why don't you just turn your phone off, like you did on our honeymoon? At least through dinner?"

He scoffed, reached for his lowball glass, and emptied it. "It's not that easy. I'm full time now, Tori. I'm the head of Logistics and Operations, and there's a major issue going on right now that affects hundreds of people and hundreds of thousands of dollars. This is my team. This is the real world. I can't just turn off my phone whenever it's convenient for me. We're not on our honeymoon anymore, beautiful. I have to be available right now."

Her eyes narrowed across the table. "It was just a suggestion. You don't need to lecture me."

"I wasn't. I mean, I wasn't trying to. I don't want to fight with you. I've got a pounding headache..."

"Then why don't you switch to water?" she clipped out.

He didn't miss the implication of her tone. She'd been on him all day about drinking water. It wasn't anything explicit, but the subtle hints that he was overindulging or that he needed to slow down were starting to grate on his nerves.

"Let's ask them to box up our meals and just go home. We can eat, then you can get a good night's sleep. Maybe we could relax in the hot tub for a bit to help you unwind?"

Rhett shook his head as the edges of anger started to take hold. This sucked. He hated all this in-between. He couldn't physically be in Virginia with his team when they needed him. He couldn't be mentally present with his wife when she was sitting across from him.

"As tempting at that sounds, I've still got hours of work ahead of me tonight. As soon as we get home, I need to get back to it."

She let out a long sigh, seemingly defeated. "Why'd we even come out tonight if you were just shoehorning me in between work calls?"

"Tori."

"No. This is stupid. If you need to go back to Virginia, just go. I'm sure Quinn can find a flight and still get you out tonight. That would honestly be better than feeling like I'm another thing you have to check off your to do list," she spit out.

He didn't understand why their conversation was escalating so quickly. He needed to recover and turn things around.

"I'm here because I want to be here, V. I need to be here for you, for Monday," he reminded her. He reached across the table to take her hand.

She recoiled and sat up straighter against the back of the booth. "Don't use me as an excuse, Everhett. Not now. Not ever. If you told me you needed to go back and be in Virginia this weekend, I would have no problem with it, and you know it. I know you're itching to be there and take care of this."

She was relentless. Why was she so insistent?

"It almost sounds like you want me to go."

She grimaced at his accusation. "What? Why would you say that?"

"Do you have other things you'd rather do this weekend than spend time with me, V? Who are you going to call up to hang out with tomorrow if I'm conveniently back in Virginia? You seemed to be having a good time hanging with Jake and Haas this morning, so I guess I have a pretty good idea about your backup plans."

Her eyes grew wide for a fraction of a second as she physically recoiled. "Stop it," she scolded in a lowered voice as she shook her head back and forth over and over again.

What the hell? Why was she worked up and defensive about him mentioning Haas? She knew he didn't like him. He didn't trust him. They both knew the other man was standing outside this very restaurant tonight, probably eager to open her car door and call her by her full name as soon as they left the restaurant.

Fucking Fielding.

She raised a hand to her face, rubbing it across her forehead a few times before sitting back up to look him dead in the eye. "You're exhausted. You're stressed out. You've been drinking most of the day."

He knew it. He fucking knew it. She couldn't let it go without getting in her own jab. A jab that cut like barbed wire, creating more damage the longer he let it fester in his mind. He hadn't been drinking "most of the day." He couldn't have been. He'd gone on a ten-mile run that morning. He'd met up with her at lunchtime.

"It's time to go home," she declared, rising to her feet and walking over to the serving station without giving him another opening.

Chapter Twenty-Four

Tori

They walked in silence from the restaurant to the valet station. Each step felt heavy, each stride lonely. She wasn't used to having to be the level-headed one. It was unnerving to see Rhett wound up and volatile. She let out a long sigh before glancing back at her husband. He was pounding out a text or email on his phone, not even aware of her eyes on him.

"I can drive us home," she offered, reaching for the valet tag he had just pulled out of his pocket.

"Not necessary," he insisted without peeling his eyes off his device.

"I just figured if you needed to be on your phone..."

"I said I'm fine." He pocketed his phone and raised his head then, his steel-grey eyes dark as graphite. His frown turned to a grimace. "Of-fucking-course," he muttered under his breath.

She turned to see Fielding jogging toward them, a genuine smile gracing his tanned and slightly freckled face.

"Hey! Anwar told me you were here, but I didn't see either of your cars in the lot."

"Hey, Field." She gave him a tight smile. "Rhett drove his dad's car tonight."

She didn't miss how Rhett's gaze narrowed when he looked up from his phone to assess Fielding. His eyes were a storm of emotions, none of them pleasant or cordial. He was in *such* a mood tonight. He held out his valet ticket without speaking a word to the other man.

"Did you have a nice dinner?" Fielding asked, accepting the ticket with a subtle head nod to Rhett. "Yo, Anwar!" he called over his shoulder. Anwar jogged over and took the ticket out of Fielding's hand before taking off in the other direction.

"We just had apps and drinks. We're taking dinner to go," Tori explained, holding up the bag of boxed food.

"Goddamnit," Rhett muttered, taking a few steps away from them as he raised his phone to his ear. He didn't bother excusing himself.

"Is he okay, Tor?"

"He's fine," she answered meekly. "There's a big emergency at work, and he really should be there, but he's here, because he thinks he has to stay for me, and... I don't know."

"Let me try again. Are you okay, Tor?"

She looked up at Fielding's lagoon-blue eyes and saw genuine concern in his expression. She could feel the worry emanating off his body, too. She could sense that he was holding back from reaching out and wrapping her in a hug. At least he had the wherewithal not to pull something like that in front of Rhett, especially tonight, although she could really use a hug at this point.

Rhett barking something into the phone caught her attention. She watched with trepidation as her husband paced over the same small patch of grass. Four steps forward. Four steps back. On the next pivot, he faltered, his balance unsteady for a few seconds before he caught himself against a tree and found his footing.

"Tori," Fielding pleaded. He obviously hadn't missed that stumble either.

She didn't look at him, choosing to ignore the question he hadn't actually asked.

"Really?"

She bit down on the inside of her cheek and raised her eyes to meet his. She narrowed her gaze, a defensive comment on the tip of her tongue.

"Tori, how much did he have to drink tonight?"

Sixteen ounces of beer at the table.

At least one double whiskey from the patio bar.

An unaccountable amount of Jameson throughout the afternoon.

"He's fine, Field," she insisted.

"Fine? You think that's fine? I've watched my mom do that same dance for years, Tori. He's not fine, and we both know it. I can't let you get in the car with him. I can call you a ride share, or I can drive you home myself. Your choice." He ran his hand through his perfectly styled blonde curls and dislodged them as he continued to stare her down.

"I said *he's fine*, Fielding. You know Rhett would never do anything to put me in danger."

"Isn't this their thing?" he snapped at her dismissal. "I thought Jake and Rhett had a whole moral stance against drinking and driving. Bro code, total control, all that alpha male shit. Or do those rules not apply to the king himself?"

"Leave it alone," she hissed. But Fielding's words were already percolating in her mind. Her husband didn't drink and drive. He didn't let anyone even drive tipsy. Being in control and ensuring everyone got home safe had been his hallmark for years. Was he about to throw that out the window?

"This is bullshit, Tori. I bet Jake would have something to say about this," he threatened as he slid his phone out of the back pocket of his khaki pants.

"What are you two whispering about?" Rhett asked as he rejoined them, wrapping an arm around her waist as he hugged her from behind.

"Just talking about our buddy Jake," Fielding replied before widening his stance and crossing his arms across his chest. A few tense seconds passed as he assessed Rhett up and down. "You good, man?"

"Yep, all good. Just need my car. It's been a long day."

Rhett either missed the challenge in Fielding's tone, or he chose to ignore it. Tori gave Fielding a pointed look, silently pleading with him to drop it as Anwar pulled the Mercedes into the circle drive.

Rhett made his way around to the driver's side to exchange keys and cash with Anwar. With her husband on the other side of the car, Fielding grasped her by the elbow, holding her in place when she attempted to reach for the passenger door. He turned his back to the vehicle and slowly met her gaze. His fingers brushed back and forth against the crease of her elbow as he wrapped his other hand around the passenger door handle without actually pulling it open.

To Rhett and Anwar, it would look like he was just opening the door for her. But Tori knew he was stalling, giving her one extra second to consider her options and change her mind.

"Text me when you get home," he whispered in her ear when he finally opened the door. She started to shrug one shoulder in defiance but softened when she glanced and saw the worry on his face. "I'm serious, Tori. If I don't hear from you in the next ten minutes, I'm coming to check on you myself."

She nodded. He squeezed her elbow once more, then finally released her arm.

She lowered herself into the luxury car and reached for her seatbelt right away. "Goodnight, Fielding." Her friend said nothing in reply, but she felt his uneasy stare through the tinted windows as they drove away.

CHAPTER TWENTY-FIVE

Rhett

"Did you know your buddy was working tonight?" he asked as calmly as possible as he coasted through the main intersection of downtown Hampton.

She sighed loudly as she turned her body toward the window. ""I don't keep track of his schedule, Rhett. And I'm not the one who picked the restaurant or made the reservation, remember?"

She had him there.

"Not our best day, huh?" he asked as he turned onto Willow Drive. He glanced over at his wife, willing her to look at him. He knew better than to throw out an apology just yet. There was still too much tension vibrating between them.

"Definitely not. But it's okay," she assured him as she typed something on her phone and continued to avoid his gaze.

"No, it's not. There's something about fighting with you that just raises my blood pressure and makes me see red. It's not you, I mean. It's the fighting."

She tucked her phone away before she finally turned to face him. "We're not fighting, Ev. We're just... going through it. Growing pains, just like you and your team. Think about it. We haven't had a normal version of a relationship since we were kids. And now here we are, suddenly married, trying to figure out our new normal. We're going to have ups and downs. You're going to have to get used to things not being perfect all the time."

"I just... I just don't feel right when we're not okay," he confessed as he eased the Mercedes into the garage. He turned the car off before turning to face her head-on. "Everything feels harder when we're not solid."

"I know. But I'm always on your team. Even when things aren't perfect, you don't have to worry. I'm not going anywhere. Not now. Not ever."

"My heart knows that. My brain forgets it sometimes."

"I get that." She reached out to cup the side of his face, running her thumb up and down his jaw as she gave him a soft smile. "Think of all the ways I pushed you away over the last six years. It makes sense if you don't completely trust everything that's happened over the last few months. Your nerves haven't had a chance to adapt to our new normal. Things between us were so messy and complicated for so long, and then everything changed so quickly over the last few months. It's okay if you're still adjusting. I'm still playing catch up, too."

They sat in silence for a few moments before he took in a deep breath and broke the silence.

"I'm so damn lucky," he mused as he leaned in for a kiss. She let him kiss her, fully and completely, reaching across the center console to wrap her arms around his neck.

"And why's that?" she teased as he moved his mouth from her full, sweet mint lips to the exposed skin stretched over her collarbone.

"Because I've got the full package right here. My wife is beautiful *and* brilliant."

"Hey," she whispered, her tone serious once again as she placed her hand under his chin to coax his head up. She held his face in both hands as she met his eyes. "I'm just going to put this out there now, rather than let it linger. No more low blows, okay? I know you're really stressed. And I know we don't see eye to eye on certain issues right now..." she trailed off instead of mentioning Fielding by name. "But you have to keep it together where my friends are concerned. It's your choice if we're going to keep having the same fight about the same people. I won't be shamed into not seeing my friends. I won't be gaslit into second-guessing my own judgement. I'm telling you right now that I'm not budging on this, so I guess you get to decide if this is a problem in our marriage or not."

He recognized her declaration for what it was. A line had been drawn. There wouldn't be any more griping around his dislike of Haas, of his displeasure in their friendship. Tori was giving him the choice: put the issue to rest for good, or prepare for this to be a perpetual problem. He wasn't willing to let Haas come between him and his wife in any way, so there wasn't even anything to consider. Accepting the other man's presence in his wife's life was the only way forward.

"There's no part of me that doesn't trust you, V. I was out of line earlier. I shouldn't have said what I said about Fielding and Jake. It *was* a low blow, and I'm sorry."

"I know. Thank you for apologizing." She nodded her acceptance, her forehead moving against his.

"And I'm sorry our date night didn't go as planned. I'll make it up to you as soon as things settle down. Let's go inside and eat before our food gets cold."

They were able to enjoy an uninterrupted dinner after all, much to Rhett's surprise. Now Tori was lounging on the sunroom couch behind him, sketching in one of her notebooks with her AirPods securely in place. Every now and then, she'd start absentmindedly humming along to whatever she was listening to. She didn't even realize she was singing out loud thanks to the noise cancellation technology. It was adorable.

He rose up from his makeshift desk and circled the mahogany bar. He refilled his tumbler with his last drink of the night, then grabbed a water bottle from the mini fridge for good measure. He looked over and watched Tori for a moment. She was completely engrossed in whatever she was sketching on the page. She'd changed out of her dress and into one of his old Archway Prep crewnecks as soon as they were done eating. The oversized sweatshirt just barely covered the top of her thighs, leaving her long, toned legs on full display along the couch.

He took a healthy swallow from his glass as he continued to watch her in reverence. It was hard to imagine that she could already be sick or that she could be sick sometime soon. She looked so healthy and vivacious from where he stood. But her follow-up tests had been inconclusive. Something wasn't right, but they had caught it early. It was the in-between that was so damn hard to deal with. He knew that even if the cancer cells weren't rapidly duplicating in her body, the constant worry about "what if" was already playing through her mind.

He watched her for another minute before he circled back around the bar and resumed his place on the bar stool. It was almost ten, and his team had finally left the office for the night. Quinn had logged back on once he got home, and together they'd spent the last two hours updating the carrier schedules for the rest of the month. They needed to get two more files updated on the shared drive, then they could finally call it a night, too.

He reached for his phone as soon as it started vibrating. But instead of Quinn's name as expected, Chandler's picture illuminated the screen.

Rhett snarled in disgust. This was the second time she had called him tonight. He knew what kind of calls came through on a Saturday night. What he didn't know is why she wouldn't take a hint and leave him the fuck alone.

He pressed the side button of his phone harder than necessary to send her to voicemail before he flipped the phone face down on the bar. He'd entered the first few characters of his password into his computer when his phone started buzzing again. He closed his eyes and steeled himself to look at his device. Maybe it was just a message coming through. Maybe it really was Quinn this time. He wished he could believe either alternative.

His gut instinct was right. She was calling him again.

"Fuck," he muttered, knowing damn well he couldn't turn his phone off for the night until he heard from his assistant.

"You okay, Ev?" Tori asked. He swiveled in his seat just in time to see her stand up and stretch her arms over her head. The full-body stretch left little to the imagination as his well-loved sweatshirt crept further up her thighs.

"Yeah, all good. Just waiting on one more update from Quinn, and then I can be really, truly done for the night and we can go to bed."

She tipped her chin toward his phone as she approached the bar. "That wasn't him?"

He sucked in a sharp breath, searching her eyes before he laid out the full truth. They had talked about Chandler, albeit weeks ago. Tori had assured him she trusted him to handle things. There wasn't any reason not to tell her about the calls.

"That was actually Chandler," he said, raising his eyebrows in frustration.

"Chandler? Really? Why would she call after all this time?"

Technically it had only been four weeks since he told Chandler he was getting married and to stop contacting him. But he recognized that it felt like longer. So much had happened so quickly over the last few weeks. It felt like a lifetime had already passed since then.

"This isn't the first time she's pulled this shit. She's called me a few times recently, including once earlier tonight and twice just now."

As if on cue, his phone started to vibrate again. He flipped it over but left it sitting on the bar, Chandler's picture on display in contrast to the rich dark brown wood of the bar top.

"Rhett..."

There was concern in her voice. Not an untrusting concern, but a genuine concern. Something akin to worry.

"That's the third time she's called tonight?"

"Fourth, if you count earlier when we were out."

Tori shifted from one leg to the other as she stared at his still-vibrating phone on the bar top. "What do you think she wants?"

"Nothing. Everything. I don't know. It's a game to her. A fucking game. If I had to guess, I bet she's wasted at some bar right now, hitting my name over and over again just to mess with me." He growled out an agitated breath as he ran his hand through his hair.

"I know things didn't end on the best terms between you, but even if she wanted to mess with you, I can't see her calling multiple times in a row. You should call her back."

He shook his head in frustration, regretting telling Tori about the calls. He was so damn tired. He had worked himself to the brink of exhaustion, and he could still feel the lingering anger that had risen up when he saw Fielding at The Grille that night. He was in no position to call anyone back at this point. He just wanted to crawl into bed with his wife and go to sleep.

"I'll call her back tomorrow," he promised as he hopped off the barstool and started to tear down his computer setup. He would just text Quinn and ask him to get the last two reports updated in the system, then he could double check everything in the morning.

He reached for his phone to text Quinn as Tori collected up their dishes. He hit the Messages app just as a new text came through.

Chandler: Everhett please call me back. I'm pregnant. Or I was. I'm at the hospital now and they think I'm having a miscarriage.

Pregnant.

Hospital.

Miscarriage.

The words registered in his brain, but he couldn't conjure up their meaning.

He reread the message once, twice, then a third time just to be certain. He flipped his phone over in his hand, staring at the case to confirm it was really his.

Fuck.

He closed out of the text, then opened it back up. But the words were the same. The message hadn't changed. The words were right there.

Fuck. Fuck. Fuck.

All her missed calls flashed through his mind. How many times had she tried to call? He couldn't even check his call log to help him remember, because he had habitually deleted every single missed call from Chandler Cunningham over the last four weeks.

There had been so many missed calls.

He didn't know how much time passed as he stood in the sunroom, staring at his phone. He couldn't move. He couldn't breathe. All he could do was stare.

"Rhett?"

Her voice called to him from far away. Her voice always called to him. She was his beacon. She was his anchor. She was everything he had ever wanted, and he had done exactly what she asked him to do to get to this point. *But at what price?*

There had been so many missed calls.

"Rhett? What's wrong?"

He tore his eyes away from the phone, away from the words that had just shoved a knife into his side and twisted.

He finally looked up at his wife. Her expression was marred with concern, her green eyes mirroring back the soul-deep love that had bound them together. They had been through so much. Would this be too much?

He didn't know what to say. He didn't know how to tell her. He didn't know anything anymore.

Horrified, and fully aware there was nothing he could do to protect her from the consequences of what they had done, he handed Tori his phone.

She glanced down at the device, glancing at it for mere seconds before her eyes shot up and her harrowing expression met his gaze.

"I—I didn't know," he stammered. "I swear I didn't know."

CHAPTER TWENTY-SIX

Pregnant.

Chandler was pregnant.

Chandler was pregnant with Rhett's child.

Chandler and Rhett were possibly losing a child.

A flurry of thoughts clashed for dominance in her mind, each one knocking on the door of her subconscious and demanding attention. She didn't know what to focus on. She didn't know how to keep her balance when it felt like the earth was literally crumbling beneath her feet.

"I—I didn't know," Rhett confessed in a whisper. He was uncharacteristically pale, his steel grey-blue eyes wider than she had ever seen them. She watched his Adam's apple work overtime as he gulped. "I swear I didn't know," he repeated.

It was then that she realized he expected her to say something. To react. To say anything.

"You have to go." She didn't even think about it. She just said it. She took three steps forward to close the space between them. As soon as she was within range, he fell into her arms.

"I swear I didn't know, V," he whispered into her ear. A confession, a muffled sob. She believed him. And yet...

Rhett had just admitted that Chandler had been calling him for weeks. He said she was playing a game. That obviously wasn't true. He said he didn't know. But he should have known.

"I believe you. But you need to call her, Ev. You need to call her right now."

He pulled away just enough to lift his phone between them. Neither of them moved any further apart. They stood toe-to-toe in the sunroom as he lifted the phone to his ear.

"Chandler," he croaked. "I just saw your text. What's going on?"

Tori watched his face contort as he absorbed what was being said.

"When did it start?"

"What did the doctor say?"

"Who's there with you now?"

Tori reached out to get his attention, placing her hand on the arm hanging at his side. "You have to go," she mouthed to him, repeating her initial reaction to the news. "You have to be there for her."

Tori watched as his expression hardened. Resolve had set in. She already knew what he needed to do. Now he knew it, too. "Text me the name of the hospital. I'll get in the car right now and be there as soon as I can." He stood up straighter as he listened to whatever she said in reply.

"Columbus?" he questioned.

Tori glanced over at the clock hanging above the mahogany bar. It was just after ten. The drive to Columbus was more than two hours from here. Her eyes trailed back down, landing on the empty lowball glass he had left on the bar.

Shit.

Rhett had been drinking all. Damn. Day. She had been willing to downplay that fact earlier when he only had to drive them five minutes through town. But then he came home and drank even more. There was absolutely no way he could drive anywhere now.

"I'll be there as soon as I can," he repeated into the phone, softer, as he ended the call and hung his head. He lifted a closed fist to his mouth and shook his head in dismay.

Tori knew he was just barely holding on. She also knew what she was about to say was possibly going to make him fly off the handle.

"Rhett…" she started, closing her eyes to conjure up the strength she needed. She had already run through all the options in her head. It was the only way. "I'll drive you."

Anger crossed his expression as he opened his mouth to object.

Tori held up a hand and looked him in the eye.

"You've been drinking. Your mind is reeling. You cannot drive yourself to Columbus right now."

"Tori," he pleaded. "I have to go. I have to be there."

"I know that. I agree. But you can't drive. You weren't in any position to drive us home earlier, then you came home and drank even more."

He stared at her a beat, then another. His face was expressionless now, his in-control mask fixed in place.

"You're my wife. I can't ask you to do this."

"You're right. I'm your wife. That's why I can't let you do this alone."

She reached around his body and picked up the empty tumbler. She let the crystal lowball glass fill her palm. The weight of it distracted her momentarily from the heaviness of everything that was crashing down around them.

Rhett's eyes moved from her face to the glass in her hand. He stared at it for a few beats as she saw a deep, guttural sadness return to his expression.

A tiny bubble of panic formed inside her as the full reality of what they were about to do settled in her gut. There was no ideal outcome to this scenario. There was nothing to even hope for based on the little she knew of what was going on. Rhett had already been so on edge. He had been toeing an invisible line for weeks. This was going to break him.

But she'd be damned before she'd let him go through it alone.

"I'll drive," she repeated more confidently this time, taking control of the situation the same way he would for her if their roles were reversed. "Go pack a few things in case we have to stay overnight.

Bring your work stuff, too, just in case. Plug your phone in now so it's charged. We can be on the road in the next twenty minutes."

Rhett stared at her for another breath before nodding once to acknowledge what she said.

"Tori…" he started as he reached for her. He wrapped one hand around her shoulder, then peeled the lowball glass out of her grasp. He held it in his hand and stared down at it for a beat, and then another, before finally lifting his head to meet her gaze. There were tears threatening to spill over, regret radiating off him. "I'm so fucking sorry, V."

Tori closed her eyes and shook her head slightly, grasping at straws and trying to find the strength to do what they were about to do. She opened her eyes to find him staring right at her still, his brow furrowed as shame and regret consumed him. Seeing her husband break down was going to break her. But she had to hold on. She had to hold on for him.

"I can't believe this. How is this even happening right now?"

Tori kept her eyes fixated on the road, focusing on the overhead streetlights as they passed under them in quick succession. Light would fill the car and she'd inhale. Then they'd be cast back into darkness until they reached the next lamp post, and she'd blow out a slow breath.

Light. Breathe in.

Darkness. Breathe out.

Rhett had been fidgeting in the passenger seat for the last hour. She knew it wasn't about her driving, but with each jerked movement, she found herself sitting up a bit straighter or tightening her grasp on the steering wheel of the Prelude. She was singularly focused on getting him where he needed to be. She couldn't bear to let herself think about anything else right now.

Light. Breathe in.

"We don't know anything yet, Ev. Let's just get there, and then we'll figure out what's next. Don't let your thoughts start spiraling."

He groaned in frustration. "I don't know what the fuck I'm supposed to think right now."

Darkness. Breathe out.

She didn't know what to say. The GPS said they still had more than an hour until they got to the hospital in Columbus. She couldn't get them there any faster, and yet she knew Rhett needed to be there now. She couldn't imagine a worse scenario for him to have to endure. Every part of this cut into the core of who he was as a person, what he stood for as a man.

Mr. Dependable. Mr. Control. Mr. Take Care of Everyone.

"I hope she doesn't lose the baby," he confessed in a broken whisper.

The baby.

His baby.

Tori gulped down the noise that threatened to rise in her throat. She wouldn't judge him. She couldn't hold it against him. All she could do was honor how he was feeling right now, knowing that his desire was completely unaligned with everything they had dreamed about for their future together.

Light. Breathe in.

She kept her eyes on the road and nodded. She had to stay steady.

"It's okay to feel that way, Ev. Of course you want your... your baby to be okay."

Darkness. Breathe out.

"Did Chandler send you anymore updates?"

He blew out a long breath as he pulled out his phone. "She texted me when we first got on the road. She said she was still waiting for an ultrasound. She's bleeding a lot, and the first doctor she saw said she was probably miscarrying. They just haven't confirmed it yet."

"I'm so sorry, Ev." And she really was. She was all too familiar with the acute pain of anticipatory grief. Of knowing the direction that things were headed, but not knowing the details of that final destination. Of knowing that things were only going to get harder, that soon everything would feel even worse. She knew what it was like to be at the lowest low and know there was still further down to go.

She was also intimately familiar with the heartache of hope. People talked about hope like it was this ethereal, everlasting ideal. Like hope was worth hanging onto. That couldn't be further from the truth in a situation like this. Hope was the fucking worst. Knowing that there was a sliver of a chance that things could work out was so much harder than just getting on with the act of grieving.

"We'll be there as soon as possible. I can't promise it'll be okay. But we'll know more soon."

She knew it wasn't enough. She knew a better woman would have sat there and promised it would all be okay, that everything would work out, that they would experience something akin to a miracle. But that just wasn't who she was. The grief of losing her mother when she was eleven, coupled with the decade-long worry that she'd succumb to the same fate, had made her too much of a realist when it came to life and death.

She wouldn't wave empty words of comfort or false hope in his face. She couldn't. She knew how this was all about to go down. She knew she was driving her husband to his undoing. She wouldn't give him hope that any of this was going to be easy or okay. She loved him too damn much to lie to him. Getting him there safely was all she could do for him now. It would have to be enough.

CHAPTER TWENTY-SEVEN

Rhett

"Chandler Cunningham's room number, please," he practically begged when they finally reached the right floor.

The woman sitting behind the nurse's station assessed him up and down.

"This floor isn't open to visitors. One immediate family member per patient only."

"I'm..." He faltered, not sure how to explain who he was to Chandler anymore or why the hell he was standing in a hospital desperate to be by her side.

"She's..." He glanced over at Tori and saw her stand up a bit straighter beside him as she took his hand. She squeezed once, reassuring him, encouraging him to keep going.

"She's pregnant with my child," he finally uttered, the words still foreign on his tongue.

The nurse behind the desk continued to assess him, as if trying to decide whether he was telling the truth or not. After a few drawn-out seconds, she blinked, picked up a clipboard, and started to rise from her seat. "Follow me," she instructed, not bothering to turn around and see if he was behind her.

"Go," Tori urged him forward before he could even get a word in. He glanced back down at their joined hands, feeling powerless to this moment that seemed to engulf them.

"I'll try to see if..." he started, only to have her interrupt him.

"No, you won't. I don't even know what you were about to say, but I know where your head's at. I'm fine, Rhett. Go. You need to be with her. Take your phone, and just text me and keep me posted. I'll be here. I'm going to sit right over there," she assured him, pointing to a cluster of hard plastic chairs.

He didn't want to do this. He didn't want to go. He could barely bring himself to take a single step forward.

She held his gaze, her face calm and steady. She squeezed his fingers one more time, then dropped his hand. "Go," she asserted again with a pointed look.

He couldn't hesitate. If he did, the fear would consume him. He looked at his wife for one more second before turning quickly and making long strides to catch up with the nurse. Every bone in his body told him to turn around, to give Tori one more glance. But he charged forward instead, not trusting that if he glanced back, he would find it in himself to keep moving forward.

"Go on, then." The nurse held out her arm toward what must have been Chandler's room. He reached for the door handle but hesitated. Chandler knew he was coming, but he had no idea the proper protocol. Should he knock? Should he text her and ask if it was okay to come in?

He didn't get to dwell on the issue because the nurse rolled her eyes and pushed into the room in front of him, letting the large wooden door bang against the door stop.

Rhett followed behind her, his eyes scanning the dimly lit area as he made his way into the room. There was a low buzzing sound coming from one of the machines pushed up against the wall, accompanied by a less frequent but higher-pitched beeping. Everything smelled sterile.

"Everhett."

He'd been so distracted by the foreign setting he hadn't even looked toward the bed yet. Chandler was sitting up, her hair thrown up in a messy, sweaty ponytail.

He strode over to her without a second thought, looking her up and down as the nurse he'd followed into the room wheeled over a computer cart toward the bed.

"Are you in pain?" he demanded when he reached her bedside. He reached out and brushed a few stray strands of hair behind her ear, noticing just how pale she looked now that he was closer. Her skin was flushed yet pallid. She had sweat all along her hairline and on her upper lip, and she had a slight grimace on her face.

"Yeah, I have really bad cramping," she admitted, winching as she sat up a little more.

"Can you give her something for the pain?" he asked, directing his question at the nurse who was starting at the screen in front of her. She finished typing, then looked up slowly before responding.

"Can you convince her to accept the pain meds?"

Rhett whipped his head back around, bewildered and blindsided. "You haven't taken anything? Chandler, if you're in pain..."

She shook her head obstinately, a look of determination in her eyes that he knew all too well. "It's not safe," she replied. "If I'm... If... It's not safe for the baby," she insisted as understanding clicked into place.

So they still hadn't confirmed anything. He hadn't missed the ultrasound she was waiting on. They still didn't know if she was miscarrying for sure.

Rhett glanced from Chandler to the nurse. "Isn't there anything you can give her that's safe? Something to take the edge off?"

The nurse pursed her lips and looked at Rhett, then back to Chandler before speaking. "Am I permitted to speak about your medical care with this man?" Chandler nodded once to confirm. "Okay, I have a form you'll need to sign saying so." Then she turned back to him. "She can have acetaminophen. It's the safest option for pregnant women, but she's refused it all."

"Chandler," he whispered, not sure whether to scold or beg or to just leave it alone. She was clearly in pain, and she'd told him earlier that she first noticed the bleeding that morning. She'd been at the hospital for hours. She met his eyes but shook her head twice in protest.

"Chandler," he growled out again. This wasn't the time to be a martyr. If she was in that much pain...

"Why do you even care, Everhett?"

He stilled at her jab, hanging his head in shame as he thought about the last in-person encounter they'd shared four weeks ago. He had been rude and borderline cruel in his efforts to get her to leave him alone. Of course she thought he didn't care.

His breathing stilled as he thought back to that day. He had spent days wondering why she had even wanted to see him in the first place. Realization dawned on him as all the pieces clicked into place.

"How far along are you?" he asked, reaching down to hold her hand.

"I would have been nine weeks tomorrow," she replied quietly without looking up to meet his gaze.

Rhett ran his thumb over the pale skin stretched between her thumb and her pointer finger. There was no point in asking anything else. The timeline made sense, even if the exact encounter was unclear in his mind. He knew with certainly the baby was his. Or had been his. Fuck.

He also knew now that all those missed calls and attempts to contact him hadn't been some game, as he had been so quick to assume. He had treated her like shit. He had treated the mother of his unborn child like shit. He had never felt so low in his entire goddamn life.

"Once they do the ultrasound, I'll take something," she relented. The defeat in her voice confirmed that she thought she was miscarrying. Not that he hadn't already come to the same conclusion just from looking at her.

"I put the ultrasound order in over two hours ago, but they must be running behind tonight," the nurse explained. "They should be here any time now."

"Who's they?" Rhett demanded.

"The ultrasound technician. They'll bring in a portable machine and conduct a transvaginal ultrasound to confirm whether or not there's a heartbeat."

"And then who do we have to wait on to tell us the results?" He knew better than to assume that the ultrasound tech would give them all the answers they needed.

"Our on-call resident will review the images and the report once the ultrasound tech is finished."

"What do I need to do to get the resident in the room while the ultrasound tech is here, so we know exactly what's going on right away?"

The nurse pursed her lips again at his question. That seemed to be her favorite expression. "That's not the standard operating proc..."

"That's not what I asked," he snapped back.

"Everhett," Chandler scolded him softly, trying to reign him in. But he wasn't going to stand for this. She'd been waiting for hours, and she was clearly in pain. He couldn't change anything about what was happening or what he'd done or not done. But he sure as hell wasn't going to idly stand by while she suffered now.

"Look," he said quietly, changing his approach. "She's been here for hours. If the worry and fear wasn't enough, she's very clearly in pain. If there's a way to call for the resident as soon as the tech arrives, that would give us the answers we need sooner. I'm not asking you to bend the rules, but we could really use a little break tonight. Please. If there's any way..."

"I'll see what I can do," the nurse conceded before wheeling her computer cart out of the room.

They were finally alone.

Rhett opened his mouth to speak first, desperate to try to chip away at the first layer of awkwardness and pain between them. But Chandler beat him to it.

"Thanks for that. And thank you for coming," she offered meekly. There was no sarcasm to her voice, but there was no warmth either. Her tone was even and transactional.

"Chandler, I'm so incredibly sorry that I..."

"Please don't," she interjected. Her tone was softer now, almost pleading. "I don't want to hear apologies or any groveling from you tonight. I've spent the last month and a half trying to call you, then finally gave up and just tried to figure shit out on my own. I'm grateful I'm not alone tonight. But tonight isn't about you. You haven't been here. You don't get to apologize to me and try to make yourself feel better right now. I'm pretty sure tonight is the night they're going to tell me I lost my baby... a baby I wasn't sure I even wanted until I saw the blood this morning. I know this is probably hard for you, too, but you don't get to pile on to my pain right now. I don't have it in me to deal with your bullshit tonight."

Silent tears streamed down her face as she gazed up at him in earnest. She was right. He hadn't been here. He had made it impossible for her to reach him. She had been alone up until this point, but not because she wanted to be. He'd been too much of an asshole to let her even get through to tell him about their baby.

Their baby.

Fuck.

Rhett assessed her for a moment as he decided his next move, then lowered himself on the edge of the bed to join her.

"Fine. I won't apologize to you tonight then. But you're not alone now, and you won't be alone through whatever comes next," he insisted, wrapping his arms around her and pulling her into a hug. The best thing he could do now—the only thing he could do really— was honor her request. Tonight wasn't about him. It was about her: about her pain and the crushing reality she was most likely facing. He couldn't give her anything else, but he could at least be with her tonight.

Chapter Twenty-Eight

1:35 a.m.

The obnoxiously loud second hand on the clock was taunting her. She didn't know what to do with her hands. She didn't know if she should sit or stand. Every movement she made set off a cacophony of sound that echoed through the small cave-like waiting area. She was the only one seated out here, alone in every way.

They'd been at the hospital for more than an hour now, and she knew nothing about what was going on down the hall in Chandler's room. Not that she was entitled to know. But the pain of not knowing and being kept in the dark was starting to take root. There was a constant ache tightening around her heart. How much longer until Rhett sent her some sort of update?

She considered going out to the car to wait. But the Prelude wasn't any comfier that the concave plastic chair she was sitting in. And she hated the idea of Rhett coming out to look for her and not finding her where she'd promised she would be. She knew cell phone reception could be spotty in a hospital. It was best if she just waited for him to find her. He'd come update her soon.

This was the first time she'd spent any real length of time in a hospital waiting room. The last hour had felt like an entire day. The heaviness of everything that had happened and everything that was still yet to come made time drag on.

She tried to pass the time playing on her phone, but all she could do was stare at the calendar on her phone. She had learned everything that was to know ovulation and the luteal phase over the last few weeks. Rhett was usually the planner, the reader, the organizer, but she had taken the reigns on all the fertility and egg retrieval research. It was her body, after all, even if it was both their futures.

Based on what little information she knew, Chandler was probably between eight and nine weeks pregnant. Meaning she had gotten pregnant seven weeks ago. Less than two months ago. The weekend of Easter. The weekend of her scans. The weekend Rhett didn't come home.

The irony wasn't lost on her. The guilt and responsibility of what she had done—about the series of events that created this situation and allowed it to happen in the first place—weighed heavily on her mind. It was a cruel and merciless Universe that pulled at the thread unraveling their lives tonight.

A noise down the hall alerted her to someone approaching. She squinted her eyes, eager to see if her husband was coming out with an update. She didn't even know what she wanted him to say; there was no right response to hope for. But just knowing *something* would be better than sitting here clueless at this point.

Instead of Rhett, the same nurse from earlier emerged in the hall. She didn't bother looking up from the file in her hand as she closed the space between them before veering left and circling around the check in desk. Tori knew that engaging her would be futile. She wouldn't know anything until Rhett texted her or came out and updated her himself.

She tried not to let her mind wander as the second hand on the clock served as a staccato metronome to her anxiety. Why hadn't she thought to bring her AirPods? Probably because she hadn't had time to think. She had just reacted.

Her husband had gotten another woman pregnant.

Her husband could have been, or was still going to be, a dad, but she was not the mother of his baby.

That role went to a woman Tori had insisted he date; A woman Tori had hand-picked because of what now seemed like a childish, absurd, ridiculous arrangement.

She blew out a long sigh, frustrated by her own immaturity and naiveté that had brought them to this place. What the hell had she been thinking, messing with their lives—with their futures and their hearts—the way she had done? Now people were hurting. No, not just hurting. Now people were suffering.

She wasn't innocent in any of this. She was the root cause of so much of this. She was the storm. Rhett got Chandler pregnant. Chandler was possibly losing the baby. And all of it— every broken branch, every downed power line, every crack of thunder— all of it was happening because of what Tori made him do.

She shoved to her feet in frustration. She couldn't sit still any longer. She knew she couldn't just take off, and it wasn't her place to go find Rhett, but she needed to do something. She needed to move.

She took a few steps out of the waiting area and cautiously glanced over at the check-in station. The nurse wasn't sitting there any longer. Tori was alone once more.

She followed a long hallway opposite the way they had come in and found a small room marked Family Lounge. The door swung open easily, so she didn't feel too bad pushing into the space. A refrigerator, sink, and a few cabinets dominated most of the room. A quick peek inside revealed a fully stocked fridge with just a few items labeled like they belonged to someone. She helped herself to a water bottle, then pulled open one of the cupboard drawers. The inside was filled to the brim with packaged snacks and candy bars. She snagged two packs of peanut M&Ms since they were Rhett's favorite, and they at least had a bit of protein to balance out the inevitable sugar high.

She looked around for a price list or donation jar but didn't see anything of the sort. *I'm sure it's all covered under the crazy hospital charges,* she thought to herself as she slipped back into the eerily quiet hallway.

Shit.

Did Chandler have health insurance? She had just graduated college a few weeks ago. Did she have a job lined up? No, wait. Maybe Rhett had told her Chandler was applying for internships at some point? Tori was embarrassed to admit just how little she knew about the other woman.

About the mother of her husband's child.

She ripped open the yellow package and dumped several pieces of candy into her mouth as she made her way back to the waiting area. She considered doing a few laps in the hallway rather than sit back down in that horribly hard chair, but she didn't want to wander too far.

She turned the corner and stopped in her tracks, freezing in place as she took in the sight before her. His legs were spread wide in the chair, his head bowed low. He had the tips of his fingers tented so he could rest his forehead in his hands. He must have come out to find her the moment she ducked into the Family Lounge.

"Ev?" she questioned, her heart fracturing as she took in the ghost of the man before her. Nothing but anguish filled his eyes when he lifted his head at the sound of her voice.

"You're still here," he breathed out.

This was exactly what she was afraid of. She wasn't going anywhere, and she needed him to know that. She made her way over to him in three strides, meeting him toe-to-toe as he rose up from the seat she had been occupying just minutes ago.

"I'm here," she promised, wrapping her arms around his torso and pulling him close. "I'm not going anywhere. I just went to get some snacks."

They didn't say anything for a few breaths, instead just holding each other. She tried to give him everything in that moment: all her love, all her strength. Every ounce of support she could pass into him, every bit of comfort she could spare. He returned her embrace, but she could feel the feebleness in his hug. He was just barely holding on.

"That's what I came out here to talk to you about, V. I think you should go home."

She pulled back and glanced up at him without dropping her arms. "Rhett..." She wasn't going to leave him. Not here. Not alone. Not like this.

"They still haven't even sent up the goddamn ultrasound tech to confirm anything," he explained. He brushed a loose hair away from her face and tucked it behind her ear out of habit. He looked so defeated, but at least his eyes weren't so hazy anymore.

"It's almost two a.m. Chandler is going to be here the rest of the night, and maybe into tomorrow, depending on what they say when they finally examine her. I think she knows it's... it's over. But she won't take any pain meds yet just in case. She's a mess, she's exhausted, and she's in a ton of pain." Tori swallowed down the thump in her throat. Finding out her husband's former hookup was pregnant with his child was hard. But standing in the hospital and listening to details of their loss was an entirely different kind of anguish.

"I think I need to stay with her." He was right. He needed to be here. Tori knew him well enough to know he'd never forgive himself if he wasn't here. She nodded in earnest, not even sure what she was agreeing to, but knowing she was willing to do whatever she could to support him.

"But I think I need to stay here alone."

Hell no. She wouldn't leave him. He was just barely hanging on. He needed to stay, and she needed to be here to support him.

"No, Rhett, I want to be here for..."

"I know, beautiful. I know. I *want* you here, too. The selfish part of me wants you to stay and hold me and just be here with me. I can't even sit in that fucking room without thinking about you out here, V. I can't stop worrying about what you're thinking, what you're feeling, what you need. I keep getting distracted thinking about how tired you probably feel after that drive. You've been up since sunrise. You've been up for almost twenty-four hours."

"So have you," she argued feebly. There was no real fight behind her words. She wanted to be here to support him, but she didn't want to be a distraction either. She wasn't willing to make things harder for him or for Chandler right now. And if she was honest with herself, she was relieved at the idea of not having to sit here all night and into tomorrow.

She watched as Rhett turned his head away from her, no doubt feeling the shame deep in his gut that he couldn't hide in his voice. He worked his jaw back and forth as he stared off down the hallway. After a few more seconds of contemplation, he finally spoke again.

"This is my mess. I did this. I screwed up so fucking bad, and now I have to deal with the consequences. I've been freaking out for the last hour, debating whether it was worse to ask you to stay or to go. But you should never have had to be here in the first place, beautiful. It's my fault you're here. It's my fault Chandler's here. It's my fault you had to drive me. It's all my fucking fault." His voice cracked on the last word, snapping all the stoicism she had worked so hard to maintain for him.

Tears silently started to fall down her face. She wasn't upset about being asked to leave. She was just so sad that this was happening. That they were here. That Chandler was in there. None of this would have ever been their reality if she hadn't made him...

"Don't," Rhett demanded, snapping her out of her thoughts. "Please, V. Please don't cry," he begged. "If you cry, I'll break. All I want to do is make this go away. To take away your pain. To take back everything I did and every choice I made that landed us here. But it's too late for that now. I can't undo what's been done. I can't undo it anymore than I can ask you to stay. I don't know if this is the right thing to do or not, but I think I have a plan."

She offered him the smallest smirk. The whole world could be crashing down around them, and Everhett Wheeler would somehow still come up with a plan.

"I'm going to stay here, in Columbus, for now. Not because I want to be here, or because I don't want to be with you—"

"I know. You don't have to spend one second worrying about that, Ev. I've already said it once tonight, but you don't have to worry about me or about our relationship. Not now. Not ever."

"I love you so goddamn much," he breathed out in a rush, crashing his mouth into hers for just a second before pulling back and looking her in the eye to finish explaining.

"I'm going to stay here, and it might be a few days, depending on what happens. Chandler told me she got dropped off at the ER tonight by someone who lives in her building. She just moved into a new apartment and started an internship this week. She doesn't know anyone in Columbus, and her parents don't even know that she's... that she was pregnant."

Tori nodded her understanding. Rhett had to stay with Chandler. He had to take care of her. She knew his heart and the fabric of his being wouldn't allow him to do anything less. That didn't make the reality of the situation burn any less.

"I don't want you driving back tonight, but I don't want you stuck here all night either. What do you think about calling Jake to come get you?"

She ran her teeth over her lower lip as she considered her options. Part of her wished Rhett would just let her take the Prelude home, but the idea of having to come back down to pick him up sometime in the next few days was almost as unappealing as waking her dad up and asking him to come get her. She knew Jake had to work in the morning—he would barely have enough time to make it to Columbus and back before the start of his early shift at Clinton's. But she also knew he would come, no questions asked. And when it was time to ask questions, she could give him honest answers, which she wouldn't feel comfortable sharing with anyone else.

Only Jake would do.

"Okay," she relented after a few more moments of consideration. She inhaled deeply. Jake was already pissed at Rhett. This whole situation, especially the reason she had to be the one to drive him here in the first place, was going to stir the pot in the worst kind of way.

"Let me call him, though," she suggested, easing back a few steps to pull her phone out of her back pocket.

"V..."

"I'm serious, Rhett. Let me handle Jake. You're dealing with enough," she insisted, already scrolling through her contacts to find his name. Now that a decision had been made, she needed to act. If she waited any longer to call, he wouldn't be able to make it to Columbus and back before his shift, and she'd be stuck at the hospital until tomorrow evening.

"Okay, yeah." He took a few steps away from her to give her space. He slumped against the frame of the entrance to the waiting area and watched her lift the phone to her ear.

It only rang twice before Jake picked up.

"Tori?" he answered in question. "What's wrong, baby?"

His voice was thick and gravelly. He had obviously been sleeping.

"I'm okay. Rhett's okay, too. But we need your help." She glanced over at her husband where he stood. His face was pained, his arms crossed across his chest. There wasn't an easy way to explain to Jake what was going on, and they both knew it. Part of her wondered if she should have sent Rhett away before making this call.

"I'm in Columbus right now, and I need a ride home. Rhett and I came down here because... because Chandler called him tonight and had an emergency."

"What the fuck? What does that even mean?" She could hear him moving around, most likely getting dressed. Of course he wouldn't hesitate.

"Chandler is pregnant," she provided, trying to sound as matter-of-fact about the statement as possible. "Or she was. She's bleeding a lot, and they think she's miscarrying, so we're at the hospital, and we're waiting for them to confirm it."

"He got her pregnant?" Jake growled into the phone. She closed her eyes, absorbing the statement and the vitriol in his voice while trying to steel her expression so Rhett wouldn't know the context of what had just been said.

"Yes," she finally replied. She lifted her eyes to meet her husband's. No matter how much she tried to protect him, he knew Jake well enough to know how his best friend was going to respond. Rhett's face was almost emotionless. Almost. She knew better than to fall for his apathetic mask.

"Can you come get me? I know you have to work tomorrow, but we drove one car down here, and we both decided that Rhett needs to stay."

"I'll be on the road in less than ten minutes, baby. Text me the address and where to park, okay?"

"Thank you, Jake." She sighed as she felt some of the tension that had built up over the last several hours dissipate.

"Is Rhett there with you right now?"

"Yes," she answered honestly.

"And yet you're the one calling me... Hey, get up," he muttered. Tori's curiosity piqued at who he was talking to on his end. Did Jake have an overnight guest? She'd have plenty of time to get it out of him during their two-hour drive back to Hampton.

"Do you want to talk to..."

"I'll talk to him when I get there," Jake declared with finality. "I've gotta stop for some caffeine, then I'll be there as soon as I can."

"Okay, drive safe."

She ended the call and sought out her husband one more time. She took a few steps forward and leaned into him, essentially boxing him in against the door jamb of the waiting room. Rhett had his gaze fixed down the hall, his posture still rigid, his arms still locked across his body. She reached out and pulled on each of his forearms to unwrap him, to force him to let her in.

"Jake will be here in a few hours," she murmured into his neck as she wrapped her arms around his torso. Rhett didn't reply, but she could feel him nod. "He wants to see you when he gets here." He stiffened slightly, then nodded again.

Wordlessly, his hand found the small of her back. He started rubbing figure eights up and down the base of her spine. It was his go-to move whenever she had cramps or needed extra comfort. Trouble was, she wasn't the one cramping or in need of his comfort right now. At least not physically.

She didn't need anything from him now. She wouldn't take what he didn't have to give. Tori could feel herself building a wall, becoming a fortress. The foundation had started as soon as she read the text from Chandler. She didn't want to come off as crass or cold, but she couldn't let herself feel anything either. She had to protect her heart and be strong for Rhett. If she let herself think too much about what was happening... about what had been at stake a few months ago and what she had been willing to gamble to prove a point and dig her heels in the night of the Jake and Rhett Party... she would crumble.

She couldn't crumble tonight. Not as her husband was breaking right in front of her eyes.

"I don't know how we're going to get through this," Rhett confessed into her hair.

She didn't know either. But she wasn't willing to admit that to him. Not tonight. Not when he had so little to hope for, so little left to cling to.

"I don't know how either, but I know we will. I promise we will."

CHAPTER TWENTY-NINE

Rhett

It was almost four in the morning, on what was arguably the worst day of his life. How many times had he seen four a.m on the clock over the last few months? What he wouldn't give to not be seeing it again now.

The ultrasound tech had finally made an appearance, only to discover that the machine wasn't charged. Of course it wasn't charged. Just when they thought they were going to get answers, when he thought she was going to get some relief... Chandler had been here for eight fucking hours without any confirmation of what was going on.

There was no urgency to anyone else's actions. The only urgency seemed to live inside him. His anxiety crested in waves, the ripple effect set off every time someone opened Chandler's door or they heard footsteps coming down the hallway.

Once Jake was on his way, Tori had encouraged him to come back to the room. He'd been dutifully sitting by Chandler's side for the last two hours, alternating between holding her hand, rubbing her back, and glaring at each and every hospital employee who dared to enter the room without an update. The janitor who came by to collect the trash had run out of the room so fast he practically fell into the hallway.

He knew Jake would be arriving soon. He kept checking to make sure he hadn't missed the text or call alerting him to the fact that his best friend was there or that his wife was about to leave.

He offered Chandler a tight smile as he squeezed her hand assuredly. "Hang in there. If the tech doesn't come back in the next ten minutes, I'll go find someone else. Someone higher up. That can't have been the only machine in the whole damn hospital."

"I'm just so tired." She sighed, closing her eyes before scrunching her nose up in pain. "If the baby had any chance of making it, things wouldn't be taking this long." Her words came out barely above a whisper, the confession seeming to be as much for herself as it was for him. She kept her eyes closed, but even while it looked like she was resting, he could tell she was hurting.

"Don't say that," he insisted. "We don't know that."

"I Googled it," she offered quietly as she opened her eyes and turned on her side to face him. She tucked her legs up into her stomach, wincing as she struggled to get comfortable. "I've bled way too much. I've been bleeding since this morning. The cramps I'm feeling aren't normal cramps. They're contractions. There's just no way..." A single tear rolled down her cheek. Rhett reached out and wiped it away with his thumb before cupping her face in his hand.

"You're strong, Chandler. You've been so fucking strong. I'm so sorry this is happening. Do you think it's time to ask for pain meds?" he suggested. "I respect your decision if you don't want to take them yet... but fuck. I can tell how much you're hurting right now, and there's nothing else I can do. Let me call the nurse and get you something for the pain."

She hesitated, then nodded feebly. Her delayed response gave him pause.

"Yes for real? This has to be your decision, Chandler." As much as he wanted her to not be in pain, he refused to be the reason she did anything she didn't want to do. It may have been his baby, but it was her body. She needed to make the choice.

"Yes. I'll take something now. Can you get the nurse?"

"On it." Rhett shot to his feet and headed for the door, grateful to be in motion and to have something to do after feeling utterly helpless for hours.

As soon as he stepped into the hall, his phone buzzed in his pocket.
V: He's here.

Rhett walked even faster to the nurse's station and let them know
Chandler was requesting something for the pain. The nurse from
earlier didn't make any comments, but he saw a flash of relief in her
eyes.

He turned on his heel and ventured back to the waiting area,
spotting his best friend hugging his wife at the end of the hall. He
was laser-focused on the two of them as he approached. He was too
far away to hear anything they were saying, but he still felt an
upwelling of calm as he watched Jake give Tori the comfort she
needed right now.

Almost as if he could sense his presence, Jake lifted his head and
met his gaze. The other man continued to hold Tori in his arms as a
look of pure contempt hit Rhett like a ton of bricks.

*I know you're pissed, bro. Give me all your loathing. I fucking
deserve it all.*

"Hey," Rhett greeted him when he was in range, alerting Tori to
his presence. She slowly pulled out of Jake's arms and turned to face
him.

"How is she?" she asked.

"The same really, but fading fast. She's exhausted. She's just in so
much pain." He looked between his wife and his best friend as he
continued. "We're still waiting on an ultrasound to confirm
everything. But she finally asked for pain meds, so..." He blew out a
long breath, not sure what else to even say.

"Hey, baby?" Jake asked. "Can I talk to your husband alone for a
few minutes?"

Tori glanced over to meet Rhett's gaze, checking in to confirm he
was okay. He nodded to her once, trying his best to convey some
semblance of calm. "I'll go to the bathroom and grab us a few more
snacks for the drive home," she offered before reaching out to take
Rhett's hand. "Don't leave until I get back, 'kay?"

"I wouldn't dare," he vowed, nodding solemnly and squeezing her hand before letting her go. She turned on her heel and headed down the opposite hall, leaving the two men to face off alone.

"Fuck, bro," Jake opened, raking a hand through his short hair as he shook his head in disbelief. "This is insane."

Rhett nodded, welcoming the criticism. He wanted Jake to verbally assail him. Part of him craved the pain. At least disappointment and shame hit different than the grief waiting for him down the hall. "I know. Thank you so much for coming..."

"Did you know?" Jake demanded, cutting him off before he could get another word in.

"Did I know what?"

"Did you know that Chandler was pregnant?"

Rhett felt himself physically recoil at the accusation disguised as a question.

"No, I didn't fucking know. You think I would keep something like this from you? From Tori?"

Jake lifted his hand to the back of his neck as he assessed him. He was looking at him like he was searching for some sort of tell. "I don't know what to think," he finally replied. "I don't know what to believe with you half the time these days..." He blew out another long breath. His comment dripped with disappointment. Rhett had never felt so small standing before his best friend.

"I didn't fucking know," Rhett growled out again. "I swear to you, bro. I haven't talked to Chandler in weeks. I don't even know when it happened."

"After our last party, when you didn't come home for weeks and weeks," Jake supplied with a pointed look. Leave it to him to have already figured out the math.

"I mean, yeah. I guess. I know based on the timing that the baby is mine. Or was mine. Fuck. There's no doubt on the timing of things. I just never thought..." he trailed off before his voice could crack. He averted his eyes to the floor and shook his head in shame. It was all too much. It was like each time he tried to wrap his head around what was happening, another realization burst into his consciousness that sent him even deeper down the path of self-loathing. He had fucked up so hard.

Jake's tone was softer as he pulled Rhett out of his own thoughts. "Hey. Bro. You're okay. I was just making sure I understood what's happening and where things stand. I believe you didn't know. I'm so sorry this is happening."

Rhett released a full breath as relief flooded his lungs. Jake believed him. He didn't know that was something he needed until now. He couldn't control anyone's judgment of the consequences of his actions, but he needed them to believe he didn't know anything about this until tonight.

"Thanks. It's... It's just been a lot. And it's not over. Listen, I'm not sure how much Tori told you, but I might need to stay down here for a few days..."

"Consider it handled. Anything you need me to do, anything she needs... I got you, bro."

Rhett bit down on the side of his cheek to keep himself from tearing up. It had been such a long, emotional night already. Knowing that Tori was going to be taken care of and that he didn't have to worry about her right now gave him a sense of temporary relief.

"Are you going to be okay if I take her back to Hampton? I know this whole situation sucks, but maybe you should..."

"You have to take her home," Rhett insisted. "She doesn't deserve to just sit here and have to deal with the consequences of all this. She's all I can think about already, and that's not fair to any of us."

"So if you don't want her mixed up in this, then why is she here?"

He stilled at the question. He dreaded what his answer would reveal. He was ashamed of the admission he didn't feel ready to admit.

"We went out to dinner tonight."

Truth.

"I had a few drinks."

Truth.

"Then when we got home, we were hanging out in the sunroom. I set up my computer at the bar because we had an emergency at work today. Tori was sketching, and we were just hanging out."

Truth.

"I didn't know anything about this until I heard from Chandler around ten p.m."

Truth.

"By then I'd had several drinks. I thought we were in for the night."

Truth.

"Once I realized I had to get to Columbus, I asked Tori to drive me."

Lie.

Jake nodded in understanding. "Okay. So you do still have a limit. Good to know."

What the hell was that supposed to mean?

"Sir?" A nurse he didn't recognize interrupted them. He turned away from Jake to give her his full attention. "Sir, the ultrasound technician is back, and they're ready now. Your wife is asking for you."

Rhett blinked in slow motion as the words cut into his severed heart. *His wife.* He didn't bother correcting her. He was wearing a wedding ring after all. And it would take too long to try and explain that his actual wife was currently somewhere else in this hospital, waiting on their mutual friend to whisk her away from this nightmare he had created for them all.

"I'll be right there," he replied to the nurse before turning back to Jake.

"Bro..." he croaked out, his voice cracking as he came face-to-face with everything he didn't want to do. How was he supposed to send Tori away, walk back to Chandler's hospital room, and sit back idly as someone confirmed the death of his child?

"I'd do anything for you, Rhett. I've got you for anything you need."

He didn't need Jake's assurances to know that. They had been best friends for twenty years. They were brothers for life. But hearing Jake say it out loud was still a small comfort as he felt the vise grip of anxiety start to squeeze.

"Tori is…"

"She'll be okay. I'll make sure she's okay," Jake promised.

"She has a doctor's appointment on Monday," he murmured, not letting his mind linger on the realization that Tori would most likely be going to her first egg retrieval appointment alone.

"I'll keep her close for the next few days or for however long this takes."

He nodded, defeated. It was all he could do.

"Fuck. I've gotta find Tori… I've gotta go…"

"I'll go wait by the elevators. Send her my way when you're done."

"Thanks, bro. Thanks for coming for her. Thanks for… thanks for everything."

Jake nodded once before turning around and walking away.

Rhett stalked down the hall he'd seen Tori walk down a few minutes ago. She was either in the restroom, or… He spotted her through the glass door panel of a room marked Family Lounge.

"Hey, V?" he asked as he pushed through the door, not wanting to startle her as he approached from behind.

She turned around slowly, revealing her tear-stained cheeks and bloodshot eyes. He was once again hit with the gut feeling that they weren't going to survive this. He let the lounge door slam behind him as he wrapped her in his arms. "I'm so sorry, V," he whispered into her hair. "I'm so fucking sorry."

His own tears started up again, the moisture falling down his face before he even had a chance to wipe it away. How anyone had any tears left to shed tonight was beyond him. But they all seemed to keep finding reserves.

"The ultrasound tech is back, so I have to go now. Jake is down by the elevators, waiting for you."

She nodded against his shirt but held him tighter, like she wasn't planning on releasing him anytime soon. A loud sob escaped her but was muffled by her mouth pressed up against his chest.

Please don't cry, beautiful. Don't break down. Don't break me. Don't let us break.

"I don't know if I can do this," she confessed through another sniffle.

Rhett stilled, then instinctively tightened his hold. They were clinging to each other with such ferocity he wouldn't be surprised if they both had bruises tomorrow. What did she mean by that? This couldn't be their breaking point. They had come too far. They had fought too hard to get here. He wouldn't let her give up on him now.

"What can't you do?" he asked hesitantly, holding his breath as he waited for her answer.

"I don't think I can walk away. I can't leave you here like this," she sobbed.

His heart broke all over again. Her tears weren't for herself. She wasn't thinking about cutting her losses or trying to get out of their marriage. Her tears were all for him. His beautiful, amazing, selfless wife was only worried about him in that moment.

"Well, aren't we a pair? I don't know if I can make you leave." He worked his hand into her hair and possessively gripped the back of her neck. She let him hold her. She let him feel her devotion. He couldn't even begin to process any of the emotions churning in his own gut. But if he could focus on Tori, if he could just be here for her now...

His phone vibrated in his pocket, pulling them both out of their trance. The reality of the situation was that he didn't have an extra second to spare. It didn't even matter who was texting him. Chandler... Jake... Hell, it could even be Quinn, informing him of another work emergency that was wreaking havoc and sending his world into even deeper turmoil. It seemed like anything was possible after the last twenty-four hours.

Tori shuffled back slightly, blinking away more tears as she raised her gaze to meet his.

Rhett bowed his head low, completely uncertain how to let go or how to convince her to leave. He kissed each of her cheeks, trying to absorb all the tears he had caused.

"Please don't hate me for this," he whispered as he rested his forehead against hers.

"Never," she replied automatically. "Not now. Not ever." She broke out of his grasp and moved toward the door, an unconvincing confidence to her gait. She turned around once more before stepping into the hall.

"I love you, Everhett Wheeler. Please come back to me as soon as you can."

CHAPTER THIRTY

Tori

"Come on, baby. Let's get you home."

Jake slung an arm around her shoulders as they stepped out of the elevator and into the hospital parking garage. She leaned into him and let him lead her, grateful for his solidness. She had lost track of time at this point, and being underground in the lower level of the parking deck was disorienting. "Are you going to be late for work?"

"Cory took the opening shift for me," he replied as he guided her down the next row of cars. "I didn't give him a reason or even mention you... just told him it was important."

Seeing Jake's black Jeep was a balm to her soul. Knowing that she was leaving Rhett when he needed her was hard, but there was still a sense of relief that washed over her as she reached for the passenger door handle.

"Hold up." He reached around her and pulled open the back door. "I brought along a surprise. You're going to want to sit back here."

Tori was too exhausted for his words to fully register, but she ducked under his arm to crawl into the backseat anyways. Instead of finding an empty bench, someone else was already in the back, offering her a megawatt grin as she climbed into the car.

"Fielding?!" She felt a grin take over her face before she even realized she was smiling. It was the first time she had done anything besides scowl or cry for hours.

"What the heck are you doing here?"

"Hey, Tor," he offered sheepishly. She couldn't tell if he was tired or uncomfortable or maybe a little of both. She scooted across the back seat and practically fell onto him with a sigh of relief. He wrapped his arms around her on contact, holding her so much tighter than she expected, but exactly as tight as she needed. He squeezed her once for emphasis, then used a firm grip on her upper arms to pull her away so he could look her in the eyes.

She hadn't looked in a mirror in hours. She could feel the raw, tender skin pulling around her eyes. She didn't shy away from Fielding's assessment, though. He had seen her at her literal worst, and he was still hanging around. She didn't need to hide anything from him.

"You good?" he asked gently, concern coating his words. Based on that question alone, she knew Jake had filled him in.

She nodded and inhaled through her nose before speaking. She trusted Jake, and they both trusted Field. It wasn't like no one was ever going to find out about this.

"I'm okay. But I'm shocked to see you right now. Why are you here?"

"I was asleep on Jake's couch when you called him."

"Yeah, this one can pass out anywhere," Jake interjected as he caught Tori's eye through the rearview mirror, "but I wasn't about to leave him unsupervised at the condo. Besides, once I woke him up and told him where I was going, he wouldn't let me leave without tagging along."

"You know I'm always up for a little Tori Recon Mission," Fielding teased as he reached around her and pulled the seatbelt across her body. "Here ya go."

She took the strap from his hand and secured the buckle in place.

"I hope it's okay that I'm here. Jake told me just the bare minimum, I think."

"Correct," the other man confirmed from the front of the car as he paid the parking meter to get out of the garage.

Fielding drummed his fingers on the middle seat between them, tapping out an anxious rhythm that was out of character for him. "I knew better than to come in. I'm really sorry about what's happening. For both of you. Or, I guess, all three of you. I'm not trying to insert myself into anything, and I have my headphones if you and Jake need to talk and you don't want me to hear. I just needed to make sure you were okay. Between this and Wheeler's stunt at The Grille..." he whispered the last part so only she could hear the worry to his words.

"I'm glad you're here," she insisted before reaching across the empty middle seat and squeezing his hand to quiet his anxious drumming.

"Chandler is or was pregnant with Rhett's baby. She started bleeding earlier today. They think she's having a miscarriage. She just moved to this area, so she's all alone. Rhett and I drove down here as soon as we found out what was going on."

There. That was the black and white, cut-and-dry version of the story. That wasn't as hard to explain as she thought. She would have told Fielding all of this eventually anyways, so it didn't bother her if he knew what was going on now.

Fielding sighed after a few beats of heavy silence. "You're a really good person, Tor."

She held back a scoff in response to his praise. She wasn't a good person. A good person wouldn't have fucked up everyone's life like this. There wasn't anything good about anything she'd done, about the deep, unforgiveable pain she had caused. If he knew that Rhett and Chandler were only ever together because of her... or that Rhett went back to Chandler when she had convinced him she had sex with Fielding a few months ago... she couldn't bear to consider what Fielding would really think of her if he knew.

Jake interrupted her spiraling thoughts as he merged the Jeep onto the highway. "Damn, I forgot how much I hate hospitals. Tori, remember that time we had to take Lia to the ER because she twisted her ankle drunkenly jumping off the pole barn?"

She knew what he was doing. He was trying to take her mind off things, to lighten the mood. She didn't feel like she deserved to feel any happiness, but she took the bait anyway. "She was *so* mad at you that night."

A grim shadow of guilt embedded in her heart as Jake set his cruise control at seventy-five MPH, heading north. She was leaving her husband in Columbus to navigate his pain alone. How the hell was she supposed to be okay with just leaving him? But she knew Rhett had been right in asking her to leave: There was no physical place for her at the hospital. He needed to focus his attention on Chandler and what they'd lost. Tori was a distraction; just an afterthought in this situation.

"Yeah, but I'd rather endure the wrath of Lia for a few hours than find out later that she broke her ankle and I did nothing. Have you ever broken anything, Field?"

"Yep. But just once, which is impressive considering I played hockey all four years at Arch. When we were six, Dempsey and I were goofin' off, and I fell into the bedframe in our parents' room. We weren't supposed to be in there, so Dem convinced me not to say anything for a few days. By the third day, I couldn't even lift my arm up to get dressed. Our mom finally noticed and took me to the doctor. My collarbone was broken in two places."

Tori hissed in a breath through her teeth. "Ouch. How the heck did you keep quiet for so long?!"

Fielding chuckled. "Dem and I may be identical twins, but he's technically older, and he's definitely bossier."

The conversation flowed easily as they settled in for the drive home. Tori was able to stay present enough to keep herself from slipping into her own anxiety about everything that had happened that night. About half an hour later that the conversation lulled and Fielding started to drift off to sleep.

His body was slumped against the window on his side, his long legs spread wide and taking up most of the foot well of the back seat.

"I know I'm just a hot, solid mass of hard muscle over here, but you can use me as a pillow if you're tired, Tor."

She smirked at his typical cockiness before adjusting her seatbelt and letting her back come to lean against his side. Fielding lifted his arm across the back of the bench seat so she could rest her head on him if she wanted to. She accepted his unspoken invitation and shifted her weight again, nestling into the gap between his arm and his chest as she took in the scent of his expensive cologne. She knew she wouldn't be able to fall asleep, but it was still soothing to lean on someone and let her body rest after being awake for almost twenty-four hours.

She glanced up to check on Jake, catching his eye in the rearview mirror. He'd been sipping an energy drink for the last hour, and she assumed it wasn't the first round of caffeine he'd had that night, so he'd be okay if they fell asleep. He held her gaze and took in her position, offering her a smile that didn't quite meet his eyes but that didn't cast any concern or judgement either.

She waited a few minutes until she felt Fielding's breathing slow before speaking up in a whisper. "Why'd you bring him, Jake?"

He raised both his eyebrows before answering. "I told you. He was at my house and…"

"Don't bullshit me. He's asleep," she confirmed as she poked Fielding in the side. Her finger dug into the hard muscle under his T-shirt, but he didn't move or make a sound.

Jake blew out a long breath before amending his answer. "He cares about you, baby. I didn't know what the hell I was about to walk into coming down here, but I figured you were going to need a friend tonight. A friend who isn't also Rhett's best friend," he clarified. "Plus, I knew I wouldn't hear the end of it if I came to get you and left him sleeping at my house without inviting him along."

"I feel like you two are having a lot of sleepovers lately," Tori mused as she caught Jake's eye in the mirror again. She raised one eyebrow in question. "Something brewing there?"

"Nah. That boy's straight as an arrow. Besides, he only has eyes for one person in this car, and it's not me."

Tori winced. She knew there was a layer of truth to Jake's observation, but there was so much more to her connection with Fielding than the surface-level attraction everyone liked to call them out on. He was the first new friend she'd made in years, one of the only people in her life who saw her for who she was as an individual instead of who she was as one half of Tori and Rhett. She couldn't lose Fielding's friendship. She wouldn't. She was determined to do everything in her power to maintain a platonic relationship with him.

"He'll get over that," she offered.

"Yeah, I know he will. We talked about it the other night because I had to be sure. He respects you and values your friendship way too much to try and pull anything. I wouldn't have brought him along if I thought there was anything to worry about."

They were both quiet for a few minutes as she let his confession settle into her mind.

"Can I ask you something that might not land well?" The question snapped her out of her own thoughts. She nodded at him through the rearview mirror.

"Do you think Rhett knew?"

She chewed on the corner of her bottom lip, seriously considering the idea that had haunted her since the moment she read Chandler's text.

"No," she asserted. "I'm positive he didn't know. I was standing next to him when he got the text."

"Wait. What? She *texted* him?"

"Well, he said she'd been trying to call him all night. And that she had tried to call him multiple times over the last few weeks. But I'm positive he didn't know anything until he read her text."

"Wow. That's really shitty."

Tori nodded her agreement. The fact that Chandler had been trying to get in touch with Rhett for weeks was cringe-worthy, given the reason for all her attempted calls.

He didn't know. But he should have known.

"And you had to drive tonight because..." Jake trailed off and let the silence fill the space between them. This was the part she'd been dreading. More than the questions about the pregnancy. More than having to talk about the miscarriage. Confessing the depth of Rhett's struggles to his best friend was such a gray area, especially because she hadn't even had the chance to talk to Rhett about any of it yet.

"He had a lot to drink throughout the day. He couldn't drive."

Jake nodded at her before shaking his head to himself. The motion was so subtle that if she hadn't been watching for his reaction, she would have missed it completely.

"This is going to hit him hard, isn't it?"

It was a revelation disguised as a question. She could barely begin to wrap her mind around what this loss was going to do to Rhett. To his plans. To his dreams. To his struggles. To the enormous ball of stress and pressure that had been building inside him ever since she first got the call about her test results and selfishly laid so many of her own baggage on him to carry. This wasn't just going to hit him hard. She knew with certainty this was going to break him. She just didn't know when, or how, or what to expect amongst the rubble. How sharp would the pieces be when he finally crumbled?

"I can't even begin to make sense of it. Jake, she was pregnant. With his baby. Rhett was going to have a *baby*, and next month, I'm going to have a *hysterectomy*." She moved to wipe away the tears that had started to flow without her permission. She wasn't the person suffering a loss tonight. She had no right to feel sorry for herself right now.

As if he could sense her pain even in his sleep, Fielding's arm lowered and encased her. His fingertips brushed against her upper arm, leaving a trail of goosebumps in their wake. He shifted her body closer and held her as she continued to silently cry.

"I'm so sorry, baby. I know this sucks. And I know it's probably going to get worse before it gets better. I'm here for you, though. You know that, right?" She nodded, not daring to meet Jake's eyes through the rearview mirror again.

"You've gotta be exhausted. Why don't you try and sleep a little? I'll get us home safe. Where do you want to go? I can drop Field off at the Valet House if you want to crash at my place?"

She hadn't thought about that until now. She shuddered involuntarily as she thought about going back to Rhett's parents' house and crawling into their empty bed. It would be easier to be alone without his scent on the sheets, without the constant reminder of who wasn't there with her.

"Just drop me off at my house. I don't think Rhett will be home anytime soon."

CHAPTER THIRTY-ONE

Rhett

He let himself into the apartment using the key fob dangling off Chandler's pink pom pom key ring. He tried to be as quiet as possible as he made his way into the kitchen.

They had finally left the hospital just a few hours ago. Once the ultrasound tech confirmed what they all suspected, Chandler was discharged with nothing more than instructions to rest as much as possible and to schedule a follow-up appointment with her OBGYN to check that her blood levels were returning to normal.

He couldn't believe that was it. They had waited in limbo for hours to just be sent on their way with an apologetic smile and a follow-up reminder. He had at least made a big enough deal about her pain to get the resident to write her a script for Vicodin. He couldn't stand to think about her physically suffering any more than necessary after going without meds the previous day and night.

Rhett made quick work of putting away the groceries he had picked up, then dug around under the sink until he found a vase for the pink roses he bought. He knew it wasn't much—nothing he could have done would be enough—but he needed to make as much of an effort as possible. He grabbed a water bottle from the fridge before picking up the pharmacy bag and letting himself into her bedroom.

"Hey," she greeted him softly from the bed. He could just make out her shape under the covers. She was curled up on her side, her knees drawn up toward her chest and her arm wedged between her pillow and her damp hair. She must have taken a shower while he was running errands.

"Hey," he replied as he made his way across the room and sat down on the edge of the bed. "How are you? Can I get you anything?"

She shook her head and gave him a small smile. "I'm okay," she said tearfully.

He knew she was anything but okay. He knew all the hopelessness and sadness festering inside him was nothing compared to what Chandler must be feeling. In addition to the emotional trauma of the miscarriage, she also had to deal with the physical pain of the loss. She was most definitely not okay. Neither of them were. But they were both trying. And he'd be damned if she wanted for anything while he was here.

"I picked up your prescription. Here, take it now, and I'll write down the time and keep track of your next dose for you."

Chandler sat up in bed and flicked on the bedside lamp before accepting the pill bottle and water. She sighed after she swallowed the medication. "I probably can't go to work tomorrow. Nothing like calling off on your second week to make a strong first impression."

"Don't worry about that right now, Chandler. It's not like you have a cold or a hangover. This is a big fucking deal. You're in a lot of pain. The doctor said you could be bleeding for at least another week. You can't drive if you're taking Vicodin anyways, which you need to be taking right now..." he trailed off as an idea took root in his mind. "Can I take care of that for you? If you give me your supervisor's email, I'll let them know you need the week off."

"I'm pretty sure having your ex email your new boss isn't standard office protocol," she quipped.

"I'll send it from my work account. I can be surprisingly persuasive when I need to be."

Chandler assessed him for a few moments before her expression softened and she nodded. "Okay. That'll be good, actually. I just don't want them to know any details."

"I understand. I'll show you the email before I send it, okay? What else can I do for you right now?"

"Would it be weird if I asked you to rub my back? This heating pad is helping the cramps, but my low back is still killing me..."

"Move over," he instructed as he kicked off his shoes. He lowered himself onto the bed beside her, trying not to disturb the mattress or jostle her too much in the process. He kneaded the knuckles of a closed fist into the fleshy part at the bottom of her spine. "Like that?"

"Yes, that's perfect." She sighed as she pushed back into the pressure of his touch. He focused his energy on her aching muscles, channeling all his frustration and sadness into offering her the faintest glimmer of relief.

"Rhett?"

"Yeah?"

"Are you going to leave soon?"

He tried to discern what she was really asking. Did she want him to stay? Or was she subtly asking him to go? He had fucked up so many things lately. He doubted his own ability to read the situation from the context clues.

"No, not unless you want me to leave. I was going to stay tonight and probably tomorrow, too. I figured I could get a hotel room or sleep on the couch..."

"Please stay," she whispered.

"Okay. I was supposed to be in Hampton until Monday night anyways, but I can have my assistant change my flight to leave from the Columbus airport on Tuesday morning instead. I have to be at the office that day for sure, but if you want me to come back later this week, I will."

He could feel himself rambling. He knew he was offering too much. But after what Chandler had just gone through—after what he had put her through—after everything she had endured because of his carelessness—it was all he had left to give.

"That would be good. Thank you," she whispered so low he barely heard it. "Can I ask you something else? Something personal?"

His kneading faltered, but only for a second. He could guess what she was going to say next. He knew it would come up eventually. There was no hope avoiding this conversation after he'd just promised to stay with her for the next few days.

"You already got married, didn't you?"

"I did," he answered cautiously, switching hands as he stalled. He instinctively looked down at his wedding ring as he continued to work that same hand into her back. He didn't want to make Chandler feel like she was prying, so he continued, "Tori and I got married two weeks ago at my parents' lake cabin. It was a super fast engagement, obviously. The only reason we weren't together over the last several years was because she refused to officially date me or make things exclusive. I know that probably sounds shitty, considering that you and I..."

"It was always her, wasn't it?"

He inhaled through his nose. Chandler's tone wasn't aggressive; it wasn't nearly as sharp or angry as he deserved. She sounded genuinely curious.

"Yes. Tori and I have a long and complicated history, but it was always her. I'm sorry I wasn't honest with you about that. I'm so fucking sorry that I..."

"Everhett," she scolded. "I told you I don't want your apologies right now. Someday, maybe. But for now, all I want is honesty. Well, that, and for you to keep pressing into that spot, because it really is helping."

Rhett clamped his lips together to physically stop himself from saying anything else. He wanted to respect her request, but that didn't stop the words from dancing on the tip of his tongue. He was so desperate to try and explain himself, to apologize over and over again for all the ways he had lied by omission and withheld the truth when they were together.

The logical part of his brain got it. She didn't want to listen to him grovel or try to defend his choices. He never expected any of it to go this way. There was so much hurt, so much physical and emotional pain caused because of what they did, because of what he agreed to do to be with Tori.

For some reason, his mind jumped back into a memory he'd worked hard to forget over the last several months. It was the night of the now infamous Jake and Rhett Party. The night Tori met Fielding. The night Chandler met Tori. The night everything shifted.

Tori had gotten drunk at the party, then locked herself in the bathroom. He'd been trying to play it cool all night, but when he heard her sobbing through the door, he lost it. He distinctly remembered the way the pain radiated up his arm when he pounded on the barrier between them. He remembered the words he spit out in frustration when she refused to face him. "*Did you really think no one would get hurt? Did you think we'd come out of this unscathed?*"

He never could have imagined they'd have to live out the consequences of their shittiest choices like this. He never imagined the depth of pain they could cause because of what happened that night.

Chandler spoke again, rattling him out of his own spiraling thoughts. "Do you think in another life it could have been you and me?"

Rhett stilled. He had never stopped to consider an actual future with Chandler. For him, it had always been Tori. Chandler was a fill-in-the-blank answer that fit into the rules of the arrangement Tori created for them. But as time carried on, Chandler had expanded into his life like insulated foam. She was convenient and companionable. He had never meant for her to be around long term or for her to consider herself his girlfriend, especially since they'd never talked about being exclusive. Their lack of communication had allowed her to fill in the blanks with the answers she liked best. In hindsight, his coolness to her was worse than callousness.

Now she was collateral damage: A victim to the mess he and Tori had made trying to outrun the fate they'd finally admitted was inevitable.

The answer to her question was no. He had never thought about a future with Chandler because he couldn't see past what he wanted most for the last ten years. But he wouldn't say anything to hurt her tonight as she lay curled up in bed with a heating pad pressed into her abdominal.

"I don't know about the what ifs, babe. I do know that I messed up a lot. I'm not going to try and apologize again tonight, but I'll never stop regretting the pain I caused you."

"You really love her, don't you?"

"Chandler," he warned. He didn't want to go there. He could talk about Tori in the abstract, but confessing his love for his wife to his ex felt too intimate.

She sighed, and he knew she wouldn't bring her up again. She inched closer instead, her head resting against the solidness of his chest as he continued to rub her low back.

"Tell me something true, Rhett."

"What do you mean?"

"I know it's never going to be you and me... never was, never will be. But even if it was never going to be you and me, what we almost had... what I lost..." She choked out a sob that lit up every frayed nerve in his body. He was trying so hard to stay strong—to let her feel her grief while trying to push down his own—but her tears slid right past that armor.

"No one else in my life even knows I was pregnant. Once you go, this is all over for me. I'll be okay. I know that. But right now, while you're here, I'm going to let myself be sad. So tell me something true, so I have something to remember when I'm alone and missing our baby that we never got to meet."

A silent tear rolled down his cheek. Watching Chandler mourn their shoddy relationship *and* mourn the child they lost shrouded him in a kind of grief he had never felt before. Sadness exuded off her aching body and found a home in him. The intensity of her grief spoke to the darkest parts of his being.

He didn't know if he'd ever be a dad. They planned to freeze embryos before Tori had her hysterectomy next month, and he had assured her they were walking that path without expectation. He had promised Tori he didn't want or need kids if he had her. That was his truth. But knowing he had so abruptly lost something he never even allowed himself to dream of still carved out a pit in his stomach and an ache in his heart. How did anyone recover from the loss of something that was never theirs to lose?

"Rhett?" Chandler implored.

He cleared his throat and tried to come up with something, anything, to help her through this. He would tell her anything he could think of if he could bring her some semblance of peace tonight.

"You would have been a really good mom."

Chandler let out a soft sob.

"And we would have figured things out. Not as a couple," he clarified, "but as a family."

Her shoulders shook against his body as she continued to cry. He held her tight and tried to absorb as much of the pain as she'd give him.

He kept talking, desperate to change the subject, trying to prevent both of them from drowning in the possibility of what could have been and what now would never be. "I remember the first night we met. You walked into Chippy's like a woman on a mission. You were wearing pink, and you smelled like vanilla. You were the sparkliest girl in the bar."

"I remember that night, too," she sniffled. "I Googled you before we met up."

"You Googled me?"

"Of course I Googled you. Your dating profile looked too good to be true. My friends were sure you had stolen a picture off the Internet and were some creeper who was going to kidnap me that night. But nope. Lo and behold, I showed up, and you were the real McCoy. Everhett Wheeler: handsome. Charming. Polite. Future CEO. Just cocky enough to be sexy. Basically every Easton University sorority girl's wet dream."

Rhett chuckled at her assessment.

"Will you promise me something?" he asked, his tone more serious now. "Obviously you don't owe me anything, and I know I'm not the model of great life choices lately, but I want you to make me a promise if you can. Don't let this destroy you, Chandler. Don't let what happened between us or this loss make you fade away. I know it feels horrible and all-consuming right now, but I promise someday things will feel better. You'll get better. And you'll find better."

"I know that, and I won't. I promise," she whispered.

"I'm sorry I lost our baby."

He was gutted by the simplicity of her words. He was also perturbed that she was allowed to apologize to him, but she refused to hear any repetencies from him.

"It's not your fault, Chandler. You heard what the doctor said. There's nothing you could have done differently or not done to change what happened."

She nodded then yawned. "I know you already said you'd stay, but can you stay in here with me while I sleep? I don't want to be alone right now. I don't even know what time it is, but I can barely keep my eyes open."

"I'll stay," he confirmed. "I'll stay, and I'll do anything else you need while I'm here. Just sleep for now. You've been through hell, and you need to rest. I'll be here when you wake up."

CHAPTER THIRTY-TWO

Rhett

Leaving Columbus was one of the hardest things he'd ever done. Every action, every step forward was a bitter and merciless reminder of what he was leaving behind. His ex, who was still bleeding from losing their child. His car, which was stranded in the long-term parking garage at the airport since he didn't know when he'd be back to Columbus.

He had stayed with Chandler on Sunday and Monday like she requested. She seemed to be improving, so much so that she had wanted to eat dinner at the table last night and then hang out in the living room while watching *The Bachelor*. She said the bleeding had slowed and the cramping was less. She hadn't even taken a Vicodin that morning before he left, insisting that Tylenol would be enough.

He was glad she'd let him handle calling her off work. A cordial but solemn email to her boss from his own work account was all it took to excuse her for the whole week with a written guarantee there would be no consequences or marks on her employee file.

Knowing how to say goodbye to her—to the would-be mother of his child—was all sorts of painful. Even the mechanics of it were awkward: he went in for a hug, she kept her arms resting at her sides. He told her to take care of herself and to let him know if she needed anything, but his parting words felt shallow.

He didn't know when he'd even see her again unless she asked him to come back to Columbus for some reason. And he didn't see that happening: She was already claiming she felt better and that she'd be able to get herself to the follow-up appointment she had scheduled for Friday. She promised to text him and keep him updated. Beyond that, they were done.

He had been so angry the last time they saw each other in a random parking lot of Easton University. He had never had a problem saying goodbye to Chandler before. This was the first time he had ever struggled to walk away.

There was a harsh duality to Chandler's confession about him leaving. Once he left her place, it was all over. He had to let go of a version of his life he didn't even know was a possibility until it was ripped out from under him. The longing to freeze a moment in time and honor the life that could have been for their baby resonated deep in his soul.

His baby.

Fuck.

How was it possible to ache for a tiny human he had never even met?

He had tortured himself over the last forty-eight hours with a million what ifs. He couldn't help it—it was just the way his mind worked. He spent all his sleepless hours scrolling on his phone while keeping an eye on Chandler, wanting to be close in case she needed anything in the night. He researched college savings plans, just out of curiosity. He read consumer reports about the best strollers and baby carriers. He even watched instructional videos on the proper way to install an infant car seat.

His mind wandered beyond the practical issues, and his subconscious peppered him with more specific questions. Where would Chandler and the baby live? How often would he have gotten to see his child? Would the baby look more like Chandler or him?

Then there was the loudest question that reverberated in his mind. The question he wouldn't allow himself to think through or answer. What would Tori think if he'd had a baby?

He felt like he had barely talked to his wife since she went home to Hampton with Jake. They had exchanged their usual daily check-ins, and he had kept her updated on his modified travel plans. But every text was cordial, every call surface-level and painstakingly formal. It felt like he hadn't *really* talked to his wife since he sent her away from the hospital. They had so much to talk about. And yet there was no time or opportunity for them to actually connect. He missed her so damn much.

To add to the density of the heartache between them, Tori had gone to her first egg retrieval appointment yesterday. Alone. The irony of the timing was a proverbial punch in the gut.

When she had first got the call about her inconclusive blood work, he had vowed that he would be by her side through everything. But he wasn't there for her yesterday, and now he wasn't sure if he could make it back to Hampton until Friday because of his unexpected time off with Chandler.

He had inadvertently broken his promise, and Tori was alone because of his choices. She was alone, going through the motions to ensure they had the option to have kids someday if they decided they wanted to, while he was alone, mourning the loss of a child he hadn't even known existed until it was too late.

Rhett fiddled with his phone as the flight attendant made a final pass through the business class cabin. They would be landing in Norfolk in the next ten minutes. He was anxious to get on the ground and into the office. He'd been in touch with Quinn over the last few days, and everything seemed to have settled in the aftermath of the storm that had disrupted so much of their operations over the weekend. But he'd feel better once he was physically there, elbows-deep in work.

Work was what he needed. A few long days at the office would help him get back on track, or at least distract him long enough to let his nervous system calm down.

"Can I get you anything else?" the flight attendant asked as she removed the empty cup and mini bottles from his tray.

"No, I'm all set. Thank you though."

Rhett continued to turn his phone over in his hand, working his jaw back and forth as the cabin pressure built up in his ears from the descent. After spending the first half of the weekend with Tori, then spending the last few days with Chandler, he hadn't been without company in days. There was a grating discomfort that came with being alone with his thoughts now. He didn't know how to shake the feeling that something else horrible was about to happen; he couldn't reel in his mind from wondering what the hell the Universe had planned for him next.

He unlatched his seatbelt as soon as he felt the wheels of the plane hit the tarmac. He was out of his seat before the flight attendant finished the announcement that it was safe to do so. He was the first person off the plane as soon as the door opened.

He strode down the jetway with purpose, switching his phone off airplane mode as he merged into the foot traffic of the crowded airport. He had texted Tori and Jake right before takeoff, but he hadn't heard back from either of them yet. He double-checked that his messages had gone through. Tori hadn't seen his message yet, and Jake had left him on read without responding. He blew out a frustrated breath as he slowed his steps and rested his carry-on bag against a row of empty seats.

He had a nagging compulsion to let someone—anyone—know where he was. He debated texting his mom or maybe Maddie. But they had gone up to Michigan to clear out the cabin, and it's not like they knew anything about his disrupted travel plans anyways.

Chandler hadn't asked him to let her know when he landed, so he wouldn't.

His dad wasn't big on texting.

His granddad would expect him in the office immediately if he knew Rhett was finally back in Norfolk.

Jake was ignoring him.

Tori hadn't seen his text.

For all intents and purposes, he was completely alone.

Unaccounted for.

He wasn't here.

This wasn't happening.

He glanced around the brightly lit, bustling terminal, letting the kinetic rush fill in some of the emptiness inside. How was it possible to feel so fucking lonely surrounded by hundreds of people?

He glanced down at his phone again, willing a message from Tori to pop up. But the only information displayed on the lock screen was the time.

9:48 a.m.

Quinn had scheduled the car service to pick him up at 10:30. He had a senior executive meeting he had to attend that afternoon, followed by a debrief with the entire Logistics and Ops Teams to go over everything from the weekend.

Once he stepped into the office, everything would start falling back into place.

Once he stepped into the office, everything would go back to normal.

Once he stepped into the office, it would be like nothing had even happened.

Rhett surveyed the terminal again, this time letting his gaze linger on the restaurants, newsstands, and souvenir kiosks that lined the perimeter. He paused on a nondescript bar, homing in on the mostly empty seats that filled the dimly-lit cavern.

Two other men were sitting at the counter, one drinking a beer, the other grasping a shot.

Good enough.

He grabbed his bag and one-handedly typed out a message to his assistant as he navigated his way through a crush of hurried bodies.

Rhett: Got held up this morning. Please reschedule the car service to pick me up at the airport at 1 pm. I'll be in for the senior exec meeting at 2.

He didn't wait for a response. He didn't allow himself to hope he'd hear from Tori anytime soon. Instead, he saddled up to one of the barstools furthest from the terminal and made eye contact with the middle-aged woman behind the bar.

"A double Jameson on the rocks, please," he ordered as he stripped off his suit jacket and folded it neatly on top of his luggage.

He positioned himself in the center of the seat, studying the bartender as she reached for the familiar green bottle. He watched with detached coolness as the deep amber liquid cascaded down the ice cubes in the cheap lowball glass. He smiled when she finally set the drink on a thin cardstock coaster in front of him.

"Do you want me to ring you up now, or do you want to start a tab?" she asked, not making eye contact as she wiped down the surface in front of her.

"Oh. Ummm," he pretended to consider out loud. "I guess I'll start a tab," he answered, as if he had just reached the decision in that moment. She nodded once and met his eyes. Rhett stared back for a few seconds, offering a practiced, empty smile. Aloofness was the only emotion he allowed to surface and register on his face. He wasn't willing to let himself feel anything else.

Not here.

Not now.

Not after everything that had happened.

Not after all the pain he had caused.

It wasn't until the familiar burn of whiskey coated his tongue that he allowed himself to settle into his seat and exhale. It wasn't until the familiar burn of whiskey slipped down his throat that he finally felt less alone.

CHAPTER THIRTY-THREE

"That's the last of them," Fielding declared as he set down the final stack of canvases next to all the others on the picnic table. They had spent the morning prepping and packing the rest of the canvases she needed for camp, then they used Fielding's SUV to transport everything in one trip. Tori had picked up the master keys from the volunteer office on their way to the small camp located right on the edge of the Cuyahoga Valley National Park. Now they were standing in the middle of the outdoor eating area, trying to get everything put away before the threatening gray sky opened up.

"Perfect. I want to put them away by size in the storage shed, then we're done for the day."

Fielding stood under the covered pavilion and looked around the outdoor common area. "This place is pretty cool. I can't believe it's so close to home and I never knew about it."

Tori walked over to the picnic table where Fielding was leaning and hoisted herself onto the tabletop. She let out an involuntary yawn. It was only mid-afternoon, but she was on day three of no caffeine because of her egg retrieval. In retrospect, she should have tried to cut back on the caffeine over the last few weeks instead of going cold turkey on Monday, but it was too late for ideas like that now.

"I know. It's even cooler when you're a kid. It's like its own little secret world, a true sanctuary. I used to pretend this place was halfway around the world instead of just twenty minutes down the road."

"How many years did you come here as a kid?" Fielding asked as he sat down and straddled the bench seat of the picnic table, peering up at her with his Caribbean blue eyes. She would have accused him of wearing colored contacts if Dempsey's weren't the exact same shade of lapis blue.

"I came for a week the first summer after my mom died. I came for the full two weeks the next year, then they let me come back four more years as a camper after that. I got to be a junior counselor for a few years before I aged out of the program. This summer will be my sixth year volunteering as a counselor."

Fielding stayed quiet for a moment, staring at her with an intense, serious gaze. He assessed her for another few seconds before offering a small smile.

"Ya know, Victoria Thompson, sometimes I think I want to be you when I grow up. It's awesome that you still want to try to help kids who are dealing with what you had to go through after all these years. They're really lucky to have you."

Tori shied at his praise, but she knew his comment was genuine. For as often as he teased her, Fielding could be surprisingly sincere when he wanted to be. He never held back from sharing what was on his mind.

"I'm really lucky they kept letting me come back year after year. I have our volunteer coordinator Maggie thank for that, really. Most kids just come for a year or two. But since I'm local, they made exceptions for me, and Maggie always reached out to let me know when it was time to register in case my dad missed the sign-ups."

"So it wasn't like sleepaway camp where you see the same kids each summer?" he asked, propping his head on his hand as he continued to gaze up at her.

"No, not at all. It's uncommon for anyone to come back more than a few summers in a row."

"That's kind of sad, isn't it? It's not like you'd just get over losing a parent after one week of tie-dying and a few rounds of Capture the Flag."

Tori reached out to swat at him for the crass joke. She knew he wasn't serious with his shallow assessment of what Camp New Hope was all about, but she wasn't going to let that slide.

"Don't even think about it!" he exclaimed as he trapped her hand against his chest. She was fast, but his reflexes were faster, so she'd didn't get to shove him in the shoulder as intended. He gripped her hand against his chest and gave her a pointed look, his eyes threatening to retaliate and turn the tables on her.

"Okay, okay, truce!" she promised as she pulled out of his grasp.

"I have a theory about why most kids don't come back to Camp New Home, actually." He nodded once to indicate he was listening. "I think grief is especially hard for preteens because they're still trying to figure out who they are. It's not that kids get over their grief after coming here for one or two years. It's that they don't prioritize their own mental health once they become teenagers. They're too concerned with hanging out with their friends or maintaining their social media to go off the grid and come to a place like this. Nowadays, we almost never see new campers over the age of twelve, even though the program is open to anyone ages eight to eighteen. I have this dream. Well, I guess it's not really a dream, because I don't know how the hell I'd ever make it happen, but I wish there was a way to make this camp more accessible and more attractive to older teens. Like, maybe separate out the age groups more, or offer different programming for the older campers."

"So you want to be the founder of Camp Old Hope?"

She groaned at his lame joke. "You're such an ass."

"You know I'm just teasing you. But now I've gotta double down on my earlier statement. You're amazing, and I want to be you when I grow up."

She smiled at his compliment but let the conversation fizzle. She really was tired, and they still had to get everything locked up in the supply shed before they could go home.

"Okay, let's get this wrapped up before it rains," she declared as she hopped off the table and peered at the darkening sky. She reached for a stack of ten or so canvases and lifted them with ease. It wasn't until she tried to hold them against her abdomen that she winced and set them back down.

"Hey, do you mind carrying all these for me?" she asked sheepishly as Fielding walked over and picked up a stack twice the size of the pile she had just set down.

"Oh, I see how it is. You just brought me along to be the muscle."

"Ha-ha," she mocked. "You know I never ask for help. But I started giving myself injections a few days ago because I'm freezing my eggs next week, and my whole stomach is already bloated and tender."

Fielding's expression shifted from playful to horrified in under than a second. "Shit. I totally forgot about that. Yeah, of course. You should have reminded me earlier..."

"Chill," she said, cutting him off before he could continue his pity party. "It's not that big of a deal, but I've never done anything like this before, and I had to stab myself four times the first night before I figured out what I was doing."

"Tori..." The sympathy in his voice was warning enough for her not to look into his eyes. She started walking over to the storage shed, knowing he would follow.

"Please don't," she requested over her shoulder once she had a bit of distance from him, not wanting his compassion to trigger her own self-pity. The fertility preservation process was foreign and confusing and stressful; it already had her on edge. To have to do it alone made everything feel ten times harder. She couldn't let herself dwell on the fact that Rhett hadn't been home to go to the initial appointment with her or to help her with the first injections. She would start to spiral if she let herself feel sorry for her own circumstances.

But Fielding wouldn't leave it alone. "I know you have Jake... and your dad and Lia... but if you need anything, I want to be there for you. Seriously, Tori. If you need someone to take you to an appointment or to help with the injections, you have to promise to call me."

"You'd actually come over and stab me in the stomach?" she challenged as she unlocked the padlock on the shed.

"I'm not saying it's the number one thing I want to do on a Saturday night... but yeah. I'd do it for you. I was pre-med, remember? And Teddy has Type 1 diabetes. He and I have been friends since high school, and I've had to help him a few times when his sugar got scary low."

Tori quickly entered the shed, not wanting Fielding to see the tears threatening to spill over. She'd only been doing the injections for a few days, so it's not like she could blame her emotional response on the hormones. She always cried when people were kind to her. She never expected it, so it caught her off guard. She was so damn lucky to have such good friends, and she was especially grateful to have Fielding in her life.

As if sensing that the moment was too heavy, he spoke up again. "Hey, you know what I just realized?" He followed her into the shed and set the canvases where she pointed, turning around and heading back to the picnic table to grab the next load.

"What's that?"

"We're super close to Valley Cream right now."

"Valley Cream?"

"Wait. Don't tell me you've lived here all your life and you've never been to Valley fucking Cream?" he exclaimed, gawking and carrying on in typical Fielding fashion. "Valley Cream is the best ice cream stand in all of northeast Ohio. It's only open seasonally, and they only have like, two flavors a day because they churn it all by hand. Fuck— it's so good, Tor. You're going to love it. I'm taking you there as soon as we're done here."

She felt bad rejecting his idea, given his child-like excitement. But they had other plans that night, and she desperately needed a shower and a nap.

"I think we have to raincheck it, Field."

He pouted—he literally stuck out his bottom lip and batted his eyelashes—as she continued.

"I'm sorry. I really am. But I'm exhausted, and I want to take a shower and rest a bit before we go to Clinton's tonight."

"Fine. But promise me we'll go soon. You can't just say raincheck to me and hope I'll forget about it. I'm relentless when it comes to Valley Cream, Tori. Fucking relentless."

"I believe that. I promise we'll go soon. For now, let's get the rest of these canvases sorted so we can go home."

"To the man we can always count on to pick up a shift, pick up the tab, and pick up anyone still single at the end of the night!" Lia proclaimed, holding up her shot glass toward the man of the hour.

"To the OG master of walk-in cooler quickies and epic hot tub parties," Cory added, a knowing smirk on his face.

"To the second-best bartender this place has ever seen!" Tori finished with a flourish.

Laughter erupted amongst the friends as Jake just shook his head in mock-shame. He was totally in his element: pouring shots, shooting the shit, being the center of attention. He was the only person standing behind the bar, holding court as all their friends toasted and roasted him. He was the king of Clinton's for just one more night.

Tori smiled as she took in the sight of everyone celebrating together. Their hangout was going a lot later than she had expected, in part because Fielding and Dempsey had shown up with a few bottles of rum after Mike had left for the night. She couldn't resist pulling out her phone and discreetly snapping a picture of Jake as he exchanged jabs with Lia.

V: It's our boy's last night at Clinton's. After this he's officially moving on to greener pastures.

"Tori! You and I have to do a shot together! Get over here!" Dempsey was drunker than she had ever seen him, which was saying something, given the amount of times she'd hung out at the Valet House over the last few months. She glanced at Fielding, who offered her a little smirk and an eyeroll at his brother's antics. Dempsey didn't know her well enough to know she rarely drank. And she was certain Field hadn't told him anything about her upcoming procedure and why she absolutely could not drink tonight.

"Sorry, Dem. You're going to have to take mine for me," she hollered back across the bar, nodding to the two shot glasses sitting in front of him. "I'm one of the only people Jake trusts to drive the Jeep, so I'm DD tonight."

"Your loss, my gain," he declared as he accepted her excuse. Tori winced as she watched Fielding's already wasted twin throw back both shots in quick succession. Her phone vibrated against the bar top as he slammed the glasses down. She picked it up to read Rhett's reply.

Ev: Good thing those greener pastures are right next door. ;) Tell him congrats for me. I'm surprised you're all still at Clinton's this late?

Only Jake and Lia had worked that night. Everyone else showed up once the restaurant was closed, and it felt like things weren't anywhere close to winding down anytime soon.

V: I'm DDing for Jake, so I don't think I'll be going home for a while. All the toasts have turned into roasts. I wish you were here. You would love it.

Ev: Text me when you get home safe. I'm sure I'll still be up. Love you.

She blew out a long breath as she reread his response. He hadn't said anything wrong—but she could tell even through his text that he was distracted. He hadn't asked how she was feeling. He hadn't asked how her injection went tonight. They had talked about the shots after her appointment on Monday, and she had sent him pictures of the needle she had to push into her stomach each night for the next several days. She honestly couldn't tell whether he was treading lightly around the subject or if she was holding back from bringing it up as not to trigger him.

Regardless, the emotional stalemate sucked. She missed her husband. She was anxious to reconnect with him. She was desperate for him to comfort her, and to be here for her like he had promised.

She had no idea when Rhett was coming to Hampton next—she'd been too worried about adding to his burden to ask—but she knew they'd sort things out once he was finally home. It was just too damn hard to have any sort of real conversation while he was in Virginia. The physical distance exacerbated the emotional distance tenfold.

"Doing okay over here?"

She had been so engrossed in her own thoughts that she hadn't seen Fielding move around the bar to sit beside her. She released her lower lip from between her teeth, willing herself to relax and stop stressing.

She glanced over at her friend and smiled. He may have supplied the liquor for their little shindig tonight, but he didn't appear to be drinking any of it either.

"I'm okay," she assured him, flipping her phone over and setting it back down on the bar. "Tired, but I got in a little nap after you dropped me off at home this afternoon, so I'm good."

"You didn't want to do shots with Dem?" he teased as he bumped his shoulder into hers. She rolled her eyes but didn't bother smothering her smile.

"Uh, yeah. That would be a no. I think the more legit question is why aren't *you* doing shots with your brother tonight?"

He shrugged as he stared at Dempsey from across the bar, replying without meeting her gaze. "We drove together, and Dem is the one who needs to blow off some stream. We got the call from our mom that she's coming home next week, so we'll both be back on babysitting duty soon. He deserves a night to let loose. He's genuinely excited about working at The Oak. I'm glad he has something new to look forward to right now, and I just wanted him to have fun tonight. Plus, I figured I could be the one to drive Jake home if you were tired and wanted to leave early."

"Careful, Fielding," she chided in a hushed tone. "If people hear you talking like this, they might think you're more than just a trust fund fuckboy."

"Field!" Jake yelled in their direction, pulling them both out of their private conversation. "You want one of these?" He nodded toward the sets of shot and pint glasses lined up in front of him. Tori gagged at the sight of what he was offering. Jägerbombs after all that rum weren't going to serve any of them well tomorrow.

"Nah, I'm driving," Fielding replied before he glanced over at her with wide eyes of disgust. He obviously shared her feelings about Jake's drink of choice. "I can't even look at Jägermeister without instantly smelling puke and poor choices," he muttered under his breath so only she could hear. Tori bit down on her lip to hold back a laugh.

"You're a good man, Fielding Haas," Jake declared dramatically as he passed around the shot glasses and partially-filled pints. Fielding nodded once to acknowledge he'd heard him before turning back to Tori.

"Okay, it's decided. I'll drive Jake home tonight. There's no way he's *not* going to puke, and I have to deal with my drunk-ass twin anyways."

"I'm not gonna fight you on that," Tori said appreciatively as she stifled another yawn. "He's right. You're a good man, Fielding Haas."

CHAPTER THIRTY-FOUR

Tori

Everything about The Oak Barrell Tavern was perfect. The nineties rock playlist and the interesting-but-not-pretentious drink menu was classic Jake. The exposed industrial beams juxtaposed against the warm lighting and surprisingly comfortable bar stools was all Mike. The Hampton High and Archway Prep sports memorabilia that decorated the walls added to the local hometown vibe and kept things from feeling too sterile. There was no doubt in her mind that this place was going to be successful.

She ran her fingers along the raw edge bar, marveling at the attention to detail they had put into all aspects of The Oak.

"I'm not sure I'm allowed to let you sit here all night and order nothing but water." She could just barely hear Dempsey over The Wallflowers song blaring through the speakers. It didn't matter that Jake had the volume all the way up: the bar was packed, and they would have had to shout to hear each other regardless.

"Guess you better go ask your new boss about that," she countered, raising her chin in Jake's direction. He was moving behind the bar with skilled precision: taking orders, refilling drinks, wiping things down. He had a genuine joyfulness to him tonight that made Tori almost tear up if she thought about it too long. That, or the hormones were really wreaking havoc on her emotions.

Dempsey refilled her etched mason jar with water before going to take the order of a group of women who had just walked in. Dem wasn't the only one of the Valet Boys that Jake had hired to work for him. Cole and Teddy were also part of the staff of Hampton's newest hangout, and it was all hands on deck tonight for the grand opening. Watching the four attractive men move around each other behind the bar in their matching black T-shirts was a sight to behold. Yeah. This place was going to be wildly successful.

"My picture is hanging outside the ladies' room," Fielding boasted as he slipped back into the bar stool beside her. He had seen a few guys he knew from high school when they first arrived together, so he'd been making the rounds for the last hour.

"Uhhh... do I even want to know?" Tori side-eyed him up and down as he just smiled smugly beside her. Over his shoulder, she could see Dempsey still chatting with the group of women who had come in a few minutes ago. Two of them had noticed Fielding sit down and were currently ogling the Haas brothers like their heads were on an oscillating fan. Tori was certain Jake had known what he was doing when he hired his staff. These boys were going to be so good for business.

"There's local sports memorabilia all over the walls. The Archway hockey team won regionals my sophomore and senior years, so our team picture is back there. It's pretty cool, actually. I feel like this place is going to be really popular."

"I think you're right. This place has Jake written all over it. I didn't realize how much he was actually doing to get things up and running, or how much Mike was letting him do, I guess."

"I mean, you've been a little busy these last few months, Tor," Fielding reminded her. "But yeah. He's been working nonstop. The only time I ever get to see him is if I come visit him when he's working, or if we meet up after work and I crash at his place. Between Clinton's and here, I bet he's worked at least seventy hours a week all summer."

Tori picked at the corner of her drink napkin as his words sunk in. She'd been so wrapped up in her own life lately. She hadn't even noticed how much Jake had been pouring into this project. Not only that, he had still managed to be there for her and for Rhett time and time again over the last few months. She silently chastised herself and promised to do better when it came to showing up and paying attention to her friends' lives.

"You kids having fun?" Mike asked as he emerged from the back room and started dumping a fresh bucket of ice into a cooler.

"This place is amazing, Mike. Congratulations."

"Well, I have this guy to thank for a lot of it," he responded as he slapped Jake on the shoulder. "Most of the concept and design came from him. I wasn't sure about the exposed beams or the unfinished bar, but..."

"That's seriously the best part! I love this bar top. It's edgy but still natural. You did good, Jake."

"Thanks, baby," he beamed in response to her praise. "I can't believe we're finally open." He was grinning from ear to ear. She felt a wave of giddiness pass through her just from seeing her friend so happy.

"You two good?" Jake asked, nodding to the glasses sitting in front of her and Field.

"I'm good," Tori confirmed.

A sly smile crept onto Fielding's face. "I'll probably have one more before I switch to water, but I'm gonna wait and harass my brother about it."

Jake smirked at Fielding and took a step back to turn away from them, but then his eyes grew wide as his gaze focused just past her shoulder.

"Bro?"

That was all the warning she got before she felt a strong, familiar body wrap around her from behind. "Hey, beautiful," Rhett murmured into her ear as she raised both her hands to clasp his arms.

"Rhett?!" she confirmed, her voice shaking slightly, his name coming out more as a question than a statement. "What are you doing here?" She was out of her seat in an instant and in his arms a moment later.

She let herself sink into the hug as she savored his distinctly familiar presence, a scent that was unmistakably Rhett. He was home. And now she was whole.

"Hi, you." He ran his hand up along her spine before working it into the hair at the nape of her neck. "Fuck, I missed you," he whispered, the proximity of his mouth to her ear the only way she was able to hear him over the music.

"What are you doing here?" she asked again. She hadn't expected him home; he hadn't given her any indication that he'd be in Hampton this weekend or anytime soon. The excitement of being in his orbit was quickly giving way to worry. *Why had he come home without telling her?*

"This is a big night for our boy," he replied, nodding to where Jake was still standing with his arms spread wide on the bar. "And I really missed my wife." He bowed his head and simultaneously lifted her chin so their kiss met in the middle. He used the hand in her hair to pull her closer, melting away all the questions and concerns that had started to swirl around her mind. He smelled like fresh rain and sandalwood; he tasted like expensive whiskey and sweet mint. She let him part her lips with his tongue, welcoming him home right in the middle of the crowded bar.

"I love you," she whispered against his mouth before pulling away. She turned around to face their friends but kept close and let Rhett hold her from behind. She was grateful for the contact she hadn't even realized she'd been missing until her body instinctively pressed back into his grasp. She inhaled deeply, trying to steady her nerves from the shock of seeing her husband for the first time since they had parted ways in Columbus last weekend.

"Congrats, bro," he said to Jake, his voice dripping with sincerity. "The parking lot and all the side streets are packed. It took me ten minutes just to find a spot. This place is incredible."

"Thanks," Jake replied coolly. Tori felt Rhett's arms tense around her at the dismissal. She knew Rhett was on Jake's shit list for a lot of reasons right now, but she didn't want that to spoil this night. She gave Jake a pointed look, silently urging him to say something else.

He sighed for a fraction of a second before continuing. "It's been a long time coming, and it was a ton of work. But I'm pretty proud of it. Make sure you check out the team pictures outside the restrooms. You'll see some familiar faces."

She felt Rhett nod behind her, but he didn't say anything else. The awkwardness between the two men was palpable. She glanced over at Fielding to see if he was picking up on the vibe, too, but he had his gaze set straight ahead.

She realized then that Rhett hadn't even acknowledged Fielding's presence. That irked her to the core, especially after everything Field had done for her over the past week. But it's not like Rhett knew that he'd been in the car when Jake came to pick her up, or that he'd been the one helping her with all the prep for Camp New Hope over the last few weeks.

"Yo! Wheeler! I didn't see you come in! Can I get you a drink?" Teddy walked up and stood shoulder to shoulder next to Jake behind the bar, his full sleeve of ink on display thanks to his form-fitting uniform shirt. She didn't miss how Jake's eyes narrowed on Rhett as they all waited for his response.

"Nah, man, not tonight. I just came in to check out the new place and to get my girl." He tightened his hold around her midsection before she could remind him that her stomach was super sensitive from the hormone injections. She winced slightly, then worked her hands under his forearms and peeled herself out of his grasp. She turned around and met his gaze. Rhett cocked his head in question.

"My stomach... it's sensitive from all the shots," she reminded him in a whisper. She assumed Jake had been watching them closely enough to catch her reaction, but she didn't want to embarrass Rhett or call him out in front of everyone else.

His eyes dropped from her face to her stomach then back again. "Fuck," he muttered to himself as he ran a hand through his hair. "I'm so sorry, V. I completely forgot."

His admission hurt worse than the injection she'd struggled to give herself that night. *He forgot?* How the hell could he just forget something that had been consuming most of her waking thoughts?

Today had been the first day she had to give herself two separate shots, and the morning shot had burned going in. She thought she was getting better with the nighttime injection, but she was jumpy and squeamish after the new shot that morning, so much so that she had almost asked Fielding to help her tonight. He'd been at the house anyways, hovering in the hallway as promised, riling up Penny and cracking jokes to lighten the mood.

She downplayed the whole thing with a flippant subject change. "No worries. I'm fine. Did you want to stick around for a bit?"

Rhett shook his head. "Not unless you do?"

"No, I'm ready to go. And I'm sure the guys will be happy to have another bar stool freed up." She looked toward Jake to find his gaze still set on the two of them, his eyes assessing Rhett up and down. So much for not letting the tension between them sour the night.

She stepped a few feet forward to talk to Fielding over the music. "Hey, I'm going to get going now that Rhett's here," she said as she leaned into his personal space.

Fielding didn't even acknowledge he heard her, instead looking over her shoulder to Jake. She watched with trepidation as they shared a quick, wordless exchange.

"Is he good, Tori?"

Awareness swept over her as she realized what Fielding was asking and what Jake had been looking for when he eyed Rhett up and down.

"He's perfectly fine, Field," she answered in a panicked rush. Rhett was standing right there. She was as insulted by their overbearing assumptions as she was worried that her husband would figure out to what they were implying. Fielding remained in his seat, his back rigid against the back of the bar stool, his gaze forward and focused. He looked calm, relaxed even. But she didn't miss the storm brewing in his eyes. And apparently, he wasn't done with his cross-examination.

"So you're saying you don't need a ride home, and you're good getting in the car with him, right? I just want to make sure we're on the same page here and you understand what I'm asking you," he pressed. Fielding was speaking as low as possible given the volume of the room, but her eyes still flicked over to her husband to confirm he couldn't hear their conversation.

She wished she could snap back at Fielding so he could fully understand her outrage. "I'm good. He's good. And you're an asshole. I have no good reason to believe Rhett's been drinking," she hissed in his ear.

"Well, I have no good reason to believe he hasn't been," he shot back.

"Goodnight, Fielding." She moved to storm away from where he sat but caught herself and turned back to say goodbye to Jake first. "Bye, Jake. Congrats again. I'm really happy for you and really proud of you, too."

Jake smiled at her and nodded once. He was obviously satisfied enough with Fielding's interrogation to let her walk out the door. She resisted rolling her eyes at the two men as she reached for her husband's hand.

"Hang on," Rhett murmured as he approached the bar to talk to Jake. "Can we hang out tomorrow, bro? I'm free anytime." He turned to Tori to confirm, and she nodded. She didn't have any plans this weekend, especially now that he was home.

Jake blew out a long breath. "Yeah, sure. I've been meaning to get with you anyways. I'll text you when I wake up, but it probably won't be before noon."

Rhett nodded in relief, and Tori let out a breath she hadn't realized she'd been holding. She was glad those two were going to have a chance to talk and get back on track. Now she just needed to find the courage to have her own heart-to-heart with Rhett while he was here.

Chapter Thirty-Five

Rhett

The blare of an alarm followed by a few yips from Penny pulled him out of a restless dream. He had been running and was out of breath, although he had no idea whether he was being pursued or was chasing something. Probably both, if his scrambled, anxious mind had any influence over the context of his dreams.

"Tori," he whispered, his voice gravelly from sleep. He ran his hand up and down her arm until she finally began to stir. "Hey, beautiful. Your alarm's going off. You don't have to work today, do you?"

He hadn't thought to ask about her work schedule for the weekend. They had both fallen asleep without talking about much of anything last night. She was exhausted from the hormones, and he was tired from working so much all week. He had actually slept for more than a few hours, which was a vast improvement over his last several nights in Virginia. He hadn't even bothered to set an alarm last night because he hoped they'd be able to sleep in as late as possible this morning.

"No," she murmured sleepily. "But I have to get up and do my morning shot."

He yawned as he watched her rise out of bed. "Want me to go start the coffee?"

"You can if you want," she replied, her arms lifting in a full body stretch. "I can't have any caffeine though."

She couldn't have caffeine? He didn't know that. He felt like shit that he didn't know that. He'd only done a little research about the egg retrieval process when they first started talking about it. He hadn't counted on not being able to go with Tori to her first appointment, to not knowing anything about the process or the side effects or what else to expect.

He watched closely as the T-shirt she'd slept in inched up her thighs, revealing her lacy black hipster panties and a small strip of stomach. He fixated on the marks on both sides of her body: the patches of purple, black, and yellow that freckled the soft skin of her tummy. She had told him about the injections over the phone, but seeing the visible proof landed differently in his mind.

"Can I bring you some peppermint tea, then? Or something else?" He had no idea what else to do for her, what else he could possibly offer.

"Tea would be good. And can you bring up a few ice cubes, too? The morning shot burns when it goes in, but Fielding read about a trick I want to try. I'm going to ice the spot for a few minutes before I actually do the injection and see if that helps."

He cleared his throat as he pulled on a T-shirt, desperate to keep his cool. "Why would Haas know something like that?"

Tori shrugged before sitting back down on the bed. "He knew I was having a hard time with the shots this week, so we looked up some stuff online yesterday when we were at his mom's pool."

The way she just nonchalantly dropped that bomb was enough to have Rhett seeing red. The fact that his wife had been casually talking to *Fielding* about *their* egg freezing procedure... None of the anger percolating inside him was aimed at Tori. There was only his dueling hatred for Fielding and his own self-loathing wrestling for dominance in his mind.

"I'll be right back," he promised as he left the bedroom and made his way downstairs to the Thompsons' kitchen. Paul must have already been up and off to work, because a mostly full pot of coffee was still hot on in the carafe. He poured himself a cup, then set to work making her tea. By the time he let Penny out and made his way back upstairs, Tori wasn't in her room anymore.

"In here," she called from the hallway bathroom.

He walked into the narrow space and handed her the mug and a little bowl of ice before perching on the edge of the tub.

He grimaced when she tied up her shirt and revealed her marked abdomen. It physically hurt him to see her body covered in bruises. She picked up a single ice cube and wrapped it in a washcloth, then held it to the skin under the left side of her belly button. Their eyes connected in the mirror, her face expressionless aside from a timid smile.

"Not exactly the sexy Saturday mornings we used to enjoy, huh?"

The meekness in her voice and the dejection in her eyes permeated into every part of his crumbling, broken heart. He wordlessly watched as she held the ice to her stomach. He gripped the edges of the tub in frustration, desperate to soothe her somehow. He couldn't just sit back as she did this alone. He wouldn't be a bystander in what was supposed to be a team effort. Decision made, Rhett pushed to his feet and padded over to join her in front of the mirror.

He stood behind her and rested his chin on her shoulder. He assessed their reflection, appreciatively taking in everything from the freckles on the tops of her shoulders to the depth of her emerald-green eyes. "You're so beautiful, V. So strong. So brave. So fucking perfect." He kissed her neck, letting his lips brush back and forth over the delicate skin stretched over her collarbone. Then he turned her around so they were standing face-to-face.

"Show me what to do," he instructed, nodding toward the vials and the new syringe laid out on the counter. He made quick work of thoroughly washing his hands before giving her his full attention.

Tori measured out the liquid and handed him the syringe. She took a few steps backwards, leaned against the closed bathroom door, then blew out a long breath.

"I'll pinch the spot where it should go. Just make sure it's in all the way, then push down on the plunger at a steady pace. This one burns, so I have to brace my back against the door. Don't stop, even if I flinch."

"Got it," he told her with false confidence. He was completely out of his element, underprepared and terrified to stick a needle in his wife's stomach. But he refused to let her see his doubt.

"Do you want a countdown or a warning?"

"Nope. Just do it."

He inhaled through his nose, inserted the needle into her pinched skin, then let out a steady exhale as his thumb injected the hormones into her body. Tori didn't move a muscle, but he didn't miss how her face screwed up in pain as the burning sensation must have hit. How she had been able to do this all by herself for the last six days was beyond comprehension.

"All done," he promised as he discarded the used needle into the sharps container sitting by the sink. "But stay there."

He leaned into her space and let his forehead rest on hers for a few moments as he held her face in his hands. He kissed her once on the forehead, once on the mouth. Then, wordlessly, he dropped to his knees.

He held her hips in his hands, careful not to touch any of the bruises. He let his fingertips brush up and down the sides of her body, against the dips of her waist, along the curve of her hips, over the lace of her panties, then softly down her thighs. He repeated the motion, caressing her over and over, worshipping every part of her midsection.

He kissed the spot he had just injected, his breath warming her iced skin, then gently nuzzled her with the tip of his nose. He found another mark a few inches lower, this one a faded yellow that was barely visible against her pale skin. He held her hips possessively as he moved from bruise to bruise. His mouth brushed over every mark, each kiss a silent apology for each one of the injections she'd had to endure alone.

"Why are there so many more bruises on this side?" he asked when he made his way across her stomach. He continued to hold her steady, peering up through his long lashes.

"It took me a couple tries to figure out what I was doing the first few nights," she explained, running her nails through his hair as he continued to pepper her with kisses. Rhett stilled as he let her words sink in. His self-loathing returned to a low boil, thanks to her confession.

"I'm so sorry you've been doing this alone, beautiful. Especially because I know this wasn't originally part of your plan. Thank you for being so strong, and for seeing this through for us."

He wrapped his arms around her, mindful not to touch any of the sensitive spots. She may have been alone all week, but she wasn't alone now. He vowed to spend the rest of the weekend reminding her that she wasn't alone in this, that she could count on him, just like he had promised.

"Why are we down here, bro? You got someone upstairs you don't want me to see?" Rhett joked as he walked through the pedestrian door of the underground garage. It was dark in the cavernous space, the only light coming from the emergency exit signs on the far ends of the basement.

"Nah, not this morning. Really the only overnight guest I've entertained lately has been Fielding anyways, and that's just because I usually pass out before he's done playing video games."

Rhett held his tongue as he endured the second reminder of Fielding Haas's existence that day.

Jake gave him a subtle head tilt, indicating Rhett should follow him deeper into the garage. "I realized last night that you're gonna need a car. The Prelude's still in Columbus, right? You can borrow one of mine until we can go get it."

Waves of gratitude caught Rhett off guard. He had figured he'd just get a rental each time he came to town until he could figure out a time to go back to Columbus. This would be so much easier and more convenient. He didn't miss how Jake offered to help him retrieve his beloved car, too, which would save him from having to ask Tori to make the drive again.

But Rhett didn't express his gratitude right away. He couldn't. He still didn't understand where things stood between him and his best friend after last night's icy reception at The Oak.

"Damn, brother. It's taken us twenty years, but I think I've finally rubbed off on you. Now you're the one making plans and thinking ahead," he joked, testing the waters and trying to gauge Jake's reaction.

Jake rolled his eyes as he hit a panel of switches on the wall. The entire garage was suddenly cast into light, illuminating the full garage.

"Yeah, well, I've been meaning to talk to you, and I figured if I let you borrow a car, maybe you'd take me more seriously."

Rhett stilled at the sharpness of his tone. What had originally felt like a generous offer was starting to feel more like a trap. "So I'm getting a car with conditions, then?"

"Something like that," Jake muttered as he strode deeper into the garage. "Here's the deal," he declared, adjusting his backwards baseball cap a few times before continuing. "You can take your pick and borrow anything you want in here"—he waved an arm around the various cars in the garage—"but you have to promise me you'll reel it in."

Rhett came to stop by a covered vehicle and leaned his forearms on the roof. The top of the car barely reached his chest, making it easy for the other man to level with him and match his stance on the other side. When Rhett didn't say anything right away, Jake continued.

"I've been watching you, bro. I've been watching things spin out of control, little by little. You're always so level-headed and steady, and you're a hell of a liar, so not many other people probably notice what's happening. But I fucking see you." Jake paused and glared at him over top of the car, an intense anger raging behind his hazel eyes. "You've been drinking more than normal, and you've been doing shit that we don't do."

Rhett caught the inside of his cheek between his molars and bit down hard. He hadn't expected to be called out like this. Not today. Not this early. And certainly not by his best friend. He turned his head to the side to avoid Jake's gaze. It wasn't worth arguing the facts —he had been struggling, drinking more and caring less about covering it up, but he still felt compelled to defend himself.

"It's been a tough week for sure," he offered, hoping to end the conversation before it went any further.

Jake grimaced and shook his head. "This has been going on for a lot longer than a week, and you and I both know it. Fielding told me about that night at The Grille."

First the ice trick. Then the sleepover comment. Now this. How was it not even noon, and Fielding Haas, who was apparently not just a fuckboy but also a snitch, had been brought up three times in conversation?

Fucking Fielding.

"You have no idea the pressure I'm under," Rhett gritted out between clenched teeth, "or what it's like to lose a child."

Jake hung his head for a breath, then another. Rhett watched as his hands fisted against the top of the car. "I feel broken inside about what happened to you, bro. I really do. But the drinking... the scene at The Grille? That was an issue *before* you went to Columbus last weekend. You are grasping at straws right now, so I'm calling you out." He looked up then, a storm of accusations and disappointment in his eyes. "Don't use your dead baby as an excuse for your shitty choices. This is all on you."

Rhett was around the car before his brain even caught up to his body. He couldn't help it. It was a guttural reaction, an immediate response triggered by a crassness he never expected from Jake.

His knuckles colliding with the other man's chiseled features ignited all the anger that'd been bubbling under the surface. His fist connected with his best friend's face in a satisfying crack. Jake stumbled back, falling into another car before righting himself. Rhett rolled his shoulder once, checking his range of motion before he struck again. It wasn't until Jake winced and cracked his neck to the side that Rhett realized Jake hadn't even raised his fists to block the blow.

What the hell was he doing? Had he really just punched his best friend?

"Feel better?" Jake taunted. But there was an underlying sincerity to his question, too.

Rhett opened and closed his hand a few times as his chest rose in deep, heaving breaths. That *had* felt good.

"There are other ways to work through shit than drowning in a bottle, bro. Join a gym in Virginia. Come over here and use the heavy bag when you're home. Just get a fucking grip. This isn't who you are. This isn't who *we* are or what we stand for."

Rhett gawked as realization dawned on him. "You did that on purpose. You made me fucking hit you."

Jake nodded as he brought his hand to his jawline. An angry red mark was already blossoming where Rhett's fist had connected with his face.

"I did. And it was too fucking easy. You're wound up too tight right now, bro. I know the wedding and Tori's surgeries and the new job all happened at once. And then Chandler... and the baby... fuck. I'm sorry, by the way. I'm so fucking sorry. I only said that because I knew it'd hit the hardest, and I needed you to react."

Rhett nodded and instantly accepted his friend's apology, anxious to end this little heart-to-heart that felt increasingly like an intervention. But Jake wasn't done.

"You're hearing me right now, yeah? You have to get it together, Rhett. You have to cut back on the drinking. You have to do it for Tori and for me. You're my family, bro. I can't watch you go down this path."

"I hear you."

"Good," Jake replied, tapping his knuckles twice on the hood of the car between them. "Do you want a hug or something?"

Rhett snorted. Leave it to Jake to manipulate him into throwing punches and then offer to hug it out at the end. "Nah. But I sort of want to hit you again now that I know it was all an act."

Jake let out a laugh. "Hell no, bro. That was your one and only free shot. We're done now. Let's get you some wheels so you can get home to your girl. What do you want to drive?"

"What are my options?" He tried to come off as casual, but he still couldn't bring himself to look Jake in the eye. He'd been slammed with a whirlwind of emotions. Anger, frustration, and shame rippled through him as he tried to process everything that had just happened.

"Literally anything in this garage. Well, except my Jeep. And I don't have insurance on the Ferrari or the Aston right now, so I guess those are out, too."

Rhett whipped his head around the cavernous space, quickly counting at least twenty covered vehicles in addition to the two Jeeps. "Wait. Do you have all of your dad's cars here?"

"All of them," Jake confirmed with a satisfied smirk.

"Do your brothers know?" Rhett couldn't hide the shock behind the question. Jake had been all but estranged from his family— including his two older brothers—since before his dad died several years ago.

"Julian drove every single one of them into this garage himself. His cheap ass got sick of paying for a storage unit, but you know Joe." Jake shrugged as he casually referred to his father by his first name. "There was a provision in his will that we had to store and keep all the cars in pristine condition so we could participate in the Hampton Days car show each year in his honor. I don't think there's any way to enforce that condition now, but Julian and Joey were always the suck-ups."

"How the hell did you convince the other residents to give up their parking spots?" The size of the garage was even more impressive now that he knew every single car belonged to Jake.

"There wasn't much convincing involved considering I own the building."

Rhett just shook his head at his best friend's nonchalance. Very few people knew that Jake owned the entire condo complex where he lived. It was one of the few no-strings-attached gifts his dad had left him in his will. Everything else—well, they didn't talk about everything else very often, about what Jake would have to do if he wanted to unlock the millions that had been conditionally left to him.

"Bro, I can't just drive one of your dad's old cars around town and risk Julian seeing me. No freakin' way." Rhett was friendly with Jake's oldest brother, but he had no desire to piss him off. As the CEO of Whitely Enterprises, Julian was a notoriously shrewd businessman. He was also almost ten years older than Rhett and Jake, and he'd always seemed larger-than-life.

"Well, in that case, your choices are limited. The only cars in here that weren't his are my old Jeep and the M3."

"You still have the M3?" The old BMW had been Jake's first car in high school. It was black, just like his Jeeps, a late 90s model that had seen its fair share of trouble on the streets of Hampton, Ohio.

"Hell yeah. That's the one and only car I've ever owned beside the Jeeps."

"I'll take it."

CHAPTER THIRTY-SIX

Rhett

He parked the BMW in front of the Thompson residence before letting himself in through the side door. He slipped off his shoes when he entered the quiet house. Paul must have still been at work, but Tori's car was in the driveway.

He peaked into her bedroom and was greeted with a lazy head lift from Penny at the foot of the bed. "Shhh," he whispered to the snoozing pup, not wanting to wake Tori if she was asleep. He peeled off his T-shirt and slipped off his belt and pants before crawling under the covers beside her. Penny hopped off the now crowded bed and trotted out of the room.

Tori rolled closer to him as soon as he settled, her body attuned to his even in sleep. He rested his hand on her upper thigh, intentionally avoiding her midsection so he wouldn't accidently graze any of the sensitive, bruised skin along her tummy.

"Hey, you," she whispered, her hand smoothing down over his arm before coming to rest on top of his.

"Hey. Go back to sleep. I didn't mean to wake you."

"I don't want to sleep all day when you're home," she objected through a yawn. "How was Jake?"

"Good, really good," he lied. He didn't feel like talking about the real reason Jake had accepted his invitation to hang out. At least not yet. "He leant me a car to use when I'm in town so we don't have to worry about going back to get the Prelude right away."

"Ahh, that was nice. What kind of car?"

"His M3."

"What? I thought his dad took that car away years ago. I literally have not seen that thing since our sophomore year of high school."

"Huh. Yeah, I guess he did have the Jeep by the time he transferred to Hampton High," Rhett mused as he ran his hand up and down her thigh. "I'll take you for a drive later if you want. We can pretend we're in high school again," he crooned into her ear.

"Yes to the ride. But no to the high school roleplaying." She wiggled her hips back and forth against his growing erection. "I like our life better now that you're my husband and we don't have to sneak around."

"Mhmm." He sighed into her hair. "I love hearing you say that word."

"Well, I love you, husband." She reached behind her and worked her hand between their bodies, wrapping her fingers around his dick through his boxer briefs. "And I want you, too," she added, giving his solid erection a squeeze.

He mirrored her actions and caressed her through the thin lace of her underwear. She was already wet, the warmth of her arousal spurring him into action. "I don't want to hurt you," he murmured as he brushed her hair away from her shoulder and started to kiss her neck. "Tell me what to do or not do."

"It's just the injection spots that bother me. As long as I don't lay on my stomach, I'll be fine. That means you can spoon me, or I can ride you, or you can spread my legs over my head and fuck me, or we can do it doggy style..."

"Well, aren't you just full of ideas." He chuckled as he nipped at her ear. He continued to tease her through her panties, applying the slightest edge of pressure each time his fingers moved over her clit as she pulled her shirt up and over her head.

"I just missed my husband," she retorted, but there was a softness to her voice now. He didn't need the reminder that she'd been alone for so long. But there it was. Even last weekend when he'd been in town he'd been distracted.

The physical distance. The emotional distance. It was all starting to feel like too much. He'd do anything—give her anything—be anything for her—to lessen the distance between them.

"I'm here now, beautiful. Use me. Show me how much you missed me."

He shifted out of his boxers and kicked them off. Then he hooked his fingers under the lacy fabric of her underwear and peeled them down her legs. He pressed up against her and stilled, waiting for her to make her move.

She reached back, this time grasping his freed cock with a steady hand. She lifted her top leg ever so slightly, then shimmied back to close all the space between them. She guided his erection between the apex of her thighs but didn't line him up at the entrance like he expected. Instead, she moved her own hand to the front of her body, reached back down between their legs, and held his dick between her folds as she started to slowly grind against him.

Fuck. She felt like heaven. Like soft, pillowy clouds. Like sunshine and laughter. Like the counterpoint to every sad and scary thing in this world.

Her slickness coated his length. Her warmth sparked his desire. His penis throbbed as she continued to work it against her pussy.

"You feel so fucking good, V," he growled into her ear. "I love it when you use me."

"I missed you. I missed this so much," she panted. It didn't even matter that he wasn't inside of her. The pressure between her hand and her core created the perfect amount of friction.

She continued to grind against him, letting out a little whimper each time the head of his dick pushed up against her clit. His hardness met her softness stroke for stroke. He was covered in her arousal, slick and smooth because of her wanting. All he could hear were her soft pants as she rhythmically pushed back into him. "Louder," he instructed from behind, knowing she needed this release just as much as he did. She moaned on cue, this time filling the room with the sound of her pleasure.

She didn't stop there. She reached around and frantically felt for his hand, guiding it up the front of her body all the way to her face and she continued to move against his cock. She sucked his pointer finger into her mouth, licking him past the second knuckle. "I want more of you," she moaned when she finally removed his hand from her mouth.

Fuck, he loved this woman. The way she shed all inhibitions and gave herself to him so completely. The way she writhed and wiggled against him, as if she could never get enough, even after all these years together. He knew what she wanted. And he was more than happy to oblige.

He trailed his hand from the base of her neck all the way down her spine before dipping into the crease of her ass. "Is this what you want, V? You want to feel me everywhere?"

He gathered up more of her arousal then let his wet finger rest against her puckered hole. He teased and caressed her ass until she was muttering a string of unintelligible words.

"Yes. Rhett. Fuck. Please."

He pushed in slightly, giving her a second to adjust to the intrusion as he waited for her cue. "More," she mewled, spreading her legs wider and finally guiding the tip of his dick into her tight channel. He thrust forward, filling her pussy to the hilt while his finger worked deeper into her ass. They both stilled for two seconds, breathing in unison as they reveled in the sensations of being so intimately connected. He could feel his own length through the thin wall inside her. Fucking incredible.

A current jolted through him when she finally began to move. He let her take the lead, savoring every second of being buried inside her. This was what he had been missing. This was all he needed. Her arousal gushed around him as he alternated thrusting his cock and his finger into her holes. He could feel her tense up, her pleasure gripping his dick as she teetered toward release.

"I'm close, I'm so close... but I- I don't know if I can get off like this," she panted as she continued in earnest to grind back against his dick and his hand.

As much as he loved being inside her like this, he wanted to make her come. Her pleasure was his primary concern. "I got you," he murmured as he moved away and gently pushed her onto her back. "I'll get you there, beautiful. Just lie back and let me take care of you."

He ran his hands up her legs before coaxing her thighs apart. She spread her legs wider, granting him deeper access. She was a sight to behold. Her entire center dripping with arousal, her clit swollen from grinding against his cock. It thrilled him that he got to be the one to get her off. That no one else got to have her like this. Her pleasure was all his.

He gave her one more appreciative glance, admiring her spread out before him, ready and wanting. They locked eyes before he lowered his head. "I love you," she moaned, her words alone edging him toward his own release. He placed his hands on either side of her pussy, and then he feasted.

He licked up her slit, relishing the way she writhed underneath him from just the touch of his tongue. He drew wide circles around her clit, alternating the motion with sharp flicks against the sensitive bud. He slipped two fingers inside her, working in tandem to caress the spot she loved while relentlessly working over her tight bundle of nerves.

"Ev... Fuck. Yes... I'm coming," she panted.

He continued to stroke her as he chuckled against her core. "Yeah, I know, beautiful. Not my first rodeo." He winked before sitting back on his knees and running a hand down his face. She reveled in her release for another minute, letting out the cutest little moans with the aftershocks of her orgasm.

"Speaking of rodeos..." She cocked one eyebrow at him suggestively before sitting up to mirror his position. "I want to ride my husband," she whispered seductively. He moved up the bed and lay back against the headboard, stroking his solid erection a few times as he waited for her to make her move.

She climbed up his body and straddled his lap. She leaned forward to kiss him, a slow, seductive kiss that pulled him deeper and fanned the building heat between them. He felt her reach down and grip his dick, lining him up just how she wanted him.

"V... you have to tell me if I hurt you," he pleaded. He brushed his hand against her stomach with a feather-light touch before grasping her by the hips.

"I will. I promise. And you won't," she added confidently.

"Then put me inside you and ride me."

She lowered herself on his erection and sat back, granting him the most perfect view of her dark blonde hair waterfalling down over her breasts.

She moved up and down on him for a minute before bending over and placing her palms against his chest. The new angle allowed her to grind her hips back and forth in his lap. Her nails dug into his pecs as her pussy clenched around him. He could feel the flutters of her walls against his dick every time she lowered down and let him fill her.

He let her ride him for a few minutes before the urge to take control overcame him. He gave in to it, gripping her ass in his hands and thrusting all the way to the hilt.

Her deep moans spurred him on. The sight of her on top sent tingles down his spine. It wasn't until she leaned in, draping her body forward to kiss him, and he felt her hand smooth down his stomach seeking her clit that his brain started to panic.

She was close. She was close to coming again. She was close, and now that he thought about it, he was close, too. He felt a cresting wave of anxiety build inside him along with his mounting release. Why was he freaking out? Why did it feel like he was going to cry instead of come?

He held his breath when she closed her eyes.

He stilled as he felt the first tremors of her pussy around his cock.

He waited until she let out a satisfied sigh.

Then, because of an internal urging he couldn't explain, he reached down, pulled out, and gave his throbbing dick a few fast, hard strokes. He groaned his own release as the warm cum spurted into his hand.

Tori stiffened, still straddling him, her eyes wide and unblinking. She looked like a deer caught in careening headlights: shocked, confused, and frozen in place.

"That's not how that usually goes..."

Rhett said nothing, too stunned by his own actions to be able to provide any sort of explanation. Instead, he carefully lifted her off his lap, rolled to his side, and reached over for the box of tissues next to the bed.

"Ev?" she questioned with a hint of panic in her voice. "What just happened?"

He took his time cleaning off his hand, not ready to turn around and face her. What the hell had just happened? What the fuck had he just done?

"Do you need one?" he offered, holding out the box of tissues without meeting her gaze.

Her response was clipped and angry. "Nope. Looks like you kept it all to yourself today."

He turned his head on instinct. Sarcasm wasn't her usual style. He met her stormy gaze and let out a long breath, but remained quiet.

"Rhett. Talk to me," she demanded.

"I don't know what you want me to say."

"Please." She reached over and took his hand, urging him back to the middle of the bed. "Please talk to me."

"I just wasn't sure with all the egg retrieval stuff if it was a good idea..." he tried.

"Nope. Not good enough."

Was she actually angry with him right now? Sure, it wasn't something they had talked about, and it was a little embarrassing, honestly, but why the hell did she care so much?

"You were at the appointment when Dr. Silko explained that my IUD would be effective through the entire egg retrieval process, and that we didn't have to worry about any other form of birth control until it comes out right before my surgery. Plus, I would have stopped you if it was an issue."

He leaned back against the headboard to match her posture, but maintained a sliver of space between them. He ran his hand through his hair over and over again, desperate to be done with this conversation. "I guess I forgot about that."

"That's bullshit. You had the forethought to ask about hurting me and about what not do. Then you had the wherewithal to pull out. So was that really even about me? About the egg retrieval?"

He said nothing. Not because he didn't want to answer her. But because he didn't have any answer to give. He had no fucking idea why he did that. The more she pressed, the more confused he felt.

"Or was that about Chandler?"

He stilled at the accusation. He hadn't thought of that.

"I... I don't know." He honestly hadn't considered pulling out in advance. It just happened. "I didn't mean for it to be about that," he swore. "I would never want you to think that's what I'm thinking about when we're together."

A charged, awkward silence stretched between them. He felt like he was about to lose it. He had already lost his baby. He was on his way to losing himself. He couldn't lose her, too.

"Come here," he pleaded, reaching across the small space between them and pulling her into his arms. "I'm sorry, V. I feel like all I can do lately is apologize to you, but I'm so fucking sorry."

"You don't have anything to apologize for. I'm not upset about you pulling out. I'm just worried because you're bottling everything up instead of talking to me. I just want you to open up and let me be here for you. Let me take care of you for once."

He looped an arm around her shoulders and shook his head back and forth as he buried his face in her hair. He had everything to apologize for. He had messed up so many fucking times. She had enough on her plate without him adding to her burden.

"You can tell me anything," she prompted. He knew that. He just didn't know where to begin, and he worried once he started, he wouldn't be able to stop.

He bit down on the inside of his cheek, working his jaw back and forth as the tension spiked inside him. She was just trying to help, but he couldn't talk about the miscarriage. Not right now. Not when he didn't have a release to work through all the feelings threatening to boil over. Not when he'd just promised Jake he'd cut down on the drinking.

"I know you're sad, Ev. I know you're upset. Those are all normal things to feel."

She was relentless. He knew she wasn't going to stop trying to grief counsel him until he gave her something. Most people hesitated when it came to talking about death and loss, choosing to tiptoe around the pain or just stay silent for fear of saying the wrong thing. Not Tori. Years of therapy and volunteering with the New Hope Foundation had armed her with an arsenal of all the right things to say.

He had to choose his words wisely. He couldn't stand to unleash the fury of emotions swirling inside him. He refused to give her his pain, but he had to give her *something* to make her feel like he wasn't shutting down completely. He decided to share the most logical thing he could think of.

"I offered to pay for all of Chandler's hospital bills."

She stilled in his arms. He could see out of the corner of his eye that she was looking up at him, but he had his gaze set on the door.

"Okay..." she prompted, waiting for him to continue. He silently cursed himself for offering so little.

"I just thought I should let you know, since I'll be paying for it from our checking account. She just started a new job a few weeks ago, and technically, she's still on her parents' health insurance. She was terrified about them finding out, so I offered to pay cash and already set it up with the hospital billing department. I don't know if we should have talked about it first or..."

"No, of course not. That was the right thing to do," she murmured. She reached down and took his hand in hers, interlacing their fingers as she leaned back onto his chest. "Anything else?"

Fuck. He shouldn't have gone so surface level... he should have shared something more intimate so they could move on.

He was desperate to not have to talk about this anymore. It shouldn't be the issue on the table right now. Not with what Tori was currently going through. Not when he thought about what came next. He had already focused enough of his time and energy on Chandler and the baby. All he wanted to do now was focus on his wife. Everything he was feeling, everything he wanted to shove down and forget about, it could wait. He had to be back in Virginia in twenty-four hours. His grief would keep until then.

He racked his brain for something else to say. Something honest, something true. Something that would be enough to end this conversation.

"I kept one of the ultrasound pictures," he finally offered. He had asked Chandler if he could have one when he came across the small strip of glossy black and white printouts in her dresser drawer. It was a picture from her first appointment at the OBGYN's office a few weeks ago. In the picture, his baby was seven weeks old. In the picture, his baby was alive.

Tori said nothing, instead shifting closer and spreading a hand across his chest, her palm resting over his heart. Rhett kept his gaze fixed on her bedroom door, but he felt her body tremble in his arms. It was the only indication she was crying.

There. That ought to do it. He knew he wouldn't have to talk about it again this weekend. His cool, stoic mask slipped back into place. It was over for now.

CHAPTER THIRTY-SEVEN

Tori

"Thanks again for coming with me today," Tori said, turning to her best friend and stifling a big yawn. She really was grateful Lia had been willing to drive her to and from the fertility clinic in her old boat of a farm truck. She could have driven herself to the appointment, but her stomach had ballooned this week because of the hormone injections, and she hated how the seatbelt cut across and rubbed her bruised tummy skin. At least in the passenger seat, she could hold the belt away from her body.

It had been Tori's second ultrasound so far that week, and she had received the exact news she was hoping to hear. Everything looked good, and they were able to schedule the procedure first thing on Friday morning. She had to give herself one more injection at eight tonight—the trigger shot—and then she just had to take it easy for the next thirty-six hours.

"Seriously, Tor. Anytime. It was a good excuse to get away from the farm for the morning. And to see you, of course."

Summer was the busiest season on the Perry's family farm. Lia's parents relied on her to work fourteen hours a day alongside the rest of the cattle farm staff. Lia's only "breaks" in the summer were the days she worked at Clinton's as a server, a job she refused to give up, much to her parents' chagrin. Tori rarely saw Lia during the warmer months unless they were both scheduled on the same shift at the restaurant.

Lia making time in her busy schedule plucked at a chord of dissonance. Rhett hadn't been around all week. She had told him it was fine, and the logical part of her brain knew it didn't make sense to expect him to be in Hampton for every single one of her appointments, given the fact that so much of the egg retrieval process had to be taken day-by-day. But at least now that she knew the end game, she could make sure Rhett would be around for the actual procedure on Friday.

She cracked her knuckles in a satisfying release while debating what she could do to fill the time and distract herself over the next few days. "What are you doing the rest of the day? Want to come over and lie out at the Wheelers' pool?"

Lia let out a frustrated breath. "I wish. I told my parents I'd only be gone for part of the morning, so I have to get back to the farm."

"Darn. Okay. Do we have time to stop at Cali Juice and get a smoothie before you drop me off? It's the least I can do for making you drive me around today."

"Are you gonna buy mine and put it on your husband's credit card?" Lia was still giddy about Tori's new tax bracket, even though Tori tried to downplay it. She got it—she really did. It was crazy to go from living from paycheck to paycheck and always being anxious about money to just being able to swipe a rose gold AmEx without giving the purchase another thought.

"I will use *my* credit card to buy you a smoothie," she corrected.

"And then let your husband pay the bill?"

She rolled her eyes but didn't bother correcting her, mostly because she wasn't wrong.

"Okay, quick stop at Cali Juice, then I'll drop you at home. What are you gonna do the rest of the day?" Lia asked.

Tori had given up all her shifts at Clinton's for the week after she woke up painfully bloated on Sunday morning. Since she didn't have to work, and all the prep was done for camp, she didn't have any real plans until Friday.

"I'm not sure. I'm supposed to take it easy, which is honestly fine by me because I don't feel like doing much of anything. I might text Field, or maybe I'll see what Jake's doing if he's not already at The Oak."

"Ohhh, Fielding..." Lia sing-songed, sitting up a little straighter as she yanked on the large steering wheel of her old truck to make a sharp turn.

Tori took the bait. "What about him?" She braced herself as she waited for what she was sure would be a less-than-positive response.

"Nothing." Lia shrugged as she pulled into a parking spot right outside the smoothie shop. "I just think he has a goofy name."

Tori burst out laughing. Out of everything her best friend could have said, that was *not* what she was expecting.

"And here I was thinking I was about to get a famous Lia Lecture.""Nope. Fielding's a-okay in my mind these days."

"Seriously?" Tori gaped.

"Yeah, seriously. Jake and I had a little chitchat about him a few weeks ago. I don't think I was *wrong* in my initial assessment of Fielding and his intentions, but I see now that he's been a good friend to you and to Jake over the last few months. So yeah. He's cool."

All she could do was stare. Never in her wildest dreams did she imagine Lia would come to accept, and maybe even like, Fielding.

"Jake seems to be all about that boy these days," Lia added with a salacious smile.

"Right?!" Tori exclaimed. "I thought the same thing! But I asked Jake about that a few weeks ago. There's nothing going on between them according to him. Just bro love."

"Speaking of bro love... how's that husband of yours?" Tori didn't miss the concern in her best friend's voice. The irony was Lia didn't even know about Chandler and the miscarriage. Her concern stemmed solely from all the apparent tension between their friends that whistled like a tea kettle whenever Rhett was around.

"He's good, or as good as can be. So much changed so quickly. Neither one of us feels settled yet, and this long distance is harder than anything we faced when he was at school."

"Is he coming home for your procedure?"

"Yes, for sure. He'll come home tomorrow and then go with me on Friday morning. Our plan is to freeze embryos, not just eggs, so he has to be here."

Lia's eyebrows shot up. "Oh. Wow. Yikes. Why does that feel like way too much information?"

"Maybe it is," Tori admitted, stifling a laugh. "Sorry. This whole thing is so clinical, I sometimes forget what we're even talking about. It's just a means to an end for now. I'll be relieved when this is all over and I can just focus on my hysterectomy."

They were both quiet then, so Tori reached for the door handle.

"I didn't think you even wanted kids," Lia mused, holding her in place with her words.

"I don't. I mean, I didn't think it would ever be an option, so I never let myself even think about it. We aren't trying to have kids anytime soon."

Tori swallowed past the lump that formed in her throat as she thought about Rhett, about his baby. The recentness of his loss made the emotions of this experience feel like they were playing in high definition.

"We decided to go for the embryo freezing so if we do ever decide we want kids, we have the option. This whole procedure is about *not* rushing into anything, if that makes sense. We just have to do it now, before I have my surgeries and the choice isn't available to us anymore."

Lia nodded thoughtfully but didn't press her any further.

"Any more questions? Or can I buy you a smoothie now?"

"Yes, bitch. And I'm getting an extra large," Lia declared.

"Of course you are. I wouldn't expect anything less."

Rhett's assistant said he had left the office more than an hour ago, but he still wasn't answering her calls. She knew he didn't have a business lunch—Quinn would have mentioned that. She hit her husband's name on the screen again, hoping the FaceTime video would finally connect.

When "Call Unavailable" popped up for the third time in less than an hour, she gave up. Frustrated and feeling extra cranky from the hormones, she shot off a text instead.

V: I tried calling a few times but can't get ahold of you. Nothing's wrong, I just wanted to tell you about my appointment this morning. Doc says everything looks good. The egg retrieval is officially scheduled for Friday at 8 am. Just one more shot tonight... This weekend can't come soon enough.

She set down her phone and putzed around her room. It had turned out to be a gorgeous summer day: sunny and eighty-two degrees with not so much as a hint of humidity in the air. She would have loved to take Penny on a long walk or to swim laps in the Wheelers' pool. Neither of those were an option based on how she was feeling and the doctor's orders to take it easy for the next few days.

She had read about all the side effects of the egg retrieval process, but nothing could have prepared her for how she felt right now. In addition to her stomach being achy from injections and hyper-sensitive to the touch, she was so bloated she couldn't put real pants on. Thankfully she had a collection of flowy dresses in her closet. Otherwise she didn't know how'd she even be able to get dressed and leave the house.

She practically leapt for the bed when her phone vibrated. It wasn't a call or a FaceTime like she was hoping for, though. It was just a text from Rhett.

Ev: Thanks for the update. I'll let Quinn know re: Friday. Love you.

She stared at the screen and tried to cool her raging temper. The message was just so... short. Dispassionate. Impersonal. It could have been typed out by anyone. It could have been sent to anyone for that matter. She flopped dramatically onto her bed, running her hand up

and down the bloated stomach that made her look like she was
pregnant.

Where was he that he was able to text, but not return her call?
How could he not even ask how she was feeling? And that thing
about Quinn... What the hell? She had already been in touch with his
assistant and confirmed that Rhett was ticketed for the early evening
flight tomorrow. All he had to do was check his email or glance at his
beloved calendar, and he would have known that. She had already
taken care of all the arrangements herself, just like she'd done almost
everything for this egg retrieval herself.

She knew she'd regret it if she texted back in anger, so she scrolled
down and opened up the next message on the screen instead.

*Tori: I'm moody and hormonal. Want to cash in that raincheck and
take me to get ice cream?*

A response came through almost immediately.

*Fielding: Can we just take a minute to appreciate the poetry of that
text? I mean, damn, Victoria Thompson. You're a temptress. With an
offer like that, how could I refuse?*

She rolled her eyes at his teasing. His second text came through
before she even had a chance to respond.

*Fielding: I'm at Jake's right now, but he just started one of his
stupid two-hour workouts, so he's not invited. Should I pick you up at
your house?*

Tori: Yep. Hurry up. I'm hungry.

She had just enough time to let Penny out and put her shoes on
before Fielding pulled into her driveway ten minutes later. She felt her
tension instantly melt away as she sank into the plush leather front
seat of his huge Infiniti SUV.

"Hey," she greeted him quickly before messing with the buttons on
the center console.

"Hey yourself," he replied, giving her a quizzical look. "Whoa, wait.
Hold up. That one's the seat warmer," he said as he tried to reach over
and turn off the button she had just pressed.

"I know that," she hissed as she swatted at his hand. "I don't need you to mansplain your car's features to me. My back is killing me. I can't take anything for it, but heat helps."

Fielding pulled away his hand like he'd been burned. "Shit. That sucks. Sorry, Tor. How'd your appointment go this morning?"

"It was fine," she huffed out. She hadn't exactly planned to go into detail about the appointment with Fielding. But no one else had asked. "Everything looks good. There are lots of follicles, and they're optimistic about what they'll be able to get. I just have to do the trigger shot tonight, then the actual retrieval is Friday morning. I can't wait for this all to be over."

"The trigger shot is the last one, right?"

They had done enough Internet research together by now that Fielding had turned into a walking encyclopedia on egg freezing. She originally teased him about it before he reminded her that he had been pre-med in college, so he already had a foundational understanding of the female reproductive cycle. He also couldn't resist making multiple dirty jokes about all the primary and secondary research he did on the female reproductive system in college, but she let those slide.

"Yep. Last one," she confirmed.

He gave her a little smirk before putting the car in reverse. "So does that mean you don't have anything to do until tonight?"

"Yes," she answered tentatively. She could see his wheels spinning.

"Good. I've got an idea."

She sighed appreciatively. Rhett was distracted. Lia was busy on the farm. And she'd already dumped enough on Jake this summer. It was nice to have Fielding's support and company. "I'll play along, but your idea better involve ice cream as promised. I wasn't kidding about being hormonal."

"I've got you," he assured her. "We'll go to Valley Cream first. But I have a grander vision for this day. I'm going to take you on an official valley cruise. Well, I guess it's not an *official* valley cruise because those usually involve a few joints. I'm guessing if you can't have ibuprofen, you probably don't want any weed? Yeah. No. Of course not," he answered his own question when she shot him a look.

"Right. So we'll do the kiddie version of the valley cruise. Here's how it works: We coast down 303 with the windows down and music up. Then we drive through the valley, singing at the top of our lungs and making all the classic stops. We'll start at Valley Cream, then we'll go eat our weight in grilled corn from that farm stand near the Tow Path. We'll end our adventure at Brandywine Falls, where we will *not* share a blunt while stuffing our faces with kettle corn."

"Oh wait, kettle corn is an option? I *do* want the kettle corn," she professed.

"Thank God," Fielding muttered as he backed out of the driveway. "You were going to break my Ohio-born-and-raised heart if you weren't up for two types of corn today."

She was struggling to keep her eyes open when her phone finally vibrated in her hand. She accepted the FaceTime call, even though this was going to be more of a one-sided video chat since she was already lying in bed in the dark. She still wanted to FaceTime, though. It made her feel a little less alone to actually see him at least once a day.

"Hey, beautiful," Rhett greeted her as she lowered the brightness on her device.

"Hi, you," she replied, too sleepy to say anything else.

"Are you already in bed?" he asked, loosening his tie and undoing the top two buttons of his shirt. He must have propped his phone up in the kitchen because she could see him moving between the sink and the stove. His hair was slightly disheveled, like he'd been running his hand through it over and over again today.

"I am." She yawned. "I'm so damn tired. And bloated. And full. So damn full." She smirked to herself as she thought about all the food she ate during Fielding's ridiculous valley cruise. There'd been no weed involved, yet they had both stuffed their faces like they had the most insatiable munchies.

"Tell me about your day," he prompted as he washed his hands at the sink. She knew she didn't have his full attention, but at least she could see him on the screen. She sighed and rolled over, trying once again to find a position that was comfortable. Between the back ache and the cramping and the bruises on her torso, something seemed to hurt regardless of how she lay, so she'd just been rolling from her back to each side and back again for the last hour.

"Lia took me to my appointment this morning." She yawned again. It wasn't even ten, but she knew she'd be out as soon as they got off the phone. "They did another ultrasound, and the doctor said everything looked great. There are lots of follicles close to being in the ideal range, and some smaller ones that might be big enough by Friday, so that increases our chances of getting a lot of eggs." She paused, not sure exactly what she was expecting him to say or ask next, but he stayed quiet.

"Anyways, everything is all set, so now we just wait. I'm super bloated, and I'm not supposed to do anything active, so it was a lazy day for me. I sent a few thank you notes for some late wedding gifts that showed up the other day, then I hung out with Field this afternoon. I came home for dinner and ended up watching four episodes of some weird survival show with my dad. I had to do the trigger shot tonight, which was somehow both the hardest and the easiest one, probably because I knew it was the last."

"You hung out with Fielding today?"

That was his first follow up question? Really?

On any other night, she would have let it slide. She would have brushed off the question, eager to keep the peace and not reignite their old fight. What did he think he was going to accomplish by picking a fight about Fielding anyways?

But tonight, she was tired and felt like shit. It shouldn't be her job to play peacekeeper by constantly skirting around his insecurities. Tonight, she wasn't willing to dismiss it.

"That's all you care about after everything I just said?" she snapped. "Yes, Rhett. I hung out with Fielding today. I also hung out with Lia this morning. I saw your mom for a little bit this afternoon, and I spent time with my dad after dinner. Oh! I almost forgot! I made eye contact with the kid working at the ice cream shop, and I smiled and said thank you to the woman who sold me a big bag of kettle corn."

"Tori..." he reprimanded on an exhale. Rhett side-eyed her through the phone, but screw that. He was the one who was preoccupied and only half-interested in everything she had to say until she had mentioned her friend.

"No. Don't 'Tori' me. You don't get to be annoyed about who I hang out with or what I choose to do while you're there. We all get to choose our own priorities, Everhett. You could have been here today. *You* could have taken me to the ultrasound, then to get ice cream. You could have helped me with that huge-ass trigger shot and then just stayed until the procedure on Friday. I wasn't supposed to do this alone, yet here I am, and there you are. You chose your priorities, so now you don't get to be pissy that I want to hang out with my friends and distract myself from this fucking nightmare that's apparently just another line item on your to-do list."

She didn't even know where all her anger was coming from, but once she started spewing it, she couldn't stop.

Rhett puffed out his cheeks and blew out a long breath as he picked up the phone, bringing it eye level. "I had to be at the office most of this week, V. You know that. We talked about it. You said you understood. I'll be home tomorrow ni..."

"You had no problem dropping everything and rearranging your schedule for Chandler."

Hot tears erupted along with the jab. It was a low blow—she regretted saying it before she finished speaking the words—but she said what she said. And now it was out there.

When he didn't respond, she doubled down. She hated that she knew exactly what to say and where to strike to drive her point home and hit him hardest.

"Honestly, Rhett? You can stop pretending we're in this together. I've done everything alone over the last few weeks, which is ironic, given your incessant insistence that you'd be here to support me. The farce that we're in this together is just insulting at this point. If you're too busy for me, don't even bother coming home tomorrow."

She ended the call before the pain finished registering on his face.

CHAPTER THIRTY-EIGHT

Rhett

He didn't know where he was supposed to be going, because Tori still hadn't answered his texts. He'd made it home to Ohio as planned. He had completely cleared his schedule and set an out of office message before leaving Virginia. Quinn knew not to call or text him unless it was a true emergency. He'd even gone as far to let his granddad know he wouldn't be available starting tonight. Everything was all set so he could focus on Tori.

She was his priority. She needed his full attention this weekend, and she deserved all of him, without distraction or reservation. They had a lot to talk about. He had so much to make up for. But they had three full days to be together, and he was determined to show her how important she was to him. How much he needed her. How much he loved her. This weekend was his best shot at making up for every shitty choice he'd made over the last few weeks. This weekend would be a turning point.

He hit the turn signal on the M3 and crossed over three lanes of empty highway. The car Jake had loaned him may have been twenty years old, but it still drove like a dream.

He pulled out his phone again, checking for the third time that it was really off airplane mode. He still hadn't heard from her, so he used the talk-to-text feature to send another message.

Ev: Hey beautiful. I'm just getting off Route 8. Where are you right now? Are we meeting at my house or yours?

He focused on the road and all the familiar scenery whizzing by as he waited for her response. Tomorrow was the first official day of summer. Everything that had been in bloom over the last few months was lush and green. There was that earthy smell in the air as he approached the main intersection in Hampton with the windows down, Oasis crooning through the speakers.

He was sitting at the stop light in the middle of downtown when Tori's response came through.

V: I'm not home right now, but I won't be out too late since I have to be up early tomorrow. I want to sleep in my own bed tonight. You can sleep over or just pick me up in the morning... your call.

He stared down at his phone, seething. They had fought last night. Or more like he got distracted and emotionally triggered by the mention of her having an ultrasound, then inadvertently pissed her off by bringing up Fielding as he floundered to save face. Again. Why did he keep doing that? Why did he double down on the one trigger that pissed her off the most?

He reread her reply. She hadn't actually told him where she was. She also hadn't given him a time when she'd be home. The sun was just starting to set. Was she going to be out for another hour or another three? Had she really given him the option to sleep with her tonight or not—was that a thing now?

Why the fuck did he catch the early evening flight back from Virginia if she was just going to make him sit around and wait for her to make an appearance?

A car honked and startled him out of his racing thoughts. He hit the gas and went straight through the intersection toward downtown instead of turning toward their neighborhood. Maybe Jake was working. And if not, a drink wouldn't hurt. He could find a way to stay busy until she decided he was worth her time.

It was only his second time walking into The Oak Barrel Tavern, but the place already felt familiar. That had to be due to do all the Archway Prep memorabilia on the walls, and not because the bar— any bar—was starting to feel like his real home.

"Wheeler! Hey, man!" Cole greeted him with a genuine smile as Rhett sat down at the long, natural-wood bar. At least someone was happy to see him tonight.

"Hey, Cole. How's it going?"

"Good, really good. We've been open for less than a week, and we've been packed every night."

"I can see that." Rhett nodded as he glanced around the establishment. It wasn't even nine p.m., and the place was almost full. "Jake in tonight?"

"Nope. This is his first night off since we opened. He had something to do with Tori, and he told us not to bother him unless shit was on fire." Cole smirked at the joke before his smile faltered slightly. Rhett watched through squinted eyes as the other man realized what he had just said.

Keep talking, buddy, he silently commanded. *I want to know everything you know about where my wife is tonight.*

"Yo! Wheeler!" Dempsey called out as he approached them. Dempsey clasped his fellow bartender on the shoulder before Cole turned around and slinked away without another word. "Are you looking for Jake?"

Rhett had always thought he and Dem were similar in a lot of ways. They'd both gone to school for business, and Dempsey had graduated from an Ivy League college. It was disconcerting to see him dressed down in jeans and a T-shirt, working behind a bar.

That was one of the things he liked least about the Haas twins: They just did whatever the hell they wanted. They were unpredictable, spontaneous. They both seemed satisfied to just hang around Hampton, working odd jobs and living off their trust funds. They had no sense of discipline. They were totally untamed.

"Yeah, I was. Cole said he's off tonight, though."

Dempsey nodded. "Want me to text him for you?"

Rhett grimaced at the offer. He didn't need someone else texting Jake on his behalf. Jake was *his* best friend, after all.

"Nah, thanks anyways, I heard he's busy. I'll just hang out here for a bit."

"Yeah, I was shocked he actually took the night off. It's the first time he hasn't been here from open to last call. But you know my brother. When he gets an idea in his head..." Dempsey trailed off and shook his head with a smirk. The guy had no idea what he'd just revealed or why it mattered.

Tori wasn't home, and she wouldn't tell him where she was.

But now it was confirmed that Tori was with Jake, and apparently Fielding was, too.

Tori would rather be with Fielding than with him tonight.

Rhett didn't have it in him to react. There was absolutely nothing he could do to channel the rage coursing through him. He wouldn't allow his doubt to fester or his fear to grow. Instead, he relished in the pain, letting everything he'd just learned transform his flurry of emotions into a silent, coiled anger.

"Can I get you something to drink?" Dempsey offered.

Rhett didn't know if he was actually making a choice or just giving in to the inevitable. He felt so far removed from his own body that he didn't really care either way.

"Double Jameson, on the rocks."

It was going to be a long night.

"I liked you a whole lot better in high school," Rhett slurred as he glared at his second least favorite Haas twin.

"Sorry, man. Bar rules. Three or more drinks gets an automatic Uber around here."

"You only served me two drinks," Rhett countered. That was true. The Oak had been busy tonight, and the bartenders had been going nonstop for the last three hours. He had used that to his advantage, making sure to alternate who he asked for each new round.

"Yeah, and Cole served you three doubles. Don't fight me on this, Wheeler. I know you live right down the road, but this isn't my rule. What it *is*, is my new job on the line. Give me your phone, and I'll order you a car."

Rhett balked at the suggestion. Dempsey already had his keys. There was no way he was handing over his fucking phone.

Last call came early at a bar in a small town, so although it was just past midnight, The Oak was closed and almost completely cleared out. Just Dempsey, Cole, and a dishwasher remained, along with Rhett and an attractive redhead who had been eye-fucking Dem for the last hour.

Rhett wasn't drunk. It took a lot more than five drinks to get him drunk nowadays. But he was loose enough to let out some of his anger and try to retaliate against Dempsey for taking his keys.

"Hey," he called out to get the woman's attention. Everything sounded louder now that the music was off and the bar was almost empty, including his own voice. "He's got a twin, you know. The fucker looks just like him. You could screw that one instead, or in addition, I guess, if that's your thing."

The woman's eyes doubled in size. She hopped off the barstool and exited the bar without saying a word.

"Nice, Wheeler. Real nice..." Dempsey muttered to himself as he watched his potential hookup scurry out the door. He blew out a long breath and scowled. "How about this?" Dempsey leveled with him, leaning his forearms on the bar, trying to play the role of the nice guy. "How about I call Tori to come get you if you don't want a ride home?"

"No." The one-word answer came out sharp and clear.

"Give me my keys," Rhett commanded. He wouldn't stand to be patronized. He wasn't drunk. These fuckers had no idea what kind of tolerance he had built up.

"Not happening." Dempsey stood to his full height and crossed his arms across his chest. Rhett smirked as he took in the tough-guy stance. Someone had obviously been taking lessons from Jake.

"We good out here?" Cole asked as he came back around the bar, interrupting their stand off.

"Not quite," Dempsey responded. "I've got his keys, but he refuses to get a ride or to call Tori to drive him home."

Rhett glared as the two men talked about him like he wasn't sitting right there. Cole met his eyes but quickly looked away. At least one of them had the decency to be intimidated. He didn't have a plan for getting home, but he knew he'd be fine walking the few miles if need be. It was a nice night, and the walk might even clear his head and help him sleep.

He wasn't interested in walking now. He wasn't going to let anyone tell him what to do. He knew his fucking limits. This wasn't it.

Rhett had sat at the bar longer than planned, letting his mind wander and the tension he was carrying unravel. But now he really needed to get home. He had two unanswered texts from Tori. Both had come through within the last hour. It was past midnight, and she needed sleep. He didn't give a shit about anything else. He just needed to get home and hold her so she could go to bed.

"Should we call Jake?" Cole asked quietly. But he wasn't quiet enough.

"Don't you fucking dare," Rhett snapped.

Neither man looked over at him. They just carried on like he wasn't right there. Rhett focused on the keys in Dempsey's grasp, the keys to the car Jake had lent him. Was he fast enough to get around the bar and snag them out of his hand? He tried to remember where he parked the M3. He was pretty sure he was in the back lot, through the alley and behind the building. He hadn't even bothered to check for a spot out front. He had just parked in the back out of habit.

"Jake said to only call him if there was a literal fire. I don't know if this counts, man. I'll text my brother. They're probably still together.

He'll tell us if Jake's still awake."

An intense enervation was starting to take hold as Rhett strained to hear what the two men were saying. All of Dempsey's words registered, but nothing stuck. He was too tired to fight them anymore. All he could do now was wait and see which one of them finally gave in and called his best friend.

"Okay. He said keep him here, and he'll come deal with it himself."

That was the last thing he heard Dempsey say before Rhett gave in to the exhaustion, folded his arms on top of the bar, and closed his eyes.

Chapter Thirty-Nine

Rhett

"Is he passed out?"

"Nah, just sleeping, I think. He had plenty to drink, but not enough to pass out."

"Motherfucker..."

Rhett couldn't discern who was speaking. The voices were too similar, their tones a perfect match. It was like listening to someone have a conversation with themselves.

He raised his head and looked around the empty bar. Either he was seeing double, or Fielding Haas was standing right next to his twin brother, staring him down.

Why is he here? Rhett returned the glare Fielding cast upon him, but he didn't utter a word. He needed to get ahead of this, to figure out what they were playing at so he could outsmart them and win.

"Give me his keys," Fielding instructed. Dempsey handed over the keys without question before circling back around the bar.

"I've gotta finish closing. Just holler if you need help," one of the men said to the other.

Help with what?

Rhett still didn't have all the rules figured out, so he stayed quiet.

Fielding stood a few feet away, his stance wide. He twirled a set of car keys obnoxiously on his finger before he finally let out an exasperated sigh. Rhett could barely hold in an eye roll at the other man's dramatics. It was like everything this fucker did was designed to piss him off.

"Come on, Wheeler. Let's get you home."

Rhett let out a low chuckle. As if he would *ever* take orders from fucking Fielding Haas.

Fielding snarled at his dismissiveness. Rhett watched intently as the other man showed his cards, each emotion marring his features: disgust. Frustration. Hatred. Then, finally, resolve.

A cool, almost cruel mask slipped over Fielding's face.

"Don't you have somewhere to be in the morning?" he taunted as he took a few measured steps to the front door. He was walking backwards, watching Rhett like he knew something he didn't.

Rhett knew it was a ploy, all part of the game. He recognized that in the logical part of his brain. But that didn't stop him from rising from the bar stool and stalking toward the other man.

He made it all the way to the door before Fielding smirked like he had the upper hand. That just pissed him off. Rhett moved to shove through the door, pushing into Fielding's chest to get out of the bar. Fielding let him push him, taking several steps back until he was pressed up against the brick wall of the narrow alley that separated Clinton's and The Oak.

"You don't know what you're talking about," Rhett growled as the other man's back hit the wall.

"No, *you* don't know what you're talking about. Tori's egg retrieval is first thing in the morning, you asshat. Where is she right now, Wheeler? Do you even know?"

Rhett balled his hands into fists at his sides. He could feel the strain in his knuckles as they itched to strike. All the stress and anger he'd been holding in for the last few weeks was coming together now. He could feel the energy radiating through his upper body, pain and grief and so much sorrow stitched together into a cloak of hatred.

"You're out here getting shitfaced, and she's home alone, hormonal and fucking miserable," Fielding informed him with a disgusted look on his face. "Some husband," he added for emphasis, pulling the trigger and giving Rhett the opening he'd been waiting to take.

His arm shot out on its own volition. What should have been a perfect jab strayed left. His fist just barely grazed Fielding's face.

The other man reacted so quickly Rhett didn't realize their positions had been reversed. Fielding checked him into the wall and held him there, pressing all the air out of his lungs.

Fuck. He had forgotten Haas had played hockey. He'd been on defense. An enforcer.

Rhett tried to land an uppercut, but that didn't work either. His brain automatically switched to defense. He raised his fists toward his face, steadying himself and preparing to block whatever came next.

Fielding's hands didn't stray from Rhett's shoulders, though, instead shoving him harder into the solid bricks of the alley. Haas was only an inch taller, so they were standing nose to nose. His face was so close Rhett could feel his breath each time he exhaled.

Fielding let out a quiet chortle as he stared him down. "Why are your hands up like that? I'm not going to hit you. I wouldn't fucking dare. What would she think of me if I knocked out her husband?" he taunted.

"Don't talk about her! You don't know anything about her! You've only been hanging around for a few months, you stupid fucker. You don't get to talk about her like you know her." Rhett's breathing was out of control, adrenaline burning through him.

"Time isn't always relevant." Fielding shrugged. "When you have a real connection with somebody..." He smirked as he let his words linger. "You want to know how I know she's home alone right now, Wheeler?" He didn't give Rhett a chance to answer before he continued. "I dropped her off a few hours ago. She wanted to leave Jake's early tonight to be with you."

The confession hit harder than any physical blow Fielding could have landed. Tori was at home waiting for him. Tori had been home for hours, waiting for him, while he was at the bar, waiting for who knows what.

"You're pathetic, you know that? It's one thing if you're in Virginia and can't be with her. But to be here, in Hampton? To not want to spend every fucking minute with her when you're home? Do you know how upset she's been these last few weeks without you here? She's gone to all these appointments alone. She's done all this egg retrieval bullshit by herself. Ever since you two came back from your honeymoon, it's like you don't give a shit about her. You fucking trapped her. You've totally checked out."

Rhett had stopped fighting against Fielding's hold. He relished the feeling of the bricks pushing through his shirt and scraping against his back. Between the pain in his body and the sting of Fielding's words, it almost felt like enough. It almost felt like what he deserved. But his ego wouldn't allow him to not respond to the other man's monologue.

"Fuck you," Rhett spat out. "You don't get to talk about my marriage. I could say the word, and she would never speak to you again," he threatened. *Was that actually true?* He didn't know anymore. But it was worth the risk to vocalize the idea if it knocked Fielding down a few pegs.

The other man took two steps back so Rhett could clearly see his face before he responded, "You could try." He smirked, calling Rhett on his bullshit.

Fielding ran his hand along the side of his face, smoothing over the spot where Rhett had attempted to punch him. "You know, the more I think about it, you don't deserve to go home and sleep next to her tonight. What's she going to think when she finally gives up on you coming home and falls asleep alone? I wonder if she'll even be surprised..."

Panic started to replace every other emotion as Rhett realized what was at stake. *No.* This wasn't happening. He *had* to get home to Tori. He had to be there, he had to hold her. He had to watch her sleep and make sure she got to her appointment tomorrow on time.

"Honestly? I think she's getting used to it, being abandoned and disappointed by you. It's only a matter of time before she sees your pattern. Before she sees you the way I see you." Fielding stalked toward him, getting right up in his face and boxing him in against the alley wall. "I promise you this, Wheeler. She *will* see you the way I see you soon enough. While you're there, I'm here. And unlike you, I won't abandon her. I'll be here when you break her heart."

Fielding pushed off the wall and chucked the car keys near his head.

"I'm not driving you home. Sleep it off in your car if you won't call a ride, you stubborn alcoholic. And don't forget to set an alarm. Tori has to be at the hospital by 7:15 a.m. tomorrow," he clipped out over his shoulder as he exited the alley.

Fucking Fielding.

Rhett fumbled with his phone, turning on the flashlight to search the ground. He finally found the car keys in a puddle a few feet from where he stood. He bent down to grab them, nausea churning in his stomach thanks to the mix of alcohol and self-loathing coursing through his veins. He righted himself and tried to take in a slow breath through his nose.

He wasn't going to let Fielding Haas keep him away from his wife. Not tonight. Not ever. He just needed a minute to collect himself, to get his head on straight, and then he would go home.

Chapter Forty

Tori

"Baby."

A familiar voice called to her through the fog of sleep. A strong grasp jostled her further into consciousness.

"Tori, I'm so sorry to wake you, but you have to get up."

Jake was crouched low, his face hovering just a few inches above her when she finally opened her eyes. She squinted from the brightness of the lamp on her bedside table.

"What? What's going on?"

"You have to get up. There's been an accident. We have to go."

She jolted upright, wincing as the quick movement sent a spark of pain through her abdomen. She reached out toward Jake, not even sure what she was reaching for until he took her hand. She tried to make eye contact through the darkness, tried to meet his gaze through the clouds of panic filling the room.

"Rhett. Is he..." She didn't know which question to ask. She didn't want to hear the answers to any of the questions racing through her mind.

"He's alive. But my buddy Drew was part of the emergency crew that responded, and he thinks he'll need surgery. They took him to City Hospital. I don't know anything else yet."

She let Jake pull her to her feet. She knew they had to go, but she couldn't will her body to move. Her mind was racing, but all she could do was be still. Jake ran a hand over his face before letting out a defeated sigh.

"Grab your phone and your charger. Do you want to change your clothes?"

She nodded, grateful he had the clarity to know what to do next. He moved toward her and pulled her into a quick hug before giving her a gentle squeeze to set her in motion.

"I'll go downstairs and make coffee. We'll leave here in five minutes, 'kay?"

"I—I can't have any caffeine," she remembered out loud. She glanced down at her bloated stomach, at the physical reminder of why she was so tired and why she couldn't have caffeine and why Rhett had come home in the first place.

"I'll get you a water, then. And I'll let Penny out. I'll leave a note for your dad."

She nodded. All she could do was nod. She had to get dressed. She had to get going.

She fumbled through her dresser for at least two minutes before giving up. Nothing in there would fit anyways. She ripped the door open to her closet, blindly grabbing for the first dress hanging in the front.

There had been an accident.

Rhett had been in an accident.

She had let herself go to bed angry. She'd been so unbelievably angry. But that anger was unwarranted: He hadn't been avoiding her or delaying coming home like she had assumed. He'd been in a fucking car accident. She would never forgive herself for being angry while he was in agony.

They made it out the door in less than five minutes. Now that she was finally in motion, she was desperate to get to him.

The weather had been so nice all week that Jake had taken the hard top off the Jeep. The humid summer air assaulted them from all sides as he drove through the abandoned streets of Hampton. Her hair whipped around her face, the seatbelt dug into her tender abdomen.

She didn't feel any of it, though. The only sensation that registered was the ache to be by Rhett's side.

"Baby." Jake had to yell to be heard over the wind. A pained look distorted his features. "There's no other quick way to get to the highway... Close your eyes now if you don't want to see it."

It defied human nature to not gawk at a car crash. There was no way she couldn't look. The flashing yellow light on top of the tow truck was her only indication they were close as they approached the train bridge that separated the more residential neighborhoods from downtown Hampton.

A small black car was suspended at an angle, strung up so it could be towed away from the scene. The left side was a crumbled, indented mess. The driver's window was shattered. The wheel well was turned in on itself. The car was destroyed, surrounded by bits of glass and metal scattered on the road like confetti.

She stared unblinking, desperate to memorize every inch of damage. But she wasn't even seeing the car as they passed. She was seeing the moment of impact. She was seeing Rhett being pulled from the vehicle.

"Tori!" Jake barked, pulling her out of her own head and forcing her to finally look away. It wasn't until she heard him scream her name that she realized she was sobbing. Her nails dug into the seatbelt she was trying so damn hard to hold away from her body. Her breathing was heavy against the unwavering torrent of wind whipping through the car.

"Tori," Jake repeated, calmer this time. "He's not in there. He's safe. He's at the hospital. We're going to him now."

She knew that. Rhett was okay. Or he would be okay. That wasn't even the dominant thought in her mind anymore. Not after seeing the car. Not after seeing the point of impact.

She turned to assess Jake's profile. She saw the truth in his hardened expression before she even asked the question.

"Where's the other car, Jake?"

A stillness filled the space between them. They were existing on a tightrope. She closed her eyes and savored the silence that she knew wouldn't keep. Once Jake answered her question, everything she thought she knew would unravel. There'd be no more denying what she so desperately didn't want to be true.

"There was no other car involved," he admitted.

She dragged in a breath before a flurry of accusations tumbled out.

"He went to a bar tonight. He was out drinking while I was waiting for him to come home to me. He got drunk the night before our egg retrieval. He drove drunk! He totaled your car!"

"We don't know any of the details for sure yet," Jake defended.

"But you know. Or you at least suspect."

"I've got texts out to my guys, yeah," he confessed. "Dempsey and Cole worked at The Oak tonight. I made a big dramatic scene telling them not to call me unless the place was on fire..."

She heard the self-blame in his words. His tone mirrored exactly how she felt. But she couldn't allow him to go there. There was only one person involved in the crash; there was only one person who made the series of decisions that led to a car crash tonight.

"You can't blame yourself for this, Jake. I don't think any of us realized how determined he was to self-destruct. Not even him."

Tears filled her eyes as she thought about the slow but deliberate downward spiral Rhett had been riding for weeks. She rested her head against the frame of the Jeep, crying silent tears for her Golden Boy who was so out of reach. This wasn't her fault. This wasn't Jake's fault. But she couldn't help but wonder what else she could have done to keep him from getting to this point.

She didn't know. But she should have known.

"We're looking for Everhett Wheeler," Jake informed the man sitting behind the check-in station of the emergency room. "He was brought in by ambulance around two a.m. They thought he was going to need surgery."

The man nodded as he stared at a computer screen. "Umm... Wheeler. There he is. It looks like he was admitted to the third floor," he informed them. "But it's family only, I'm afraid."

"I'm his wife," Tori said without missing a beat. She held up her left hand for emphasis, as if her wedding band could magically grant her access to his room.

"And I'm his brother," Jake added, grasping Tori's right hand and giving it a squeeze.

"Take that elevator to the third floor, then turn left. He's in room 305."

An involuntary sob escaped her when they entered the room. She hadn't been prepared for him to look so broken. Jake had to steady her shoulders and walk behind her just to get her past the bed.

Rhett's left arm was braced against his body in a sling. His right wrist was wrapped, and he had stitches running from just above his ear lobe all the way into his hairline. There were other marks on his body, his face marred with scrapes and blossoming bruises.

She approached the bed, taking in the monitors and screens that surrounded him. An IV was stuck in his arm, with EKG wires laced under his hospital gown. Her fingers itched to pull back the sheet and analyze every shattered piece of his broken body, but she knew it was futile without having anyone in the room to answer her questions.

"If he just got out of surgery, he might be out of it for a while." Jake placed an arm across her shoulders. "Come on," he urged, titling his head toward the small plastic couch in the corner. "You should try to rest while he's asleep."

She nodded wordlessly but couldn't bring her body to move. Jake tried to guide her backwards, but her feet were planted in place.

Sighing, he walked around her and grunted. A moment later, he was behind her again, this time with the couch in his outstretched arms. She let out an unexpected cackle, clamping her hand over her own mouth once she realized the sound was coming from her. Nothing about this was funny, but the absurdity of watching Jake carry a couch across the room finally cracked her shellshock. He set the furniture down gently, then pushed it across the vinyl floor a few more inches, positioning it as physically close as possible to the hospital bed.

"Sit," he instructed. This time, she obeyed.

The next few hours passed in a hazy blur. A few nurses came in to check Rhett's vitals, but no one would tell them anything. They all kept reassuring her he was okay. They all kept telling her the doctor would be by with a full report in the morning.

All she knew for sure was that he had a concussion and he'd had two surgeries—one on his shoulder, one on his spleen. Oh, and that it was unlikely that he'd be charged with any sort of driving under the influence charges, because no one mentioned a word about his blood alcohol level. She had no idea how Jake had pulled that one off, but it seemed like a foregone conclusion that he had it handled.

She had been huddled up on the couch and half-asleep when she heard the first tolls of the alarm on her phone. Jake startled awake beside her.

"Baby?" he tried, his voice deep and gravelly with sleep.

She didn't open her eyes. She didn't move a muscle. Her alarm had been set for a very specific reason this morning. She wasn't ready to face this day. Not alone. Not without Rhett.

"Tori. That's your alarm." He nudged his knee against hers, urging her to turn it off.

"I know," she breathed out, grasping at the frayed ends of her resolve. Weeks ago when they agreed to move forward with embryo freezing, she never could have predicted it would end like this.

"What do we need to do?" He sounded just as exhausted and despondent as she felt. "I know your procedure is supposed to be this morning. It's here in this building, isn't it?"

"Yes," she choked out, a silent tear rolling down her cheek as she thought about the irony of what she was about to do. The man she needed today was lying just a few feet away. He had come home to bring her here. And yet they were already at the hospital, not for her procedure, but because of him.

"Are you still going to go through with it?"

She snapped her head to glare at him for the preposterous suggestion. She'd come so far, endured so much to get to this point. She couldn't just not go through with the egg retrieval. She didn't think delaying it was even an option. She loathed the idea of having to start over and endure the shots and hormones for another cycle. She shuddered at the thought of having to move back her hysterectomy.

She took a steadying breath. She had to keep her head straight. She had to go through with the procedure, and she had to do it on her own. She had always planned to go through everything alone, anyways. She knew she had it in her.

"I don't think not going through with it is an option," she replied calmly. "I'll head up there in a few minutes and then just come back down here when I'm done. Will you stay with him for me?"

Jake's face contorted in anger. "Is someone supposed to go with you?" he demanded. "Tell me the truth, Tori. Are you supposed to have someone up there?"

He stared at her and she returned his gaze. They were locked in a stalemate, Jake refusing to fill the silence as she refused to answer to his question.

"Goddamnit..." he muttered before letting out a huff of a breath and pushing to his feet. He removed the baseball hat he was wearing for just long enough to run his hand through his hair. It was a very Rhett-like gesture that struck a nerve buried deep in her subconscious.

"I'm going up there with you," he declared as he replaced the hat on his head and turned to face her.

"No, Jake, you can't. They won't even let you in the room. I want you to stay here with..."

"No way. He came home for this procedure. I know this is a big deal. You're being put under, aren't you?"

Tori nodded, her throat clenching up at the thought of everything the procedure entailed. She would be put under. There would be pain. And they told her to expect a fair amount of bloating and cramping for the next few days. Go home and rest, they said. She hadn't counted on having to stay at the hospital afterwards.

"That's what I thought. I'm going with you. This isn't a debate, baby, so save your fucking breath."

"What if someone finally comes in to talk to us while I'm up there?" she protested as she wiped a tear of gratitude from her cheek. "What if he wakes up when we're gone?"

"I don't give a shit if he wakes up alone. I can barely look at him right now. You don't want me in this room alone with him when he comes to," Jake clipped.

"We'll talk to the nurse before we head upstairs and ask that they can wait to do rounds until we get back. Don't worry about that. Cleaning up Rhett's messes is turning into somewhat of a specialty of mine," he deadpanned.

"Did someone text you back?" she asked, already knowing the answer without his confirmation. She'd watched him respond to a flurry of texts about an hour ago. She'd been afraid to ask for an update.

"Yeah. Cole and Dempsey both texted me. Rhett got wasted at my bar last night, fought with everyone who tried to help him, then had the audacity to get behind the wheel and ram my car into the train bridge."

She nodded solemnly, accepting all the revelations she already knew. Now that the consequences of his actions were playing out in front of them, all the other truths they'd been dancing around all summer seemed even more obvious.

Her husband had been drinking in excess. Her husband had been hiding his drinking. And last night, her husband chose to get wasted at a bar, then he chose to get behind the wheel.

"The icing on the fucking cake is that he did all that *knowing* that your appointment was today. I don't know if I'll ever be able to forgive him." The words came out low and sincere, the room suddenly feeling heavier than it had all night.

"Let's go find the nurse," Jake suggested, gently pulling her to her feet. Every part of her body ached, from her head to her feet, from her midsection to her low back, from her stomach to her heart. But at least the physical and emotional pain was a distraction from the actual procedure she was about to endure.

She let him lead her to the door but froze in place when she glanced back and thought she saw Rhett move. "Wait," she whispered, pulling on Jake's hand in protest before he could exit the room.

"V..." Rhett rasped out as he attempted to sit up in bed. She almost tripped over her own feet as she staggered back across the room to reach him.

"Shhhh," she soothed, running her hand through his hair on the uninjured side of his head. "I'm here, I'm here."

Tears streamed down her face as she watched him struggle to come to. His face contorted into a grimace that only seemed to get worse with each inhalation. She hadn't even thought about all the internal injuries he may have suffered. He'd had surgery on his spleen for sure —how big was the incision? Did he have bruising or any cracked ribs?

She had been so angry—she still was so angry—but seeing him hurting like this awakened the desire to wrap him in her arms and kiss it all better. She wanted to crawl into his lap and consume all of his pain.

She knew they didn't have much time, though, so she settled on letting her palm rest on the side of his face. She stroked her thumb against his cheek, willing him to feel some sense of comfort. On contact, he relaxed into her touch. Finally, he opened his eyes.

"Tori?" It was a question. It was a testimony. It was an apology and a plea.

"You're okay," she promised through unrelenting tears. "I'm here, Ev. You're okay."

"Where..." he tried in vain to scoot up the bed. But his left arm was in a sling, and his right wrist was wrapped in a brace with an IV that inhibited his range of motion. He couldn't move. He wasn't going anywhere. She watched as his body seized up in panic as that realization dawned on him. He started to breathe heavier as he continued to struggle.

"Hey, don't. Don't try to sit up. You have a concussion. It's okay. You're in the hospital. You're safe."

"What happened?" he pleaded for clarity.

Did he really not know? Or did he need someone else to spell it out for him?

"You crashed my fucking car, bro." It was the first time Jake had said anything since Rhett had woken up. He was hovering by the door, giving them their space. She could tell he was seething by the way he was positioned, one foot resting against the wall behind him with his arms defiantly crossed over his chest.

She didn't know if Rhett could see him clearly from where he laid, but that was irrelevant. Jake's tone was enough; his anger was palpable.

Rhett closed his eyes and sucked in a shaky breath, no doubt still processing what had happened and where he was. She wondered what it must be like, to wake up and not have any clue about the damage he had caused or the destruction he left in his wake. Had this happened before? Had he woken up so unaware that he had to piece back together the consequences of his choices?

She didn't know. But she should have known.

"Baby, you're going to be late," Jake reminded her. She had forgotten about the whole procedure over the last two minutes as she poured herself into Rhett's pain. It was so easy to lose herself in him. It was too easy to only worry about him when he was like this.

She closed her eyes and steeled her spine, nodding without turning around to face their friend. She thought seeing Rhett awake would calm the anxiety that had found a home in her, but instead it had the opposite effect. She hadn't stopped touching him since he woke up. Her body craved the reminder that he was alive.

"I have to go upstairs now. I have to go to our appointment..."

Tori watched in horror as Rhett groaned and attempted to swing his legs over the side of the hospital bed. His efforts were in vain as his body refused to cooperate. She didn't know if it was the grogginess from the anesthesia or the haziness from the alcohol that held him strapped to the hospital bed.

"You have to stay here, Rhett. You can't go with me," she explained.

"But I'm supposed to be there. I need to be there for you, and I have an appointment, too," he choked out.

Did he really think he was going to be able to participate in the embryo freezing process now? Was he really that disconnected from the reality of what was happening, what he had done? He had been in a serious car crash hours ago, and he had just come out of surgery. His blood alcohol level was probably still registering over the legal limit.

There was no way Rhett could leave this room, let alone go to his appointment. And that was on him. He did this. He was the reason that their plan to freeze embryos wasn't going to happen today. She was disgusted by the cruel irony of the whole situation. She'd felt so alone through everything over the last two weeks.

"You can't go with me," she repeated.

She watched as her strong, normally steady, always stable Golden Boy let defeat wash over him. He closed his eyes in anguish. She knew the depth of his pain because it matched the bottomless pit of her own.

A single tear tracked down his cheek. "Jake," he croaked, calling on the only support he could provide by proxy.

"I'm already planning to go up there with her. She's not going to be fucking alone through anything else."

Tori swallowed past the lump in her throat, desperate to keep some semblance of peace in the emotionally charged room. "I'll come back to you as soon as I can," she vowed to her husband. But even as she whispered what should have been parting words, she couldn't bring herself to leave his side.

She looked over her shoulder and locked eyes with Jake, silently begging him to come to her aid. He assessed her up and down, his gaze shifting from her face to Rhett then back again. Then he nodded, understanding without any spoken words exactly what she needed from him.

He pushed off the wall and strode across the room with purpose, coming to stand right behind her. He gripped her left shoulder as he reached over to place his right hand on top of hers. He gently lifted it from Rhett's face, guiding her back toward the door.

His tone was soft and gentle, a complete contrast to how he's just spoken to Rhett. "He's okay. He's awake," he crooned in her ear. His words were a comfort, the reminders a balm. "He's going to be fine. We'll be back." All she could do was nod through her tears and let herself be pulled away. It wasn't until they reached the door that Rhett spoke up again. His voice was so low she almost didn't hear him.

"V, I'm so sorry. I didn't forget. I swear. I just... I... I tried, beautiful," he choked out in a muffled sob. "I tried so fucking hard to get back to you."

A fresh wave of pain that had nothing to do with the side effects of the hormones gripped her insides. Their bodies had always been so attuned to each other, and that proved true even now. The pain that was seeded inside him was taking root in her. His pain was her pain. And because of his choices, they were both drowning in it now.

"I know. I know you tried." She didn't know what else to say without losing herself. She couldn't get swept into the undercurrent of his suffering. She had to keep going. She had to push herself to finish what they'd started, even if it meant burying both their pain and moving forward on her own.

The entire procedure happened under the cast of a deep fog. She was so tired: mentally, physically, and emotionally worn down from everything that had transpired. She had enough wherewithal to explain that she had to change the retrieval plan when she checked in at the front desk. The nurse side-eyed Jake, no doubt assuming he was her partner and that he was the reason she would only be doing egg freezing instead of embryo freezing. He ignored the nurse's judgmental gaze and dutifully helped her fill out the required paperwork, forging Rhett's signature next to hers on all the forms.

She was alone for the actual procedure, but they let Jake be by her side in recovery. He sat with her and held her hand, patiently waiting the required amount of time before they could leave. They had removed thirteen eggs that would be flash-frozen as just eggs. She didn't let herself dwell on the unexpected change of plans. It was over. It didn't matter now. She didn't even know if it would matter in the future. But at least it was done.

As soon as the nurse gave her the all-clear, she was on her feet. She was sore and bloated as expected, but grateful to finally be able to take something for the pain. Jake suggested they stop at the cafeteria so she didn't have to take pain meds on an empty stomach, but she wouldn't even consider it. She promised to eat and drink anything he brought her as long as he helped her get back to Rhett right away.

Jake accepted all the aftercare paperwork and instructions from the receptionist, forging Rhett's signature one more time before they left. He grasped her shoulder and held her tight as they walked slowly through the hospital halls. They had to stop twice because the overwhelming fullness in her stomach made each step feel like she was on the brink of bursting. Nausea from the anesthesia was also taking its toll.

She slumped against Jake's side when she saw room 305. It was the combination of relief and exhaustion that finally made her succumb. She was already leaning on him with almost all her weight when she stumbled. She clung to him, unable to physically take another step.

"Tori!" he gasped.

"I'm fine," she insisted as she gripped his shoulders tighter. "Really. I'm fine," she repeated for emphasis. She saw a flash of terror register on his face. She didn't think she was going to pass out, but at least they were already in a hospital if she did.

"I just feel a little lightheaded," she clarified. "I think I'm just... done."

"It's all over now, baby. I've got you," he murmured as he hooked his arm under her knees and lifted her with ease, carrying her over the threshold of the dimly lit hospital room.

Rhett was asleep when they entered. His six-one frame was partially upright and only taking up half the bed. Even in his hungover, post-anesthesia haze, he knew she'd be back. He'd always saved space for her.

"Bed or couch?" Jake asked without any infliction in his voice. His tone may have been passive, but his question held so much weight.

"Bed," she replied without hesitation. Her life felt like a farce right now, but there was no doubt in her mind that lying in Rhett's arms was still the only place she wanted to be. That was her truth. This was their fate. A connection had been written in the stars and forged across a broken fence years ago. Even when facing the worst of the worst, there was nothing that could come between their love.

Jake lowered her onto the empty side of the narrow hospital bed, taking care not to bump or jostle either of them in the process. He kissed her forehead and squeezed her hand before grabbing the edge of the thin hospital blanket and covering them both.

Did he have to work today? Had he even slept last night? She was too tired to ask him about his plans. She met his gaze and cocked her head to the side in question.

"I'm not going anywhere," he announced as he flopped down onto the plastic couch next to the bed. "But just so we're clear, I'm here for *you*. Try to sleep, baby. I'll be here when you wake up."

Tori nodded, overwhelmed with gratitude but still feeling the bone-tired exhaustion from everything that had transpired over the last four hours. She didn't know how they had gotten here. She didn't know how they would ever come back from here.

She didn't know, but she should have known.

All the unknowns would have to wait. For now, she'd just do what Jake said and try to sleep. She lifted Rhett's arm as carefully as possible, placing it across her own body, assuming the position he had held her in hundreds of times before. She felt her eyes try to flutter closed, but she refused to surrender before she whispered a promise to the man beside her.

"I don't know if you can even hear me... but I'm here, Rhett. I'm right here. You belong to me, and I'm not going to let anyone or anything tear us apart. Not even you."

Afterword

WHAT. A. RIDE!

Are you alright? It's okay if you're not alright. Thank you for going on this journey, and for experiencing the rollercoaster that is Tori and Rhett's epic love.

Up next will be a bit of a palette cleanser-- When You're Home for the Holidays is a short novella that's low on angst but still big on feels and steam. There's a time hop between the end of this book and the start of that novella, so prepare to flash forward. Also, don't stress. YES, the title of the final book for Rhett and Tori's story is When You're Gone, but it will be okay. I promise! It's Ev + V against the world. Right? RIGHT?!

If you're interested in receiving updates, bonus scenes, and sale alerts you can sign up for my email list here. I would also love to connect with you on social media! You'll find all my contact information in the back of the book.

Finally, if you loved this story, it would mean the world to me if you'd leave a review on Goodreads, Amazon, BookBub, or any other retailer website. Rave reviews are a huge deal to an independent author. Thank you for sharing the love!

UP NEXT FROM ABBY MILLSAPS

When You're Home for the Holidays
Coming November 2021

When You're Gone
Coming Early 2022

Mr. Brightside (Jake's story)
Coming Spring 2022

Acknowledgments

I sincerely believe every story is worth sharing. Even if it's messy. Even if it's hard to write. Even if it hurts. Bringing Rhett and Tori's love to life on these pages is a dream fulfilled in so many ways. A sincere thank you to the following people, and to everyone who helped make this book possible.

David- My anchor and my lighthouse and the wind under my sails. Thank you for seeing all of me, and loving me through it all. This book (and life in general!) wouldn't be possible without your encouragement and unrelenting support. Thank you for being my Rhett, my Jake, and my Fielding, depending on the day. All of me loves all of you.

My girls- Your little hands on my face telling me you're proud of me is the best review I could ever hope for. Thank you for witnessing this journey. I hope through this experience you learn what's possible when you dream your wildest dreams.

Ethan- Your disdain for my characters makes me a better writer. Truly. Thank you for reading and critiquing and helping me whip the Hampton gang into shape. Let it be known that because of you, Fielding threw the damn keys.

Sam Wiggle- Thank you for answering all my car questions. Your sincere interest in my writing makes my heart happy. PS- your girlfriend is amazing. You should marry that woman.

My critique partner and beta readers- Thank you for slogging through the mess that was the first draft. Your time and attention to detail is so appreciated. Who knew that one flippant remark about "no spice in the first chapter?" would lead to an entire Chapter One rewrite. My readers (and Rhett and Tori) thank you.

My ARC Readers and Promo Team, aka the greatest people on the Internet and maybe planet earth- Thank you for reading. Thank you for sharing. Thank you for every review and post and graphic. The indie publishing world is what it is because of your passion and creativity. You inspire me!

Krystal- Thank you for loving my characters so hard and feeling everything right alongside me. Your support for this series keeps me going. I'm so lucky to call you my friend.

Yvette- I am honored that you shared your real-life love story with me. Your courage to love and be loved is an inspiration. I will be forever grateful that I know you.

About The Author

Abby Millsaps is an author and storyteller who loves to write messy, steamy, emo romance. Her characters are relatable, lovable, and occasionally confused about the distinction between right and wrong. Her books are set in picturesque small towns that feel like home.

Abby started writing romance in 7th grade. Sure, it was Newsies-inspired fanfic and short stories about slow dancing to 'This I Promise You', but like all good love stories, they always ended in happily ever after. She met her husband at a house party the summer before her freshman year of college. He had a secret pizza stashed in the trunk of his car that he was saving for a midnight snack— how was she supposed to resist? When she's not writing Abby enjoys spending time with her family and traveling to her favorite theme park destinations.

Connect with Abby Online

Website: www.authorabbymillsaps.com
Instagram: @abbymillsaps
TikTok: @authorabbymillsaps
Facebook: Author Abby Millsaps

Made in the USA
Monee, IL
20 October 2021